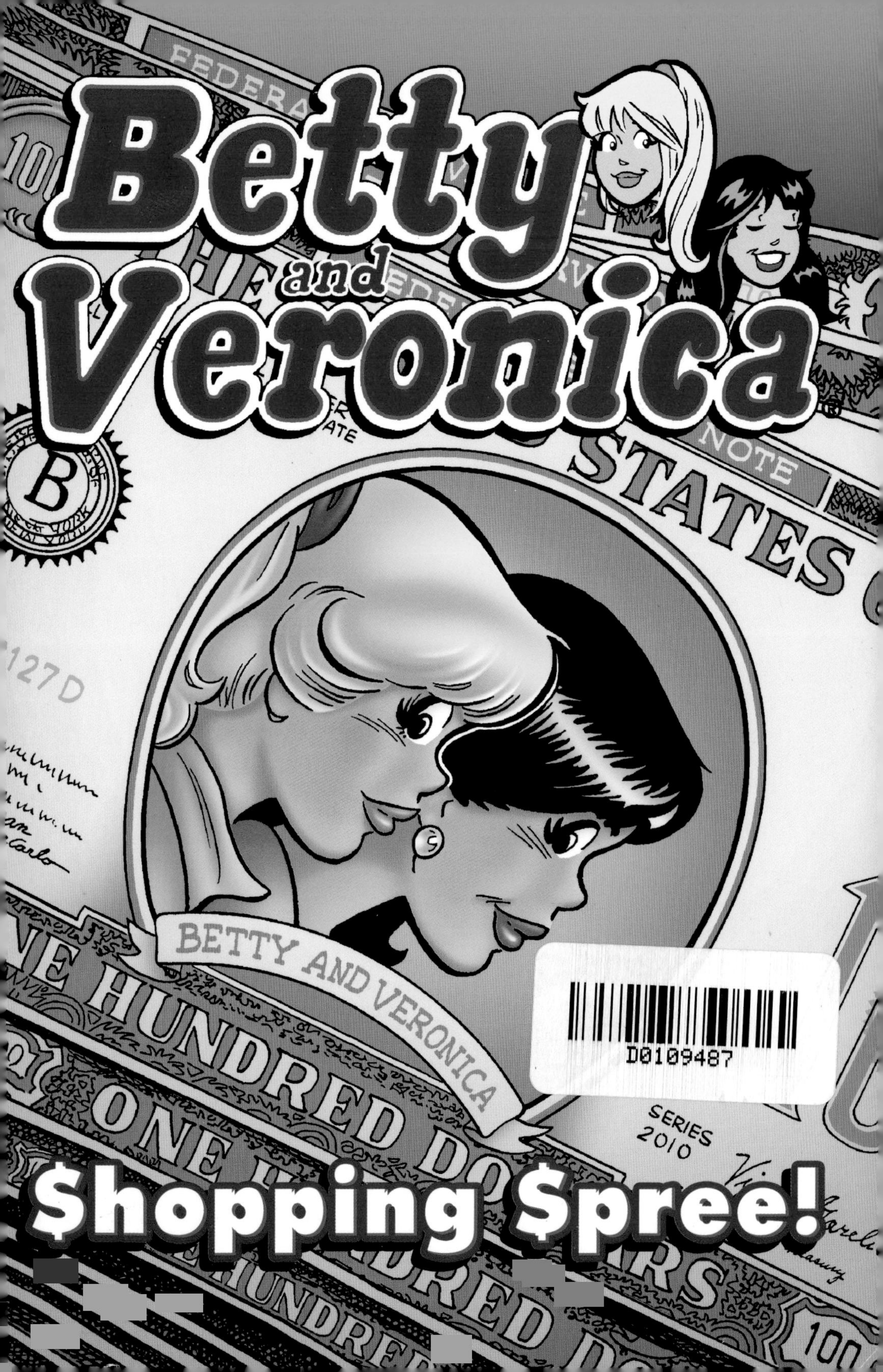
Betty and Veronica®
STATES
NOTE
BETTY AND VERONICA
ONE HUNDRED DOLLARS
SERIES 2010
$hopping $pree!
D0109487

ARCHIE GRAPHIC NOVEL CHECKLIST

Available at your local comic book store, fine bookstores near you, and online @ ArchieComics.com!

OVER 50 GRAPHIC NOVELS AVAILABLE AND COUNTING • BILLIONS OF ARCHIE COMICS SOLD

BEST OF ARCHIE

Collects the best stories
from throughout the over
70-year history of Archie Comics.

- [ ] Best of Archie Comics Book 1(978-1-879794-84-9)
- [ ] Best of Archie Comics Book 2 (978-1-935975-20-4)
- [ ] Best of Archie Comics Book 3 (978-1-936975-61-7)
- [ ] Best of Archie Comics Book 4 (978-1-61988-942-2)
- [ ] Best of Archie Comics starring Betty & Veronica (978-1-936975-88-4)

BETTY & VERONICA

The ladies of Archie Comics
take center stage in this awesome
collection of graphic novels.

- [ ] B&V: Storybook (978-1-879794-60-3)
- [ ] B&V's Princess Storybook (978-1-936975-71-6)
- [ ] B&V: Prom Princesses (978-1-936975-30-3)
- [ ] B&V: Best Friends Forever (978-1-879794-76-4)
- [ ] B&V: Shopping Spree (978-1-61988-904-0)

HOT TITLES

Collecting the hottest and newest stories.

- [ ] Archie: A Rock 'N' Roll Romance (978-1-936975-33-4)
- [ ] Archie: Rockin' the World (978-1-61988-907-1)
- [ ] Archie meets KISS (978-1-936975-14-3) HC
- [ ] Archie meets KISS (978-1-936975-04-4) SC
- [ ] Archie meets GLEE (978-1-936975-45-7)
- [ ] Archie's Pal: Kevin Keller (978-1-879794-93-1)
- [ ] Kevin Keller: Welcome to Riverdale (978-1-936975-23-5)
- [ ] Kevin Keller: Drive Me Crazy (978-1-936975-58-7)

THE MARRIED LIFE

Find out what happens after the "I do"s!
Collects the complete story from the most critically
acclaimed storyline Archie has ever published!

- [ ] Archie: The Married Life Book 1 (978-1-936975-01-3)
- [ ] Archie: The Married Life Book 2 (978-1-879794-99-3)
- [ ] Archie: The Married Life Book 3 (978-1-936975-35-8)
- [ ] Archie: The Married Life Book 4 (978-1-936975-69-3)
- [ ] Archie: The Married Life Book 5 (978-1-61988-902-6)
- [ ] Archie: The Married Life Book 6 (978-1-61988-945-3)

SUPER VALUE

Super, high-value digest collections of great
Archie comics, only available while supplies last.

- [ ] Archie: 1000 page Comics Bonanza (978-1-61988-903-3)
- [ ] Archie: 1000 page Comics Explosion (978-1-61988-939-2)
- [ ] Archie Giant Comics Digest (978-1-61988-947-7)
- [ ] Archie Comics Spectacular: It's A Date (978-1-936975-70-9)
- [ ] Archie Comics Spectacular: Sports Time (978-1-936975-84-6)

ARCHIE COMICS

ARCHIECOMICS.COM

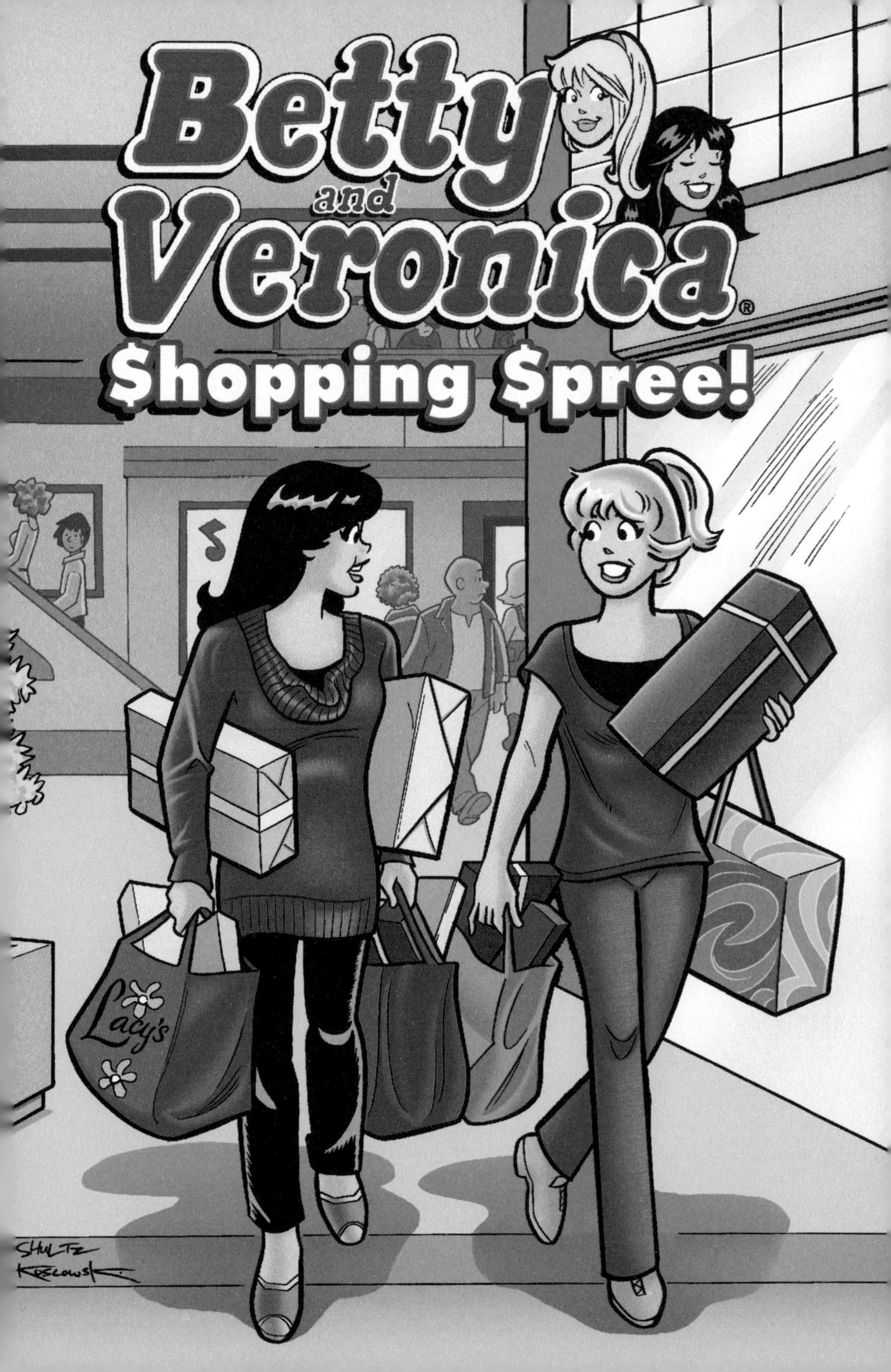
Betty and Veronica®
$hopping $pree!
Lacy's

Archie & Friends All-Stars Series: Volume 23
BETTY & VERONICA: SHOPPING SPREE!
Published by Archie Comic Publications, Inc.
325 Fayette Avenue, Mamaroneck, NY 10543-2318

ISBN: 978-1-61988-904-0

Printed in USA.

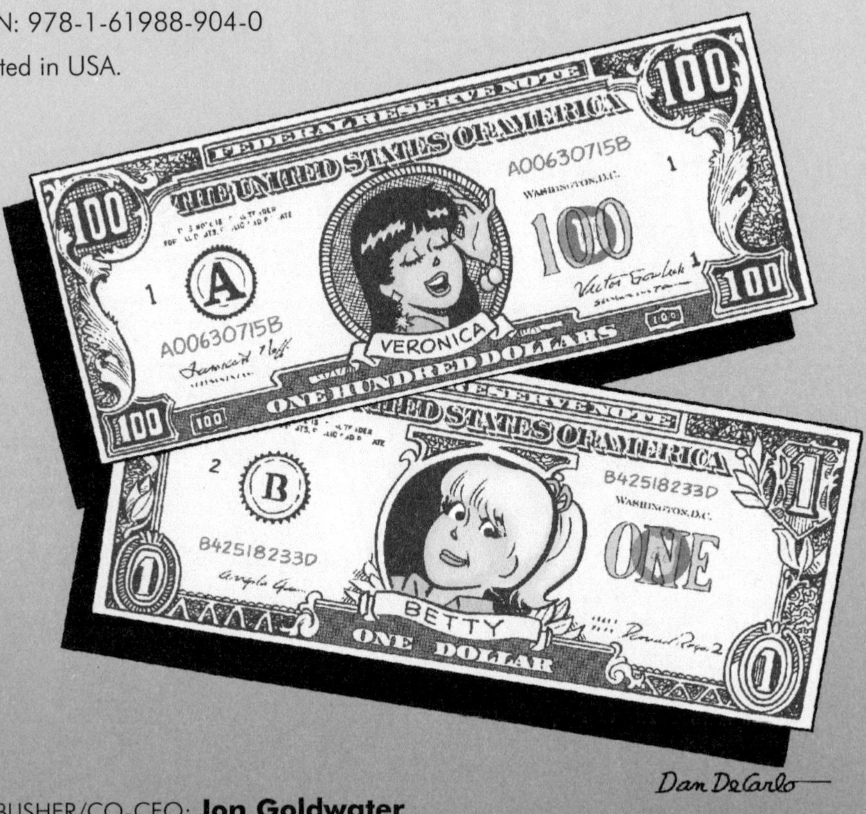
100
THE UNITED STATES OF AMERICA
A00630715B
VERONICA
ONE HUNDRED DOLLARS
B425182233D
ONE
BETTY
ONE DOLLAR
Dan DeCarlo

PUBLISHER/CO-CEO: **Jon Goldwater**
CO-CEO: **Nancy Silberkleit**
PRESIDENT: **Mike Pellerito**
CO-PRESIDENT/EDITOR-IN-CHIEF: **Victor Gorelick**
CHIEF CREATIVE OFFICER: **Roberto Aguirre-Sacasa**
SENIOR VICE PRESIDENT, SALES & BUSINESS DEVELOPMENT: **Jim Sokolowski**
SENIOR VICE PRESIDENT, PUBLISHING & OPERATIONS: **Harold Buchholz**
SENIOR VICE PRESIDENT, PUBLICITY & MARKETING: **Alex Segura**
EXECUTIVE DIRECTOR OF EDITORIAL: **Paul Kaminski**
PRODUCTION MANAGER: **Stephen Oswald**
PROJECT COORDINATOR/BOOK DESIGN: **Duncan McLachlan**
EDITORIAL ASSISTANT/PROOFREADER: **Jamie Lee Rotante**

SCRIPTS:

Dan Parent, Frank Doyle, George Gladir, Angelo DeCesare, Craig Boldman, Joe Edwards, Kathleen Webb, Mike Pellowski, Barbara Slate, Greg Crosby

PENCILS:

Dan Parent, Dan DeCarlo, Tim Kennedy, Pat Kennedy, Jeff Shultz, Doug Crane

INKS:

Jon D'Agostino, Henry Scarpelli, Rich Koslowski, Jimmy DeCarlo, Jim Amash, Rudy Lapick, Al Milgrom, Mike Esposito

LETTERS:

Bill Yoshida, Jon D'Agostino, Jack Morelli, John Workman

COLORS:

Barry Grossman, Rosario "Tito" Peña, Digikore Studios

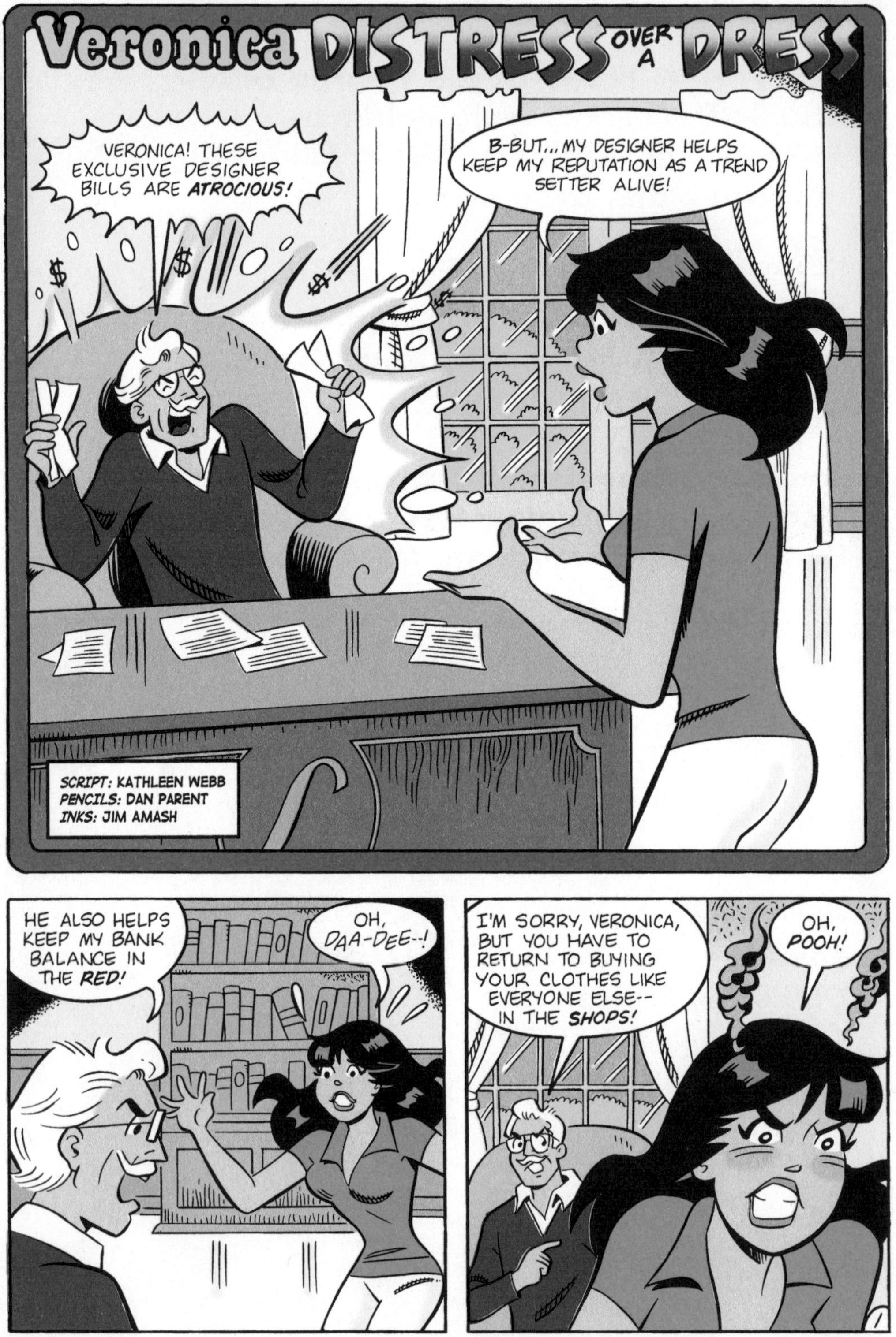
Veronica
DISTRESS OVER A DRESS
VERONICA! THESE EXCLUSIVE DESIGNER BILLS ARE *ATROCIOUS!*
B-BUT... MY DESIGNER HELPS KEEP MY REPUTATION AS A TREND SETTER ALIVE!
SCRIPT: KATHLEEN WEBB
PENCILS: DAN PARENT
INKS: JIM AMASH
HE ALSO HELPS KEEP MY BANK BALANCE IN THE *RED!*
OH, *DAA-DEE--!*
I'M SORRY, VERONICA, BUT YOU HAVE TO RETURN TO BUYING YOUR CLOTHES LIKE EVERYONE ELSE-- IN THE *SHOPS!*
OH, *POOH!*

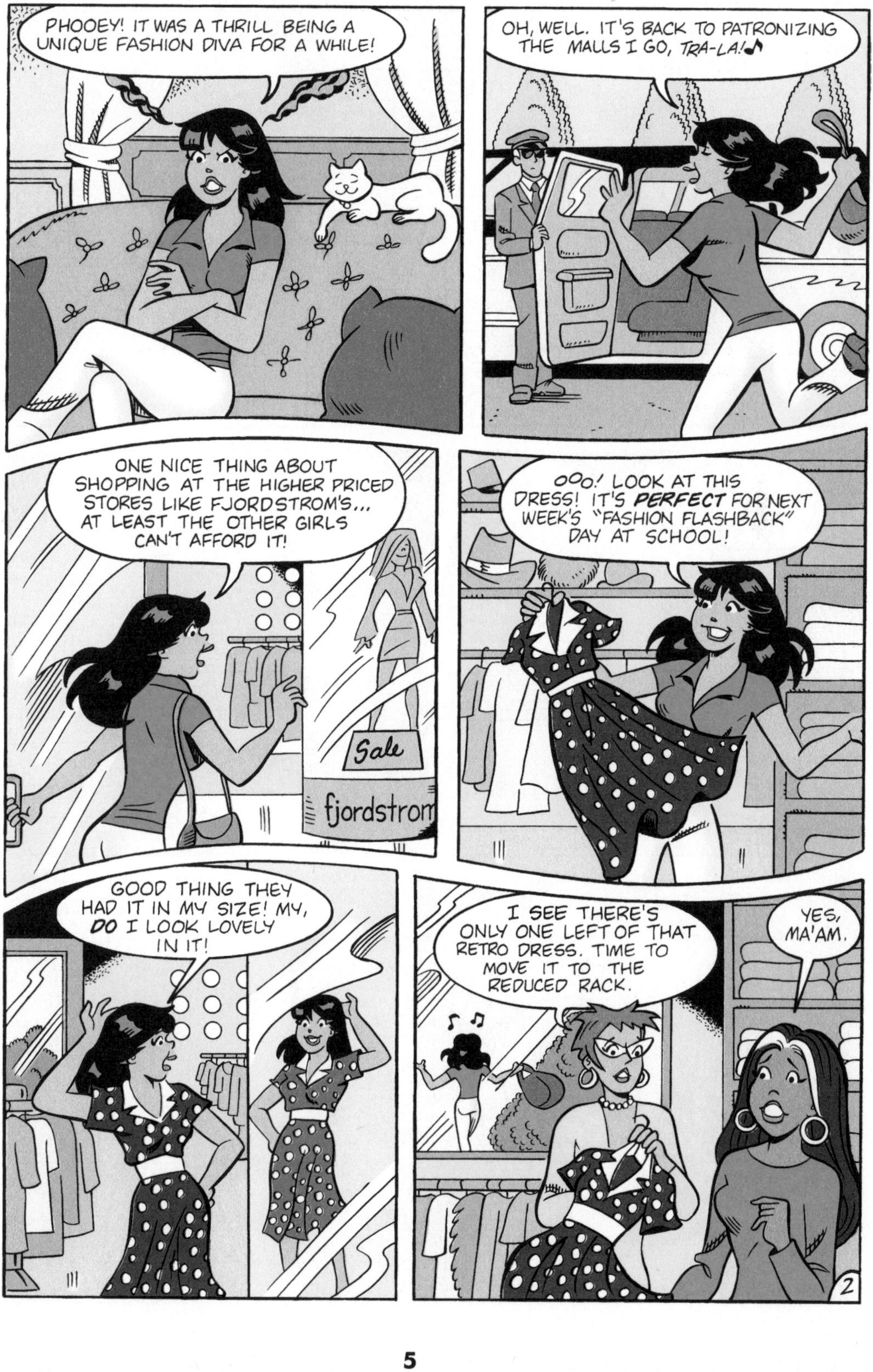
PHOOEY! IT WAS A THRILL BEING A UNIQUE FASHION DIVA FOR A WHILE!
OH, WELL. IT'S BACK TO PATRONIZING THE MALLS I GO, TRA-LA! ♪
ONE NICE THING ABOUT SHOPPING AT THE HIGHER PRICED STORES LIKE FJORDSTROM'S... AT LEAST THE OTHER GIRLS CAN'T AFFORD IT!
Sale
fjordstrom
OOO! LOOK AT THIS DRESS! IT'S PERFECT FOR NEXT WEEK'S "FASHION FLASHBACK" DAY AT SCHOOL!
GOOD THING THEY HAD IT IN MY SIZE! MY, DO I LOOK LOVELY IN IT!
I SEE THERE'S ONLY ONE LEFT OF THAT RETRO DRESS. TIME TO MOVE IT TO THE REDUCED RACK.
YES, MA'AM.
2

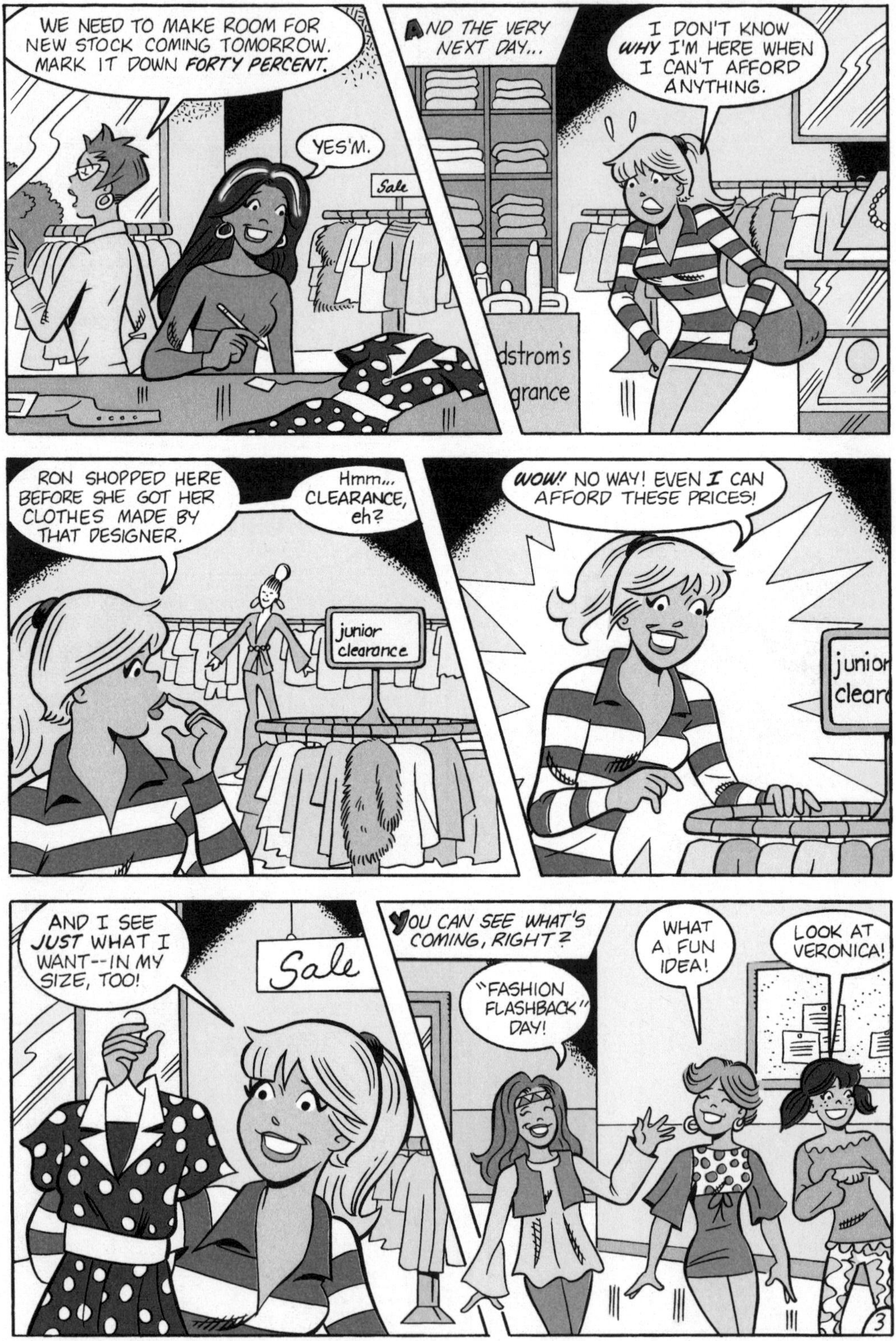
WE NEED TO MAKE ROOM FOR NEW STOCK COMING TOMORROW. MARK IT DOWN FORTY PERCENT.
YES'M.
Sale
AND THE VERY NEXT DAY...
I DON'T KNOW WHY I'M HERE WHEN I CAN'T AFFORD ANYTHING.
dstrom's
grance
RON SHOPPED HERE BEFORE SHE GOT HER CLOTHES MADE BY THAT DESIGNER.
Hmm... CLEARANCE, eh?
junior clearance
WOW! NO WAY! EVEN I CAN AFFORD THESE PRICES!
junior
clear
AND I SEE JUST WHAT I WANT--IN MY SIZE, TOO!
Sale
YOU CAN SEE WHAT'S COMING, RIGHT?
"FASHION FLASHBACK" DAY!
WHAT A FUN IDEA!
LOOK AT VERONICA!
3

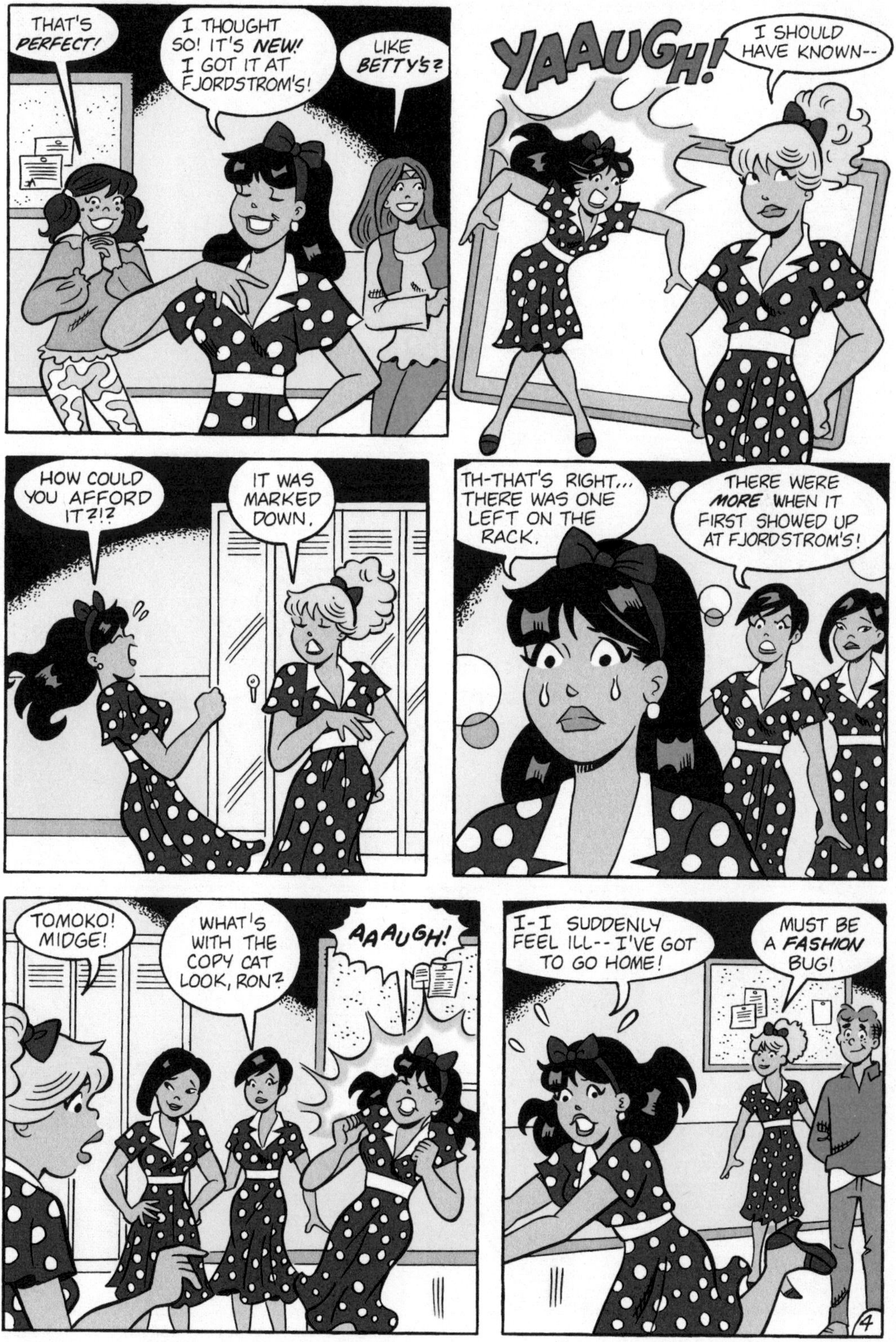

THAT'S PERFECT!
I THOUGHT SO! IT'S NEW! I GOT IT AT FJORDSTROM'S!
LIKE BETTY'S?
YAAAUGH!
I SHOULD HAVE KNOWN--
HOW COULD YOU AFFORD IT?!?
IT WAS MARKED DOWN.
TH-THAT'S RIGHT... THERE WAS ONE LEFT ON THE RACK.
THERE WERE MORE WHEN IT FIRST SHOWED UP AT FJORDSTROM'S!
TOMOKO! MIDGE!
WHAT'S WITH THE COPY CAT LOOK, RON?
AAAUGH!
I-I SUDDENLY FEEL ILL-- I'VE GOT TO GO HOME!
MUST BE A FASHION BUG!
4

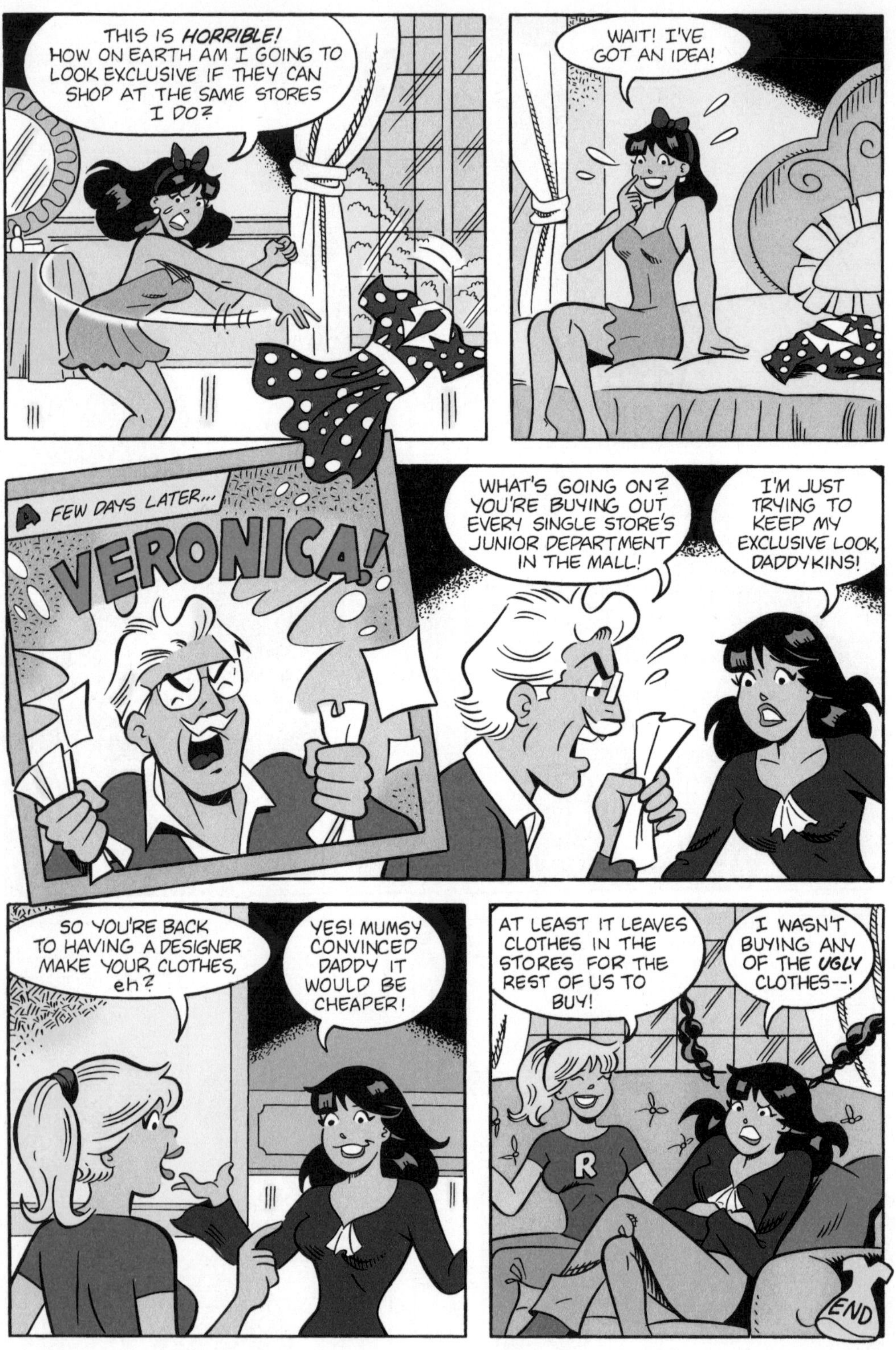

THIS IS HORRIBLE! HOW ON EARTH AM I GOING TO LOOK EXCLUSIVE IF THEY CAN SHOP AT THE SAME STORES I DO?
WAIT! I'VE GOT AN IDEA!
A FEW DAYS LATER...
VERONICA!
WHAT'S GOING ON? YOU'RE BUYING OUT EVERY SINGLE STORE'S JUNIOR DEPARTMENT IN THE MALL!
I'M JUST TRYING TO KEEP MY EXCLUSIVE LOOK, DADDYKINS!
SO YOU'RE BACK TO HAVING A DESIGNER MAKE YOUR CLOTHES, eh?
YES! MUMSY CONVINCED DADDY IT WOULD BE CHEAPER!
AT LEAST IT LEAVES CLOTHES IN THE STORES FOR THE REST OF US TO BUY!
I WASN'T BUYING ANY OF THE UGLY CLOTHES--!
R
END

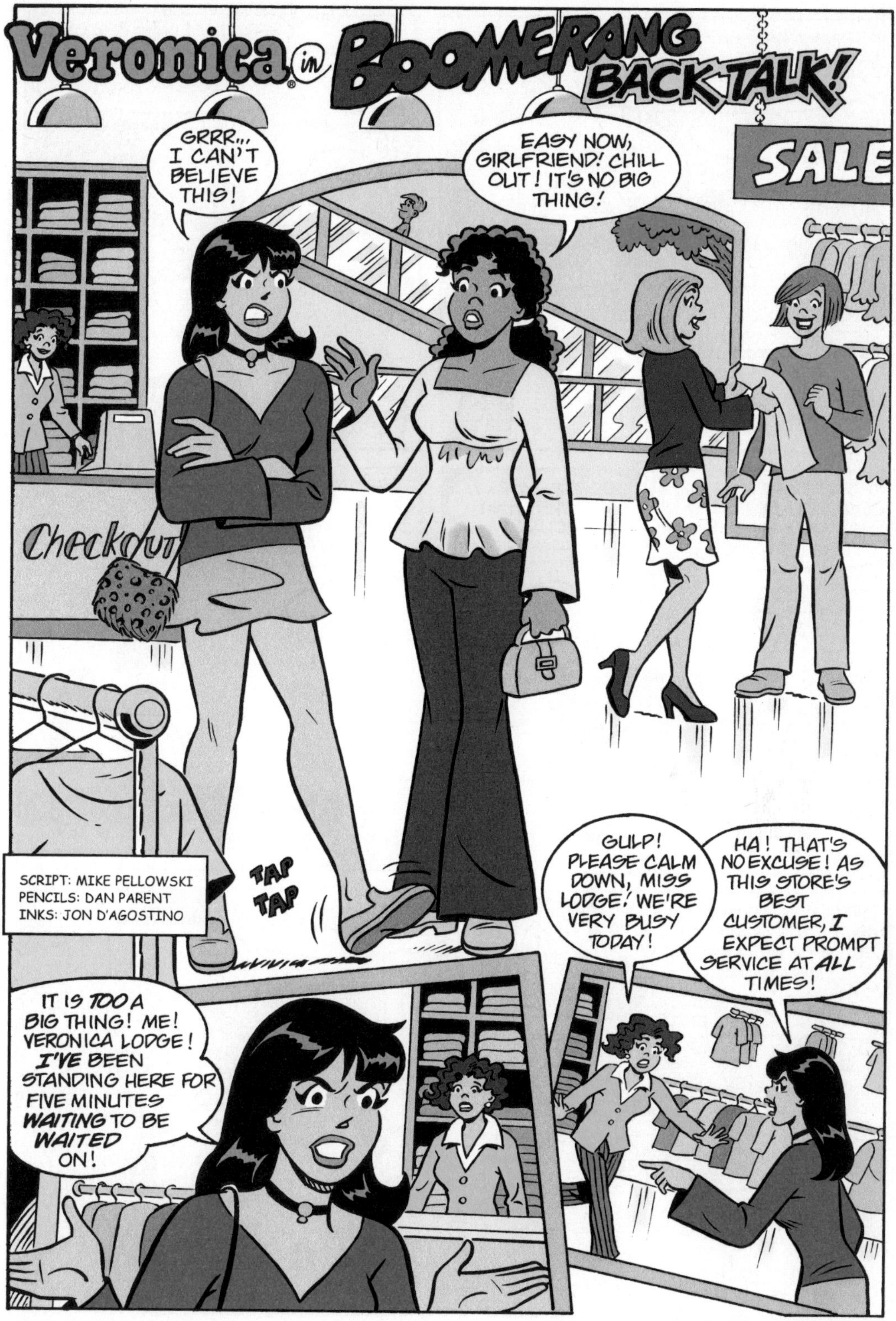
Veronica in BOOMERANG BACK TALK!
SALE
GRRR... I CAN'T BELIEVE THIS!
EASY NOW, GIRLFRIEND! CHILL OUT! IT'S NO BIG THING!
Checkout
TAP TAP
SCRIPT: MIKE PELLOWSKI
PENCILS: DAN PARENT
INKS: JON D'AGOSTINO
IT IS TOO A BIG THING! ME! VERONICA LODGE! I'VE BEEN STANDING HERE FOR FIVE MINUTES WAITING TO BE WAITED ON!
GULP! PLEASE CALM DOWN, MISS LODGE! WE'RE VERY BUSY TODAY!
HA! THAT'S NO EXCUSE! AS THIS STORE'S BEST CUSTOMER, I EXPECT PROMPT SERVICE AT ALL TIMES!

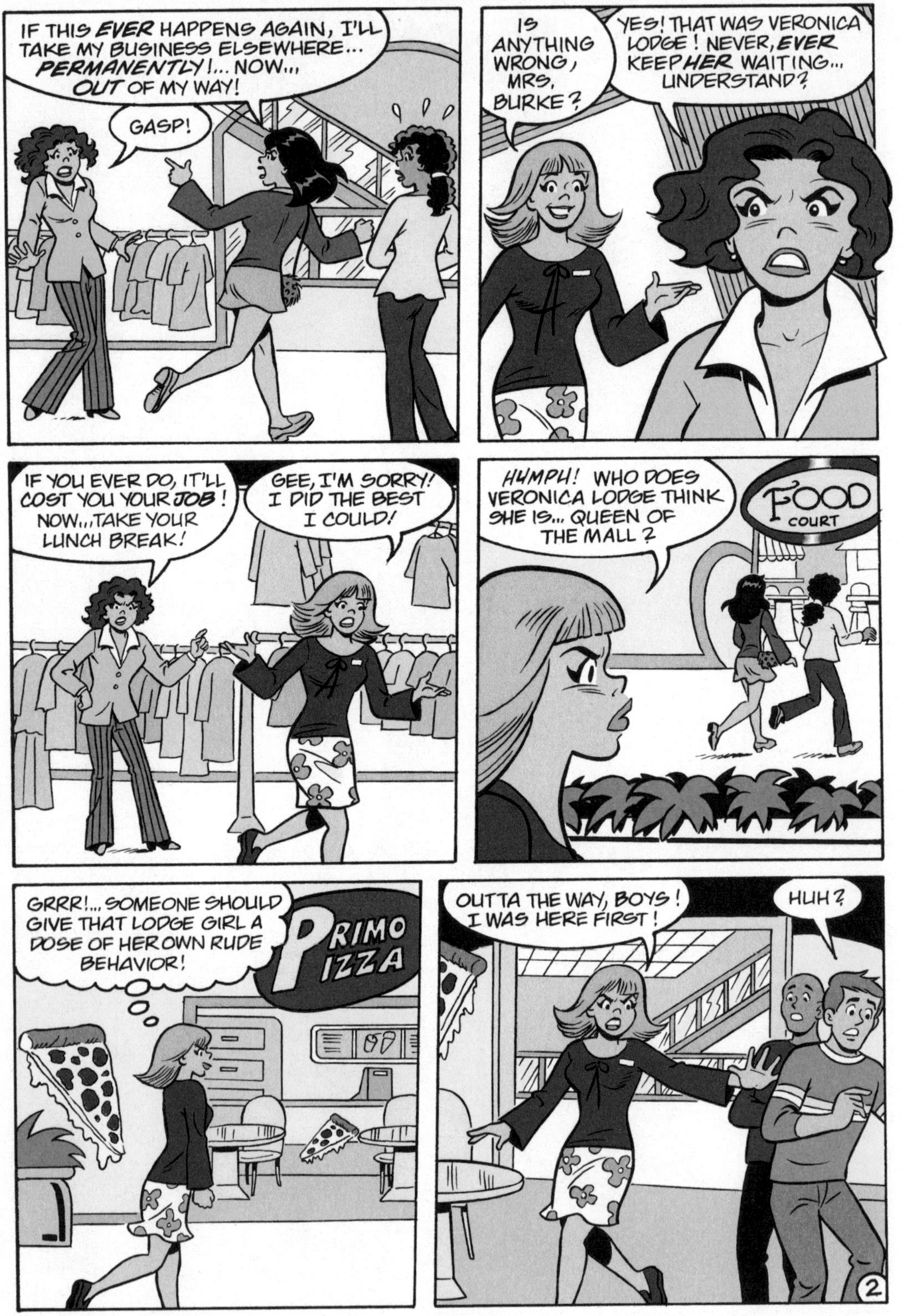
IF THIS EVER HAPPENS AGAIN, I'LL TAKE MY BUSINESS ELSEWHERE... PERMANENTLY!... NOW... OUT OF MY WAY!
GASP!
IS ANYTHING WRONG, MRS. BURKE?
YES! THAT WAS VERONICA LODGE! NEVER, EVER KEEP HER WAITING... UNDERSTAND?
IF YOU EVER DO, IT'LL COST YOU YOUR JOB! NOW... TAKE YOUR LUNCH BREAK!
GEE, I'M SORRY! I DID THE BEST I COULD!
HUMPH! WHO DOES VERONICA LODGE THINK SHE IS... QUEEN OF THE MALL?
FOOD COURT
GRRR!... SOMEONE SHOULD GIVE THAT LODGE GIRL A DOSE OF HER OWN RUDE BEHAVIOR!
PRIMO PIZZA
OUTTA THE WAY, BOYS! I WAS HERE FIRST!
HUH?
2

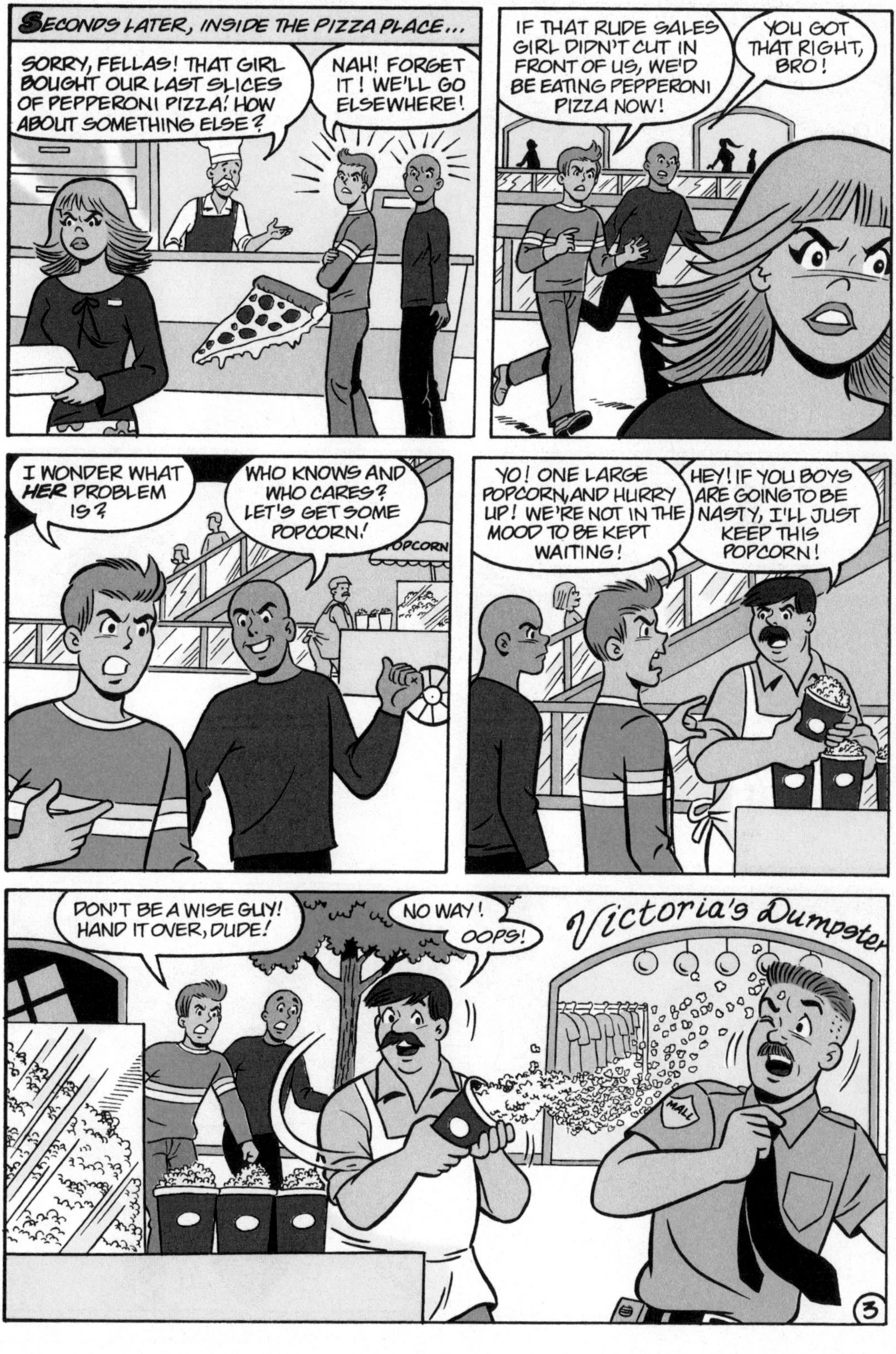
SECONDS LATER, INSIDE THE PIZZA PLACE...
SORRY, FELLAS! THAT GIRL BOUGHT OUR LAST SLICES OF PEPPERONI PIZZA! HOW ABOUT SOMETHING ELSE?
NAH! FORGET IT! WE'LL GO ELSEWHERE!
IF THAT RUDE SALES GIRL DIDN'T CUT IN FRONT OF US, WE'D BE EATING PEPPERONI PIZZA NOW!
YOU GOT THAT RIGHT, BRO!
I WONDER WHAT HER PROBLEM IS?
WHO KNOWS AND WHO CARES? LET'S GET SOME POPCORN!
POPCORN
YO! ONE LARGE POPCORN, AND HURRY UP! WE'RE NOT IN THE MOOD TO BE KEPT WAITING!
HEY! IF YOU BOYS ARE GOING TO BE NASTY, I'LL JUST KEEP THIS POPCORN!
DON'T BE A WISE GUY! HAND IT OVER, DUDE!
NO WAY!
OOPS!
Victoria's Dumpster
MALL
3

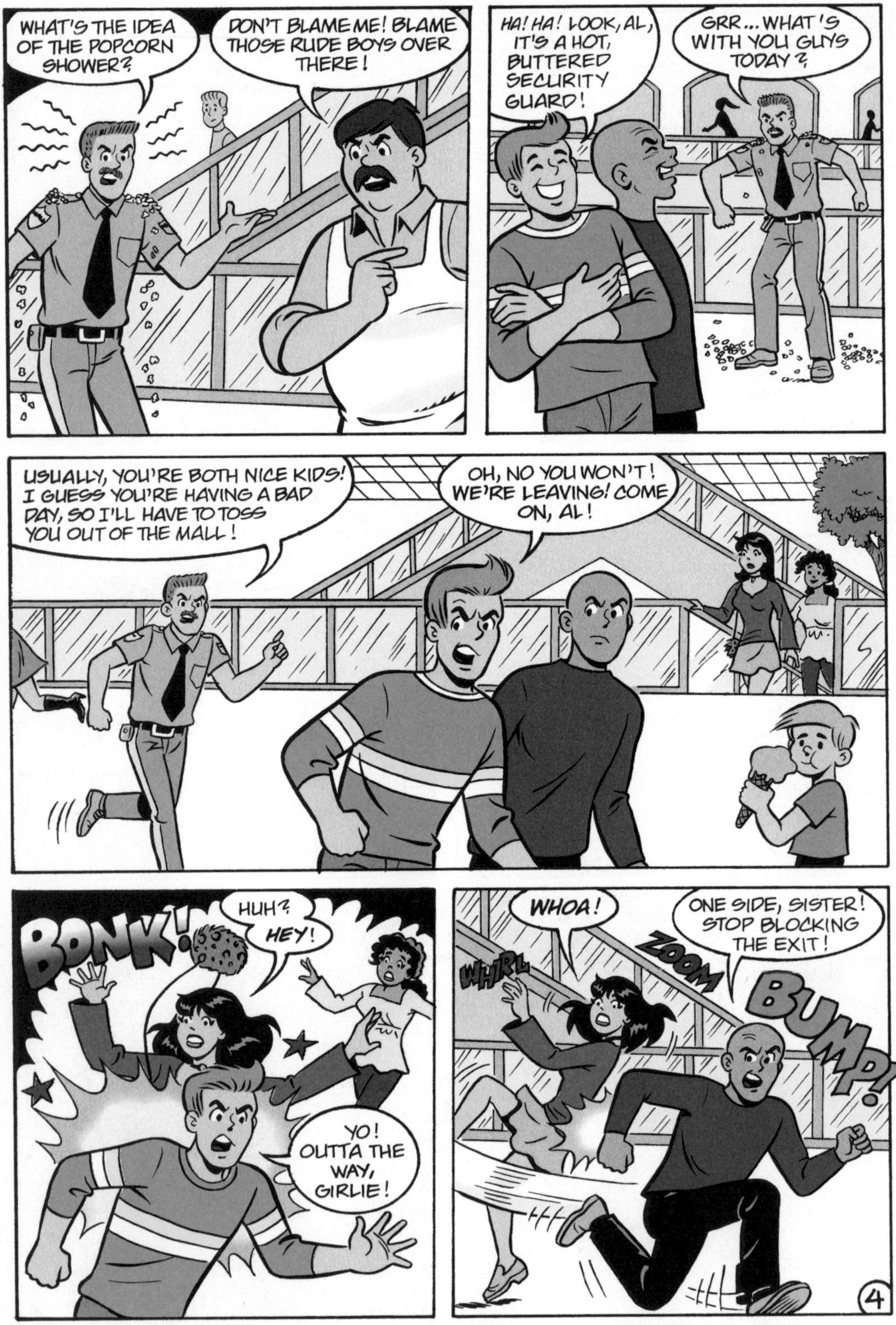
WHAT'S THE IDEA OF THE POPCORN SHOWER?
DON'T BLAME ME! BLAME THOSE RUDE BOYS OVER THERE!
HA! HA! LOOK, AL, IT'S A HOT, BUTTERED SECURITY GUARD!
GRR... WHAT'S WITH YOU GUYS TODAY?
USUALLY, YOU'RE BOTH NICE KIDS! I GUESS YOU'RE HAVING A BAD DAY, SO I'LL HAVE TO TOSS YOU OUT OF THE MALL!
OH, NO YOU WON'T! WE'RE LEAVING! COME ON, AL!
BONK!
HUH? HEY!
YO! OUTTA THE WAY, GIRLIE!
WHOA!
WHIRL
ZOOM
ONE SIDE, SISTER! STOP BLOCKING THE EXIT!
BUMP!
4

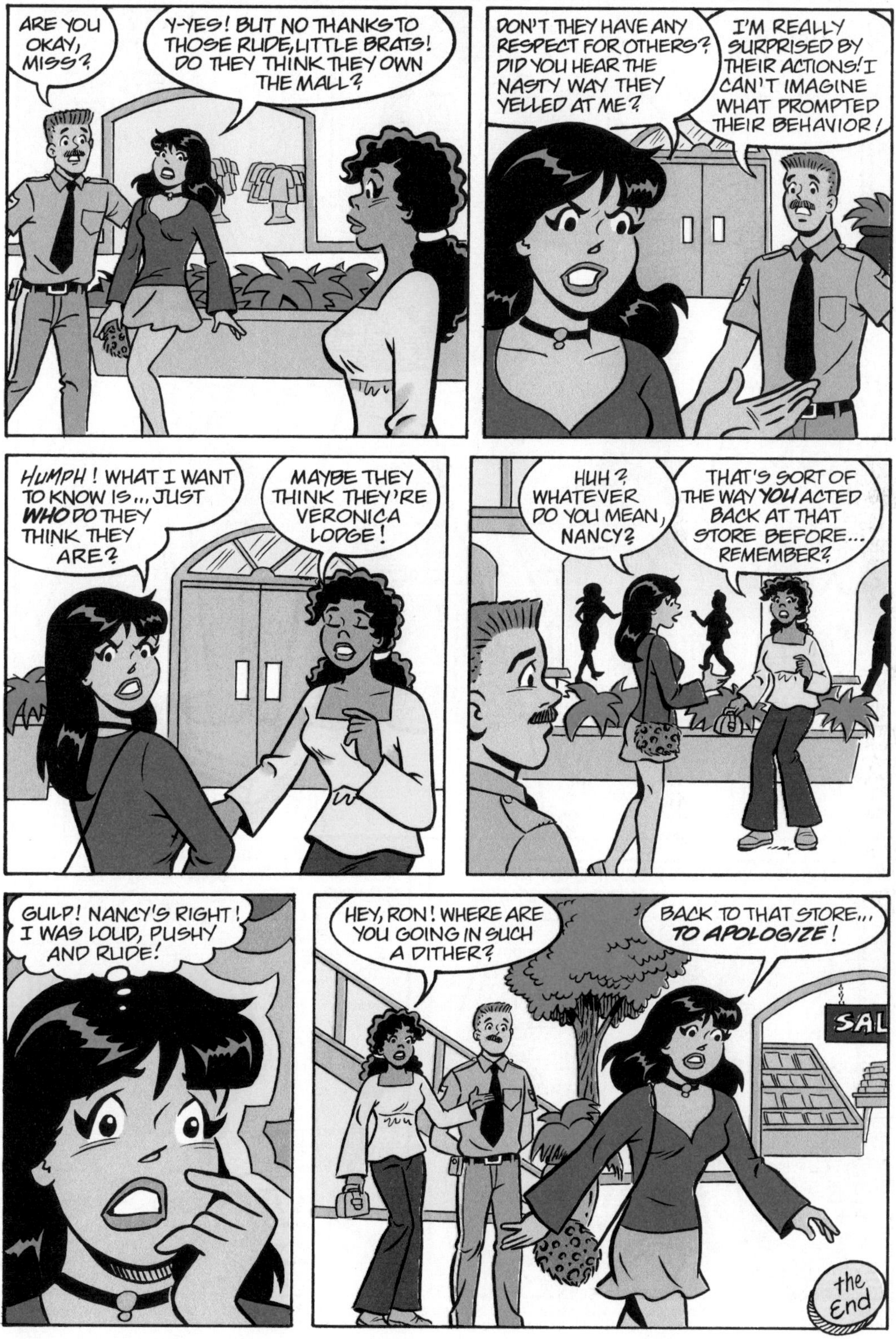
ARE YOU OKAY, MISS?
Y-YES! BUT NO THANKS TO THOSE RUDE, LITTLE BRATS! DO THEY THINK THEY OWN THE MALL?
DON'T THEY HAVE ANY RESPECT FOR OTHERS? DID YOU HEAR THE NASTY WAY THEY YELLED AT ME?
I'M REALLY SURPRISED BY THEIR ACTIONS! I CAN'T IMAGINE WHAT PROMPTED THEIR BEHAVIOR!
HUMPH! WHAT I WANT TO KNOW IS... JUST WHO DO THEY THINK THEY ARE?
MAYBE THEY THINK THEY'RE VERONICA LODGE!
HUH? WHATEVER DO YOU MEAN, NANCY?
THAT'S SORT OF THE WAY YOU ACTED BACK AT THAT STORE BEFORE... REMEMBER?
GULP! NANCY'S RIGHT! I WAS LOUD, PUSHY AND RUDE!
HEY, RON! WHERE ARE YOU GOING IN SUCH A DITHER?
BACK TO THAT STORE... TO APOLOGIZE!
SAL
the End

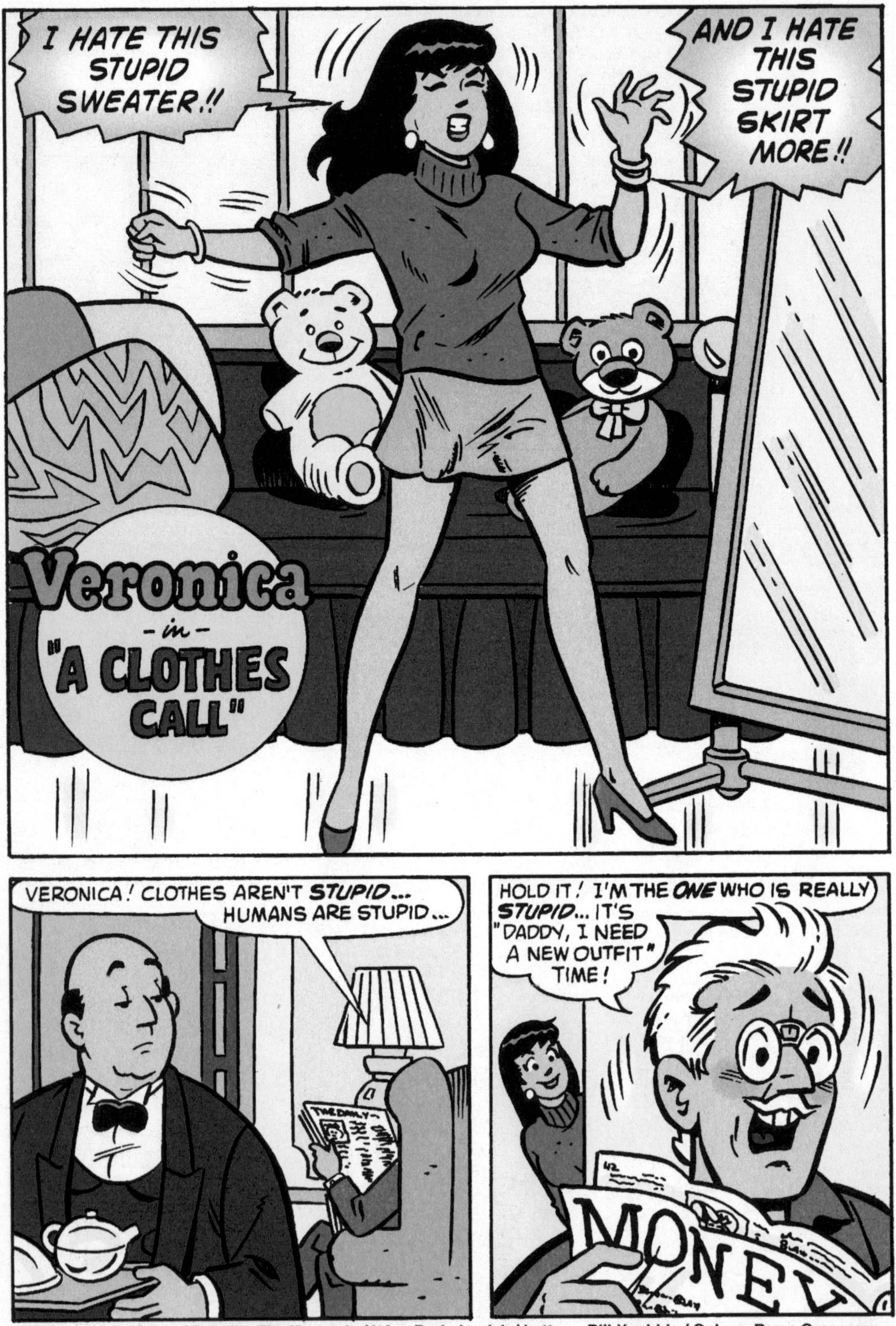
I HATE THIS STUPID SWEATER.!!
AND I HATE THIS STUPID SKIRT MORE!!
Veronica
-in-
"A CLOTHES CALL"
VERONICA! CLOTHES AREN'T STUPID... HUMANS ARE STUPID...
THE DAILY
HOLD IT! I'M THE ONE WHO IS REALLY STUPID... IT'S "DADDY, I NEED A NEW OUTFIT" TIME!
MONEY

Script: Joe Edwards / Pencils: Tim Kennedy / Inks: Rudy Lapick / Letters: Bill Yoshida / Colors: Barry Grossman

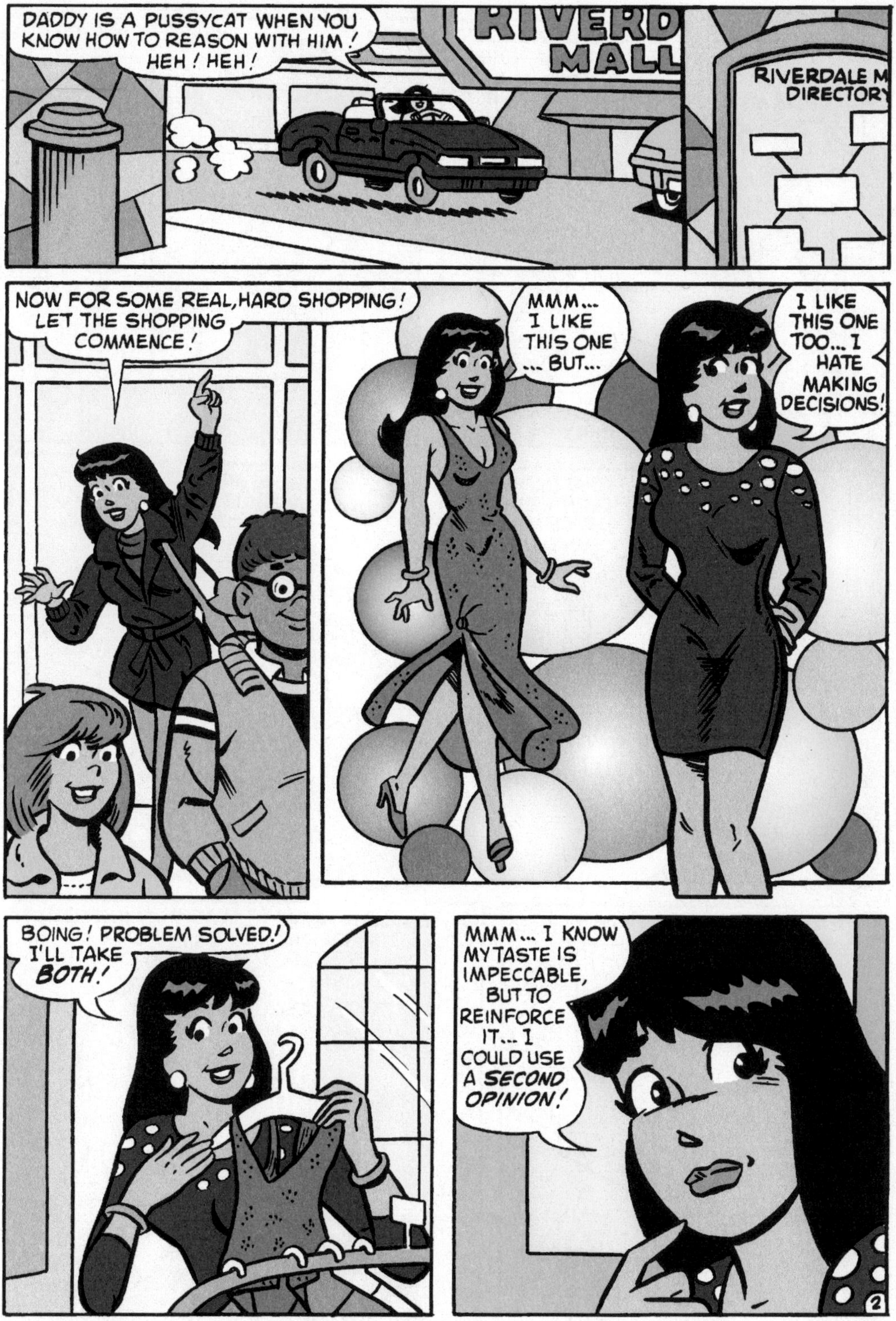
DADDY IS A PUSSYCAT WHEN YOU KNOW HOW TO REASON WITH HIM! HEH! HEH!
RIVERD MALL
RIVERDALE M DIRECTORY
NOW FOR SOME REAL, HARD SHOPPING! LET THE SHOPPING COMMENCE!
MMM... I LIKE THIS ONE ... BUT...
I LIKE THIS ONE TOO... I HATE MAKING DECISIONS!
BOING! PROBLEM SOLVED! I'LL TAKE *BOTH*!
MMM... I KNOW MY TASTE IS IMPECCABLE, BUT TO REINFORCE IT... I COULD USE A *SECOND OPINION*!
2

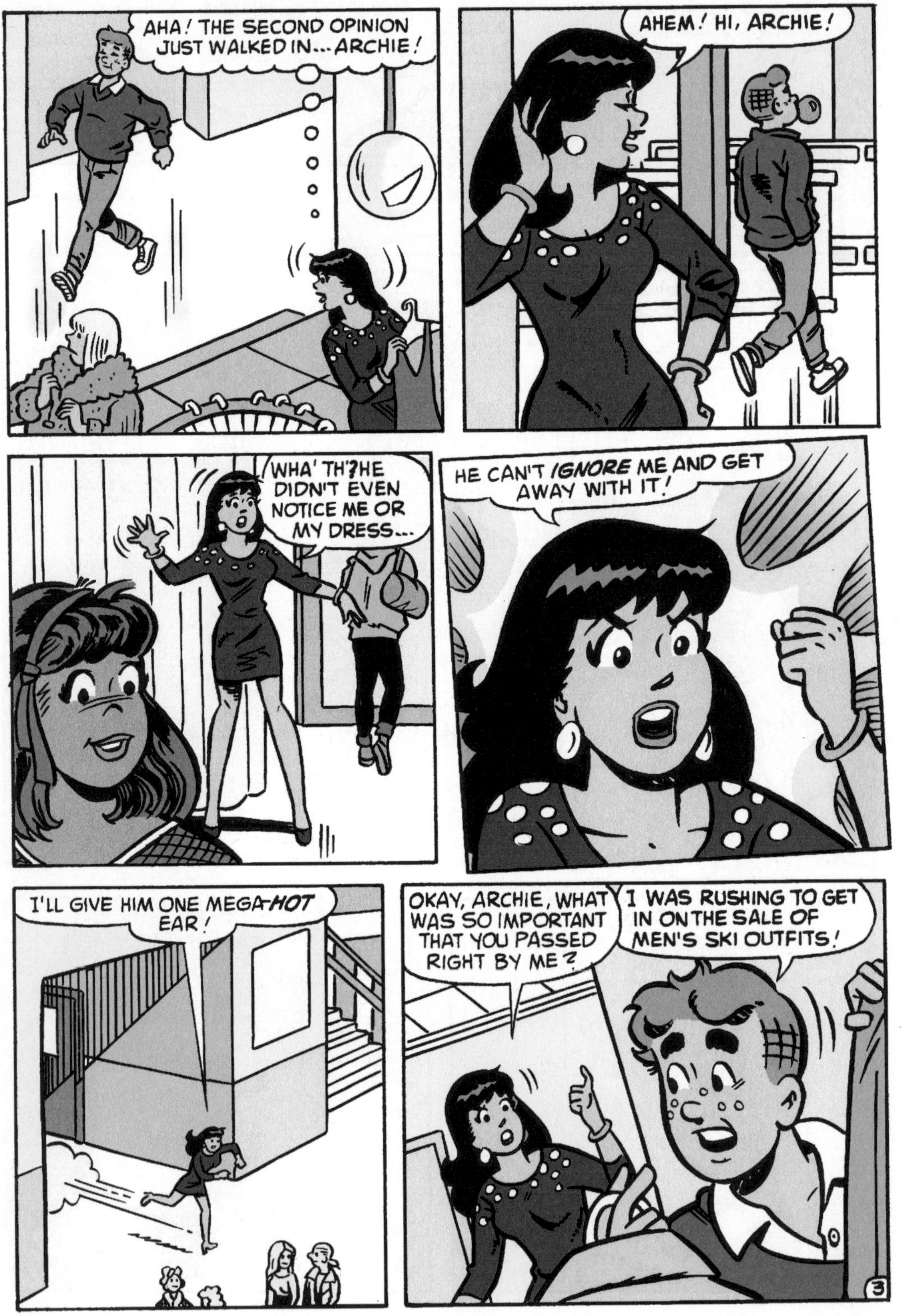
AHA! THE SECOND OPINION JUST WALKED IN... ARCHIE!
AHEM! HI, ARCHIE!
WHA' TH'? HE DIDN'T EVEN NOTICE ME OR MY DRESS...
HE CAN'T IGNORE ME AND GET AWAY WITH IT!
I'LL GIVE HIM ONE MEGA-HOT EAR!
OKAY, ARCHIE, WHAT WAS SO IMPORTANT THAT YOU PASSED RIGHT BY ME?
I WAS RUSHING TO GET IN ON THE SALE OF MEN'S SKI OUTFITS!
3

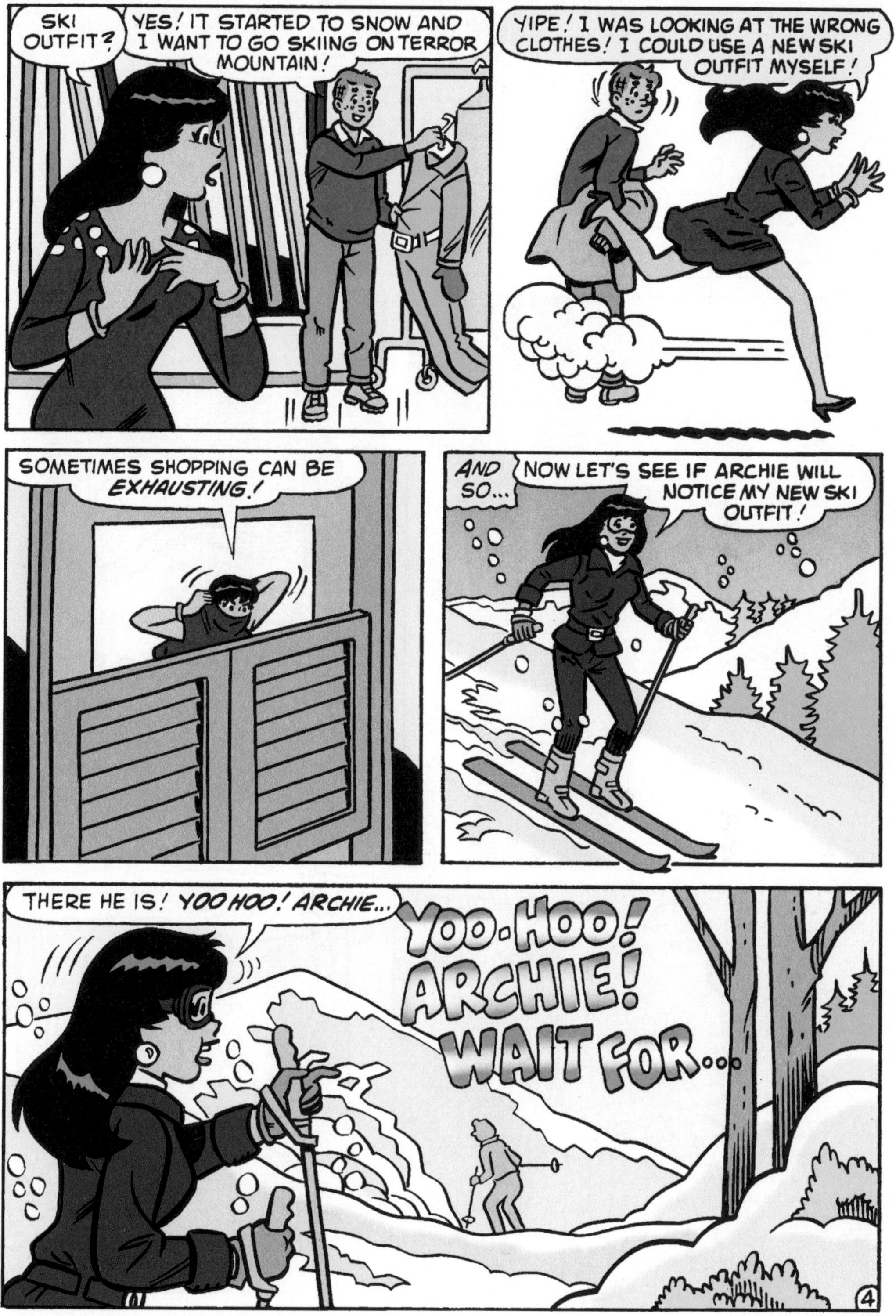
SKI OUTFIT?
YES! IT STARTED TO SNOW AND I WANT TO GO SKIING ON TERROR MOUNTAIN!
YIPE! I WAS LOOKING AT THE WRONG CLOTHES! I COULD USE A NEW SKI OUTFIT MYSELF!
SOMETIMES SHOPPING CAN BE *EXHAUSTING*!
AND SO...
NOW LET'S SEE IF ARCHIE WILL NOTICE MY NEW SKI OUTFIT!
THERE HE IS! *YOO HOO! ARCHIE*...
YOO-HOO! ARCHIE! WAIT FOR...
4

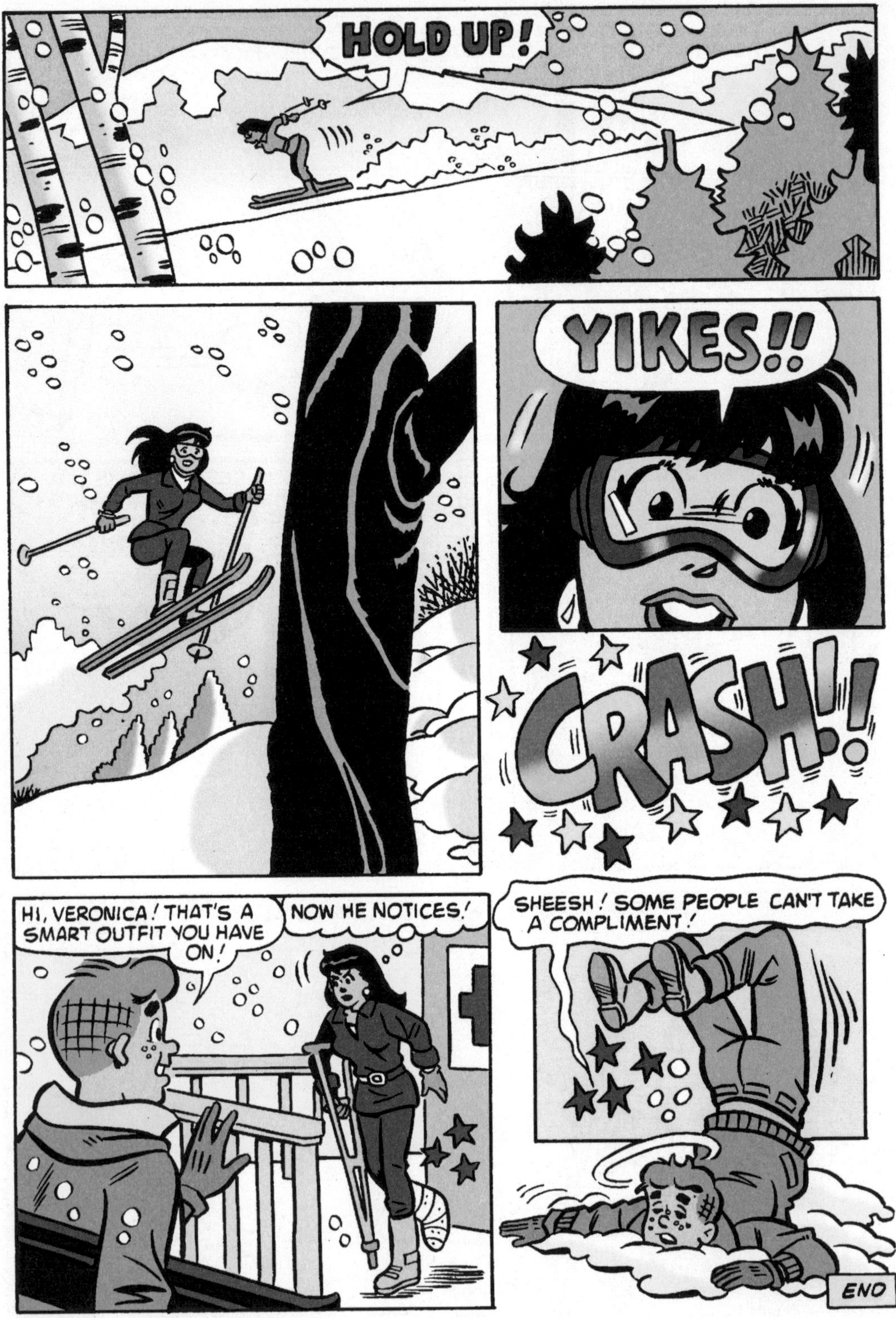
HOLD UP!
YIKES!!
CRASH!!
HI, VERONICA! THAT'S A SMART OUTFIT YOU HAVE ON!
NOW HE NOTICES!
SHEESH! SOME PEOPLE CAN'T TAKE A COMPLIMENT!
END

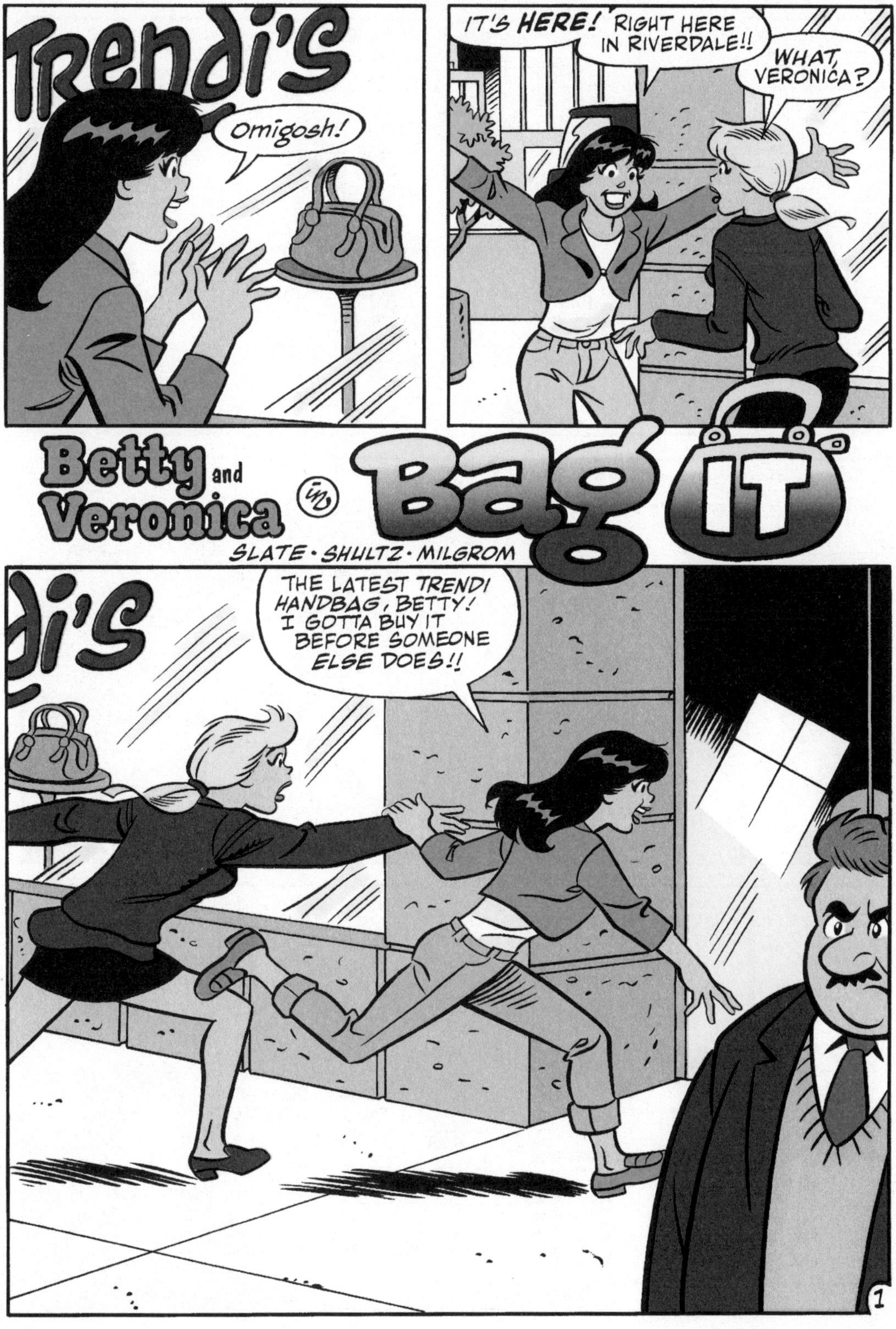
TRENDI'S
Omigosh!
IT'S HERE! RIGHT HERE IN RIVERDALE!!
WHAT, VERONICA?
Betty and Veronica in Bag IT
SLATE · SHULTZ · MILGROM
THE LATEST TRENDI HANDBAG, BETTY! I GOTTA BUY IT BEFORE SOMEONE ELSE DOES!!
1

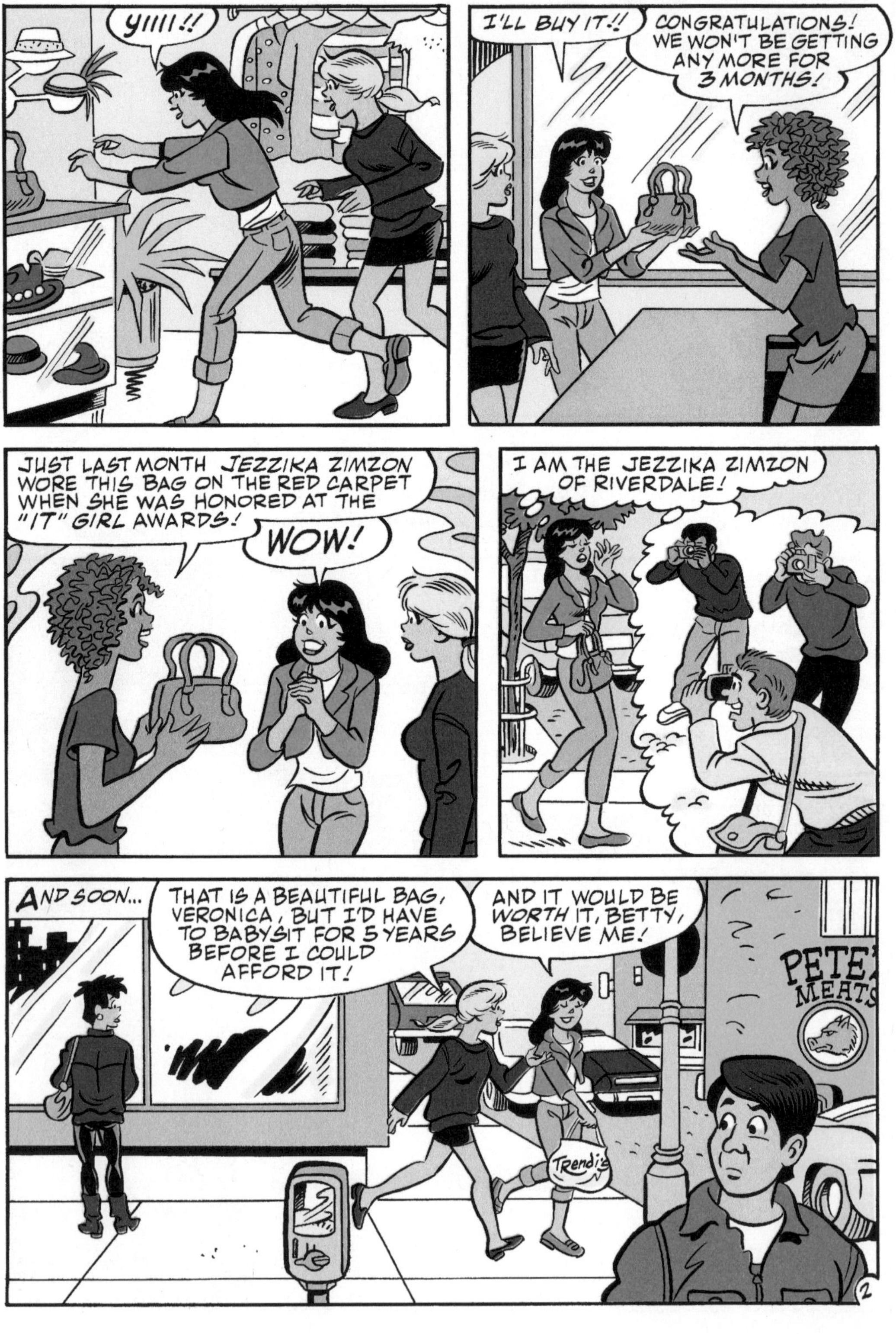
YIIII!!
I'LL BUY IT!!
CONGRATULATIONS! WE WON'T BE GETTING ANY MORE FOR 3 MONTHS!
JUST LAST MONTH JEZZIKA ZIMZON WORE THIS BAG ON THE RED CARPET WHEN SHE WAS HONORED AT THE "IT" GIRL AWARDS!
WOW!
I AM THE JEZZIKA ZIMZON OF RIVERDALE!
AND SOON...
THAT IS A BEAUTIFUL BAG, VERONICA, BUT I'D HAVE TO BABYSIT FOR 5 YEARS BEFORE I COULD AFFORD IT!
AND IT WOULD BE WORTH IT, BETTY, BELIEVE ME!
PETE'
MEATS
Trendi's
2

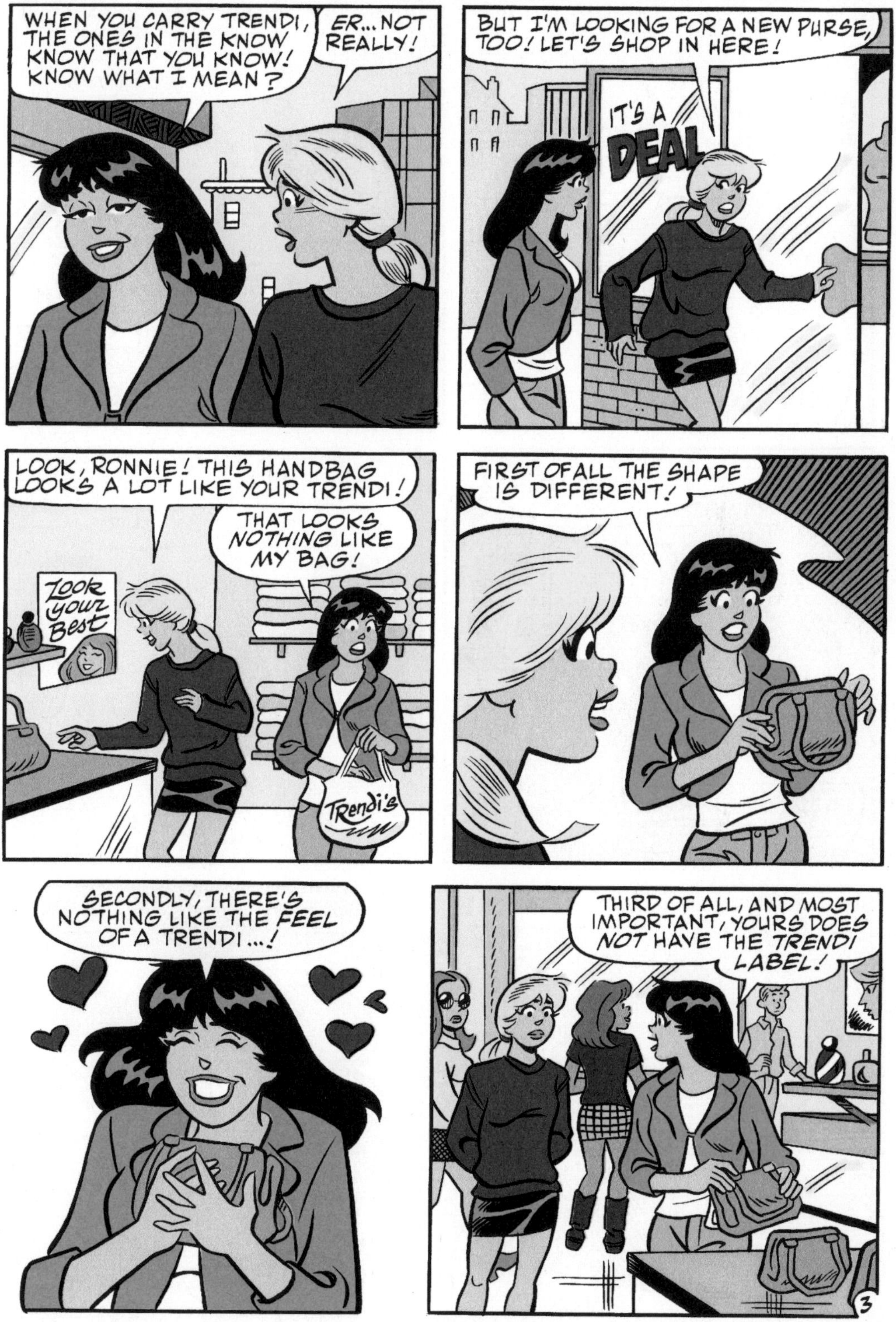
WHEN YOU CARRY TRENDI, THE ONES IN THE KNOW KNOW THAT YOU KNOW! KNOW WHAT I MEAN?
ER...NOT REALLY!
BUT I'M LOOKING FOR A NEW PURSE, TOO! LET'S SHOP IN HERE!
IT'S A DEAL
LOOK, RONNIE! THIS HANDBAG LOOKS A LOT LIKE YOUR TRENDI!
THAT LOOKS NOTHING LIKE MY BAG!
Look your Best
Trendi's
FIRST OF ALL THE SHAPE IS DIFFERENT!
SECONDLY, THERE'S NOTHING LIKE THE FEEL OF A TRENDI...!
THIRD OF ALL, AND MOST IMPORTANT, YOURS DOES NOT HAVE THE TRENDI LABEL!
3

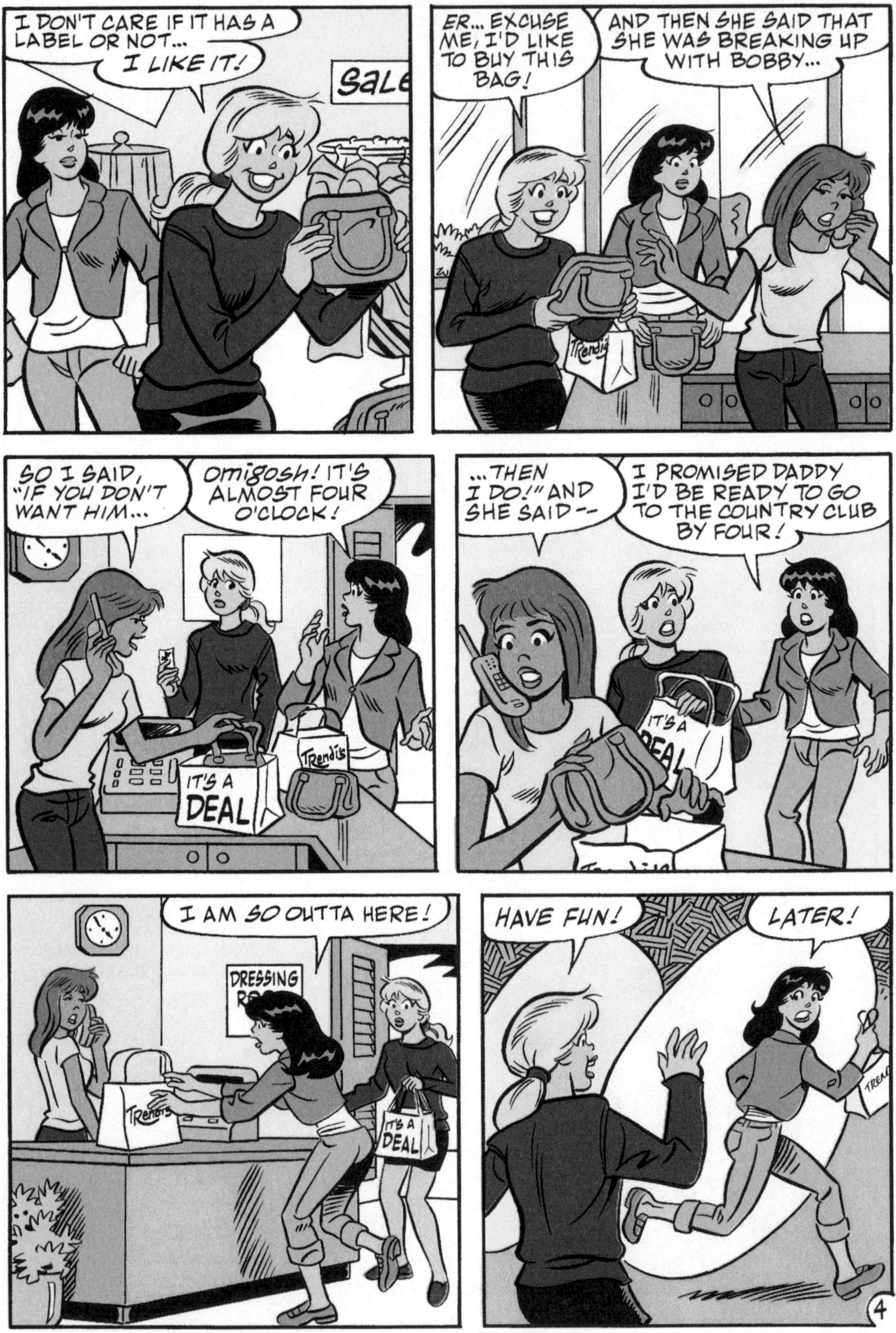
I DON'T CARE IF IT HAS A LABEL OR NOT... I LIKE IT!
SALE
ER... EXCUSE ME, I'D LIKE TO BUY THIS BAG!
AND THEN SHE SAID THAT SHE WAS BREAKING UP WITH BOBBY...
TRENDI'S
SO I SAID, "IF YOU DON'T WANT HIM...
OMIGOSH! IT'S ALMOST FOUR O'CLOCK!
IT'S A DEAL
TRENDI'S
...THEN I DO!" AND SHE SAID--
I PROMISED DADDY I'D BE READY TO GO TO THE COUNTRY CLUB BY FOUR!
IT'S A DEAL
I AM SO OUTTA HERE!
DRESSING
TRENDI'S
IT'S A DEAL
HAVE FUN!
LATER!
4

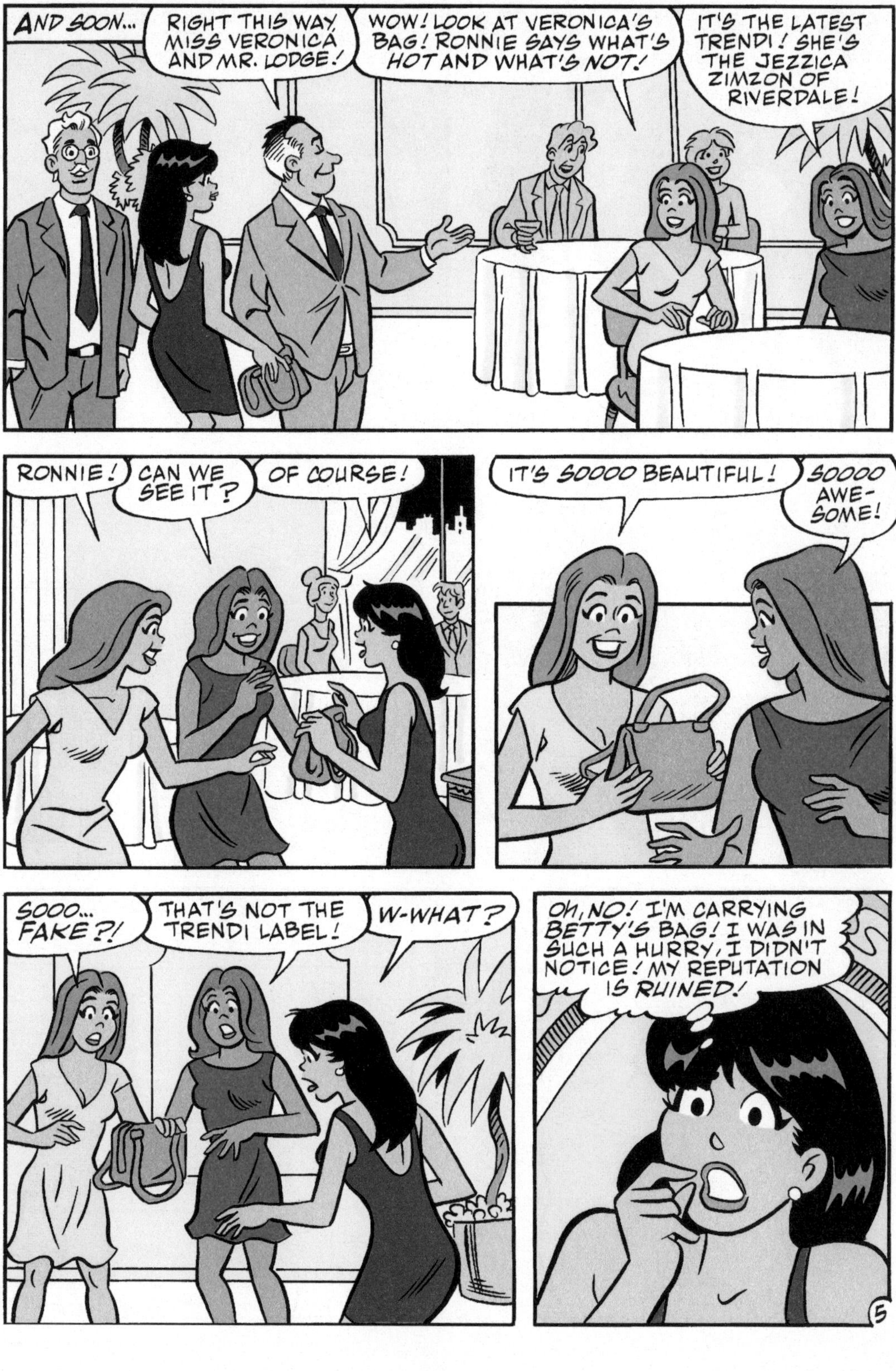
AND SOON...
RIGHT THIS WAY, MISS VERONICA AND MR. LODGE!
WOW! LOOK AT VERONICA'S BAG! RONNIE SAYS WHAT'S HOT AND WHAT'S NOT!
IT'S THE LATEST TRENDI! SHE'S THE JEZZICA ZIMZON OF RIVERDALE!
RONNIE!
CAN WE SEE IT?
OF COURSE!
IT'S SOOOO BEAUTIFUL!
SOOOO AWE-SOME!
SOOO... FAKE?!
THAT'S NOT THE TRENDI LABEL!
W-WHAT?
OH, NO! I'M CARRYING BETTY'S BAG! I WAS IN SUCH A HURRY, I DIDN'T NOTICE! MY REPUTATION IS RUINED!
5

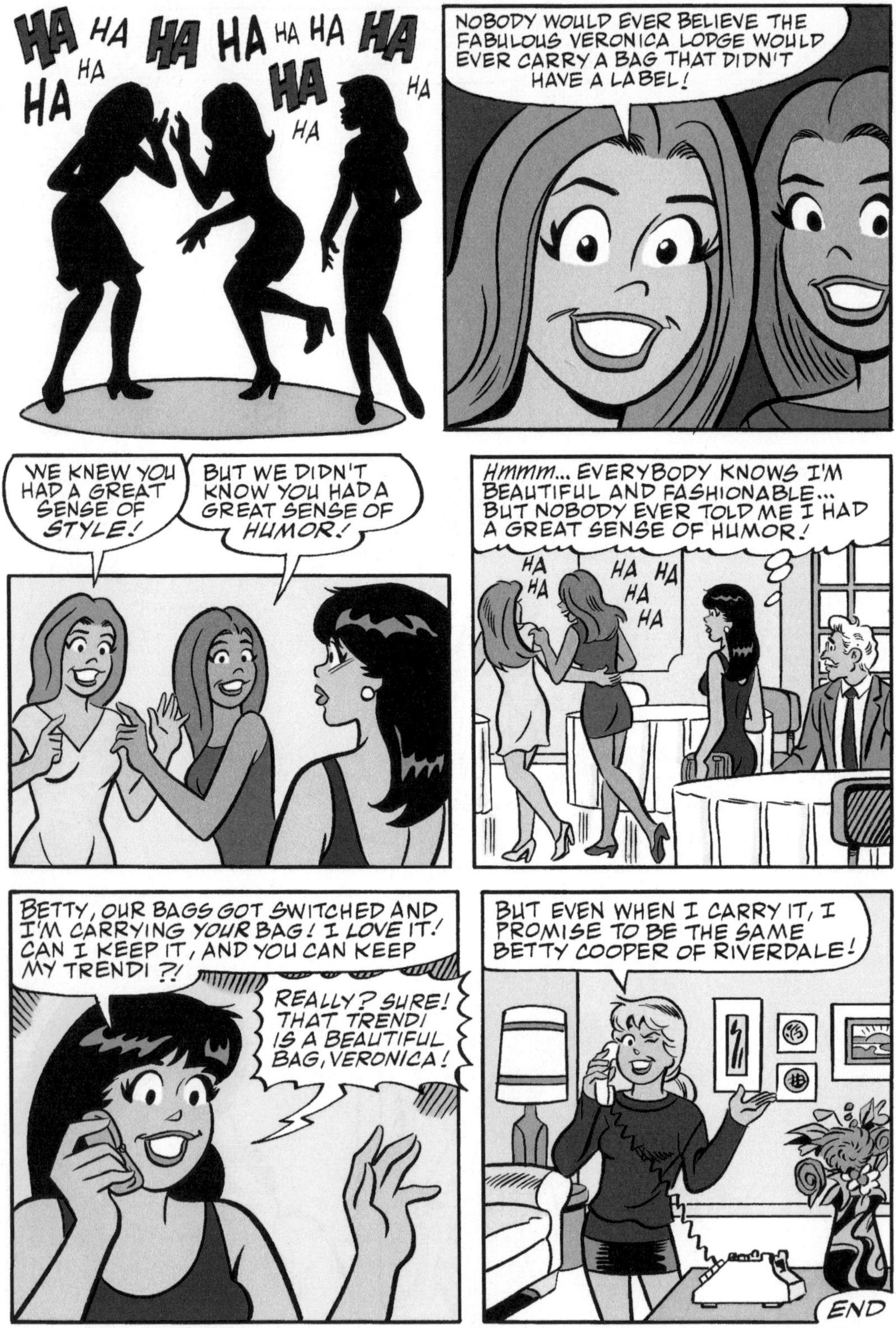
HA HA HA HA HA HA HA HA HA HA HA HA HA
NOBODY WOULD EVER BELIEVE THE FABULOUS VERONICA LODGE WOULD EVER CARRY A BAG THAT DIDN'T HAVE A LABEL!
WE KNEW YOU HAD A GREAT SENSE OF STYLE!
BUT WE DIDN'T KNOW YOU HAD A GREAT SENSE OF HUMOR!
Hmmm... EVERYBODY KNOWS I'M BEAUTIFUL AND FASHIONABLE... BUT NOBODY EVER TOLD ME I HAD A GREAT SENSE OF HUMOR!
HA HA HA HA HA HA HA
BETTY, OUR BAGS GOT SWITCHED AND I'M CARRYING YOUR BAG! I LOVE IT! CAN I KEEP IT, AND YOU CAN KEEP MY TRENDI ?!
REALLY? SURE! THAT TRENDI IS A BEAUTIFUL BAG, VERONICA!
BUT EVEN WHEN I CARRY IT, I PROMISE TO BE THE SAME BETTY COOPER OF RIVERDALE!
END

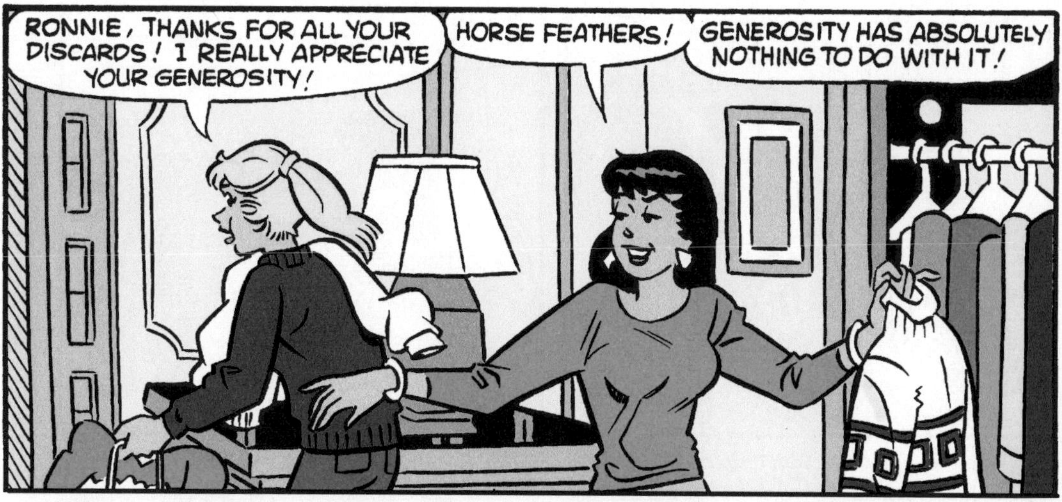
RONNIE, THANKS FOR ALL YOUR DISCARDS! I REALLY APPRECIATE YOUR GENEROSITY!
HORSE FEATHERS!
GENEROSITY HAS ABSOLUTELY NOTHING TO DO WITH IT!

SCRIPT: GEORGE GLADIR PENCILS: TIM KENNEDY INKS: RUDY LAPICK
COLORS: BARRY GROSSMAN LETTERS: BILL YOSHIDA

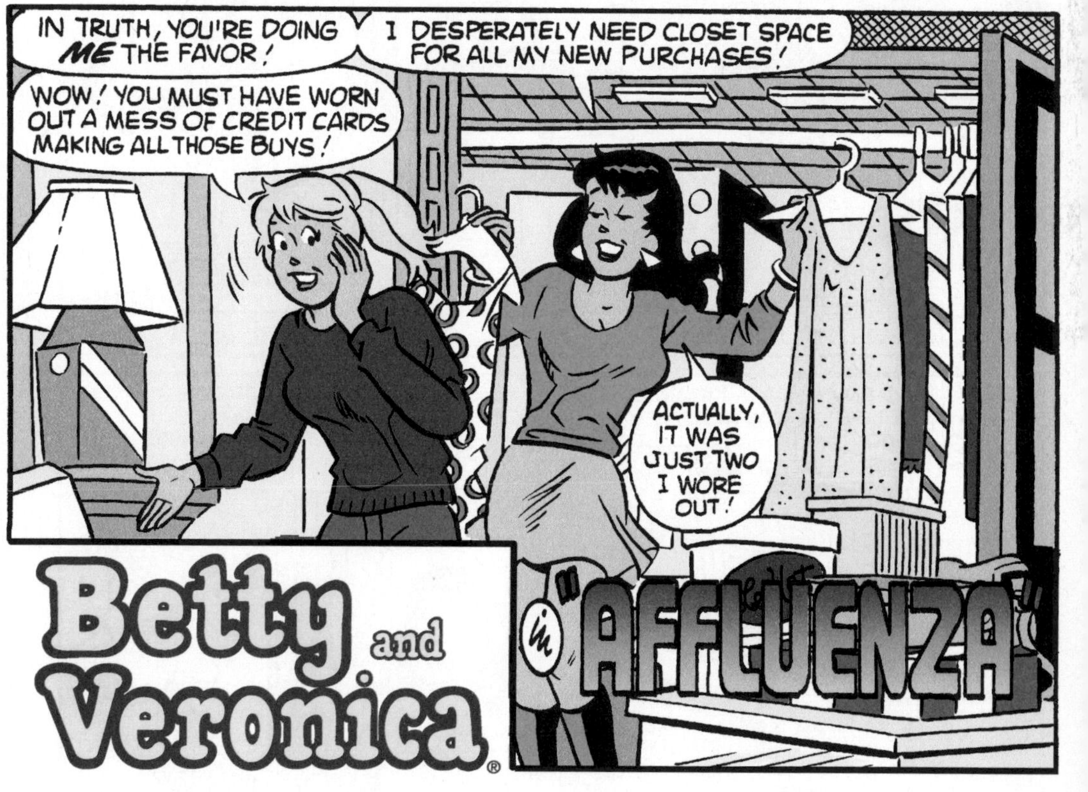
IN TRUTH, YOU'RE DOING *ME* THE FAVOR!
I DESPERATELY NEED CLOSET SPACE FOR ALL MY NEW PURCHASES!
WOW! YOU MUST HAVE WORN OUT A MESS OF CREDIT CARDS MAKING ALL THOSE BUYS!
ACTUALLY, IT WAS JUST TWO I WORE OUT!
Betty and Veronica®
in "AFFLUENZA"

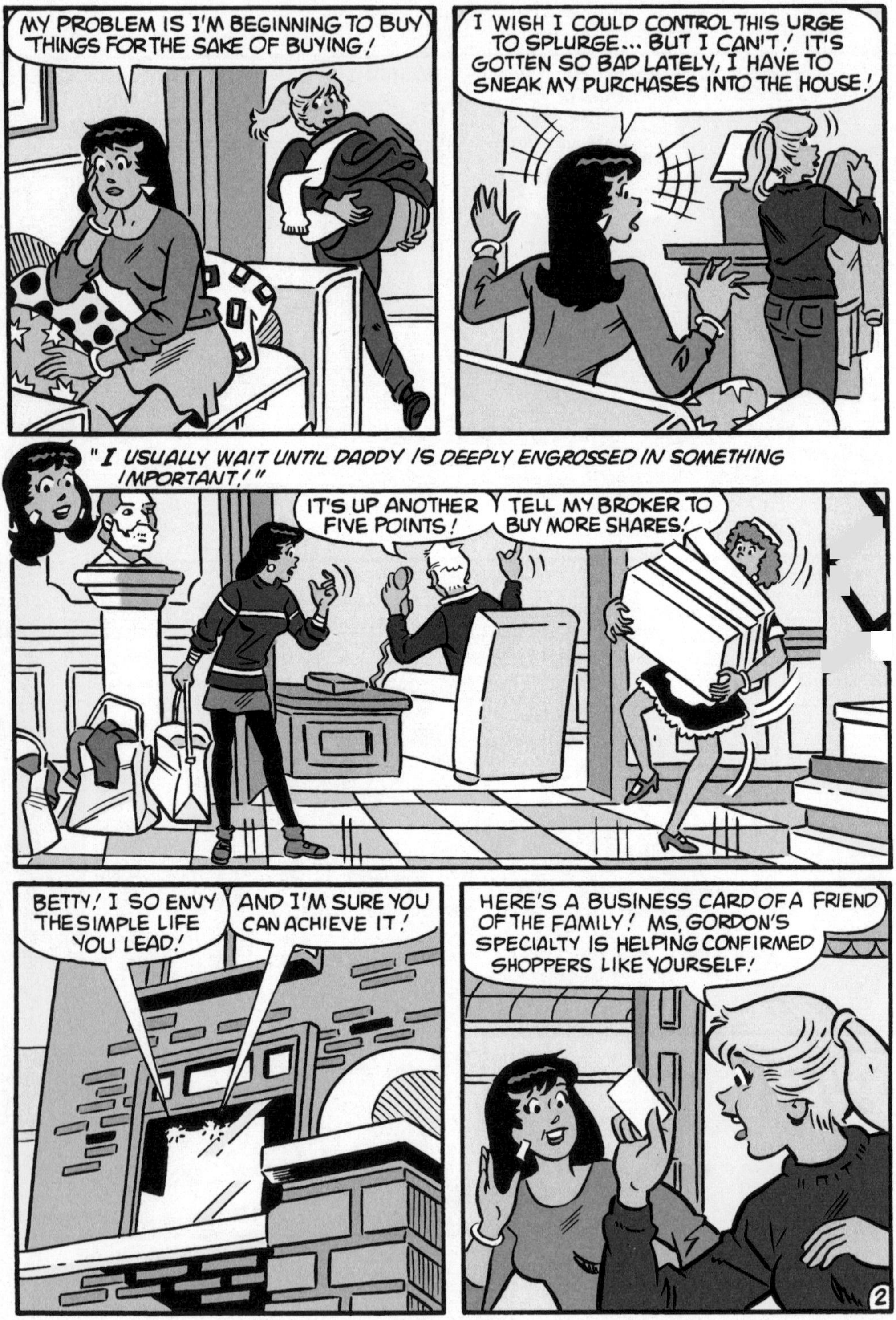
MY PROBLEM IS I'M BEGINNING TO BUY THINGS FOR THE SAKE OF BUYING!
I WISH I COULD CONTROL THIS URGE TO SPLURGE... BUT I CAN'T! IT'S GOTTEN SO BAD LATELY, I HAVE TO SNEAK MY PURCHASES INTO THE HOUSE!
"I USUALLY WAIT UNTIL DADDY IS DEEPLY ENGROSSED IN SOMETHING IMPORTANT!"
IT'S UP ANOTHER FIVE POINTS!
TELL MY BROKER TO BUY MORE SHARES!
BETTY! I SO ENVY THE SIMPLE LIFE YOU LEAD!
AND I'M SURE YOU CAN ACHIEVE IT!
HERE'S A BUSINESS CARD OF A FRIEND OF THE FAMILY! MS. GORDON'S SPECIALTY IS HELPING CONFIRMED SHOPPERS LIKE YOURSELF!
2

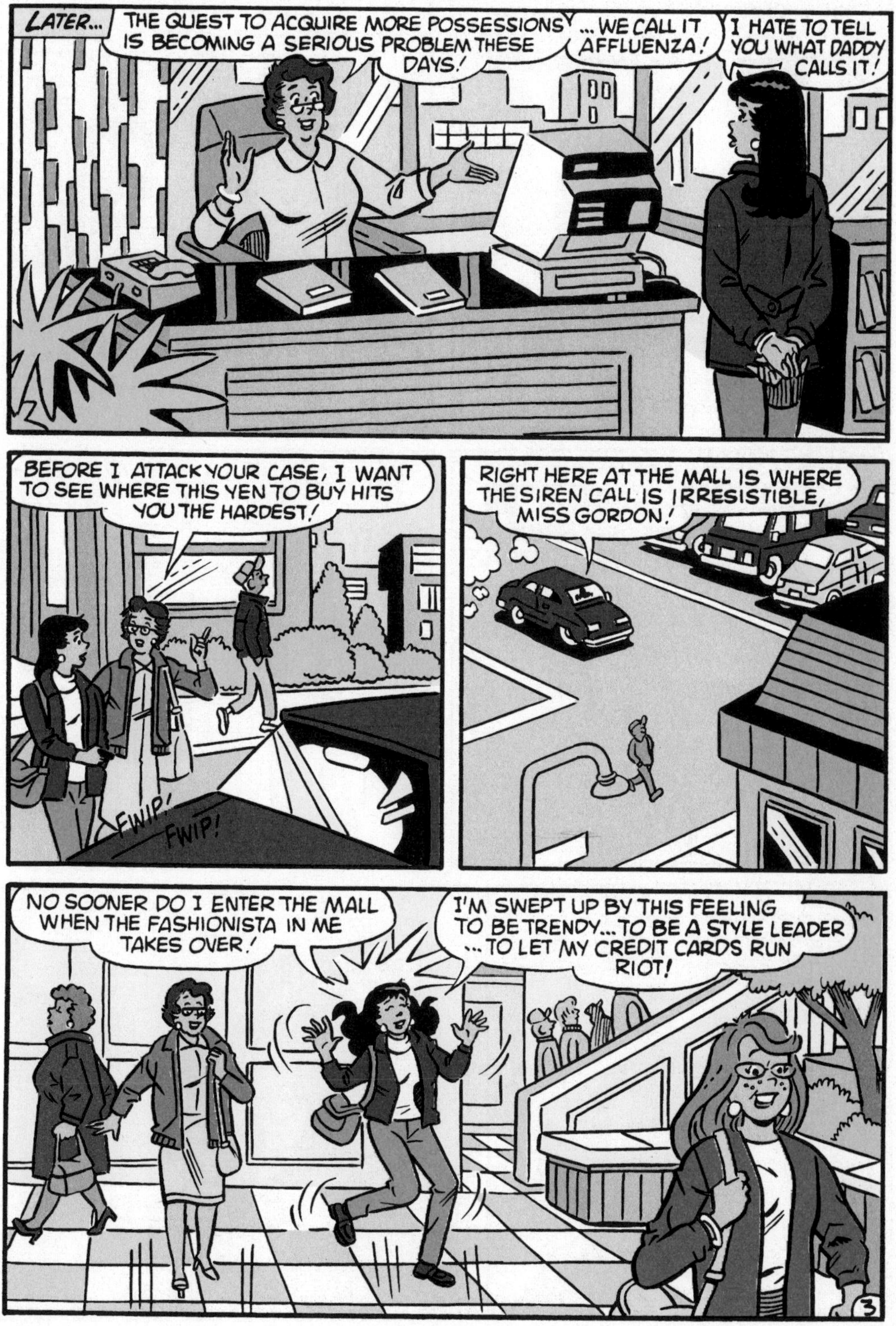
LATER...
THE QUEST TO ACQUIRE MORE POSSESSIONS IS BECOMING A SERIOUS PROBLEM THESE DAYS!
...WE CALL IT AFFLUENZA!
I HATE TO TELL YOU WHAT DADDY CALLS IT!
BEFORE I ATTACK YOUR CASE, I WANT TO SEE WHERE THIS YEN TO BUY HITS YOU THE HARDEST!
FWIP! FWIP!
RIGHT HERE AT THE MALL IS WHERE THE SIREN CALL IS IRRESISTIBLE, MISS GORDON!
NO SOONER DO I ENTER THE MALL WHEN THE FASHIONISTA IN ME TAKES OVER!
I'M SWEPT UP BY THIS FEELING TO BE TRENDY...TO BE A STYLE LEADER ...TO LET MY CREDIT CARDS RUN RIOT!
3

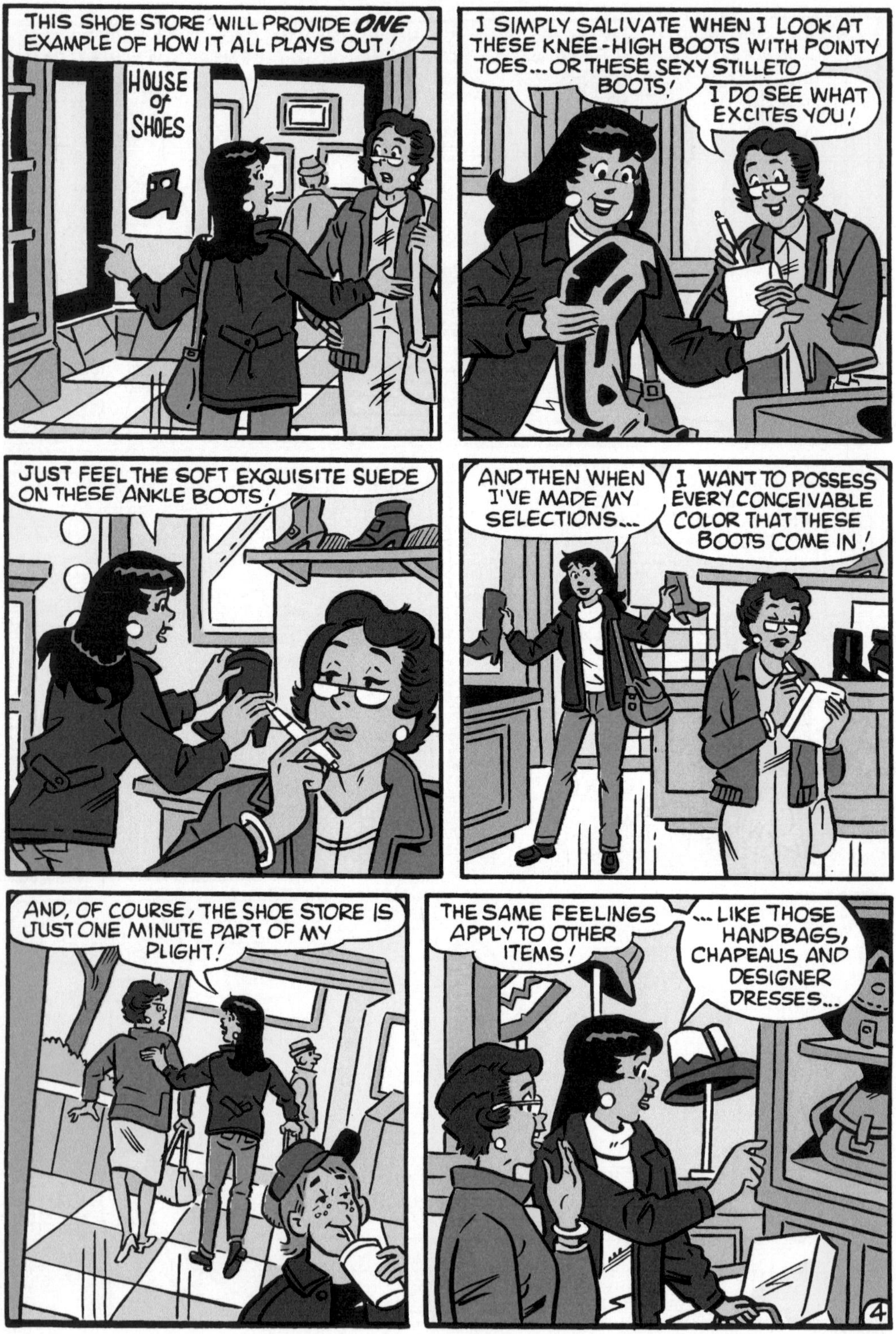
THIS SHOE STORE WILL PROVIDE ONE EXAMPLE OF HOW IT ALL PLAYS OUT!
HOUSE of SHOES
I SIMPLY SALIVATE WHEN I LOOK AT THESE KNEE-HIGH BOOTS WITH POINTY TOES...OR THESE SEXY STILLETO BOOTS!
I DO SEE WHAT EXCITES YOU!
JUST FEEL THE SOFT EXQUISITE SUEDE ON THESE ANKLE BOOTS!
AND THEN WHEN I'VE MADE MY SELECTIONS...
I WANT TO POSSESS EVERY CONCEIVABLE COLOR THAT THESE BOOTS COME IN!
AND, OF COURSE, THE SHOE STORE IS JUST ONE MINUTE PART OF MY PLIGHT!
THE SAME FEELINGS APPLY TO OTHER ITEMS!
...LIKE THOSE HANDBAGS, CHAPEAUS AND DESIGNER DRESSES...
4

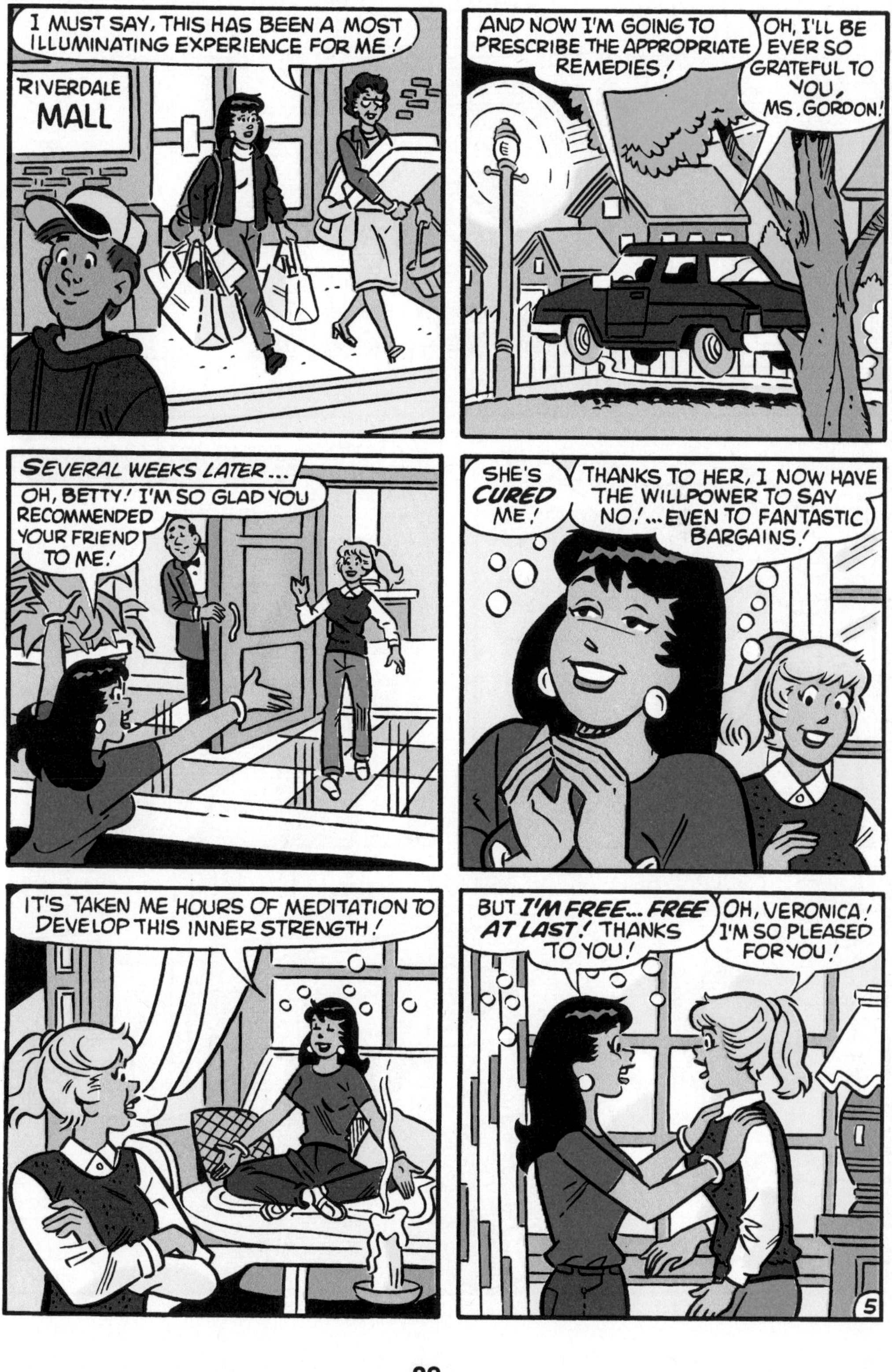
I MUST SAY, THIS HAS BEEN A MOST ILLUMINATING EXPERIENCE FOR ME!
RIVERDALE MALL
AND NOW I'M GOING TO PRESCRIBE THE APPROPRIATE REMEDIES!
OH, I'LL BE EVER SO GRATEFUL TO YOU, MS. GORDON!
SEVERAL WEEKS LATER...
OH, BETTY! I'M SO GLAD YOU RECOMMENDED YOUR FRIEND TO ME!
SHE'S CURED ME!
THANKS TO HER, I NOW HAVE THE WILLPOWER TO SAY NO!...EVEN TO FANTASTIC BARGAINS!
IT'S TAKEN ME HOURS OF MEDITATION TO DEVELOP THIS INNER STRENGTH!
BUT I'M FREE... FREE AT LAST! THANKS TO YOU!
OH, VERONICA! I'M SO PLEASED FOR YOU!
5

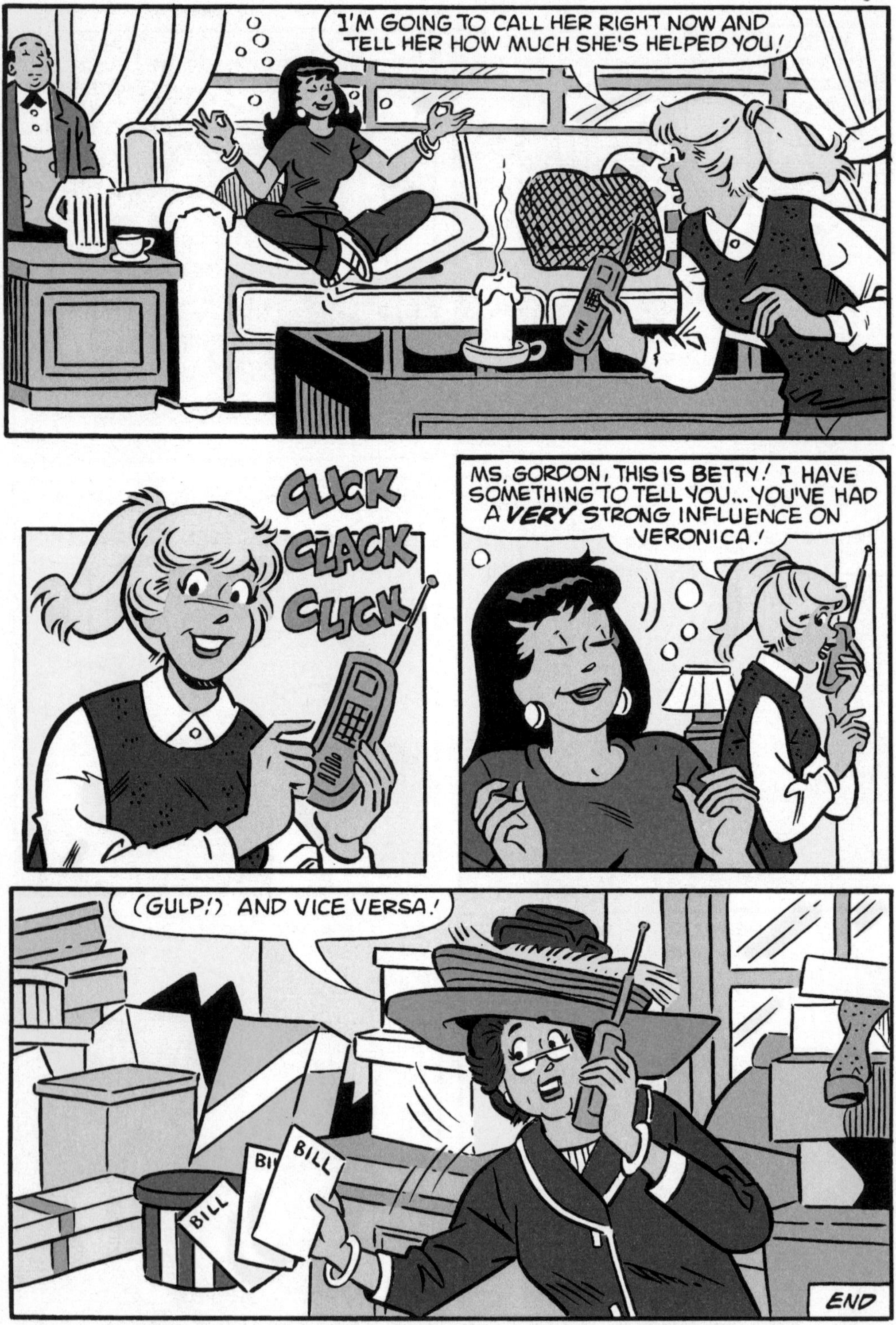
I'M GOING TO CALL HER RIGHT NOW AND TELL HER HOW MUCH SHE'S HELPED YOU!
CLICK
CLACK
CLICK
MS. GORDON, THIS IS BETTY! I HAVE SOMETHING TO TELL YOU... YOU'VE HAD A VERY STRONG INFLUENCE ON VERONICA!
(GULP!) AND VICE VERSA!
BILL
BILL
END

Veronica in "A Wise Shopper"

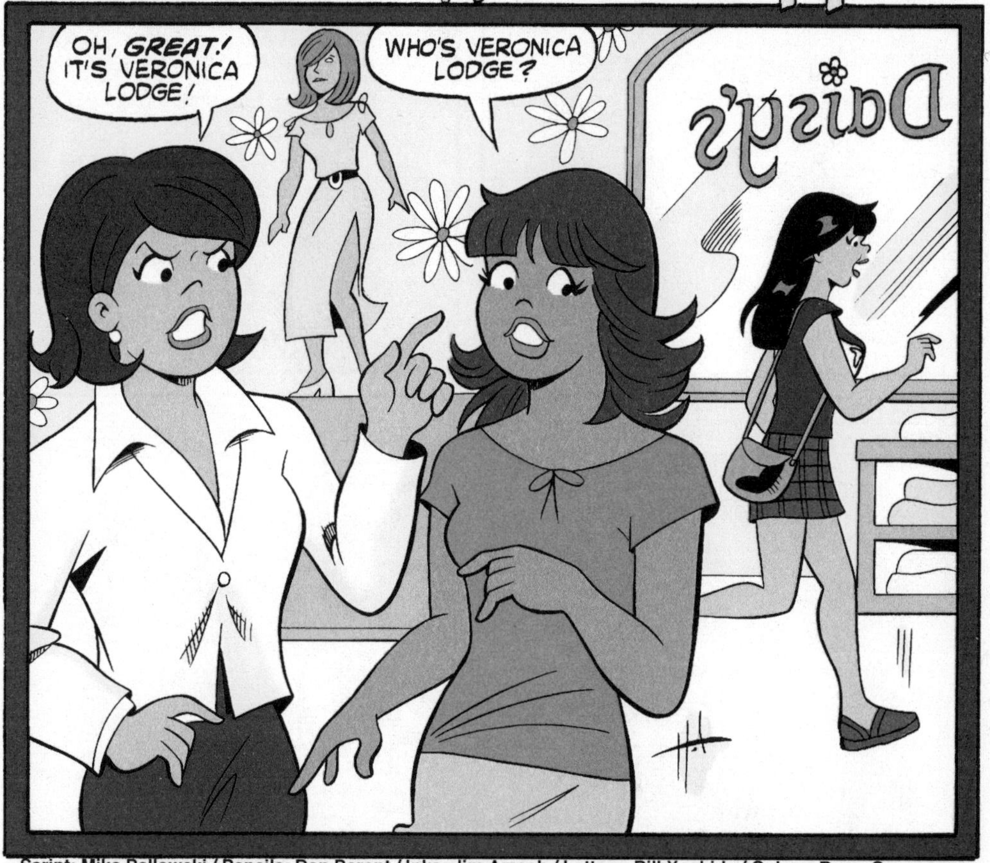

OH, GREAT! IT'S VERONICA LODGE!
WHO'S VERONICA LODGE?
Daisy's

Script: Mike Pellowski / Pencils: Dan Parent / Inks: Jim Amash / Letters: Bill Yoshida / Colors: Barry Grossman

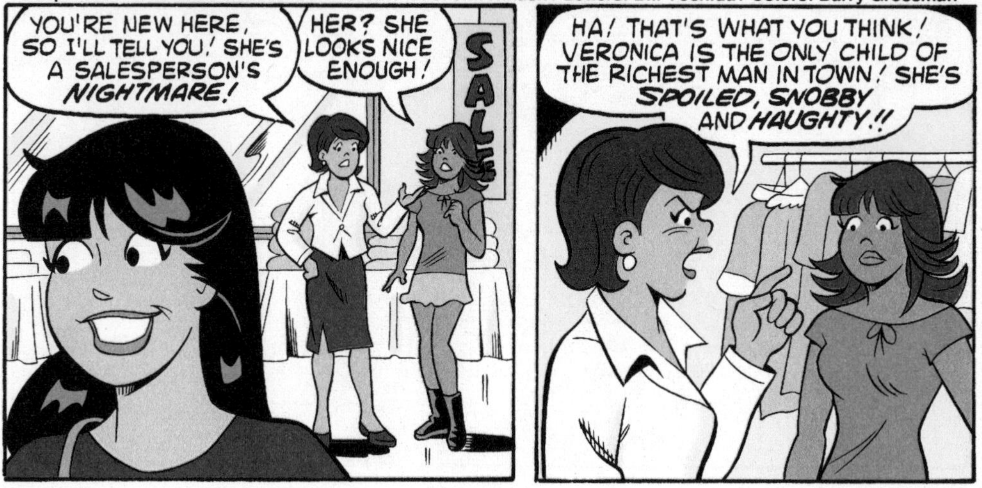

YOU'RE NEW HERE, SO I'LL TELL YOU! SHE'S A SALESPERSON'S NIGHTMARE!
HER? SHE LOOKS NICE ENOUGH!
SALE
HA! THAT'S WHAT YOU THINK! VERONICA IS THE ONLY CHILD OF THE RICHEST MAN IN TOWN! SHE'S SPOILED, SNOBBY AND HAUGHTY!!

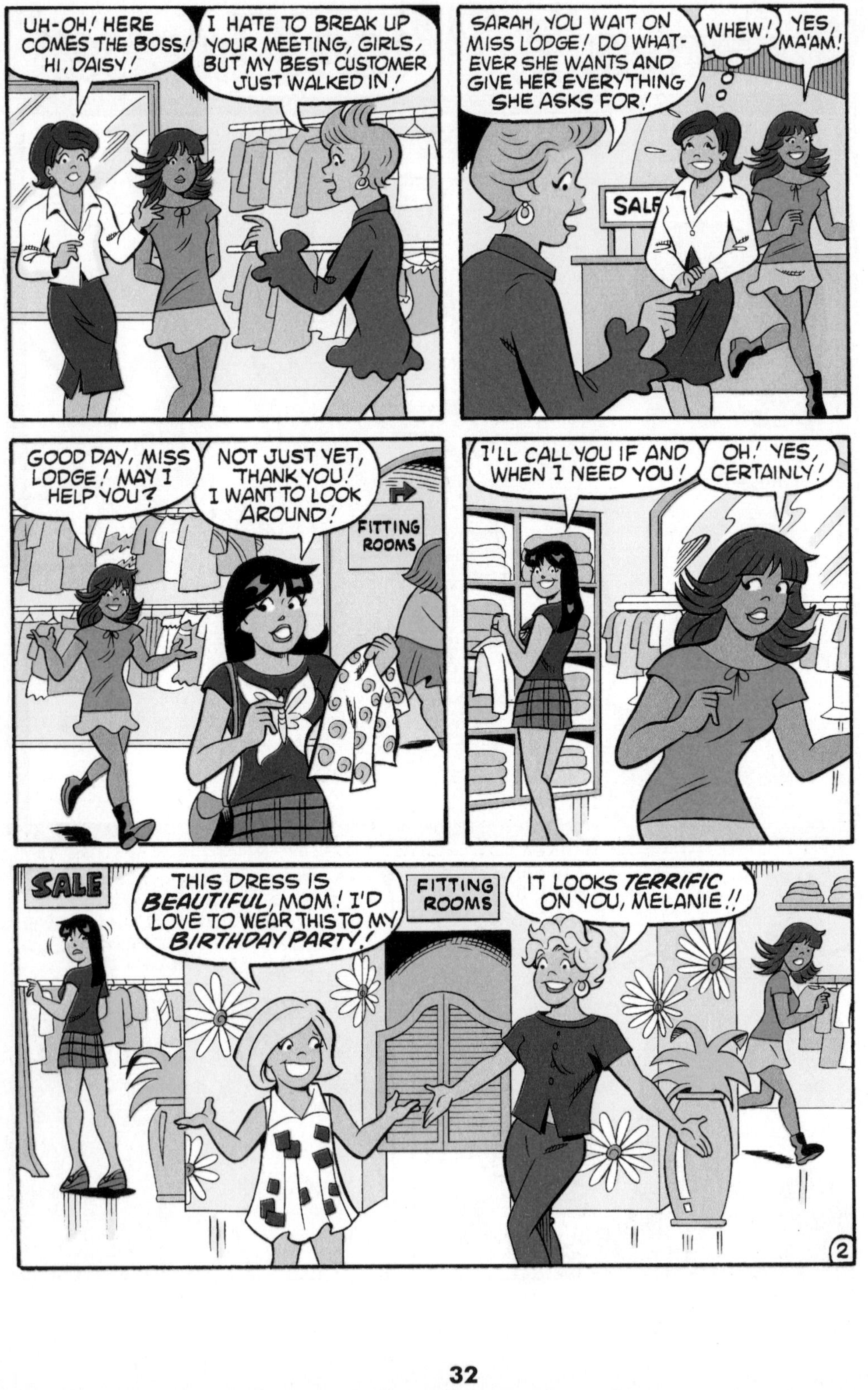
UH-OH! HERE COMES THE BOSS! HI, DAISY!
I HATE TO BREAK UP YOUR MEETING, GIRLS, BUT MY BEST CUSTOMER JUST WALKED IN!
SARAH, YOU WAIT ON MISS LODGE! DO WHAT-EVER SHE WANTS AND GIVE HER EVERYTHING SHE ASKS FOR!
WHEW!
YES, MA'AM!
SALE
GOOD DAY, MISS LODGE! MAY I HELP YOU?
NOT JUST YET, THANK YOU! I WANT TO LOOK AROUND!
FITTING ROOMS
I'LL CALL YOU IF AND WHEN I NEED YOU!
OH! YES, CERTAINLY!
SALE
THIS DRESS IS *BEAUTIFUL*, MOM! I'D LOVE TO WEAR THIS TO MY *BIRTHDAY PARTY*!
FITTING ROOMS
IT LOOKS *TERRIFIC* ON YOU, MELANIE!!
2

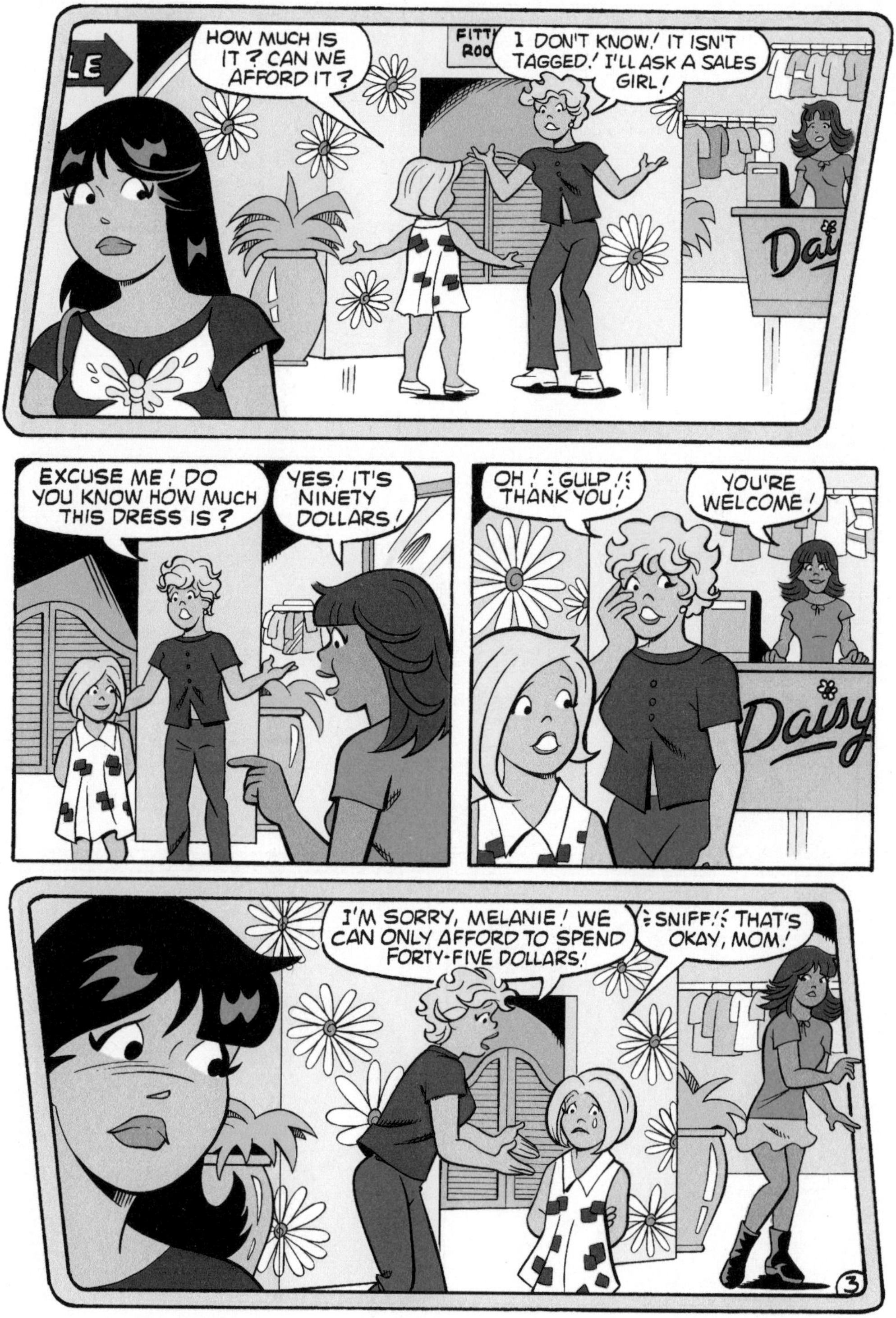
HOW MUCH IS IT ? CAN WE AFFORD IT ?
I DON'T KNOW! IT ISN'T TAGGED! I'LL ASK A SALES GIRL!
Daisy
EXCUSE ME! DO YOU KNOW HOW MUCH THIS DRESS IS ?
YES! IT'S NINETY DOLLARS!
OH! GULP! THANK YOU!
YOU'RE WELCOME!
Daisy
I'M SORRY, MELANIE! WE CAN ONLY AFFORD TO SPEND FORTY-FIVE DOLLARS!
SNIFF! THAT'S OKAY, MOM!
3

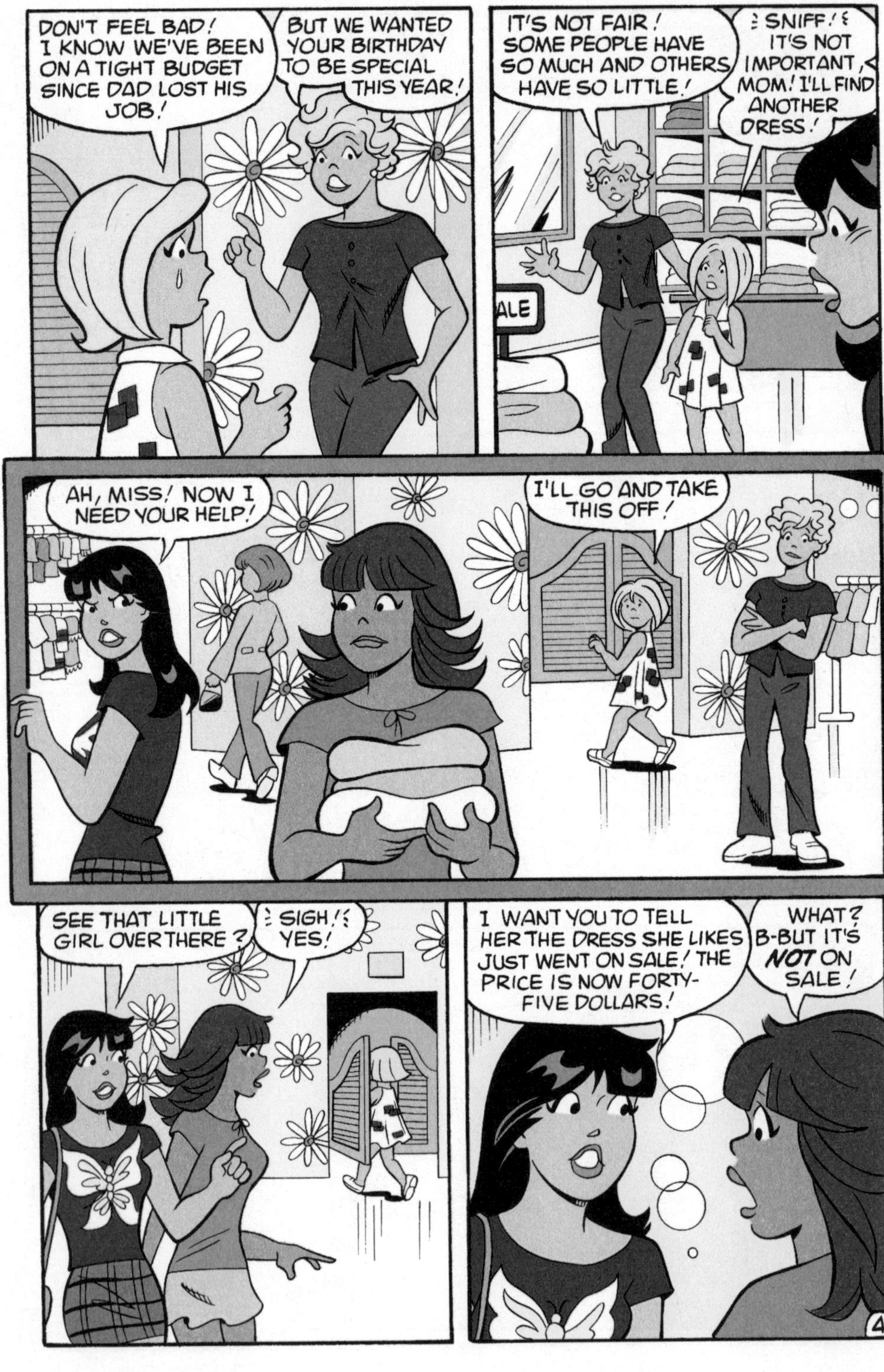
DON'T FEEL BAD! I KNOW WE'VE BEEN ON A TIGHT BUDGET SINCE DAD LOST HIS JOB!
BUT WE WANTED YOUR BIRTHDAY TO BE SPECIAL THIS YEAR!
IT'S NOT FAIR! SOME PEOPLE HAVE SO MUCH AND OTHERS HAVE SO LITTLE!
SNIFF! IT'S NOT IMPORTANT, MOM! I'LL FIND ANOTHER DRESS!
ALE
AH, MISS! NOW I NEED YOUR HELP!
I'LL GO AND TAKE THIS OFF!
SEE THAT LITTLE GIRL OVER THERE?
SIGH! YES!
I WANT YOU TO TELL HER THE DRESS SHE LIKES JUST WENT ON SALE! THE PRICE IS NOW FORTY-FIVE DOLLARS!
WHAT? B-BUT IT'S ***NOT*** ON SALE!
4

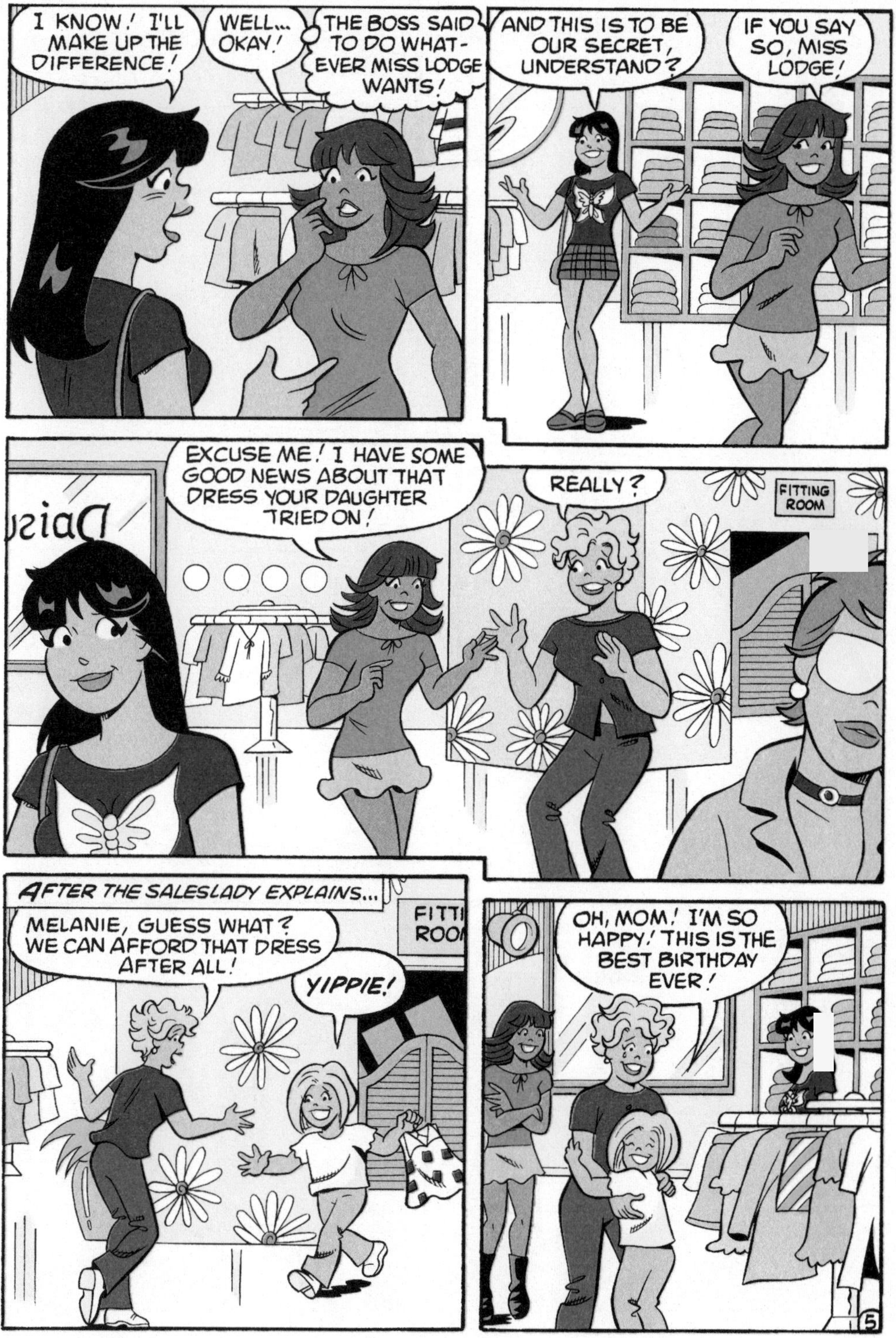
I KNOW! I'LL MAKE UP THE DIFFERENCE!
WELL... OKAY!
THE BOSS SAID TO DO WHAT-EVER MISS LODGE WANTS!
AND THIS IS TO BE OUR SECRET, UNDERSTAND?
IF YOU SAY SO, MISS LODGE!
EXCUSE ME! I HAVE SOME GOOD NEWS ABOUT THAT DRESS YOUR DAUGHTER TRIED ON!
REALLY?
FITTING ROOM
AFTER THE SALESLADY EXPLAINS...
MELANIE, GUESS WHAT? WE CAN AFFORD THAT DRESS AFTER ALL!
YIPPIE!
OH, MOM! I'M SO HAPPY! THIS IS THE BEST BIRTHDAY EVER!
5

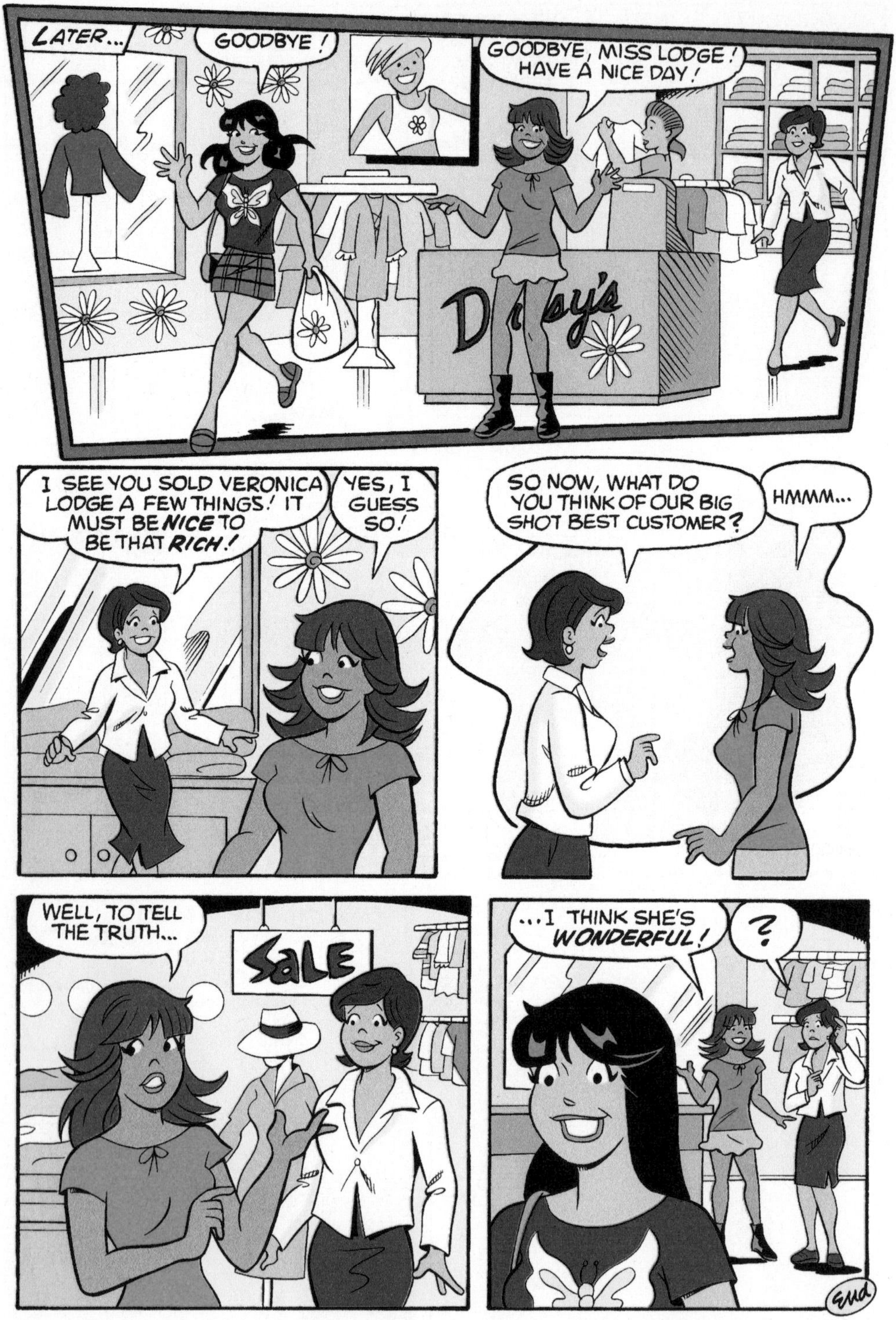
LATER...
GOODBYE!
GOODBYE, MISS LODGE! HAVE A NICE DAY!
I SEE YOU SOLD VERONICA LODGE A FEW THINGS! IT MUST BE NICE TO BE THAT RICH!
YES, I GUESS SO!
SO NOW, WHAT DO YOU THINK OF OUR BIG SHOT BEST CUSTOMER?
HMMM...
WELL, TO TELL THE TRUTH...
SALE
...I THINK SHE'S WONDERFUL!
?
END

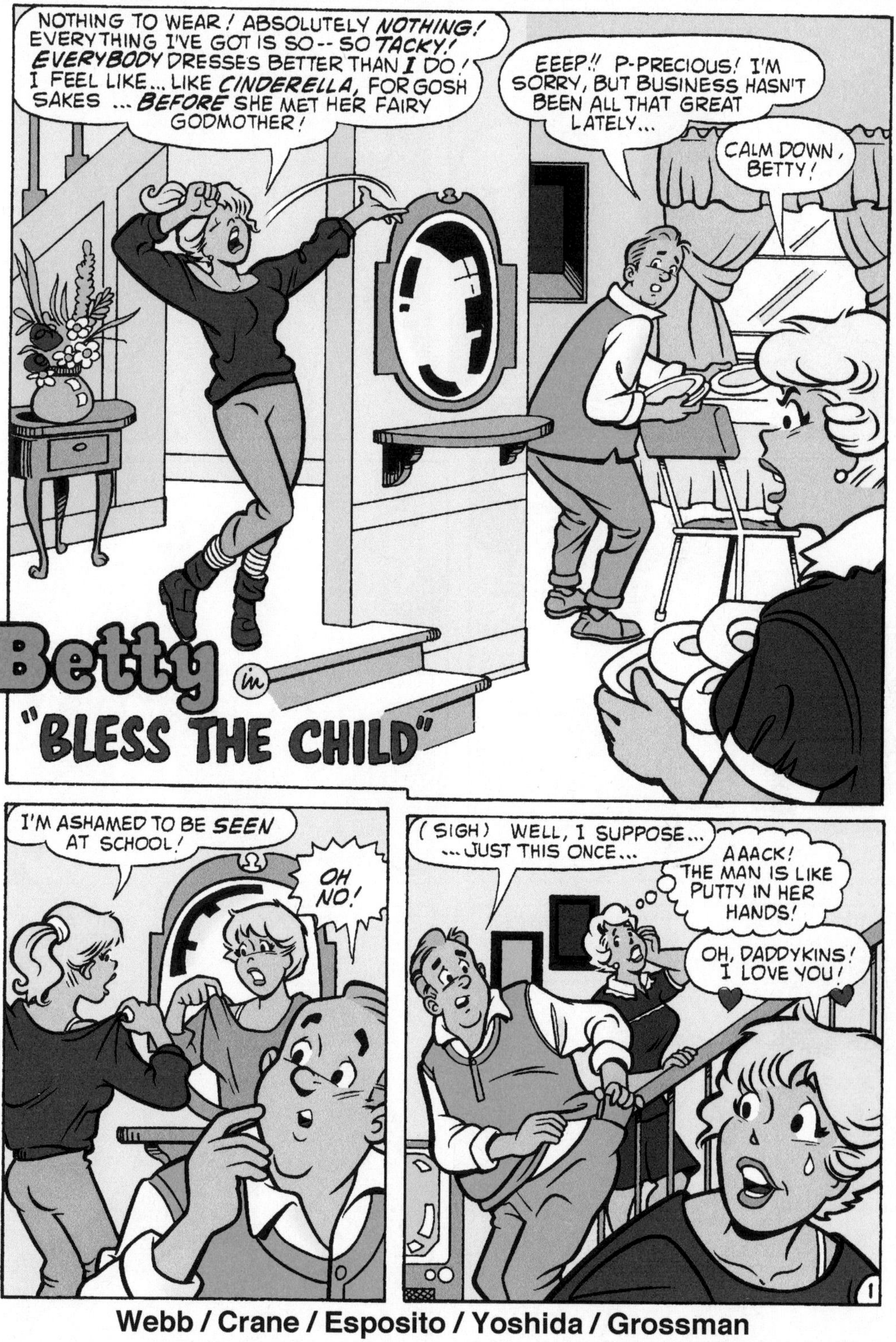
NOTHING TO WEAR! ABSOLUTELY NOTHING! EVERYTHING I'VE GOT IS SO-- SO TACKY! EVERYBODY DRESSES BETTER THAN I DO! I FEEL LIKE... LIKE CINDERELLA, FOR GOSH SAKES ...BEFORE SHE MET HER FAIRY GODMOTHER!
EEEP!! P-PRECIOUS! I'M SORRY, BUT BUSINESS HASN'T BEEN ALL THAT GREAT LATELY...
CALM DOWN, BETTY!
Betty in
"BLESS THE CHILD"
I'M ASHAMED TO BE SEEN AT SCHOOL!
OH NO!
(SIGH) WELL, I SUPPOSE... ...JUST THIS ONCE...
AAACK! THE MAN IS LIKE PUTTY IN HER HANDS!
OH, DADDYKINS! I LOVE YOU!
1

Webb / Crane / Esposito / Yoshida / Grossman

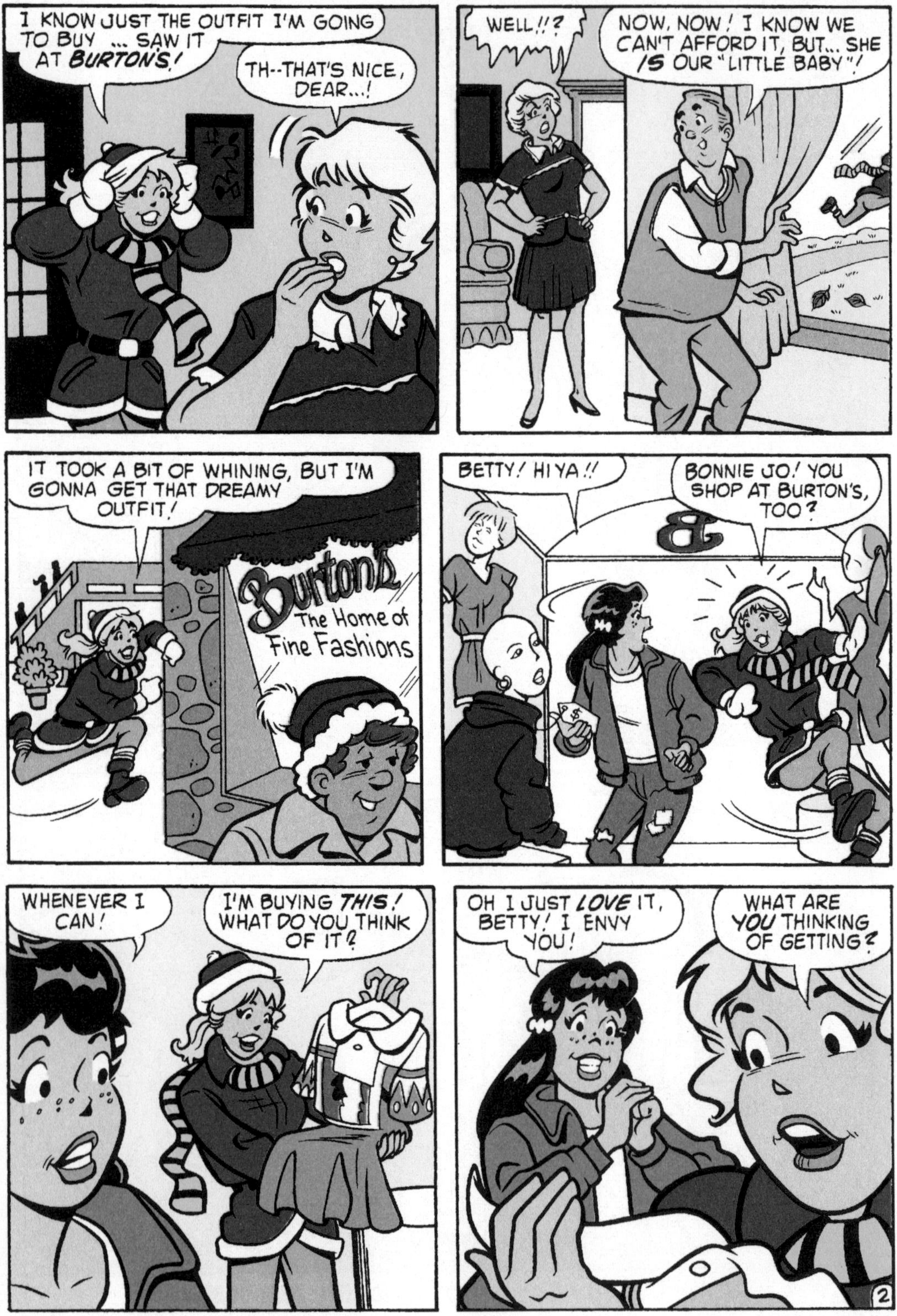
I KNOW JUST THE OUTFIT I'M GOING TO BUY ... SAW IT AT BURTON'S!
TH--THAT'S NICE, DEAR...!
WELL!!?
NOW, NOW! I KNOW WE CAN'T AFFORD IT, BUT... SHE IS OUR "LITTLE BABY"!
IT TOOK A BIT OF WHINING, BUT I'M GONNA GET THAT DREAMY OUTFIT!
Burton's The Home of Fine Fashions
BETTY! HI YA!!
BONNIE JO! YOU SHOP AT BURTON'S, TOO?
WHENEVER I CAN!
I'M BUYING THIS! WHAT DO YOU THINK OF IT?
OH I JUST LOVE IT, BETTY! I ENVY YOU!
WHAT ARE YOU THINKING OF GETTING?
2

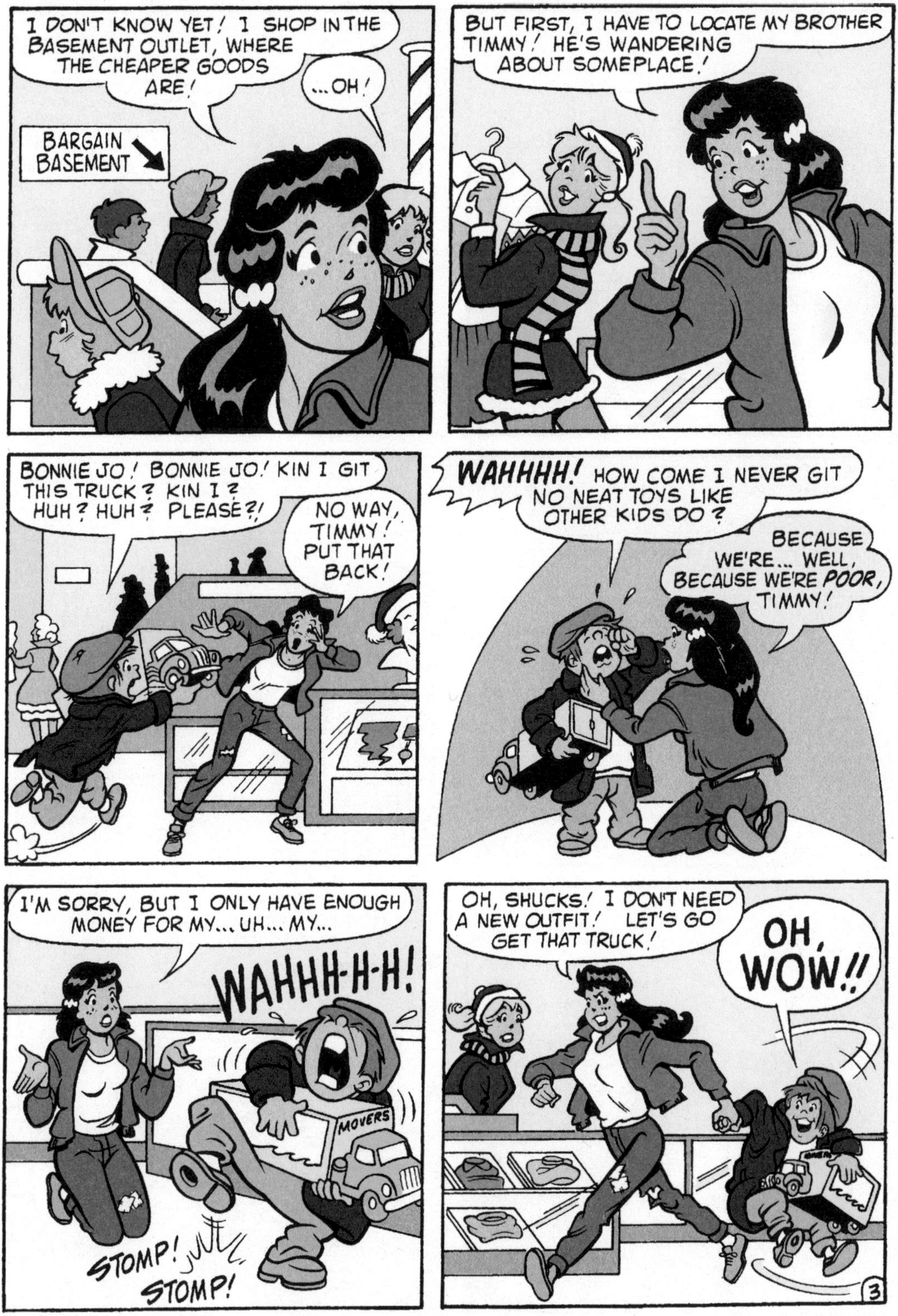

I DON'T KNOW YET! I SHOP IN THE BASEMENT OUTLET, WHERE THE CHEAPER GOODS ARE!
...OH!
BARGAIN BASEMENT
BUT FIRST, I HAVE TO LOCATE MY BROTHER TIMMY! HE'S WANDERING ABOUT SOMEPLACE!
BONNIE JO! BONNIE JO! KIN I GIT THIS TRUCK? KIN I? HUH? HUH? PLEASE?!
NO WAY, TIMMY! PUT THAT BACK!
WAHHHH! HOW COME I NEVER GIT NO NEAT TOYS LIKE OTHER KIDS DO?
BECAUSE WE'RE... WELL, BECAUSE WE'RE *POOR*, TIMMY!
I'M SORRY, BUT I ONLY HAVE ENOUGH MONEY FOR MY... UH... MY...
WAHHH-H-H!
MOVERS
STOMP!
STOMP!
OH, SHUCKS! I DON'T NEED A NEW OUTFIT! LET'S GO GET THAT TRUCK!
OH, WOW!!
3

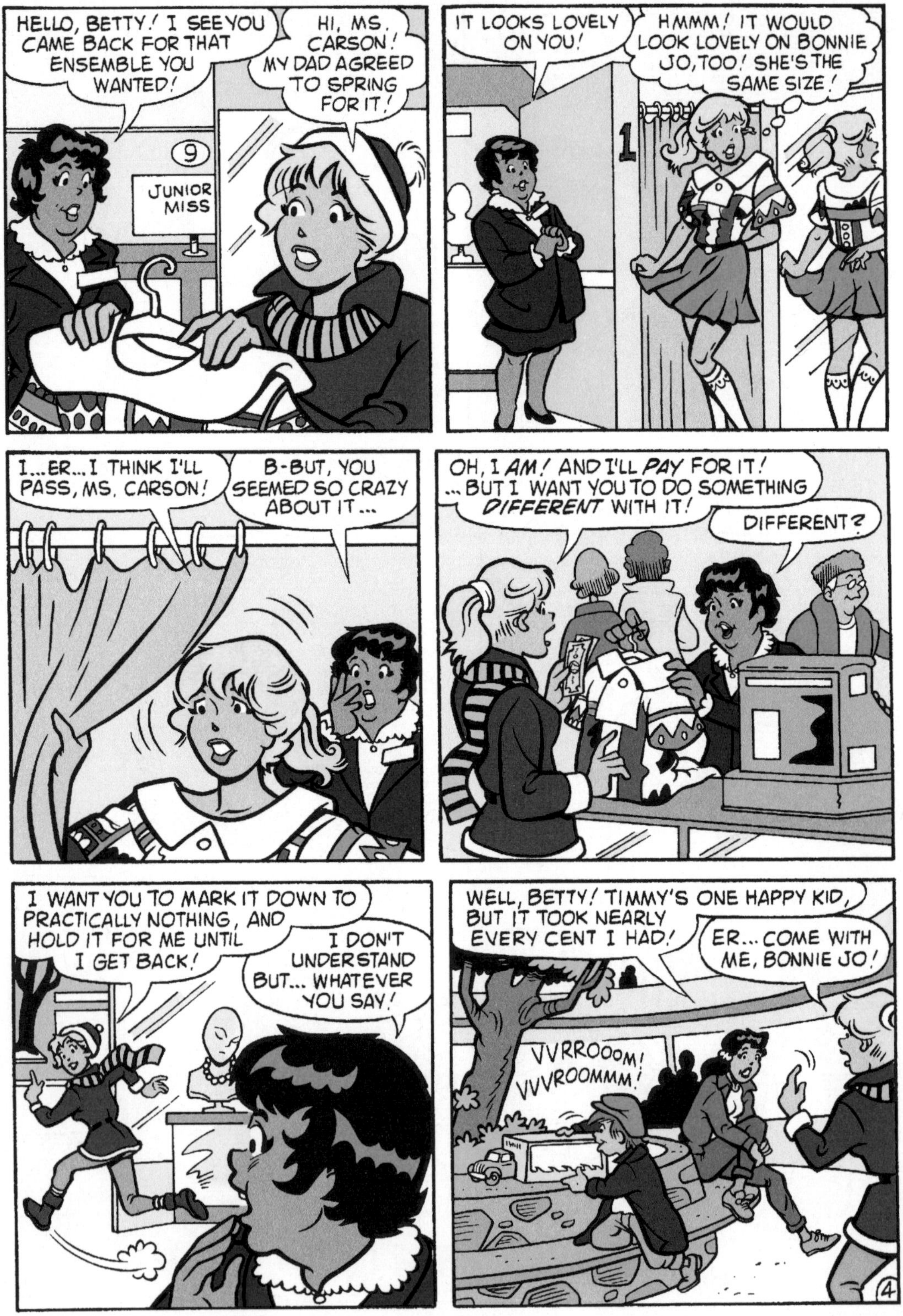
HELLO, BETTY! I SEE YOU CAME BACK FOR THAT ENSEMBLE YOU WANTED!
HI, MS. CARSON! MY DAD AGREED TO SPRING FOR IT!
9
JUNIOR MISS
IT LOOKS LOVELY ON YOU!
HMMM! IT WOULD LOOK LOVELY ON BONNIE JO, TOO! SHE'S THE SAME SIZE!
1
I...ER...I THINK I'LL PASS, MS. CARSON!
B-BUT, YOU SEEMED SO CRAZY ABOUT IT...
OH, I AM! AND I'LL PAY FOR IT! ...BUT I WANT YOU TO DO SOMETHING DIFFERENT WITH IT!
DIFFERENT?
I WANT YOU TO MARK IT DOWN TO PRACTICALLY NOTHING, AND HOLD IT FOR ME UNTIL I GET BACK!
I DON'T UNDERSTAND BUT... WHATEVER YOU SAY!
WELL, BETTY! TIMMY'S ONE HAPPY KID, BUT IT TOOK NEARLY EVERY CENT I HAD!
ER... COME WITH ME, BONNIE JO!
VVRROOOM! VVVROOMMM!
4

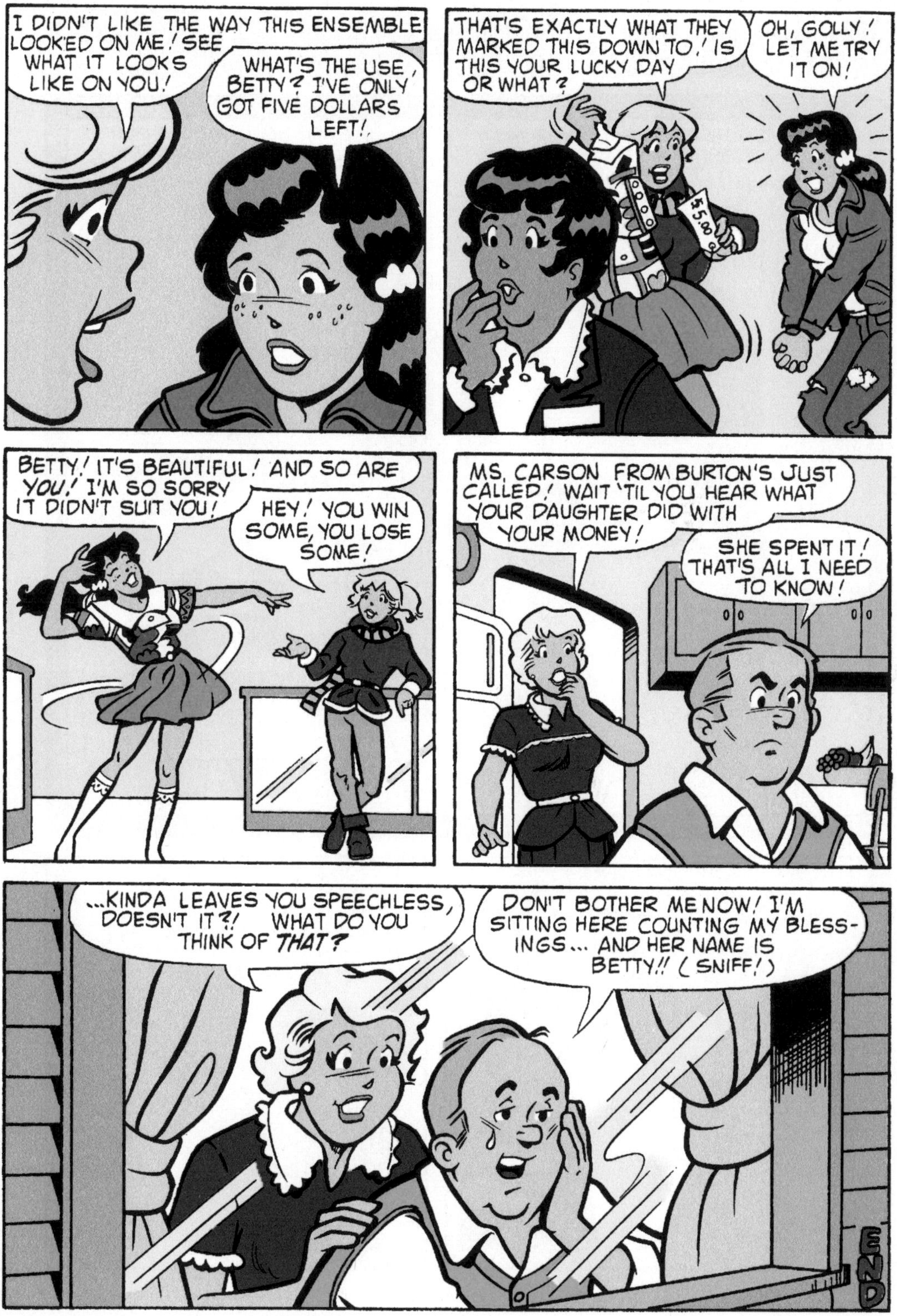
I DIDN'T LIKE THE WAY THIS ENSEMBLE LOOKED ON ME! SEE WHAT IT LOOKS LIKE ON YOU!
WHAT'S THE USE, BETTY? I'VE ONLY GOT FIVE DOLLARS LEFT!
THAT'S EXACTLY WHAT THEY MARKED THIS DOWN TO! IS THIS YOUR LUCKY DAY OR WHAT?
$5.00
OH, GOLLY! LET ME TRY IT ON!
BETTY! IT'S BEAUTIFUL! AND SO ARE *YOU!* I'M SO SORRY IT DIDN'T SUIT YOU!
HEY! YOU WIN SOME, YOU LOSE SOME!
MS. CARSON FROM BURTON'S JUST CALLED! WAIT 'TIL YOU HEAR WHAT YOUR DAUGHTER DID WITH YOUR MONEY!
SHE SPENT IT! THAT'S ALL I NEED TO KNOW!
...KINDA LEAVES YOU SPEECHLESS, DOESN'T IT?! WHAT DO YOU THINK OF *THAT?*
DON'T BOTHER ME NOW! I'M SITTING HERE COUNTING MY BLESSINGS... AND HER NAME IS BETTY!! (SNIFF!)
END

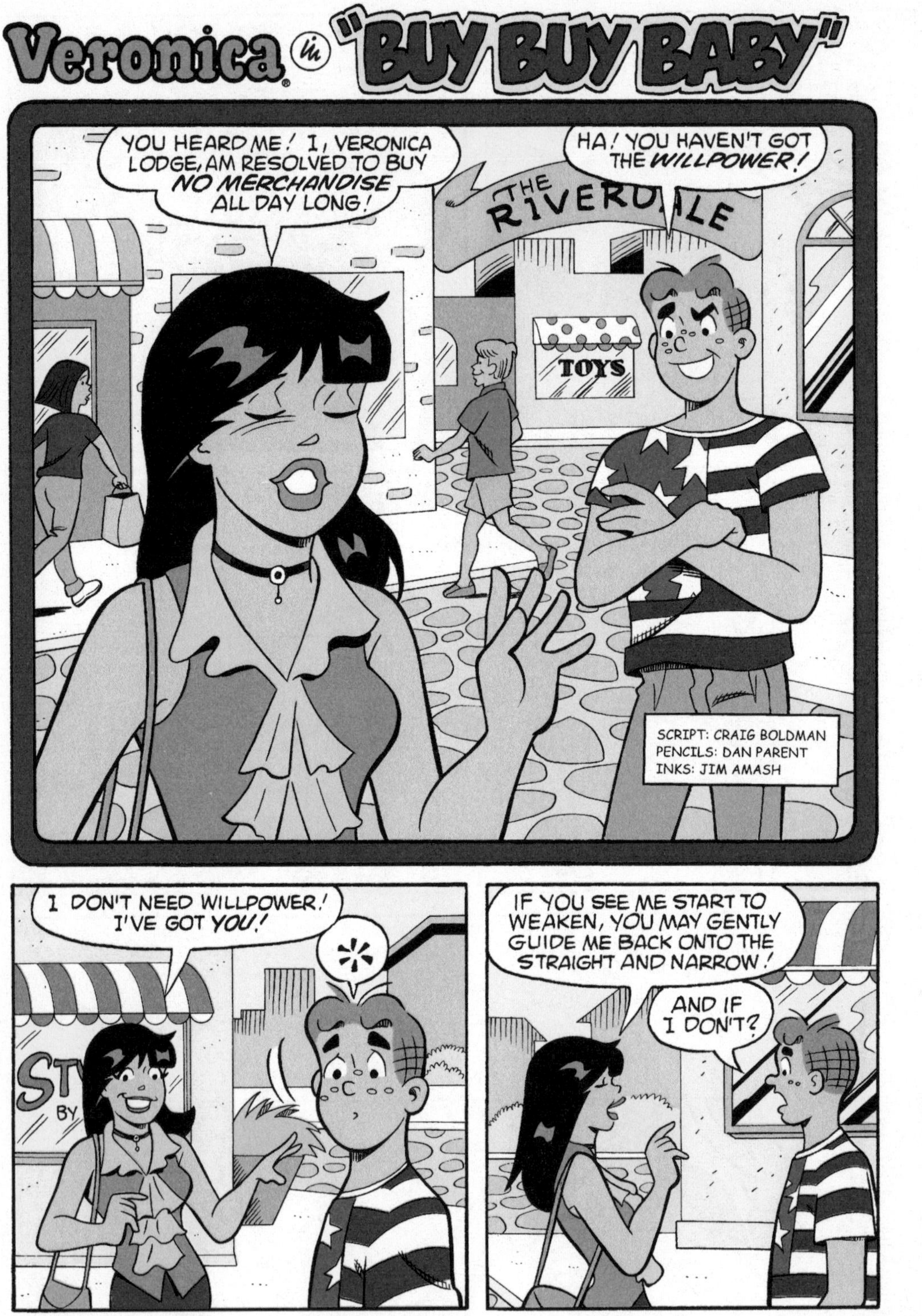
Veronica in "BUY BUY BABY"
YOU HEARD ME! I, VERONICA LODGE, AM RESOLVED TO BUY NO MERCHANDISE ALL DAY LONG!
HA! YOU HAVEN'T GOT THE WILLPOWER!
THE RIVERDALE
TOYS
SCRIPT: CRAIG BOLDMAN
PENCILS: DAN PARENT
INKS: JIM AMASH
I DON'T NEED WILLPOWER! I'VE GOT YOU!
IF YOU SEE ME START TO WEAKEN, YOU MAY GENTLY GUIDE ME BACK ONTO THE STRAIGHT AND NARROW!
AND IF I DON'T?

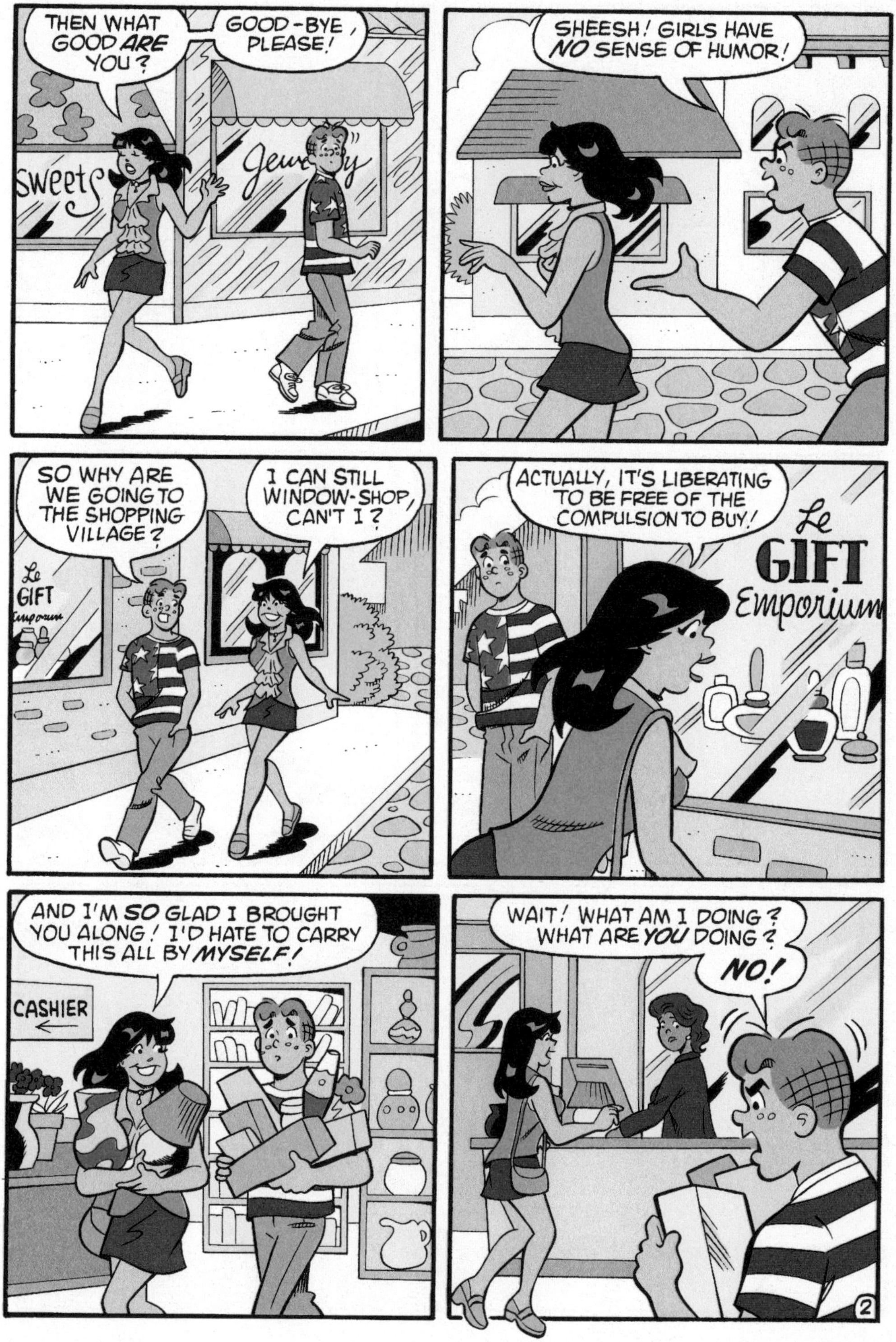
THEN WHAT GOOD ARE YOU?
GOOD-BYE, PLEASE!
Sweets
Jewelry
SHEESH! GIRLS HAVE NO SENSE OF HUMOR!
SO WHY ARE WE GOING TO THE SHOPPING VILLAGE?
I CAN STILL WINDOW-SHOP, CAN'T I?
ACTUALLY, IT'S LIBERATING TO BE FREE OF THE COMPULSION TO BUY!
Le GIFT Emporium
AND I'M SO GLAD I BROUGHT YOU ALONG! I'D HATE TO CARRY THIS ALL BY MYSELF!
CASHIER
WAIT! WHAT AM I DOING? WHAT ARE YOU DOING?
NO!
2

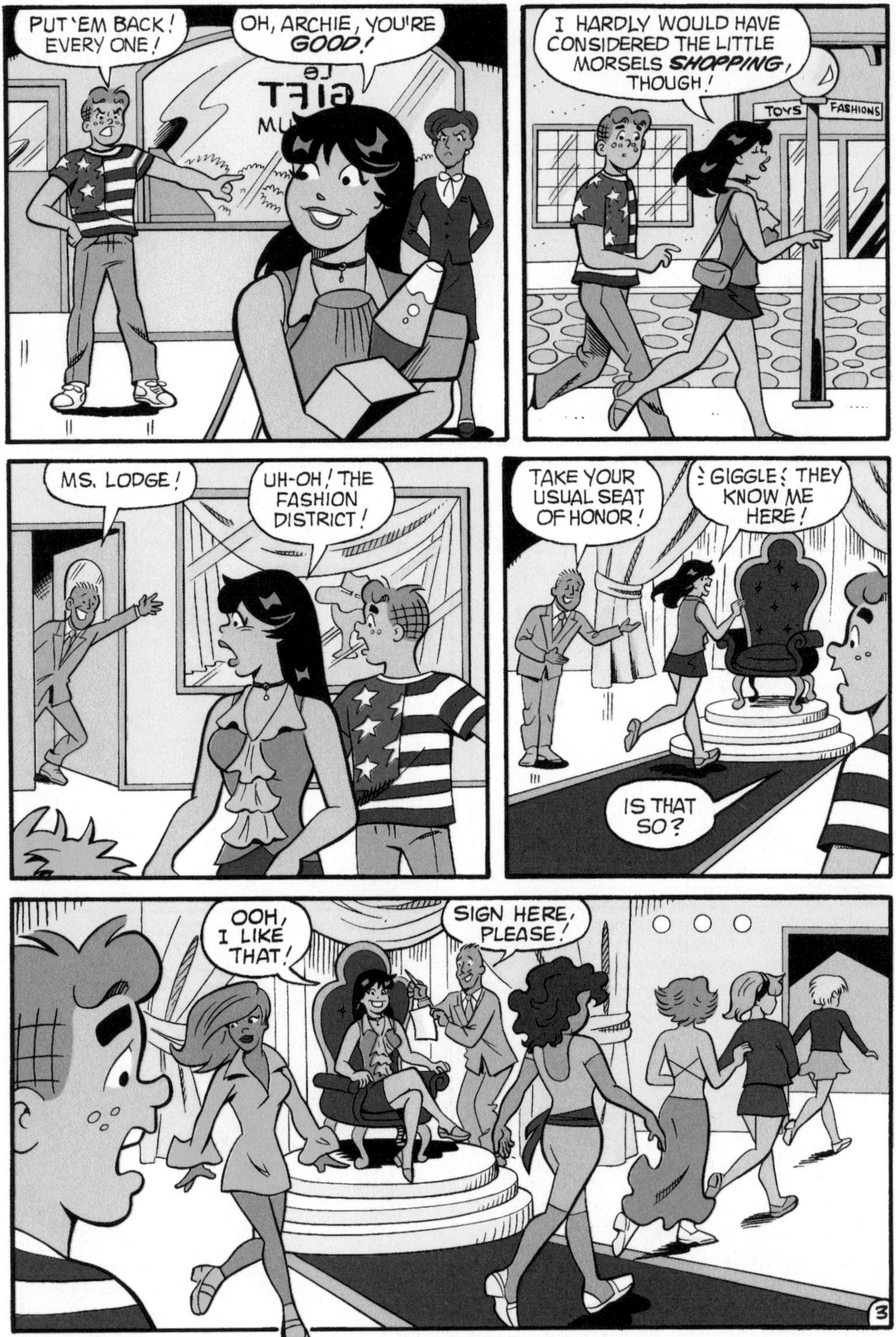
PUT 'EM BACK! EVERY ONE!
OH, ARCHIE, YOU'RE GOOD!
LE GIFT
I HARDLY WOULD HAVE CONSIDERED THE LITTLE MORSELS SHOPPING, THOUGH!
TOYS
FASHIONS
MS. LODGE!
UH-OH! THE FASHION DISTRICT!
TAKE YOUR USUAL SEAT OF HONOR!
GIGGLE! THEY KNOW ME HERE!
IS THAT SO?
OOH, I LIKE THAT!
SIGN HERE, PLEASE!
3

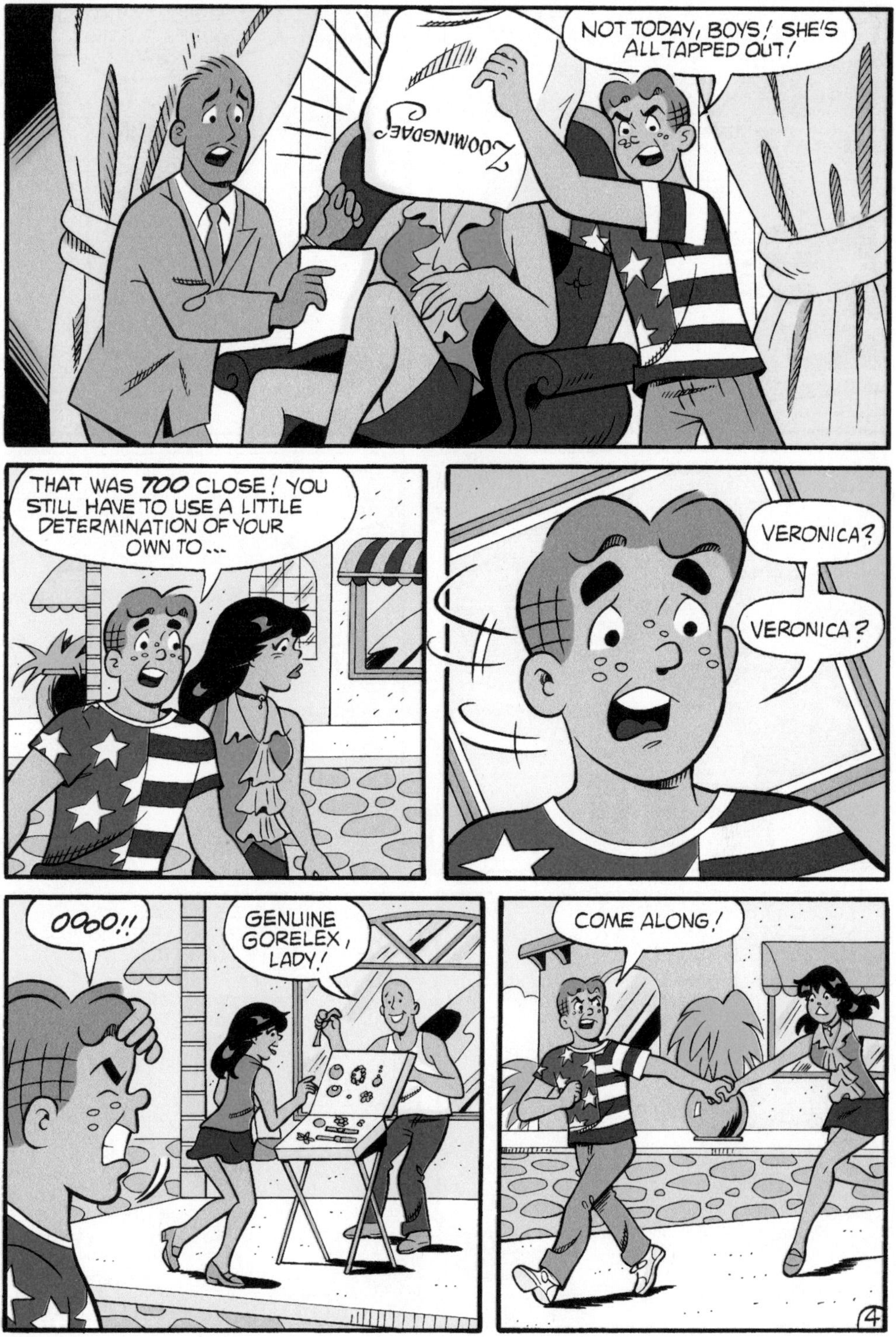
NOT TODAY, BOYS! SHE'S ALLTAPPED OUT!
ZOOMINGDAE'S
THAT WAS TOO CLOSE! YOU STILL HAVE TO USE A LITTLE DETERMINATION OF YOUR OWN TO...
VERONICA?
VERONICA?
OOOO!!
GENUINE GORELEX, LADY!
COME ALONG!
4

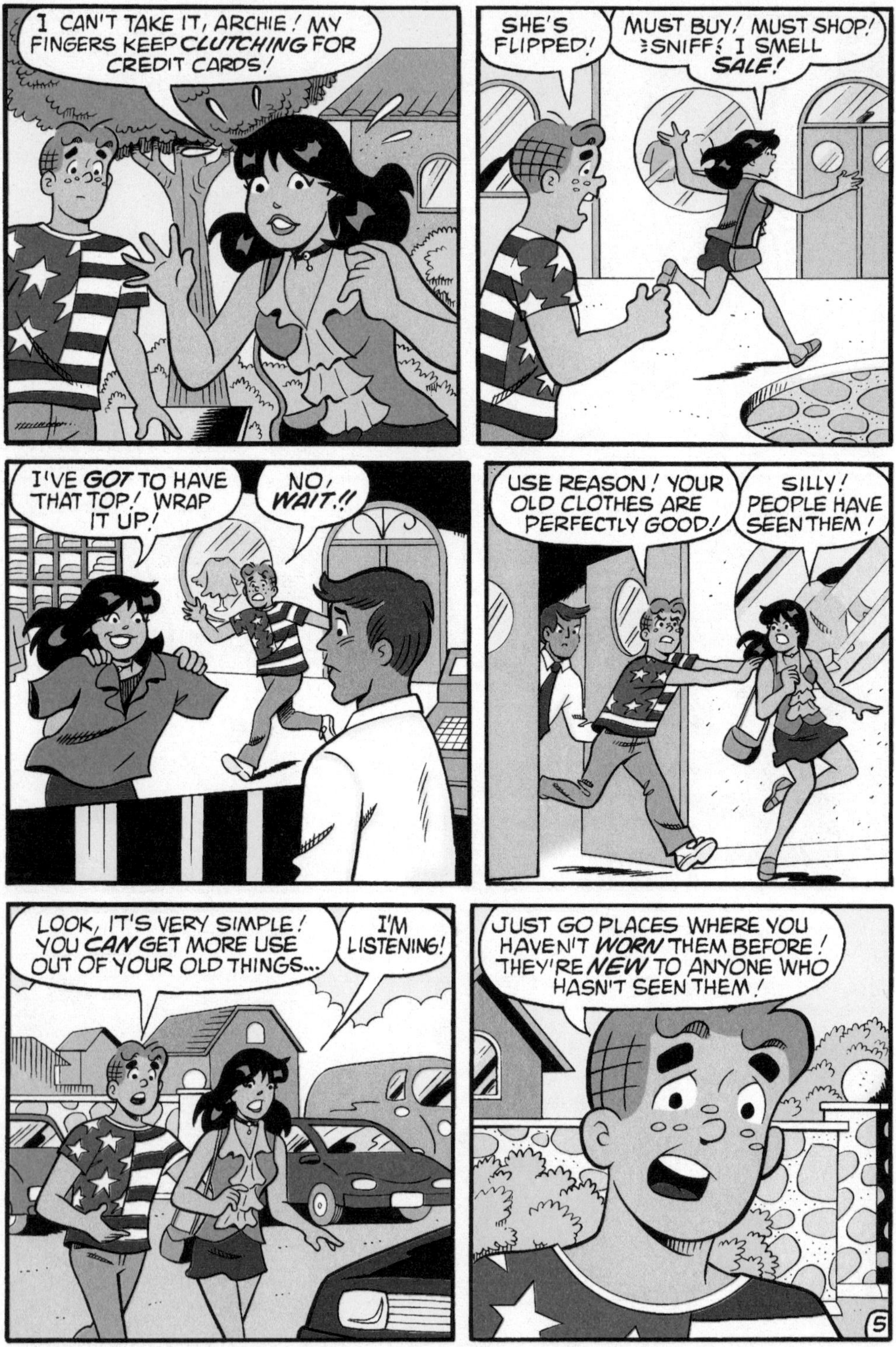
I CAN'T TAKE IT, ARCHIE! MY FINGERS KEEP CLUTCHING FOR CREDIT CARDS!
SHE'S FLIPPED!
MUST BUY! MUST SHOP! SNIFF! I SMELL SALE!
I'VE GOT TO HAVE THAT TOP! WRAP IT UP!
NO, WAIT!!
USE REASON! YOUR OLD CLOTHES ARE PERFECTLY GOOD!
SILLY! PEOPLE HAVE SEEN THEM!
LOOK, IT'S VERY SIMPLE! YOU CAN GET MORE USE OUT OF YOUR OLD THINGS...
I'M LISTENING!
JUST GO PLACES WHERE YOU HAVEN'T WORN THEM BEFORE! THEY'RE NEW TO ANYONE WHO HASN'T SEEN THEM!
5

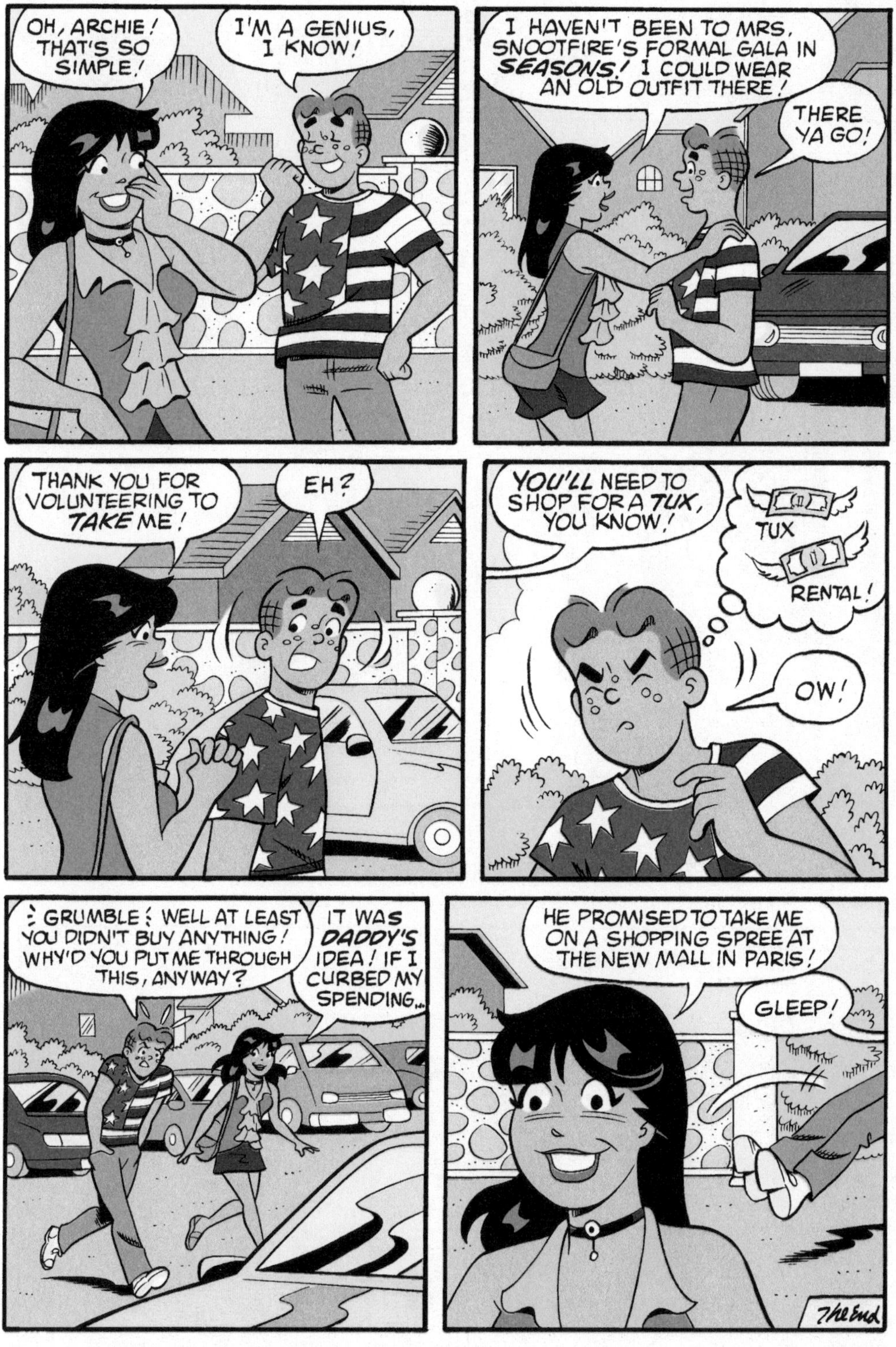
OH, ARCHIE! THAT'S SO SIMPLE!
I'M A GENIUS, I KNOW!
I HAVEN'T BEEN TO MRS. SNOOTFIRE'S FORMAL GALA IN SEASONS! I COULD WEAR AN OLD OUTFIT THERE!
THERE YA GO!
THANK YOU FOR VOLUNTEERING TO TAKE ME!
EH?
YOU'LL NEED TO SHOP FOR A TUX, YOU KNOW!
TUX
RENTAL!
OW!
GRUMBLE! WELL AT LEAST YOU DIDN'T BUY ANYTHING! WHY'D YOU PUT ME THROUGH THIS, ANYWAY?
IT WAS DADDY'S IDEA! IF I CURBED MY SPENDING...
HE PROMISED TO TAKE ME ON A SHOPPING SPREE AT THE NEW MALL IN PARIS!
GLEEP!
The End

Betty and Veronica in "Common Bond!"

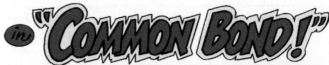

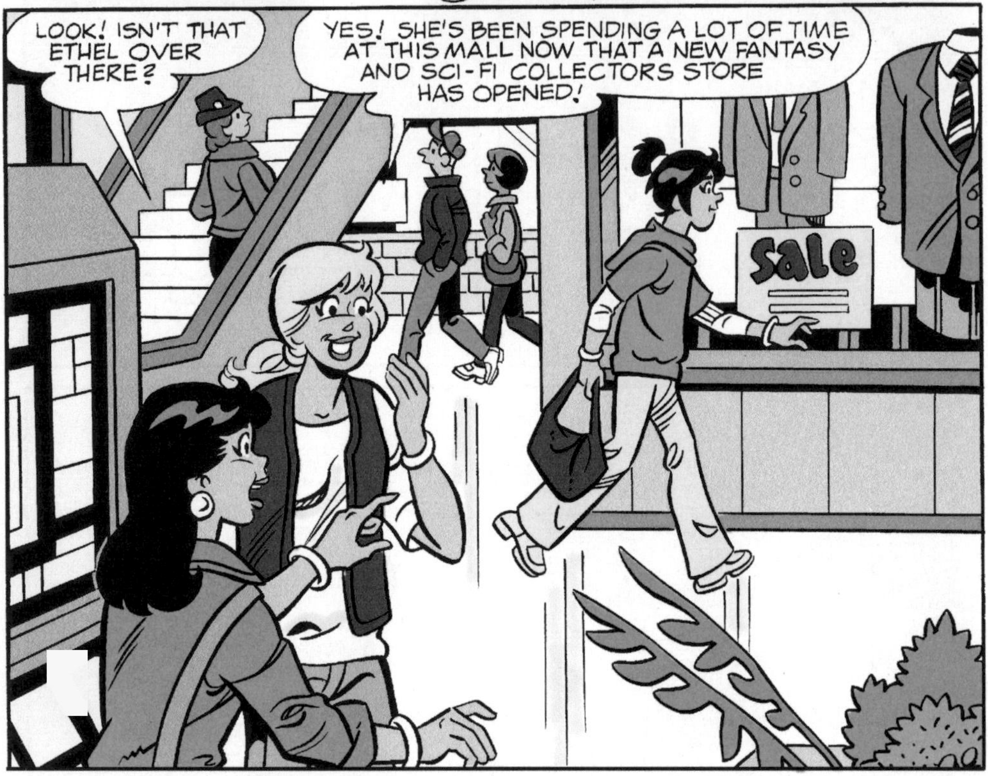
LOOK! ISN'T THAT ETHEL OVER THERE?
YES! SHE'S BEEN SPENDING A LOT OF TIME AT THIS MALL NOW THAT A NEW FANTASY AND SCI-FI COLLECTORS STORE HAS OPENED!
SALE

SCRIPT: MIKE PELLOWSKI PENCILS: TIM KENNEDY INKS: AL MILGROM
COLORS: BARRY GROSSMAN LETTERS: JON D'AGOSTINO

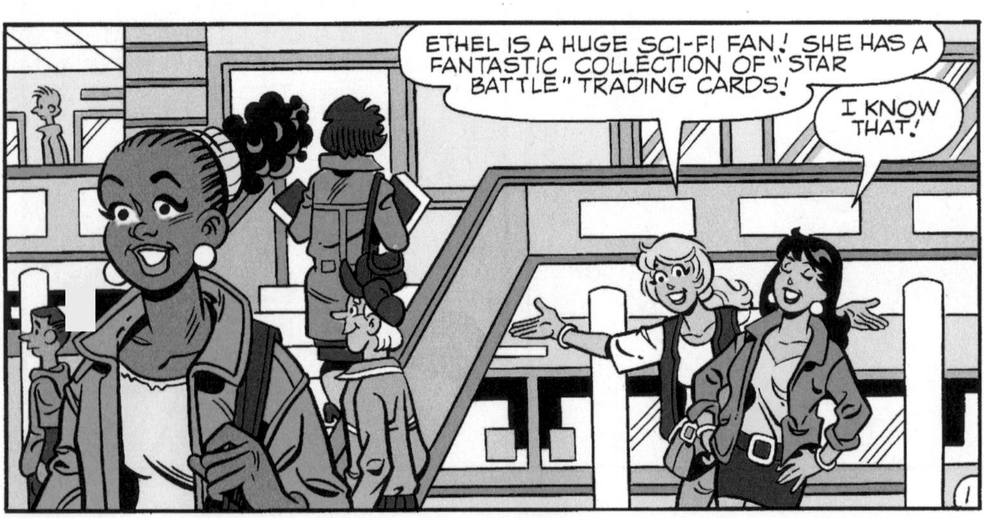
ETHEL IS A HUGE SCI-FI FAN! SHE HAS A FANTASTIC COLLECTION OF "STAR BATTLE" TRADING CARDS!
I KNOW THAT!

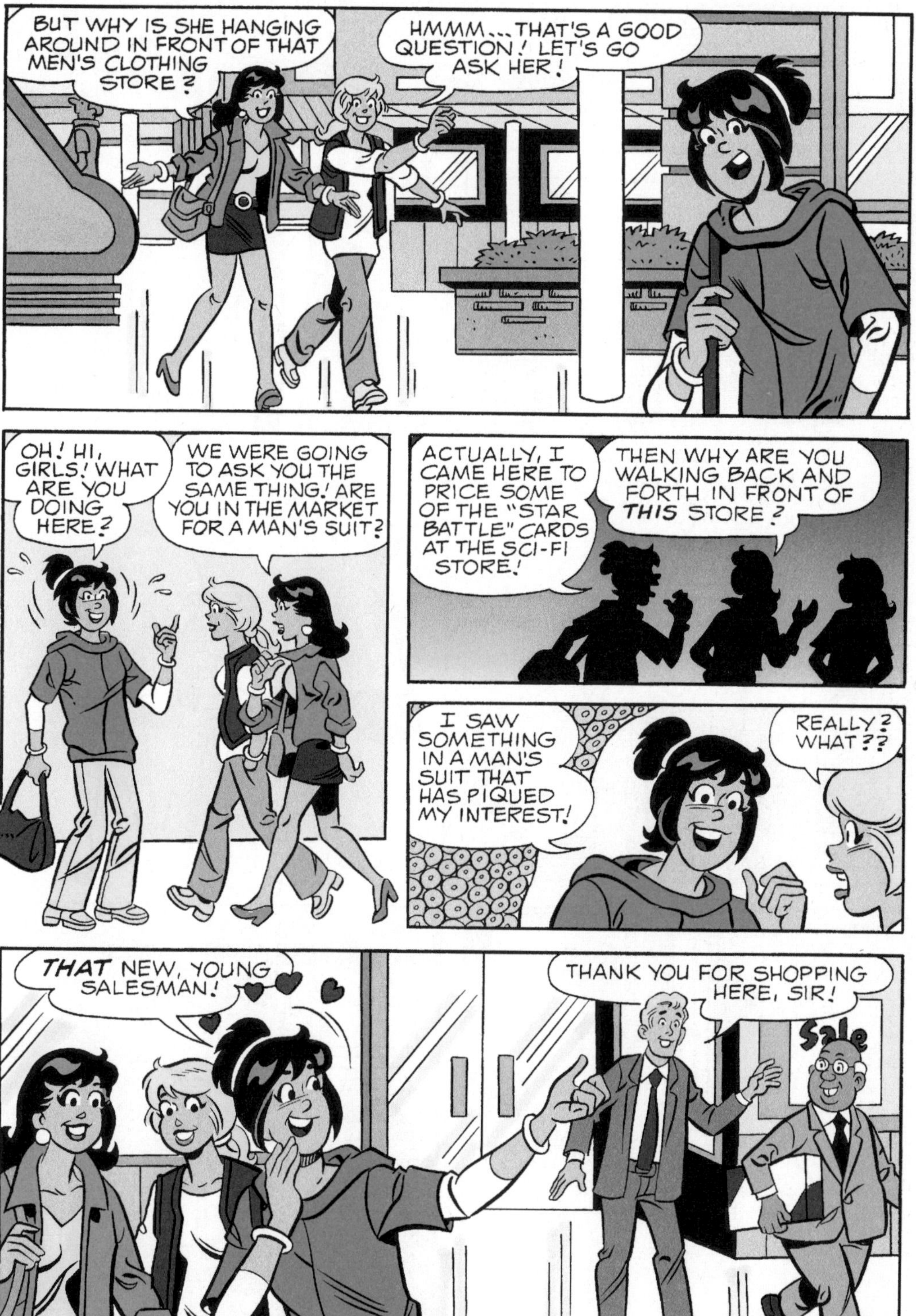

BUT WHY IS SHE HANGING AROUND IN FRONT OF THAT MEN'S CLOTHING STORE?
HMMM... THAT'S A GOOD QUESTION! LET'S GO ASK HER!
OH! HI, GIRLS! WHAT ARE YOU DOING HERE?
WE WERE GOING TO ASK YOU THE SAME THING! ARE YOU IN THE MARKET FOR A MAN'S SUIT?
ACTUALLY, I CAME HERE TO PRICE SOME OF THE "STAR BATTLE" CARDS AT THE SCI-FI STORE!
THEN WHY ARE YOU WALKING BACK AND FORTH IN FRONT OF THIS STORE?
I SAW SOMETHING IN A MAN'S SUIT THAT HAS PIQUED MY INTEREST!
REALLY? WHAT??
THAT NEW, YOUNG SALESMAN!
THANK YOU FOR SHOPPING HERE, SIR!
Sale
2

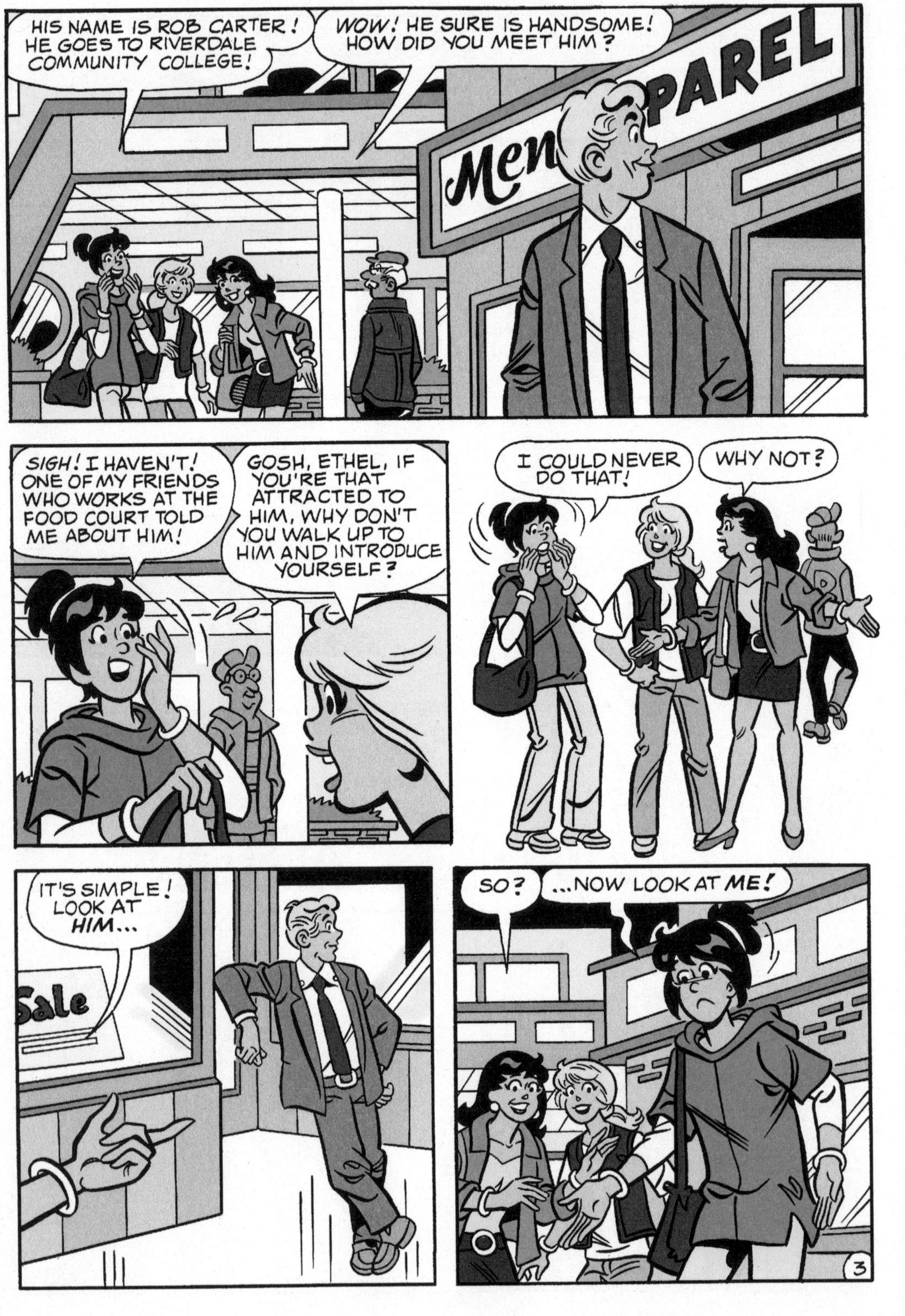
HIS NAME IS ROB CARTER! HE GOES TO RIVERDALE COMMUNITY COLLEGE!
WOW! HE SURE IS HANDSOME! HOW DID YOU MEET HIM?
Men PAREL
SIGH! I HAVEN'T! ONE OF MY FRIENDS WHO WORKS AT THE FOOD COURT TOLD ME ABOUT HIM!
GOSH, ETHEL, IF YOU'RE THAT ATTRACTED TO HIM, WHY DON'T YOU WALK UP TO HIM AND INTRODUCE YOURSELF?
I COULD NEVER DO THAT!
WHY NOT?
IT'S SIMPLE! LOOK AT HIM...
Sale
SO?
...NOW LOOK AT ME!
3

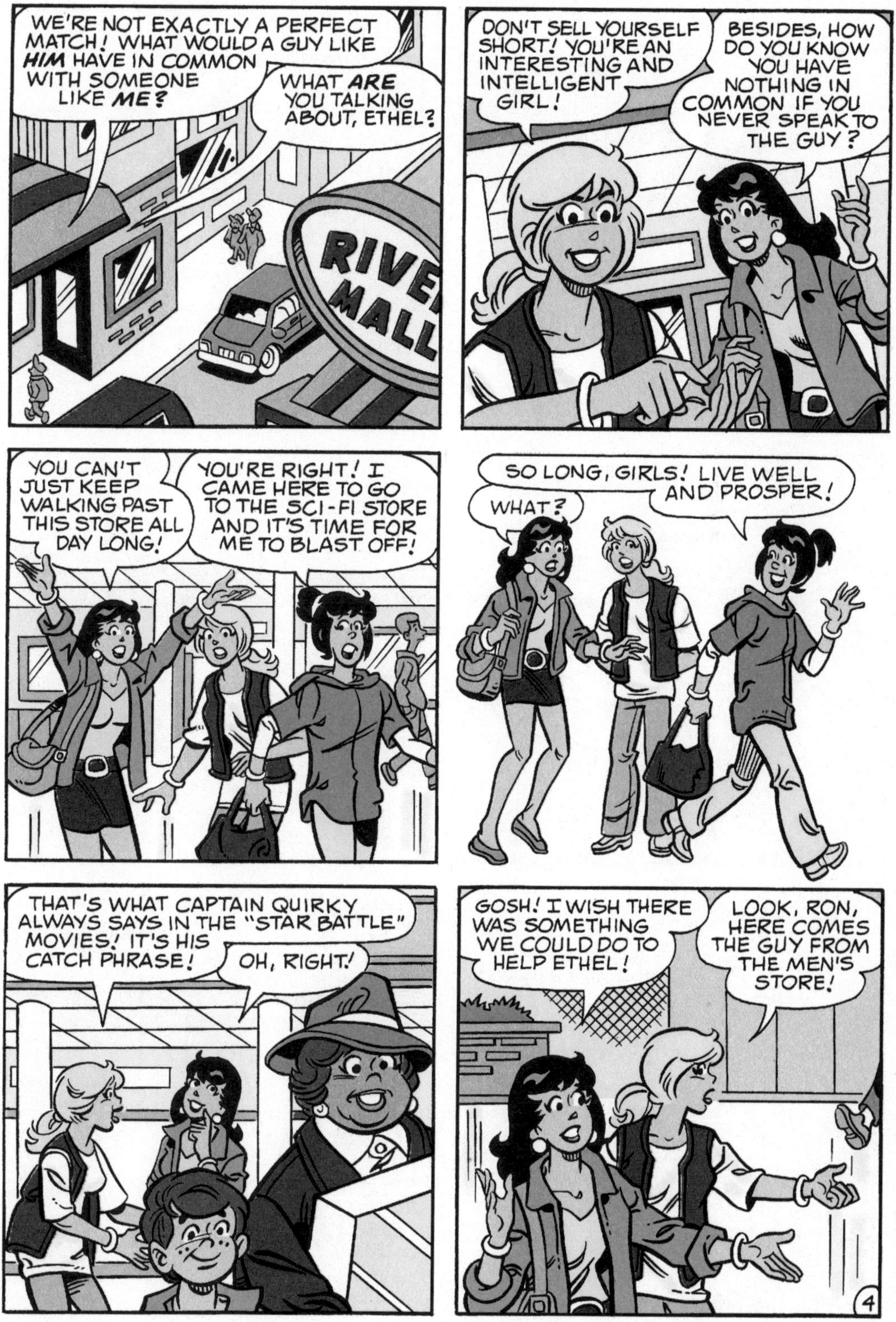
WE'RE NOT EXACTLY A PERFECT MATCH! WHAT WOULD A GUY LIKE HIM HAVE IN COMMON WITH SOMEONE LIKE ME?
WHAT ARE YOU TALKING ABOUT, ETHEL?
RIVER MALL
DON'T SELL YOURSELF SHORT! YOU'RE AN INTERESTING AND INTELLIGENT GIRL!
BESIDES, HOW DO YOU KNOW YOU HAVE NOTHING IN COMMON IF YOU NEVER SPEAK TO THE GUY?
YOU CAN'T JUST KEEP WALKING PAST THIS STORE ALL DAY LONG!
YOU'RE RIGHT! I CAME HERE TO GO TO THE SCI-FI STORE AND IT'S TIME FOR ME TO BLAST OFF!
SO LONG, GIRLS! LIVE WELL AND PROSPER!
WHAT?
THAT'S WHAT CAPTAIN QUIRKY ALWAYS SAYS IN THE "STAR BATTLE" MOVIES! IT'S HIS CATCH PHRASE!
OH, RIGHT!
GOSH! I WISH THERE WAS SOMETHING WE COULD DO TO HELP ETHEL!
LOOK, RON, HERE COMES THE GUY FROM THE MEN'S STORE!
4

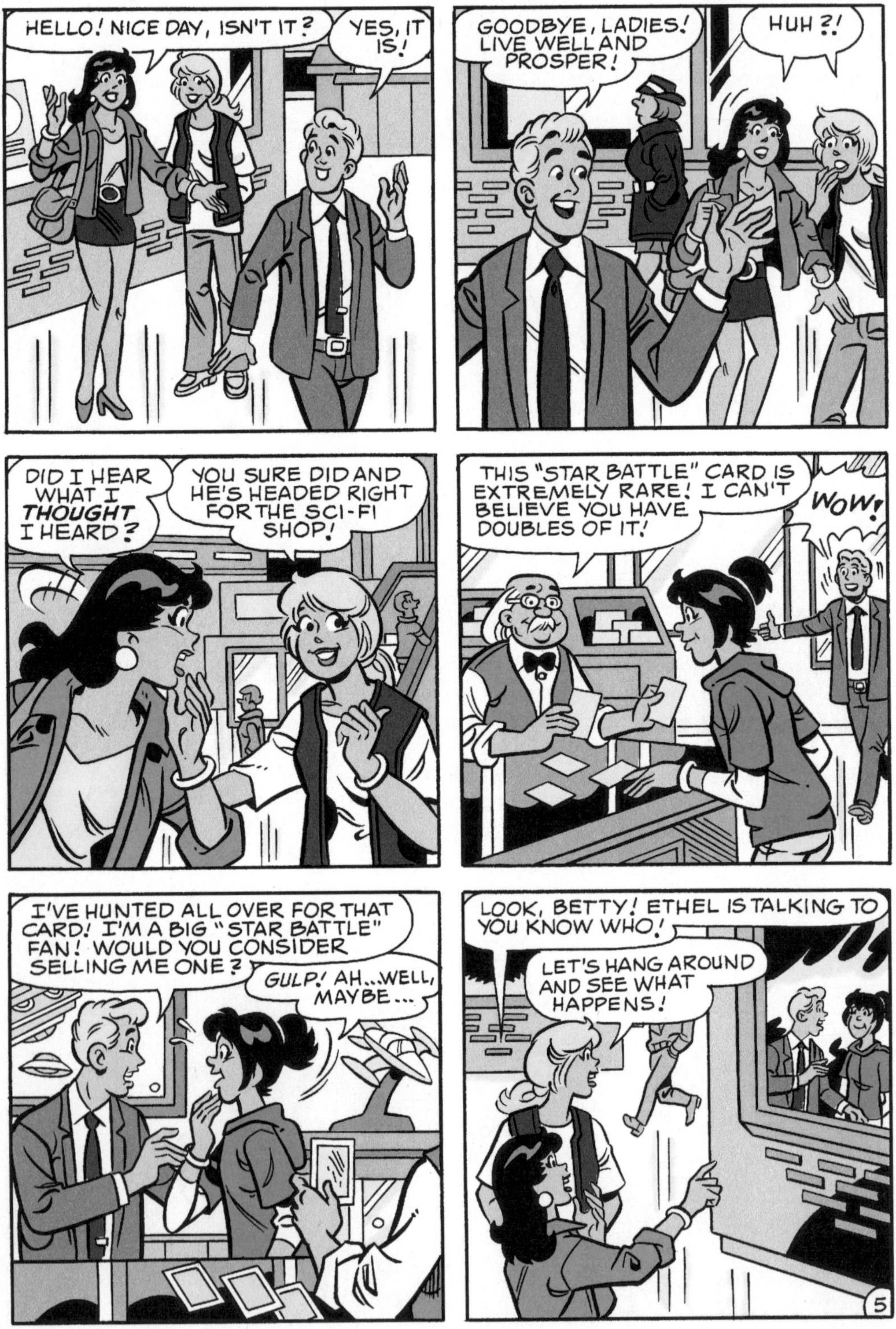
HELLO! NICE DAY, ISN'T IT?
YES, IT IS!
GOODBYE, LADIES! LIVE WELL AND PROSPER!
HUH?!
DID I HEAR WHAT I *THOUGHT* I HEARD?
YOU SURE DID AND HE'S HEADED RIGHT FOR THE SCI-FI SHOP!
THIS "STAR BATTLE" CARD IS EXTREMELY RARE! I CAN'T BELIEVE YOU HAVE DOUBLES OF IT!
WOW!
I'VE HUNTED ALL OVER FOR THAT CARD! I'M A BIG "STAR BATTLE" FAN! WOULD YOU CONSIDER SELLING ME ONE?
GULP! AH...WELL, MAYBE...
LOOK, BETTY! ETHEL IS TALKING TO YOU KNOW WHO!
LET'S HANG AROUND AND SEE WHAT HAPPENS!
5

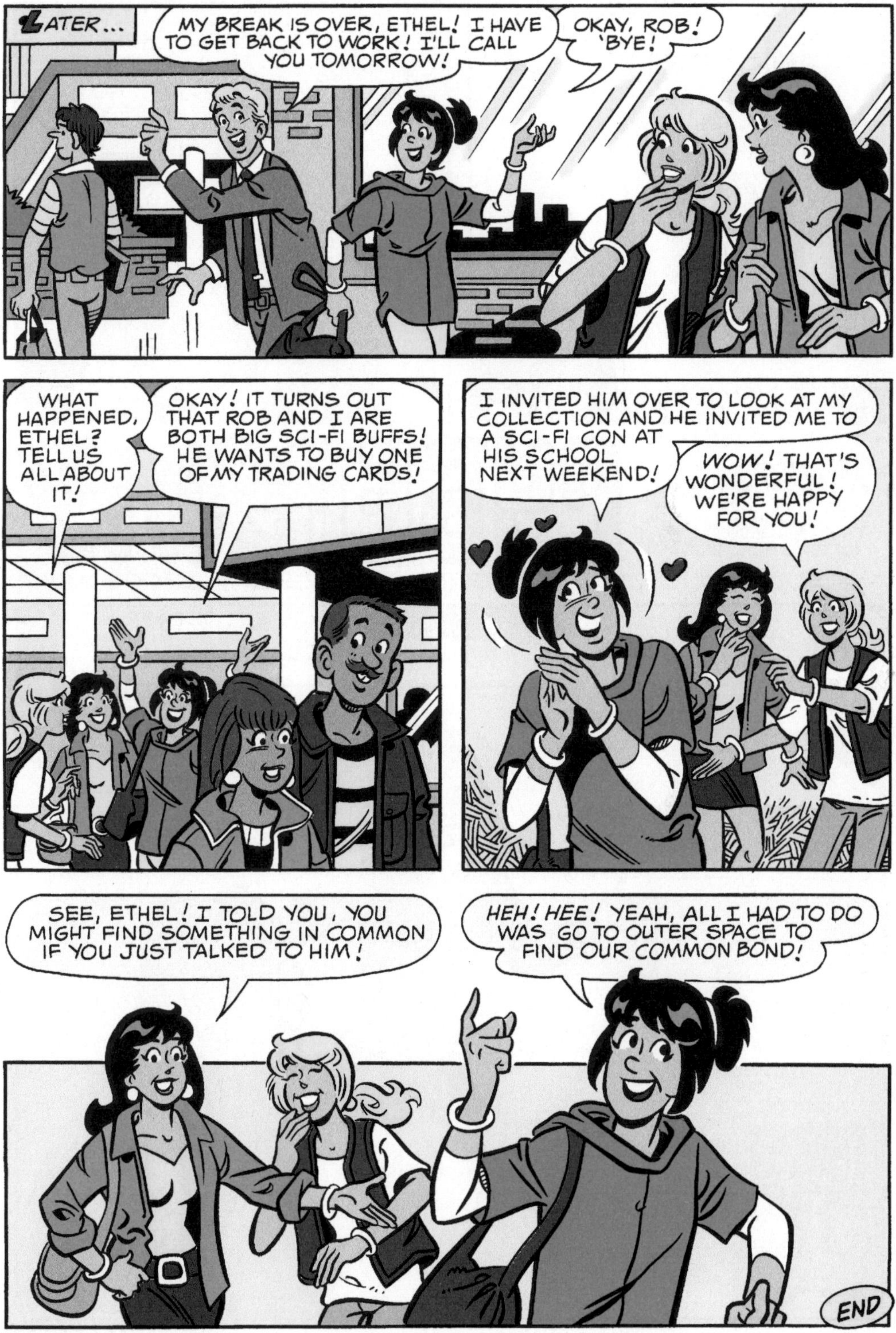
LATER...
MY BREAK IS OVER, ETHEL! I HAVE TO GET BACK TO WORK! I'LL CALL YOU TOMORROW!
OKAY, ROB! 'BYE!
WHAT HAPPENED, ETHEL? TELL US ALL ABOUT IT!
OKAY! IT TURNS OUT THAT ROB AND I ARE BOTH BIG SCI-FI BUFFS! HE WANTS TO BUY ONE OF MY TRADING CARDS!
I INVITED HIM OVER TO LOOK AT MY COLLECTION AND HE INVITED ME TO A SCI-FI CON AT HIS SCHOOL NEXT WEEKEND!
WOW! THAT'S WONDERFUL! WE'RE HAPPY FOR YOU!
SEE, ETHEL! I TOLD YOU, YOU MIGHT FIND SOMETHING IN COMMON IF YOU JUST TALKED TO HIM!
HEH! HEE! YEAH, ALL I HAD TO DO WAS GO TO OUTER SPACE TO FIND OUR COMMON BOND!
END

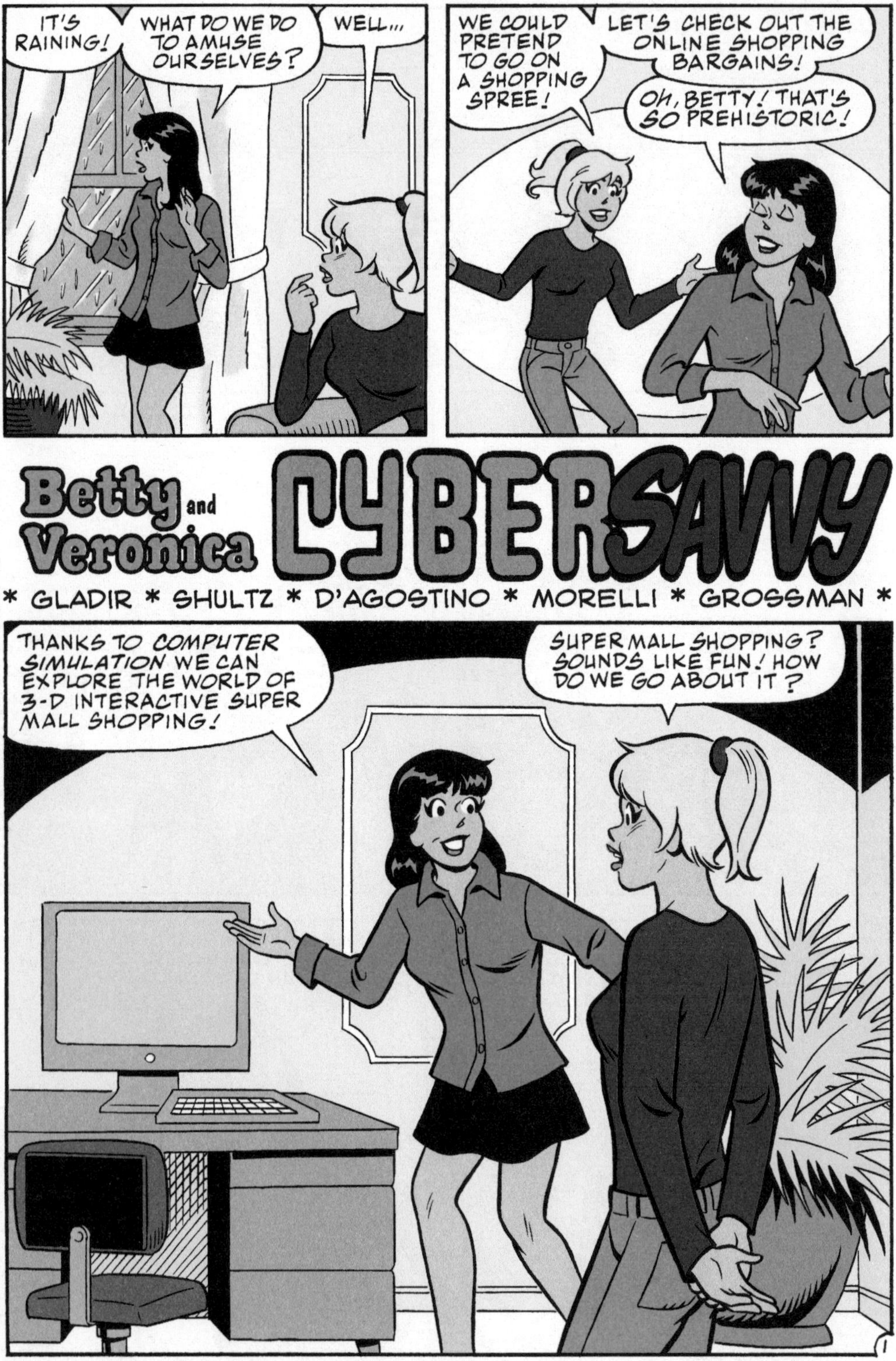
IT'S RAINING!
WHAT DO WE DO TO AMUSE OURSELVES?
WELL...
WE COULD PRETEND TO GO ON A SHOPPING SPREE!
LET'S CHECK OUT THE ONLINE SHOPPING BARGAINS!
OH, BETTY! THAT'S SO PREHISTORIC!
Betty and Veronica
CYBER SAVVY
* GLADIR * SHULTZ * D'AGOSTINO * MORELLI * GROSSMAN *
THANKS TO COMPUTER SIMULATION WE CAN EXPLORE THE WORLD OF 3-D INTERACTIVE SUPER MALL SHOPPING!
SUPER MALL SHOPPING? SOUNDS LIKE FUN! HOW DO WE GO ABOUT IT?
1

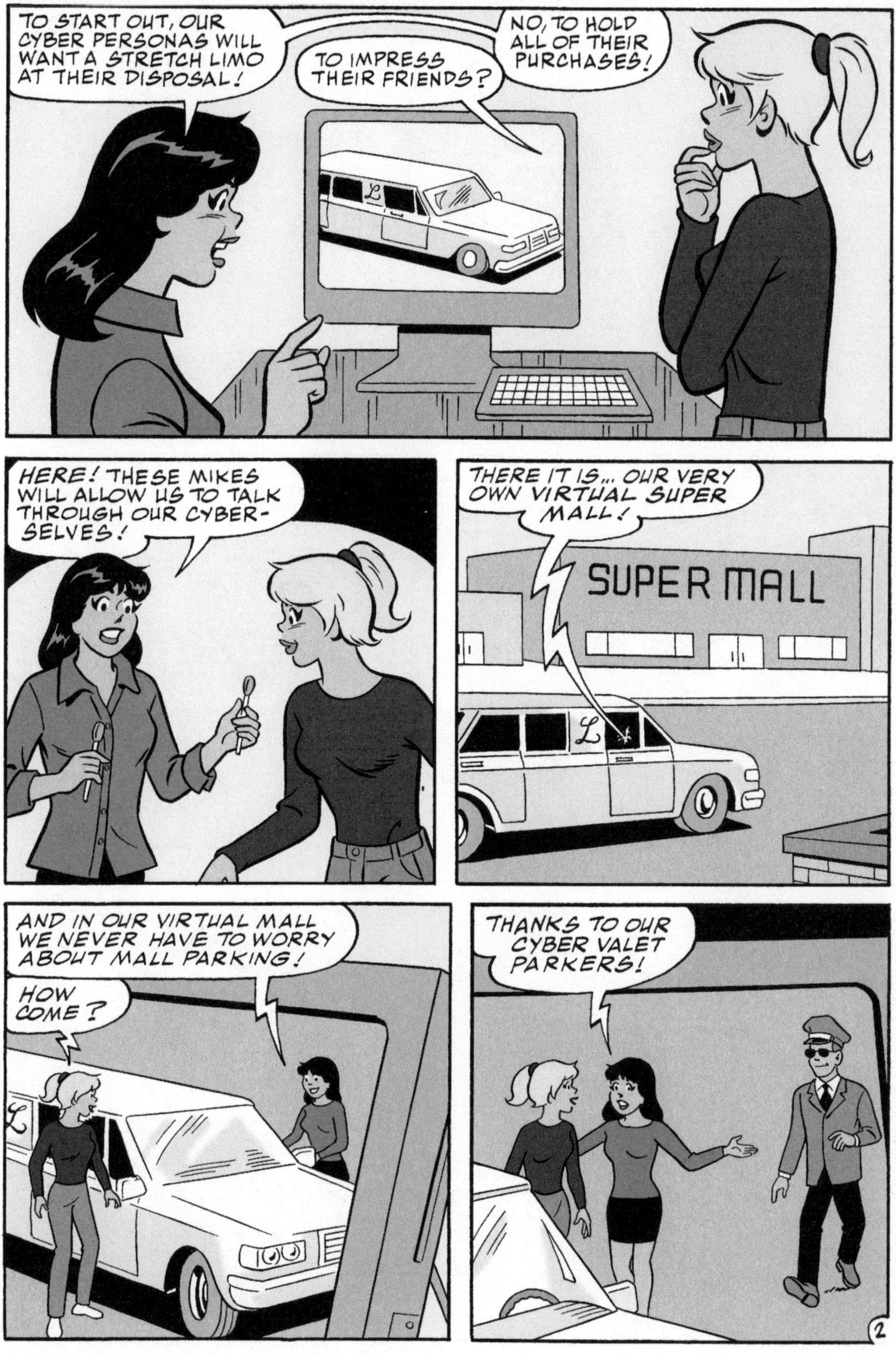
TO START OUT, OUR CYBER PERSONAS WILL WANT A STRETCH LIMO AT THEIR DISPOSAL!
TO IMPRESS THEIR FRIENDS?
NO, TO HOLD ALL OF THEIR PURCHASES!
HERE! THESE MIKES WILL ALLOW US TO TALK THROUGH OUR CYBER-SELVES!
THERE IT IS... OUR VERY OWN VIRTUAL SUPER MALL!
SUPER MALL
AND IN OUR VIRTUAL MALL WE NEVER HAVE TO WORRY ABOUT MALL PARKING!
HOW COME?
THANKS TO OUR CYBER VALET PARKERS!
2

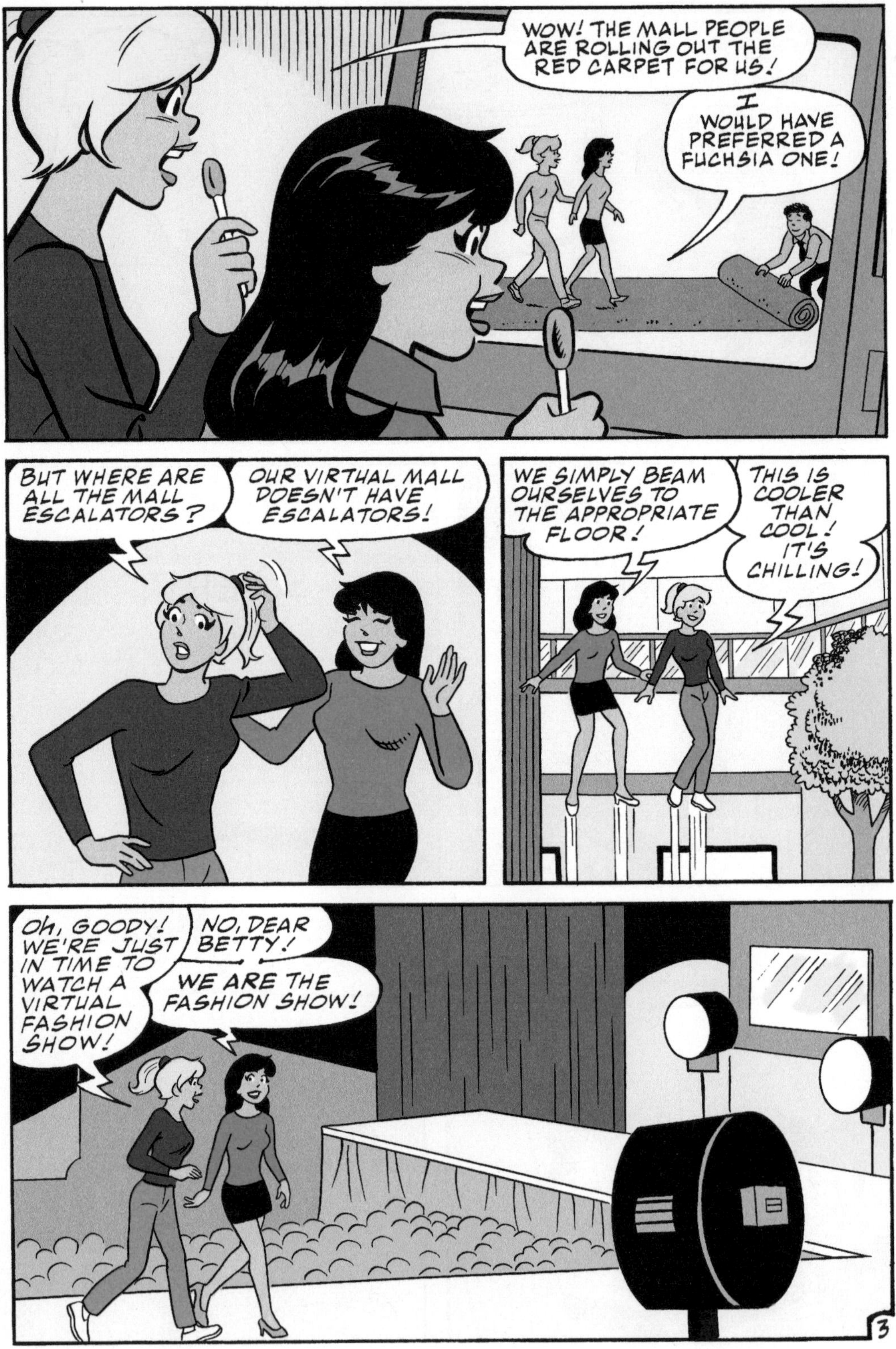
WOW! THE MALL PEOPLE ARE ROLLING OUT THE RED CARPET FOR US!
I WOULD HAVE PREFERRED A FUCHSIA ONE!
BUT WHERE ARE ALL THE MALL ESCALATORS?
OUR VIRTUAL MALL DOESN'T HAVE ESCALATORS!
WE SIMPLY BEAM OURSELVES TO THE APPROPRIATE FLOOR!
THIS IS COOLER THAN COOL! IT'S CHILLING!
OH, GOODY! WE'RE JUST IN TIME TO WATCH A VIRTUAL FASHION SHOW!
NO, DEAR BETTY!
WE ARE THE FASHION SHOW!
3

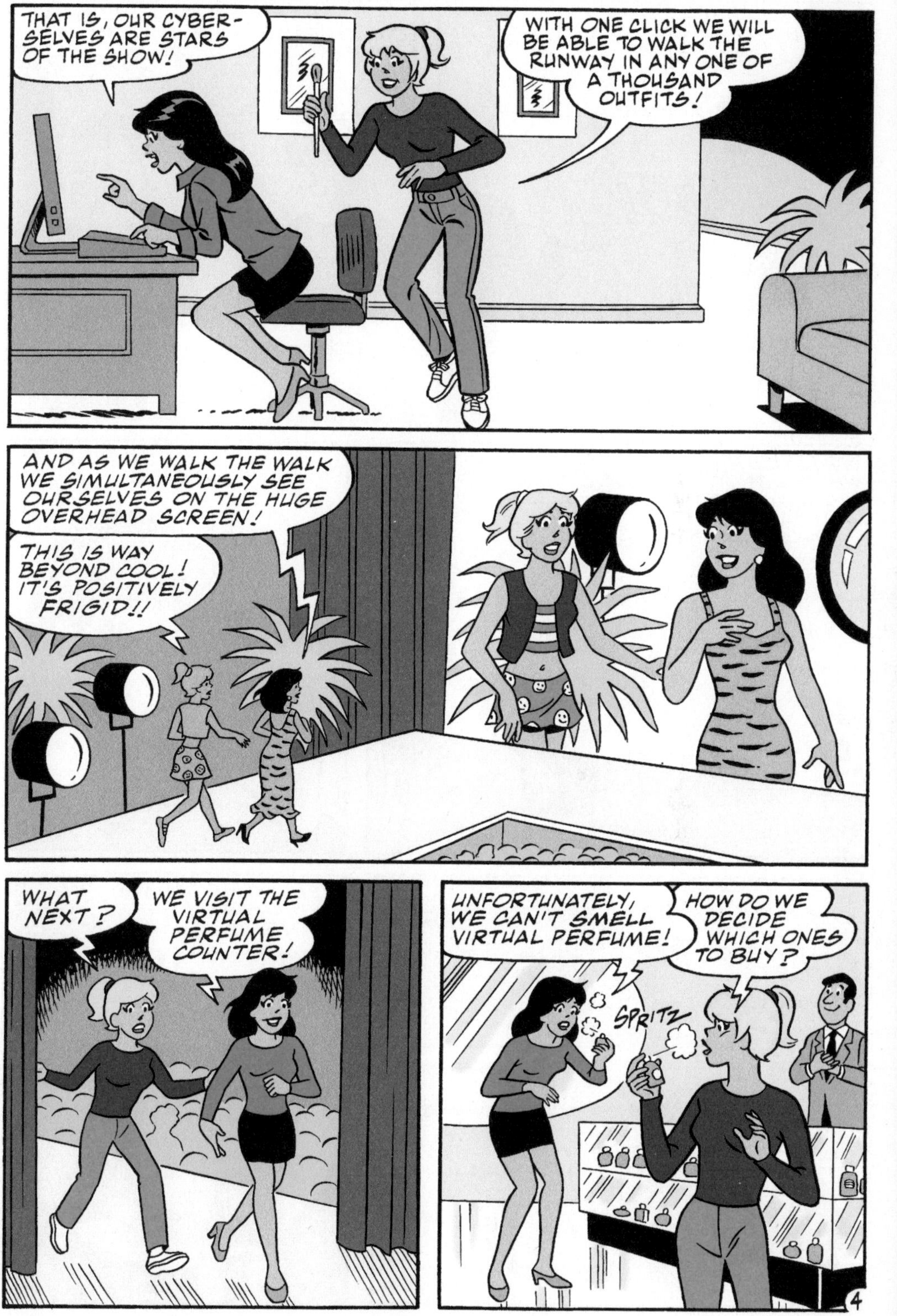
THAT IS, OUR CYBER-SELVES ARE STARS OF THE SHOW!
WITH ONE CLICK WE WILL BE ABLE TO WALK THE RUNWAY IN ANY ONE OF A THOUSAND OUTFITS!
AND AS WE WALK THE WALK WE SIMULTANEOUSLY SEE OURSELVES ON THE HUGE OVERHEAD SCREEN!
THIS IS WAY BEYOND COOL! IT'S POSITIVELY FRIGID!!
WHAT NEXT?
WE VISIT THE VIRTUAL PERFUME COUNTER!
UNFORTUNATELY, WE CAN'T SMELL VIRTUAL PERFUME!
HOW DO WE DECIDE WHICH ONES TO BUY?
SPRITZ
4

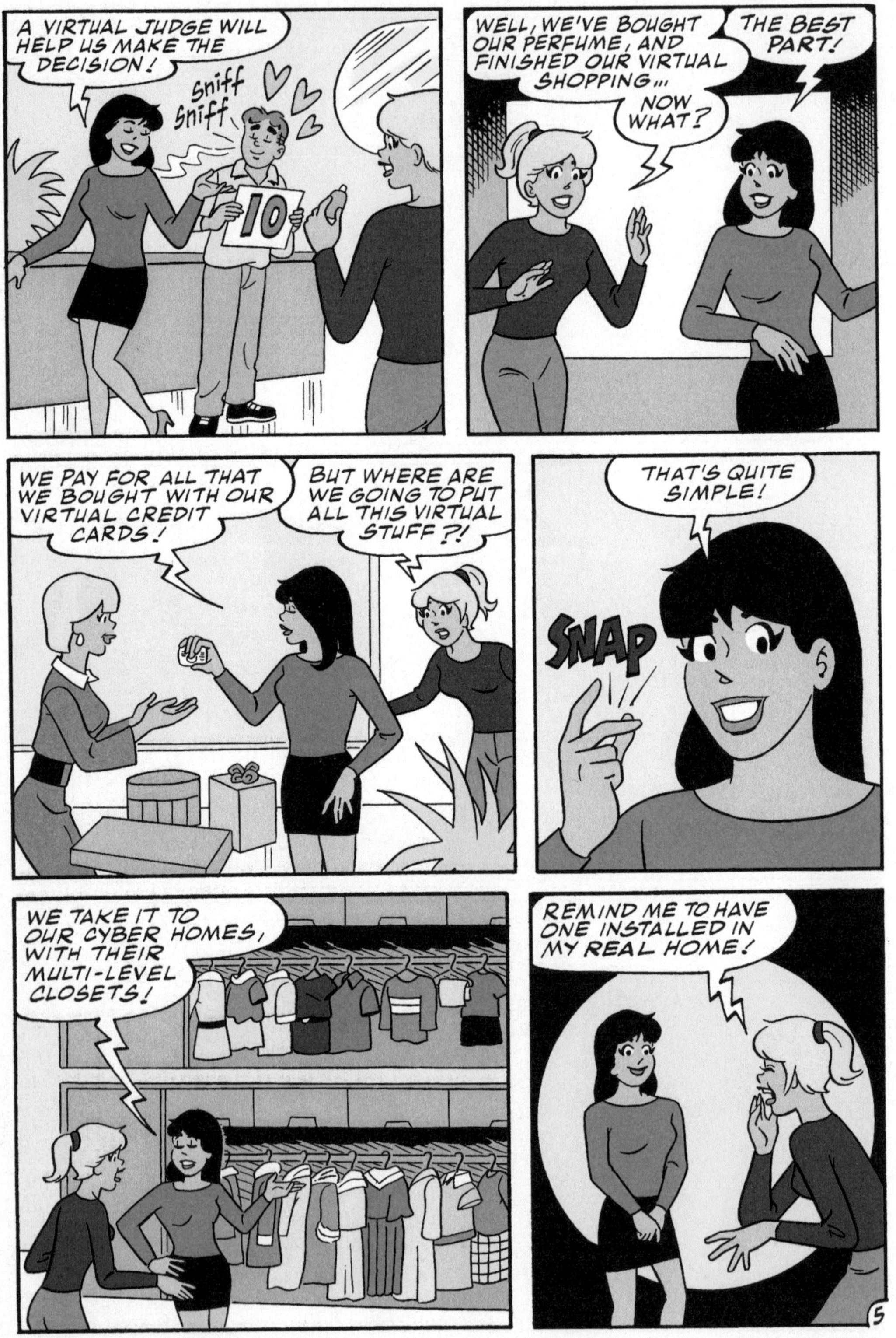

A VIRTUAL JUDGE WILL HELP US MAKE THE DECISION!
Sniff Sniff
10
WELL, WE'VE BOUGHT OUR PERFUME, AND FINISHED OUR VIRTUAL SHOPPING...
NOW WHAT?
THE BEST PART!
WE PAY FOR ALL THAT WE BOUGHT WITH OUR VIRTUAL CREDIT CARDS!
BUT WHERE ARE WE GOING TO PUT ALL THIS VIRTUAL STUFF ?!
THAT'S QUITE SIMPLE!
SNAP
WE TAKE IT TO OUR CYBER HOMES, WITH THEIR MULTI-LEVEL CLOSETS!
REMIND ME TO HAVE ONE INSTALLED IN MY REAL HOME!
5

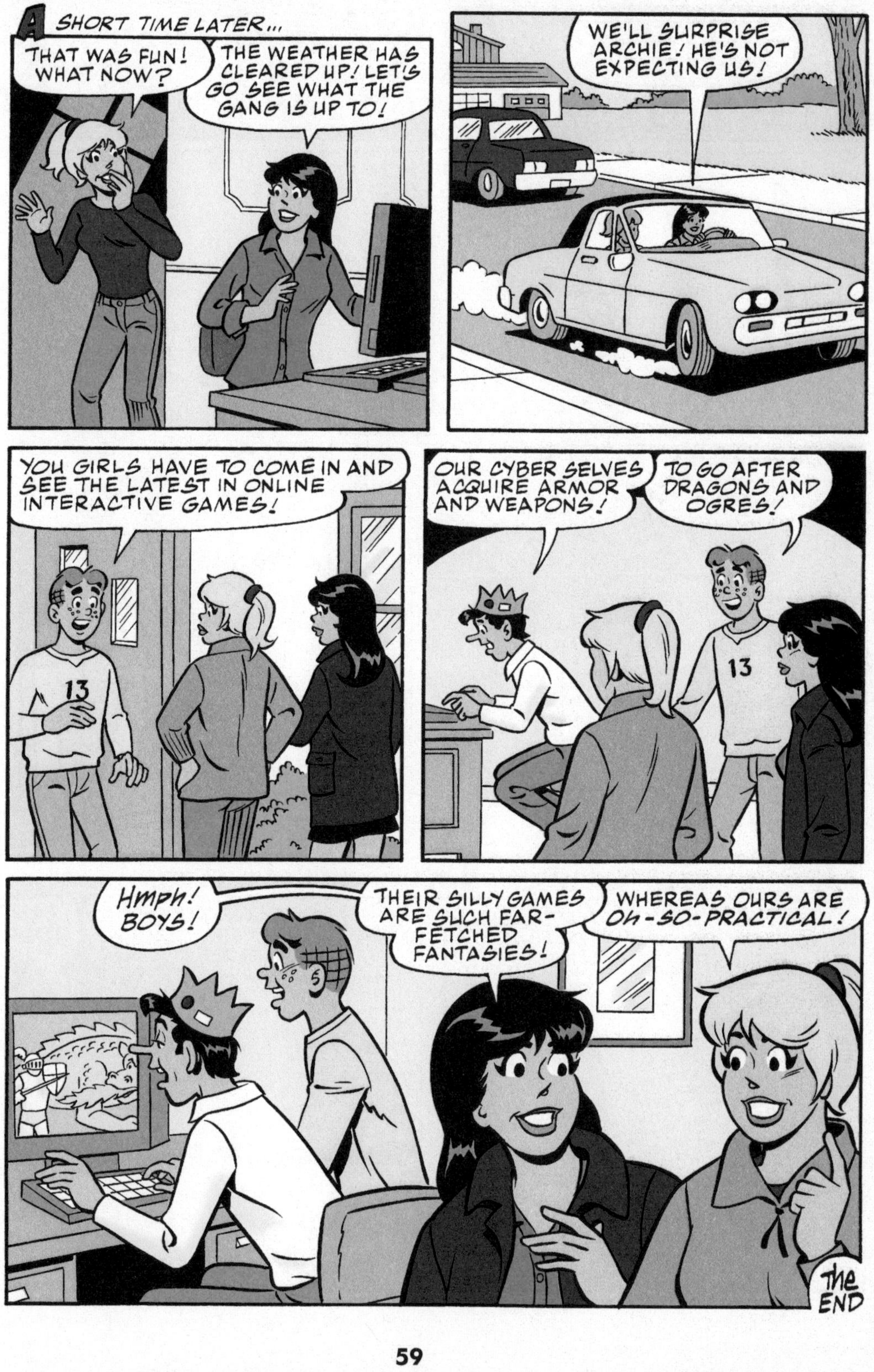
A SHORT TIME LATER...
THAT WAS FUN! WHAT NOW?
THE WEATHER HAS CLEARED UP! LET'S GO SEE WHAT THE GANG IS UP TO!
WE'LL SURPRISE ARCHIE! HE'S NOT EXPECTING US!
YOU GIRLS HAVE TO COME IN AND SEE THE LATEST IN ONLINE INTERACTIVE GAMES!
OUR CYBER SELVES ACQUIRE ARMOR AND WEAPONS!
TO GO AFTER DRAGONS AND OGRES!
Hmph! BOYS!
THEIR SILLY GAMES ARE SUCH FAR-FETCHED FANTASIES!
WHEREAS OURS ARE Oh-SO-PRACTICAL!
THE END

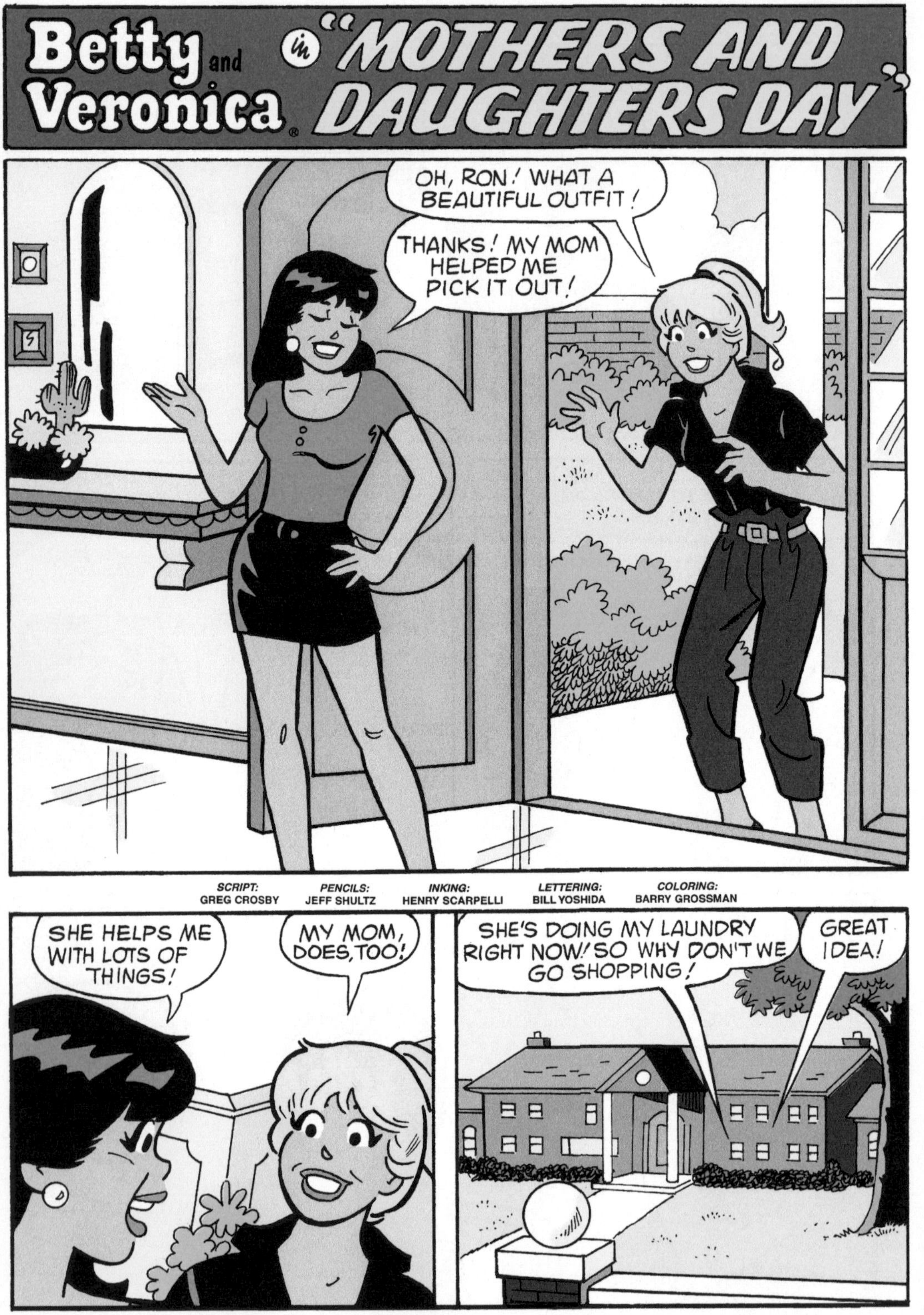
Betty and Veronica
in "MOTHERS AND DAUGHTERS DAY"
OH, RON! WHAT A BEAUTIFUL OUTFIT!
THANKS! MY MOM HELPED ME PICK IT OUT!
SHE HELPS ME WITH LOTS OF THINGS!
MY MOM, DOES, TOO!
SHE'S DOING MY LAUNDRY RIGHT NOW! SO WHY DON'T WE GO SHOPPING!
GREAT IDEA!

SCRIPT: GREG CROSBY PENCILS: JEFF SHULTZ INKING: HENRY SCARPELLI LETTERING: BILL YOSHIDA COLORING: BARRY GROSSMAN

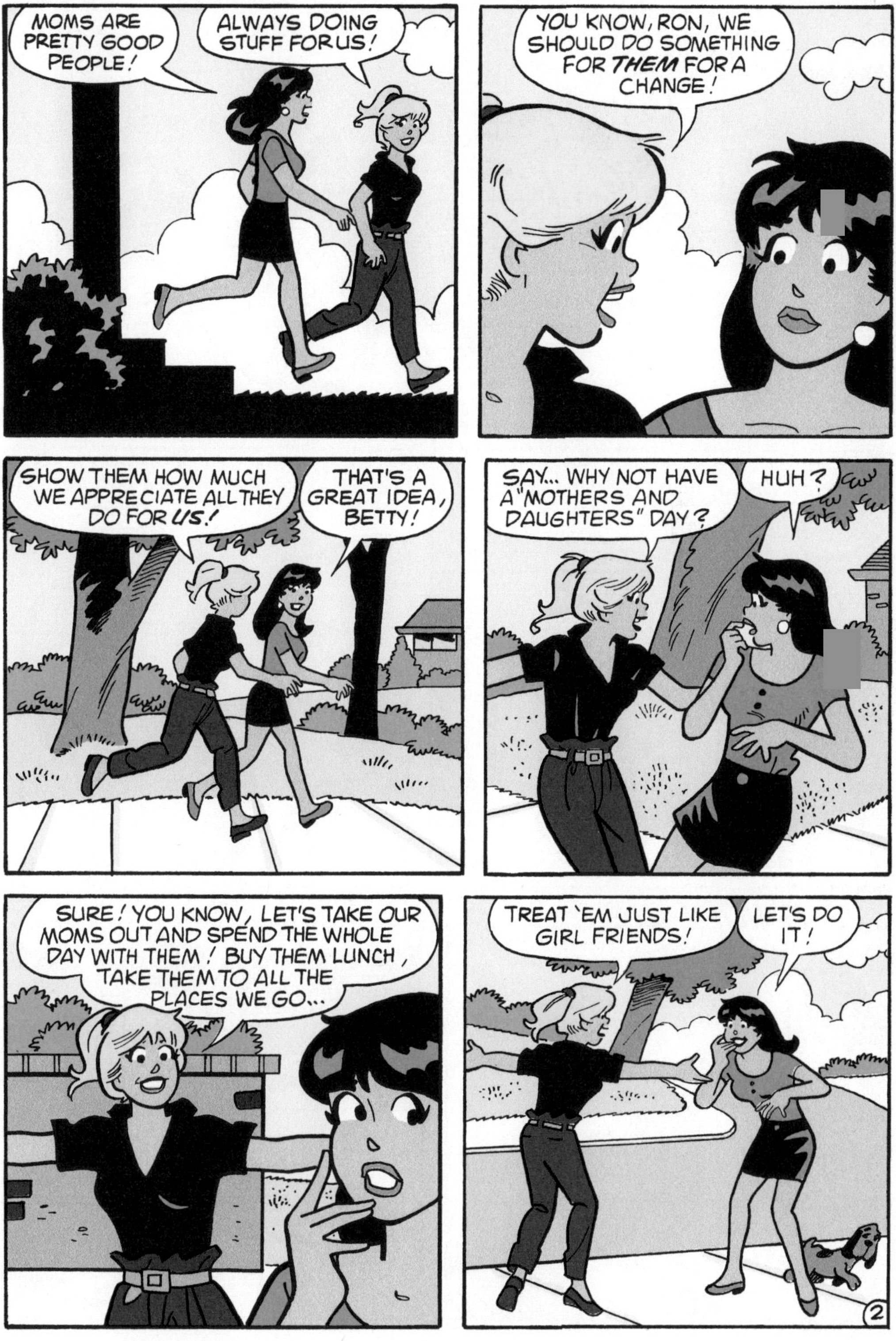
MOMS ARE PRETTY GOOD PEOPLE!
ALWAYS DOING STUFF FOR US!
YOU KNOW, RON, WE SHOULD DO SOMETHING FOR THEM FOR A CHANGE!
SHOW THEM HOW MUCH WE APPRECIATE ALL THEY DO FOR US!
THAT'S A GREAT IDEA, BETTY!
SAY... WHY NOT HAVE A "MOTHERS AND DAUGHTERS" DAY?
HUH?
SURE! YOU KNOW, LET'S TAKE OUR MOMS OUT AND SPEND THE WHOLE DAY WITH THEM! BUY THEM LUNCH, TAKE THEM TO ALL THE PLACES WE GO...
TREAT 'EM JUST LIKE GIRL FRIENDS!
LET'S DO IT!
2

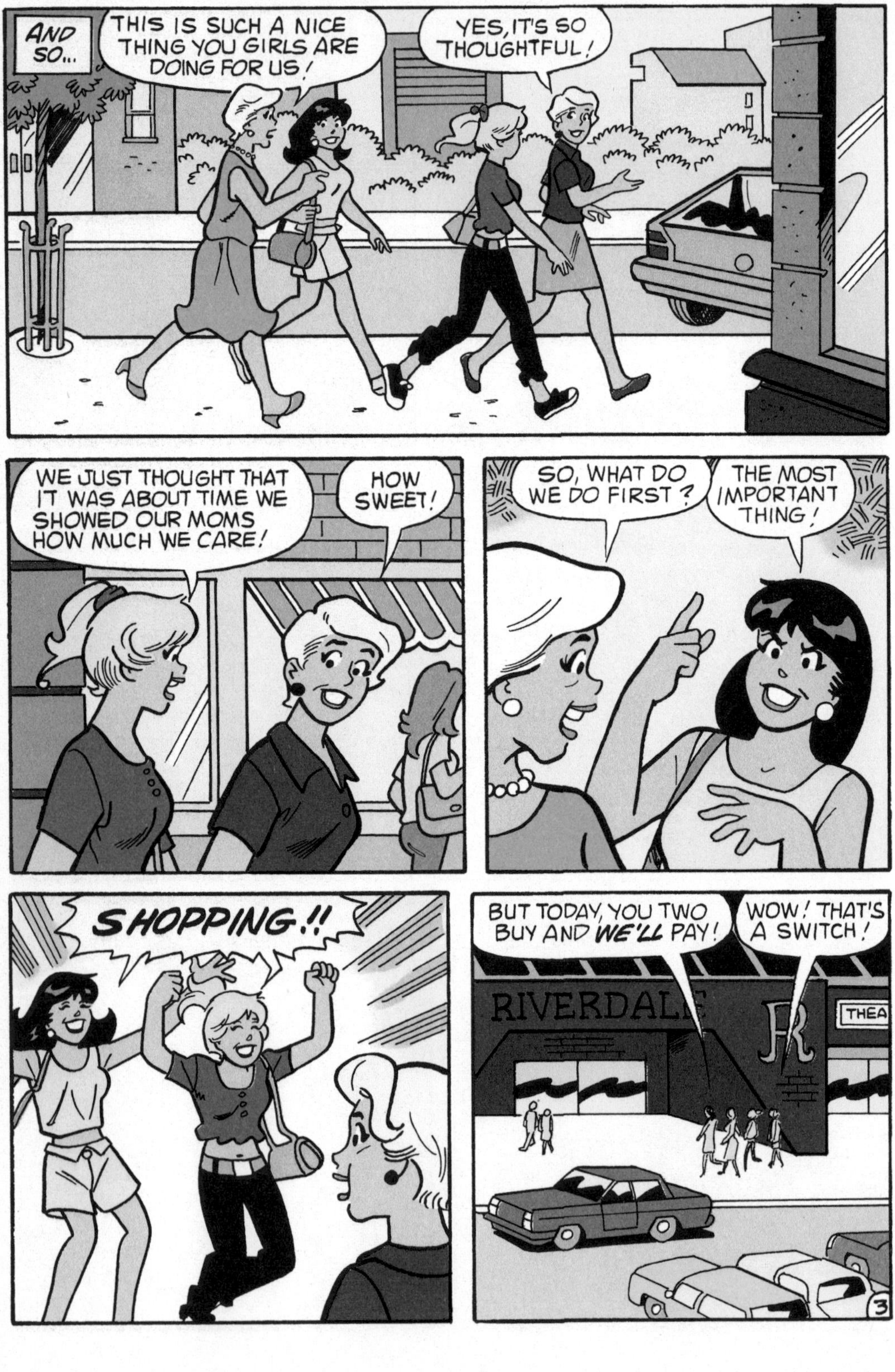
AND SO...
THIS IS SUCH A NICE THING YOU GIRLS ARE DOING FOR US!
YES, IT'S SO THOUGHTFUL!
WE JUST THOUGHT THAT IT WAS ABOUT TIME WE SHOWED OUR MOMS HOW MUCH WE CARE!
HOW SWEET!
SO, WHAT DO WE DO FIRST?
THE MOST IMPORTANT THING!
SHOPPING!!
BUT TODAY, YOU TWO BUY AND WE'LL PAY!
WOW! THAT'S A SWITCH!
RIVERDALE
THEA
3

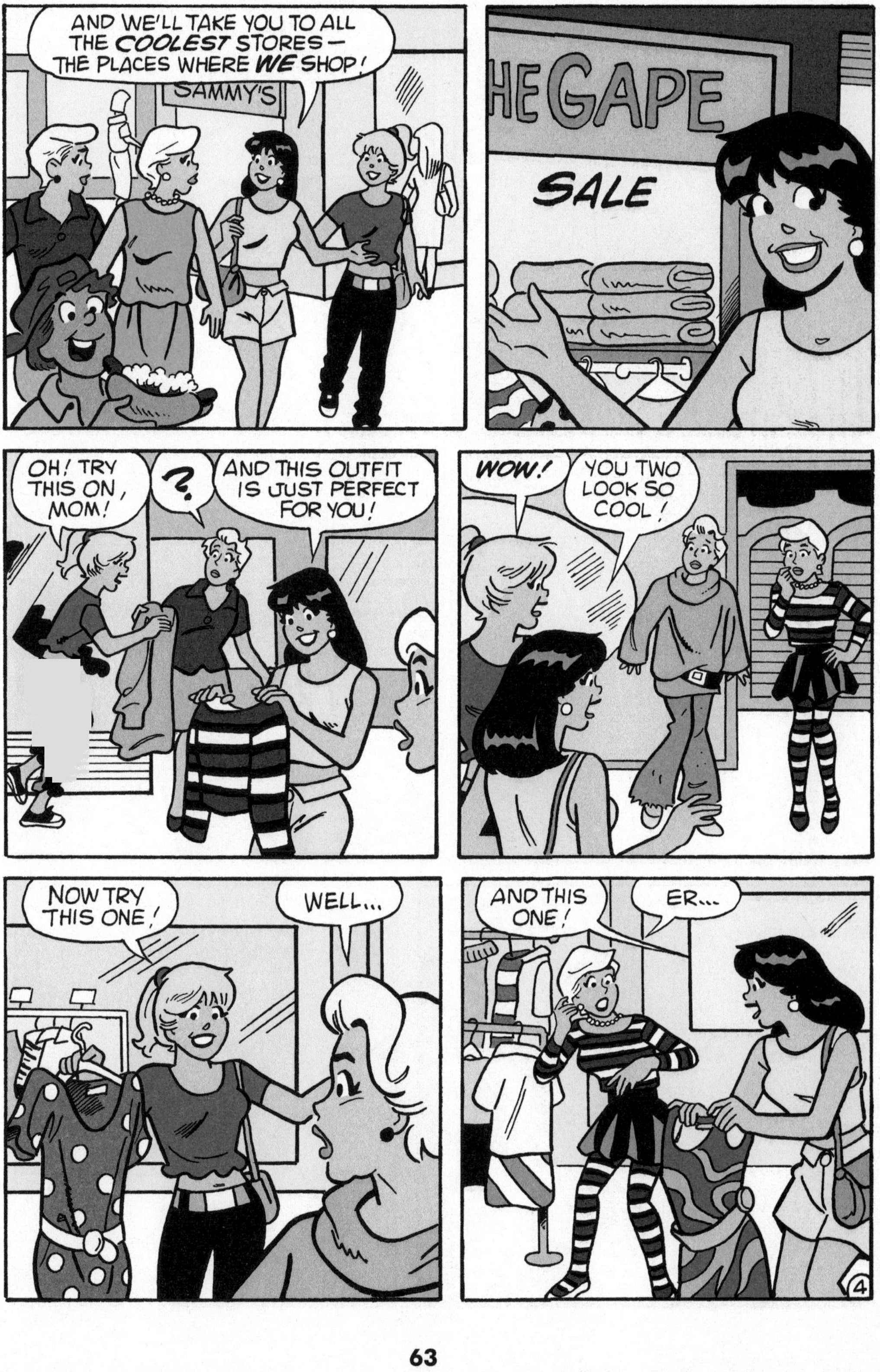
AND WE'LL TAKE YOU TO ALL THE COOLEST STORES — THE PLACES WHERE WE SHOP!
SAMMY'S
HE GAPE
SALE
OH! TRY THIS ON, MOM!
?
AND THIS OUTFIT IS JUST PERFECT FOR YOU!
WOW!
YOU TWO LOOK SO COOL!
NOW TRY THIS ONE!
WELL...
AND THIS ONE!
ER...
4

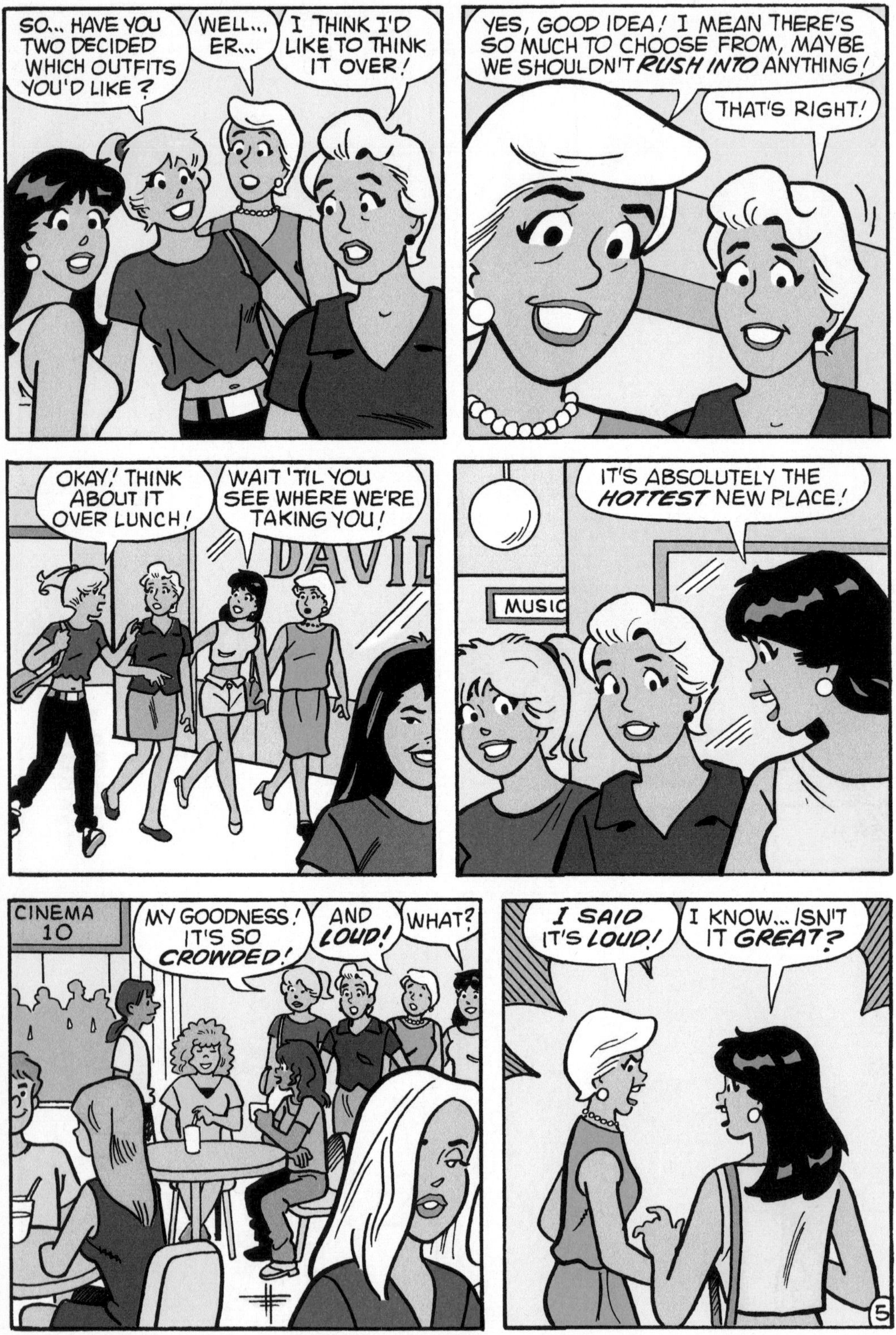
SO... HAVE YOU TWO DECIDED WHICH OUTFITS YOU'D LIKE?
WELL..., ER...
I THINK I'D LIKE TO THINK IT OVER!
YES, GOOD IDEA! I MEAN THERE'S SO MUCH TO CHOOSE FROM, MAYBE WE SHOULDN'T RUSH INTO ANYTHING!
THAT'S RIGHT!
OKAY! THINK ABOUT IT OVER LUNCH!
WAIT 'TIL YOU SEE WHERE WE'RE TAKING YOU!
DAVID
IT'S ABSOLUTELY THE HOTTEST NEW PLACE!
MUSIC
CINEMA 10
MY GOODNESS! IT'S SO CROWDED!
AND LOUD!
WHAT?
I SAID IT'S LOUD!
I KNOW... ISN'T IT GREAT?
5

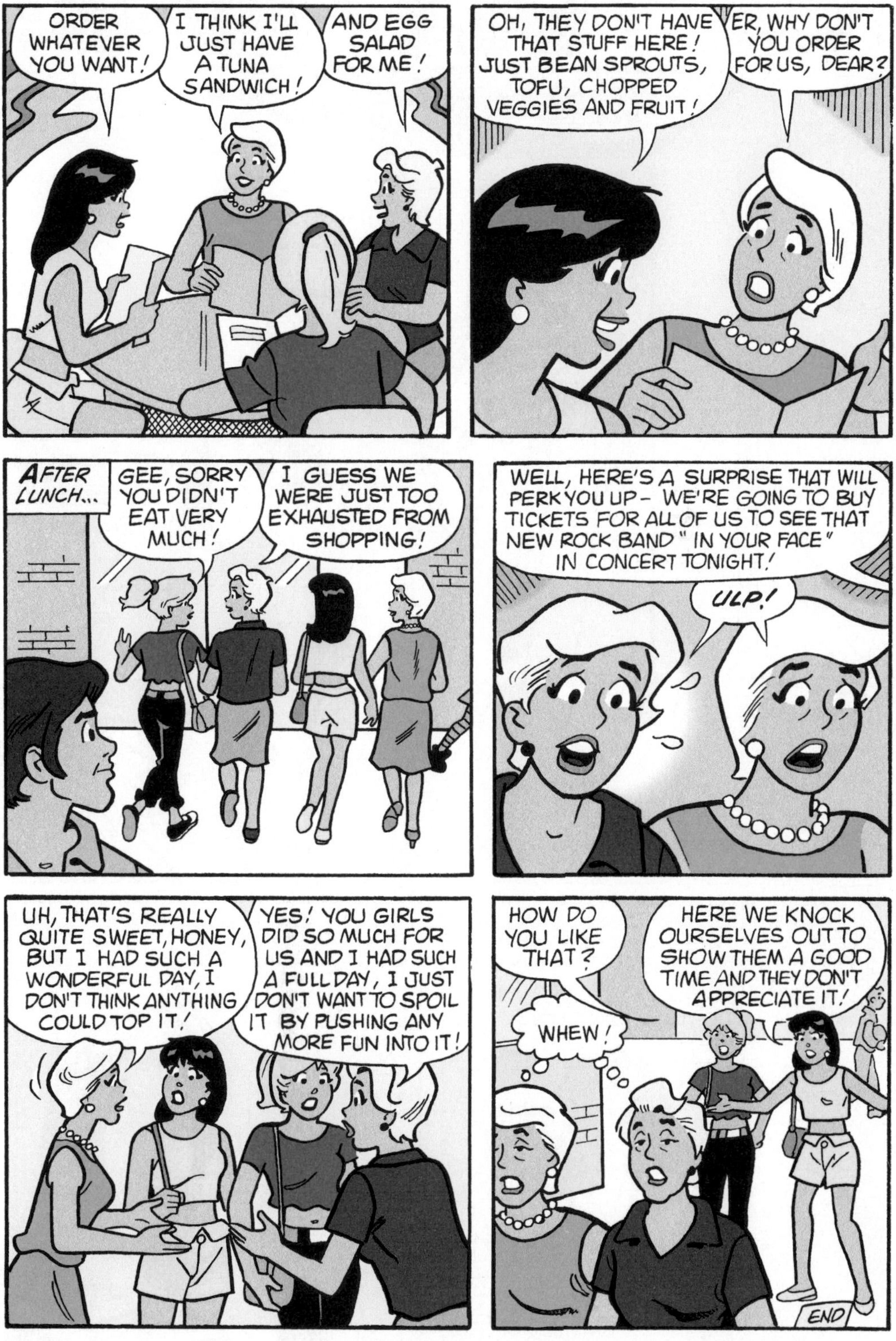
ORDER WHATEVER YOU WANT!
I THINK I'LL JUST HAVE A TUNA SANDWICH!
AND EGG SALAD FOR ME!
OH, THEY DON'T HAVE THAT STUFF HERE! JUST BEAN SPROUTS, TOFU, CHOPPED VEGGIES AND FRUIT!
ER, WHY DON'T YOU ORDER FOR US, DEAR?
AFTER LUNCH...
GEE, SORRY YOU DIDN'T EAT VERY MUCH!
I GUESS WE WERE JUST TOO EXHAUSTED FROM SHOPPING!
WELL, HERE'S A SURPRISE THAT WILL PERK YOU UP- WE'RE GOING TO BUY TICKETS FOR ALL OF US TO SEE THAT NEW ROCK BAND " IN YOUR FACE" IN CONCERT TONIGHT!
ULP!
UH, THAT'S REALLY QUITE SWEET, HONEY, BUT I HAD SUCH A WONDERFUL DAY, I DON'T THINK ANYTHING COULD TOP IT!
YES! YOU GIRLS DID SO MUCH FOR US AND I HAD SUCH A FULL DAY, I JUST DON'T WANT TO SPOIL IT BY PUSHING ANY MORE FUN INTO IT!
HOW DO YOU LIKE THAT?
HERE WE KNOCK OURSELVES OUT TO SHOW THEM A GOOD TIME AND THEY DON'T APPRECIATE IT!
WHEW!
END

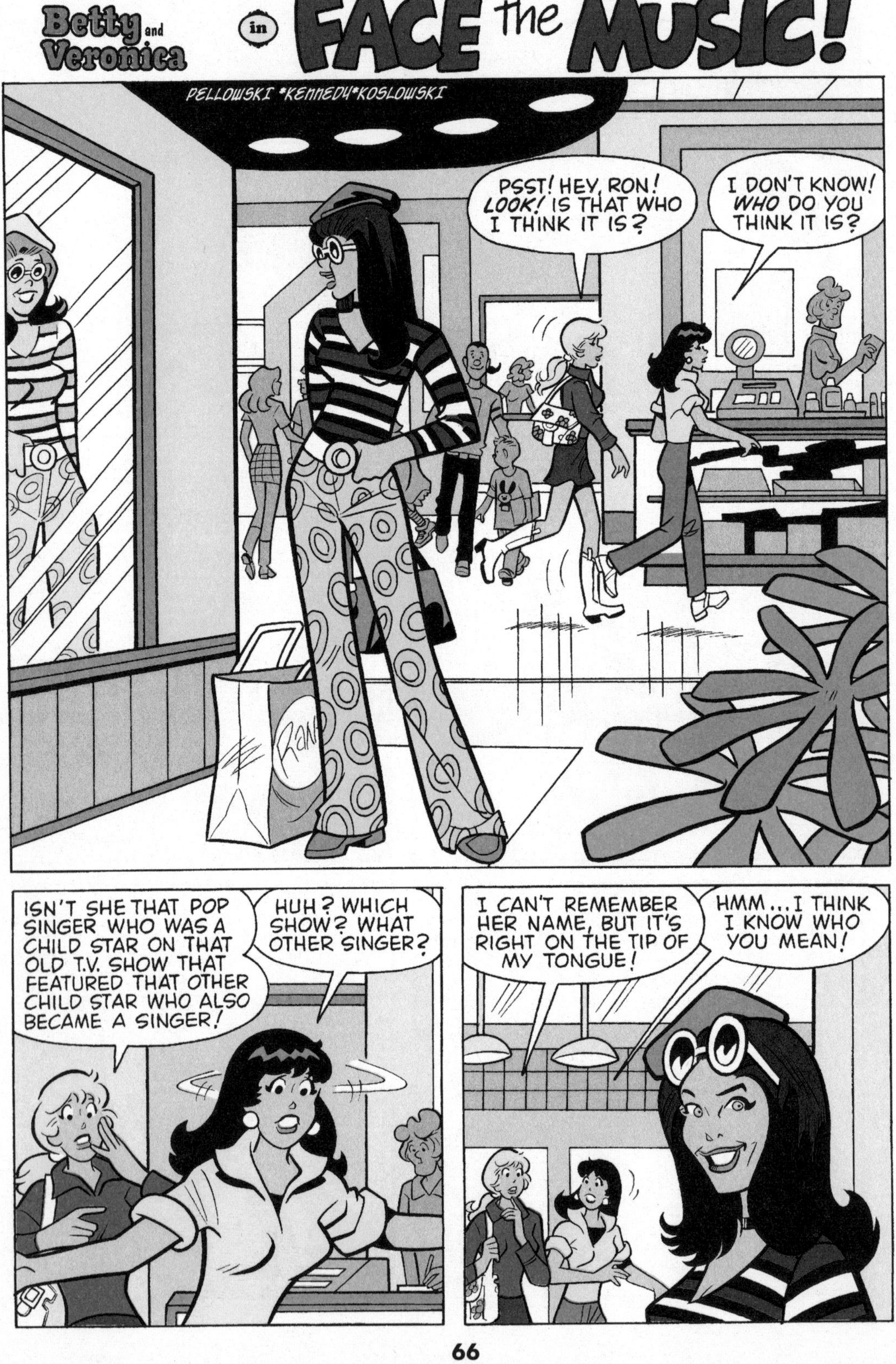
Betty and Veronica in FACE the MUSIC!
PELLOWSKI *KENNEDY*KOSLOWSKI
PSST! HEY, RON! LOOK! IS THAT WHO I THINK IT IS?
I DON'T KNOW! WHO DO YOU THINK IT IS?
ISN'T SHE THAT POP SINGER WHO WAS A CHILD STAR ON THAT OLD T.V. SHOW THAT FEATURED THAT OTHER CHILD STAR WHO ALSO BECAME A SINGER!
HUH? WHICH SHOW? WHAT OTHER SINGER?
I CAN'T REMEMBER HER NAME, BUT IT'S RIGHT ON THE TIP OF MY TONGUE!
HMM...I THINK I KNOW WHO YOU MEAN!

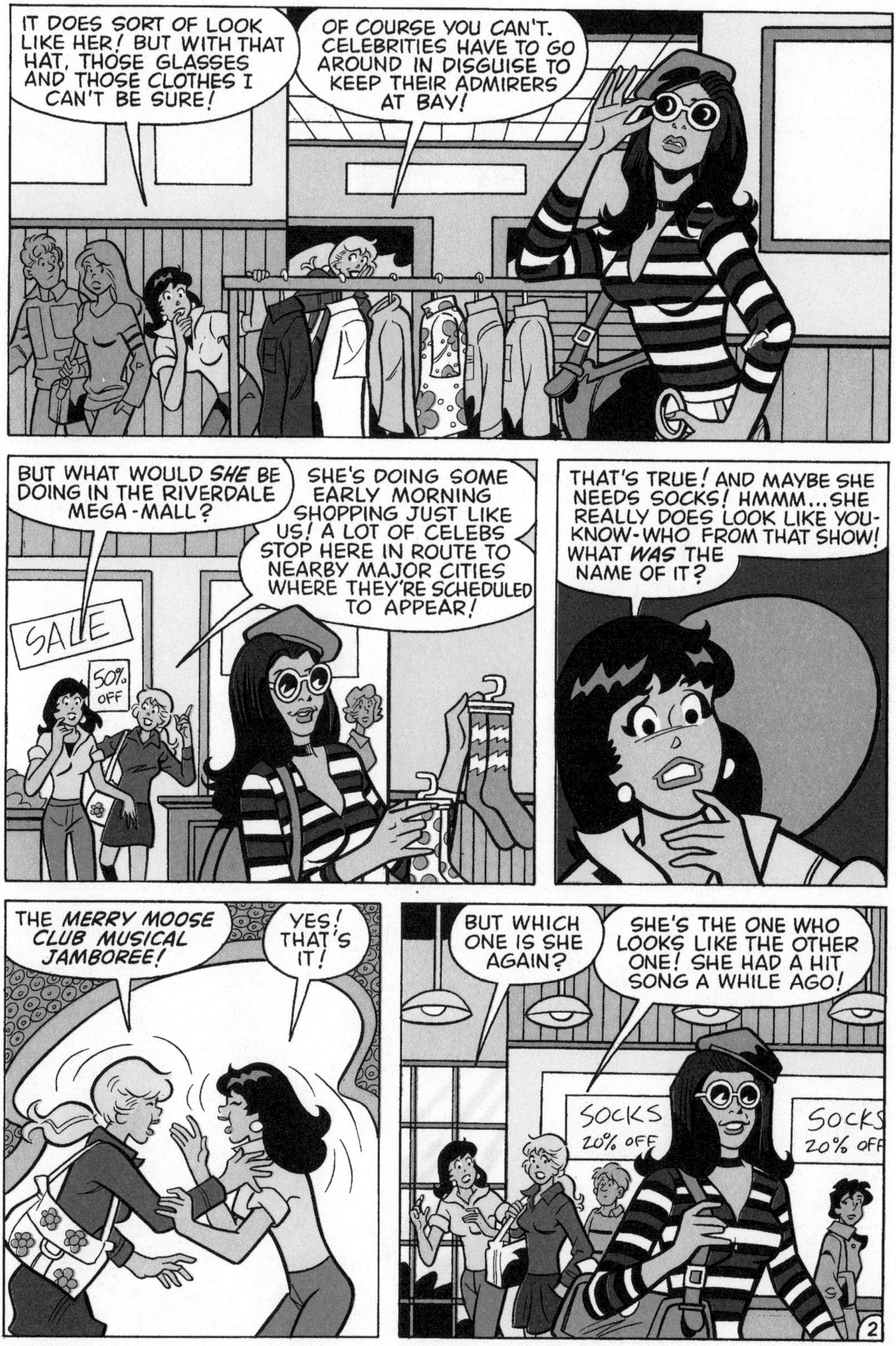
IT DOES SORT OF LOOK LIKE HER! BUT WITH THAT HAT, THOSE GLASSES AND THOSE CLOTHES I CAN'T BE SURE!
OF COURSE YOU CAN'T. CELEBRITIES HAVE TO GO AROUND IN DISGUISE TO KEEP THEIR ADMIRERS AT BAY!
BUT WHAT WOULD *SHE* BE DOING IN THE RIVERDALE MEGA-MALL?
SHE'S DOING SOME EARLY MORNING SHOPPING JUST LIKE US! A LOT OF CELEBS STOP HERE IN ROUTE TO NEARBY MAJOR CITIES WHERE THEY'RE SCHEDULED TO APPEAR!
SALE
50% OFF
THAT'S TRUE! AND MAYBE SHE NEEDS SOCKS! HMMM...SHE REALLY DOES LOOK LIKE YOU-KNOW-WHO FROM THAT SHOW! WHAT *WAS* THE NAME OF IT?
THE *MERRY MOOSE CLUB MUSICAL JAMBOREE!*
YES! THAT'S IT!
BUT WHICH ONE IS SHE AGAIN?
SHE'S THE ONE WHO LOOKS LIKE THE OTHER ONE! SHE HAD A HIT SONG A WHILE AGO!
SOCKS 20% OFF
SOCKS 20% OFF
2

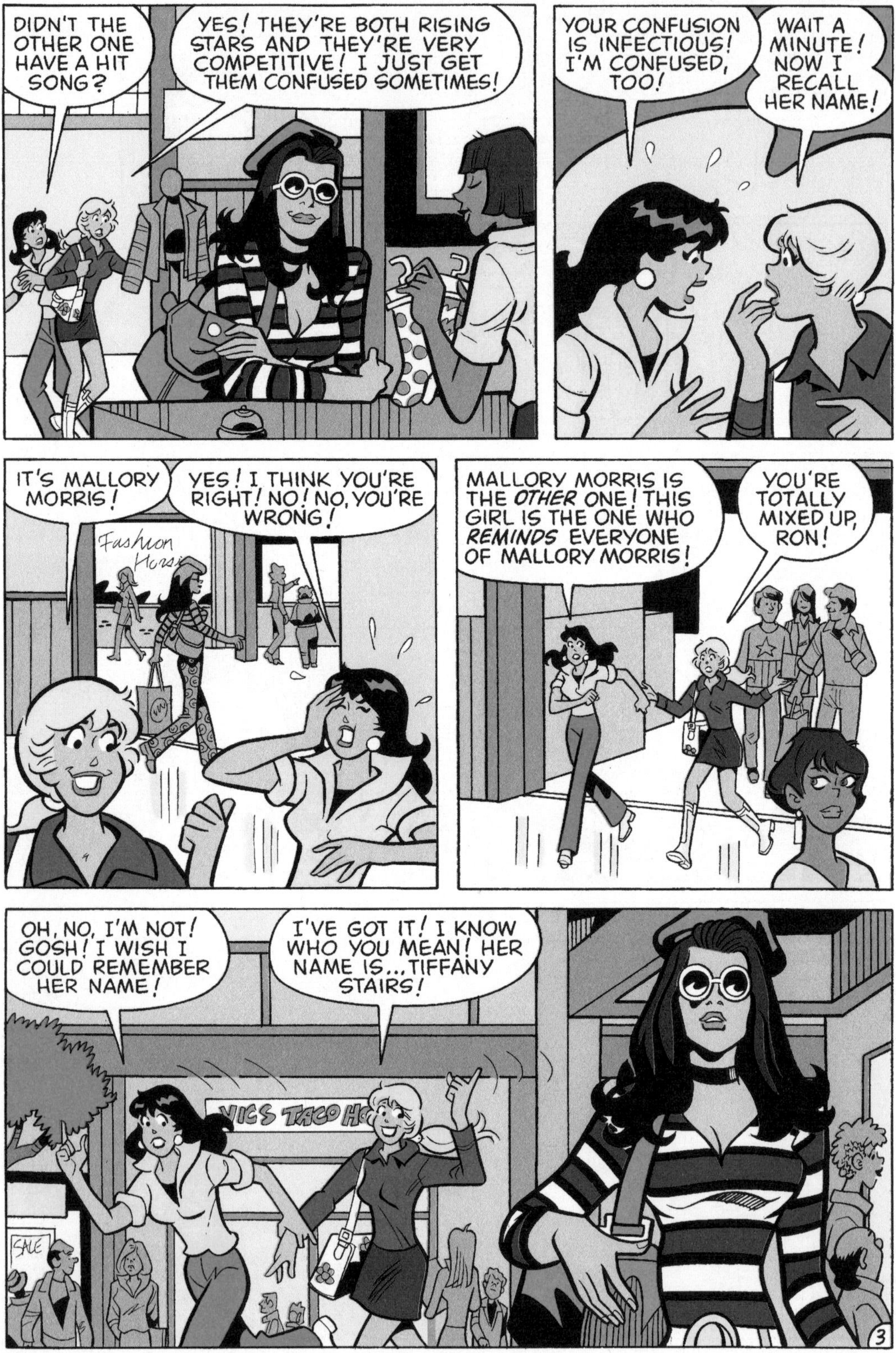

DIDN'T THE OTHER ONE HAVE A HIT SONG?
YES! THEY'RE BOTH RISING STARS AND THEY'RE VERY COMPETITIVE! I JUST GET THEM CONFUSED SOMETIMES!
YOUR CONFUSION IS INFECTIOUS! I'M CONFUSED, TOO!
WAIT A MINUTE! NOW I RECALL HER NAME!
IT'S MALLORY MORRIS!
YES! I THINK YOU'RE RIGHT! NO! NO, YOU'RE WRONG!
Fashion Horse
MALLORY MORRIS IS THE *OTHER* ONE! THIS GIRL IS THE ONE WHO *REMINDS* EVERYONE OF MALLORY MORRIS!
YOU'RE TOTALLY MIXED UP, RON!
OH, NO, I'M NOT! GOSH! I WISH I COULD REMEMBER HER NAME!
I'VE GOT IT! I KNOW WHO YOU MEAN! HER NAME IS... TIFFANY STAIRS!
VIC'S TACO H
SALE
3

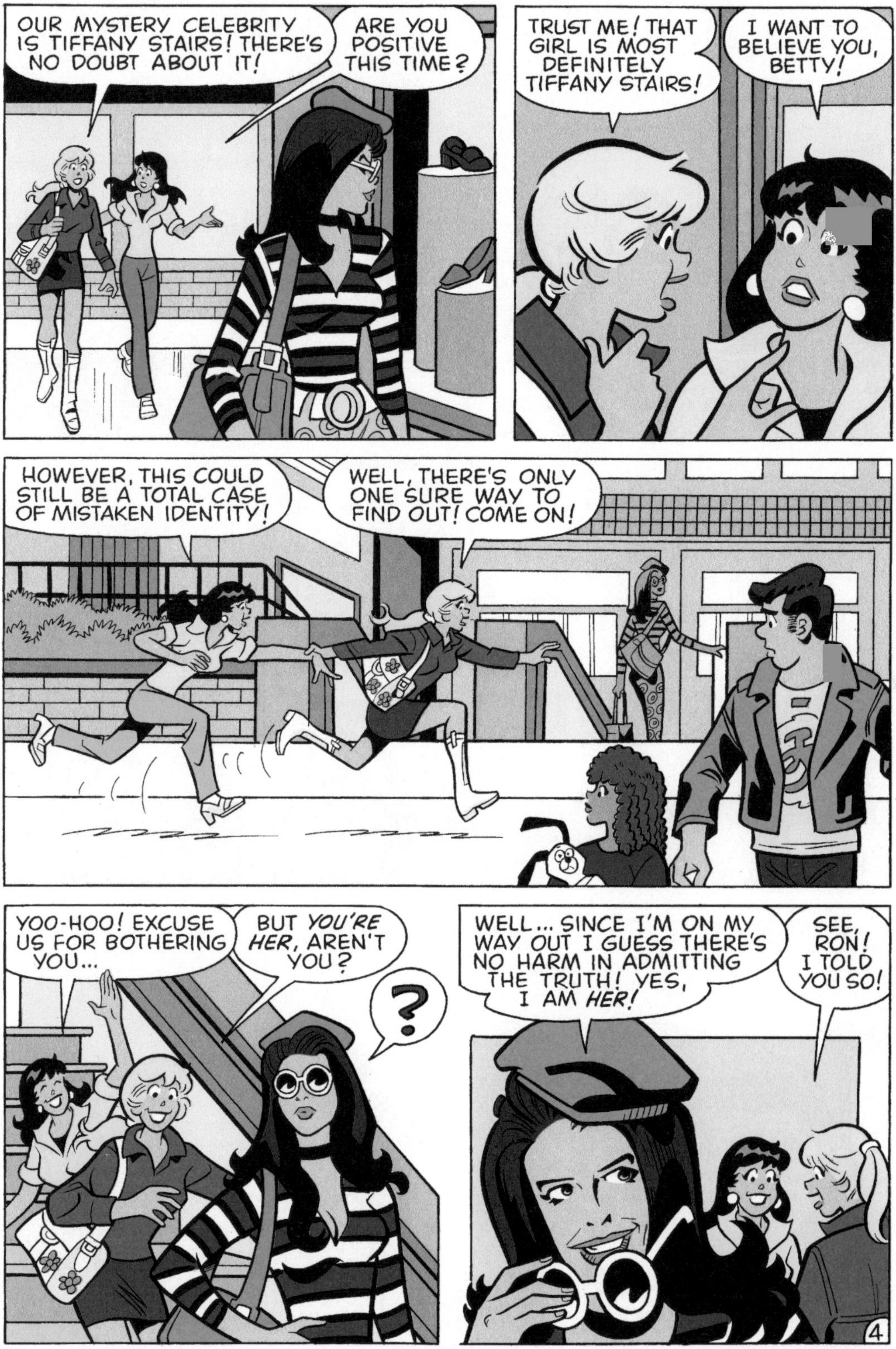
OUR MYSTERY CELEBRITY IS TIFFANY STAIRS! THERE'S NO DOUBT ABOUT IT!
ARE YOU POSITIVE THIS TIME?
TRUST ME! THAT GIRL IS MOST DEFINITELY TIFFANY STAIRS!
I WANT TO BELIEVE YOU, BETTY!
HOWEVER, THIS COULD STILL BE A TOTAL CASE OF MISTAKEN IDENTITY!
WELL, THERE'S ONLY ONE SURE WAY TO FIND OUT! COME ON!
YOO-HOO! EXCUSE US FOR BOTHERING YOU...
BUT *YOU'RE HER*, AREN'T YOU?
?
WELL... SINCE I'M ON MY WAY OUT I GUESS THERE'S NO HARM IN ADMITTING THE TRUTH! YES, I AM *HER*!
SEE, RON! I TOLD YOU SO!
4

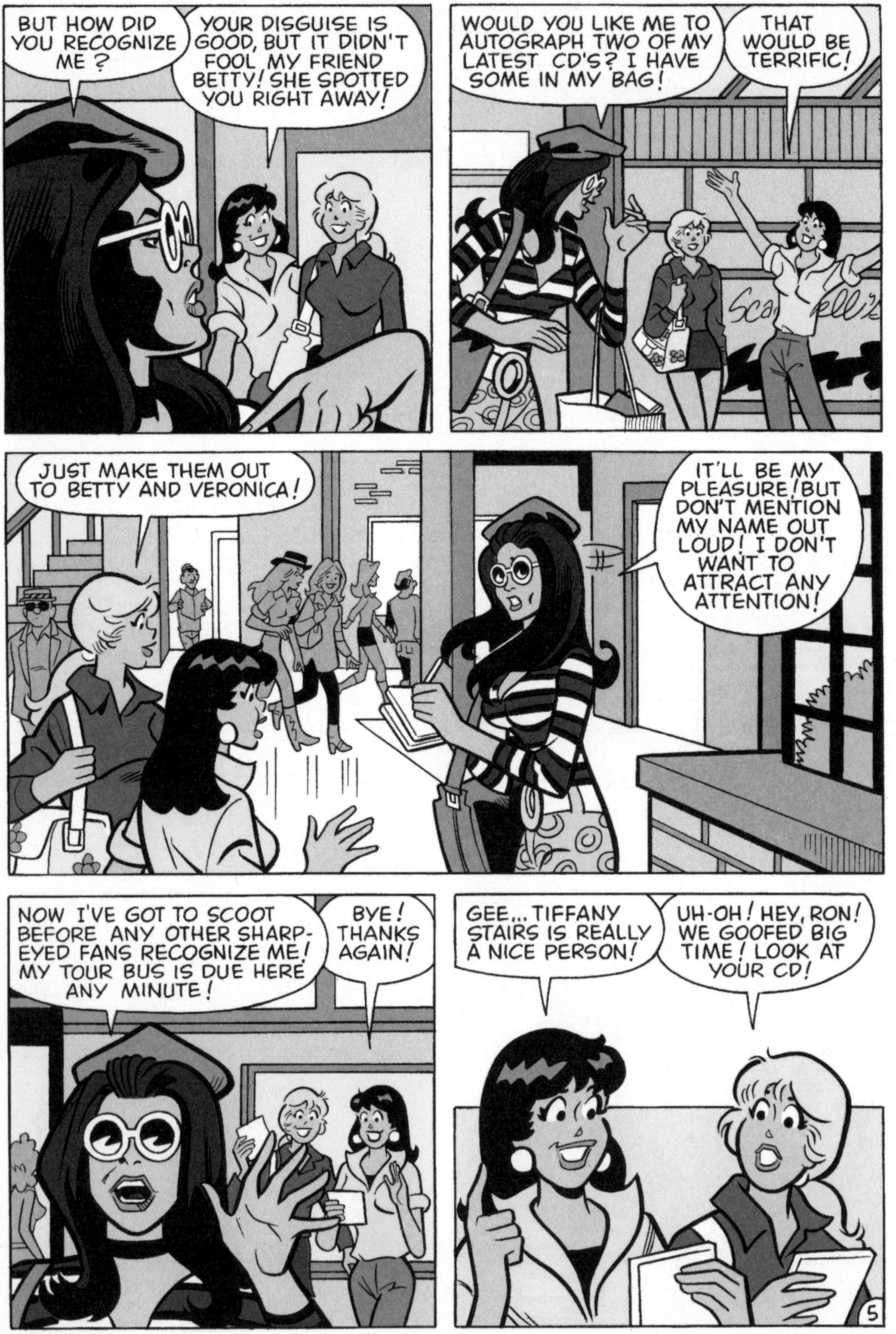

BUT HOW DID YOU RECOGNIZE ME?
YOUR DISGUISE IS GOOD, BUT IT DIDN'T FOOL MY FRIEND BETTY! SHE SPOTTED YOU RIGHT AWAY!
WOULD YOU LIKE ME TO AUTOGRAPH TWO OF MY LATEST CD'S? I HAVE SOME IN MY BAG!
THAT WOULD BE TERRIFIC!
Scarpelli's
JUST MAKE THEM OUT TO BETTY AND VERONICA!
IT'LL BE MY PLEASURE! BUT DON'T MENTION MY NAME OUT LOUD! I DON'T WANT TO ATTRACT ANY ATTENTION!
NOW I'VE GOT TO SCOOT BEFORE ANY OTHER SHARP-EYED FANS RECOGNIZE ME! MY TOUR BUS IS DUE HERE ANY MINUTE!
BYE! THANKS AGAIN!
GEE... TIFFANY STAIRS IS REALLY A NICE PERSON!
UH-OH! HEY, RON! WE GOOFED BIG TIME! LOOK AT YOUR CD!
5

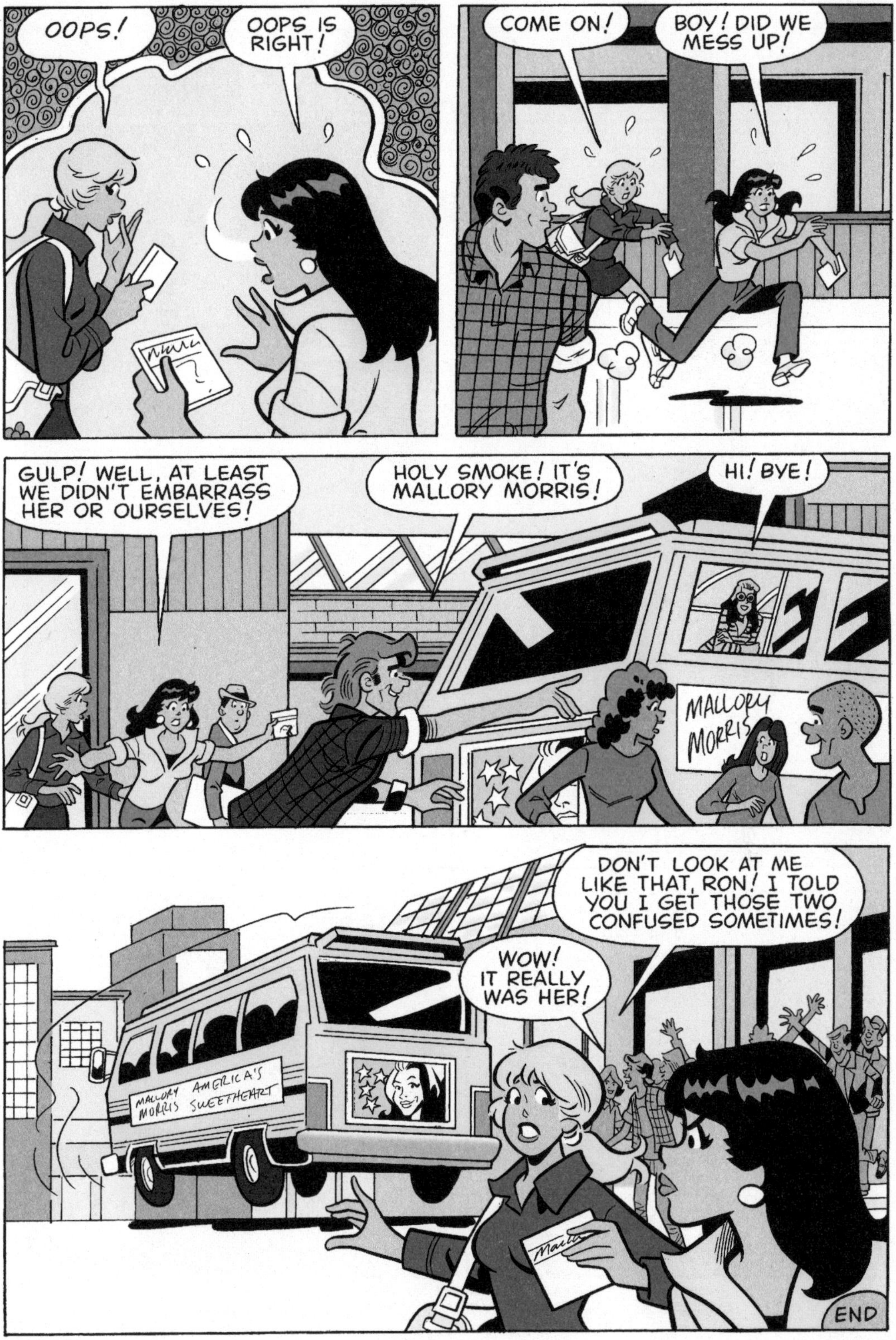
OOPS!
OOPS IS RIGHT!
COME ON!
BOY! DID WE MESS UP!
GULP! WELL, AT LEAST WE DIDN'T EMBARRASS HER OR OURSELVES!
HOLY SMOKE! IT'S MALLORY MORRIS!
HI! BYE!
MALLORY MORRIS
WOW! IT REALLY WAS HER!
DON'T LOOK AT ME LIKE THAT, RON! I TOLD YOU I GET THOSE TWO CONFUSED SOMETIMES!
MALLORY MORRIS AMERICA'S SWEETHEART
END

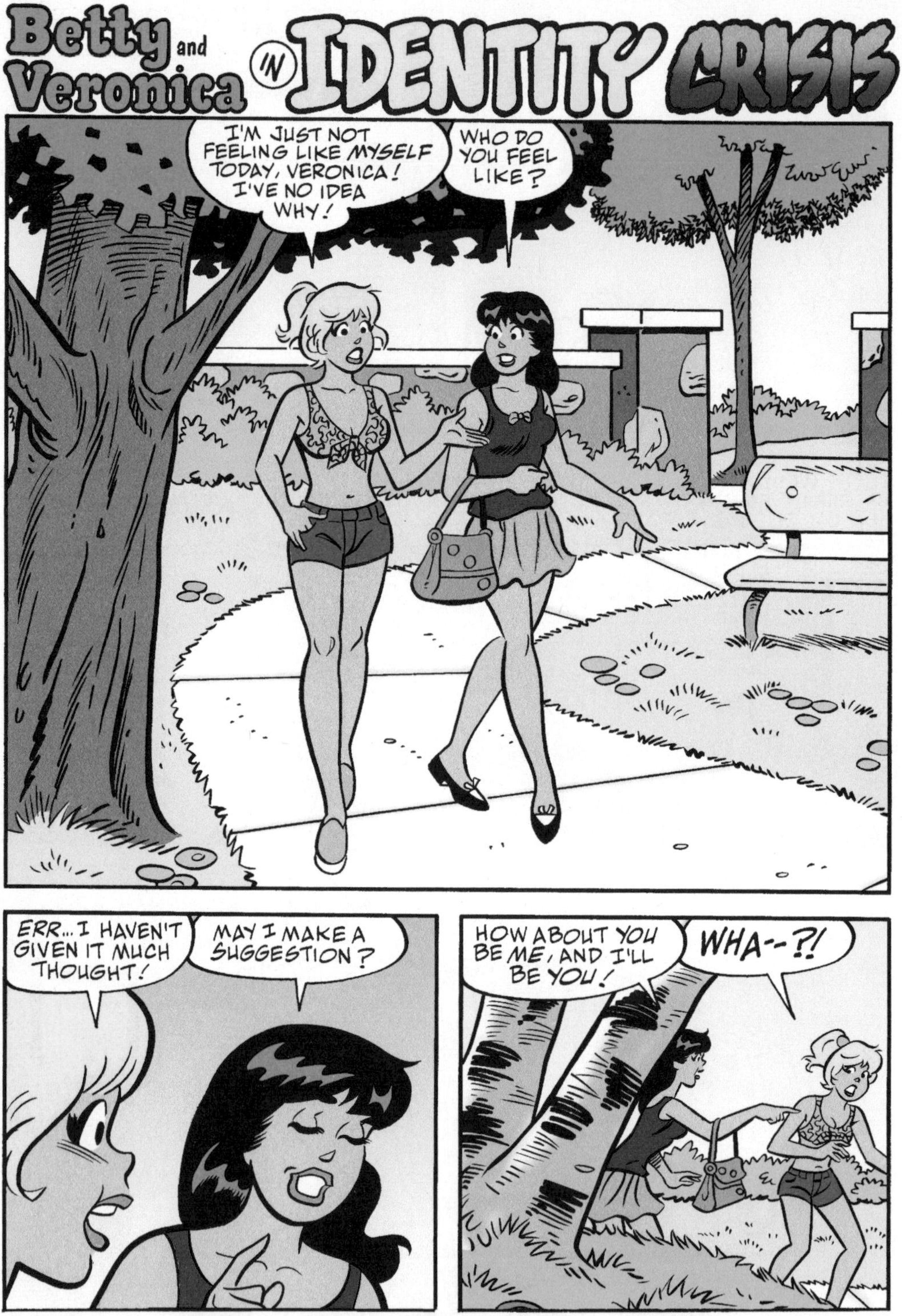
Betty and Veronica IN IDENTITY CRISIS
I'M JUST NOT FEELING LIKE MYSELF TODAY, VERONICA! I'VE NO IDEA WHY!
WHO DO YOU FEEL LIKE?
ERR... I HAVEN'T GIVEN IT MUCH THOUGHT!
MAY I MAKE A SUGGESTION?
HOW ABOUT YOU BE ME, AND I'LL BE YOU!
WHA--?!

SCRIPT: KATHLEEN WEBB PENCILS: JEFF SHULTZ INKING: AL MILGROM LETTERING: JACK MORELLI COLORING: BARRY GROSSMAN

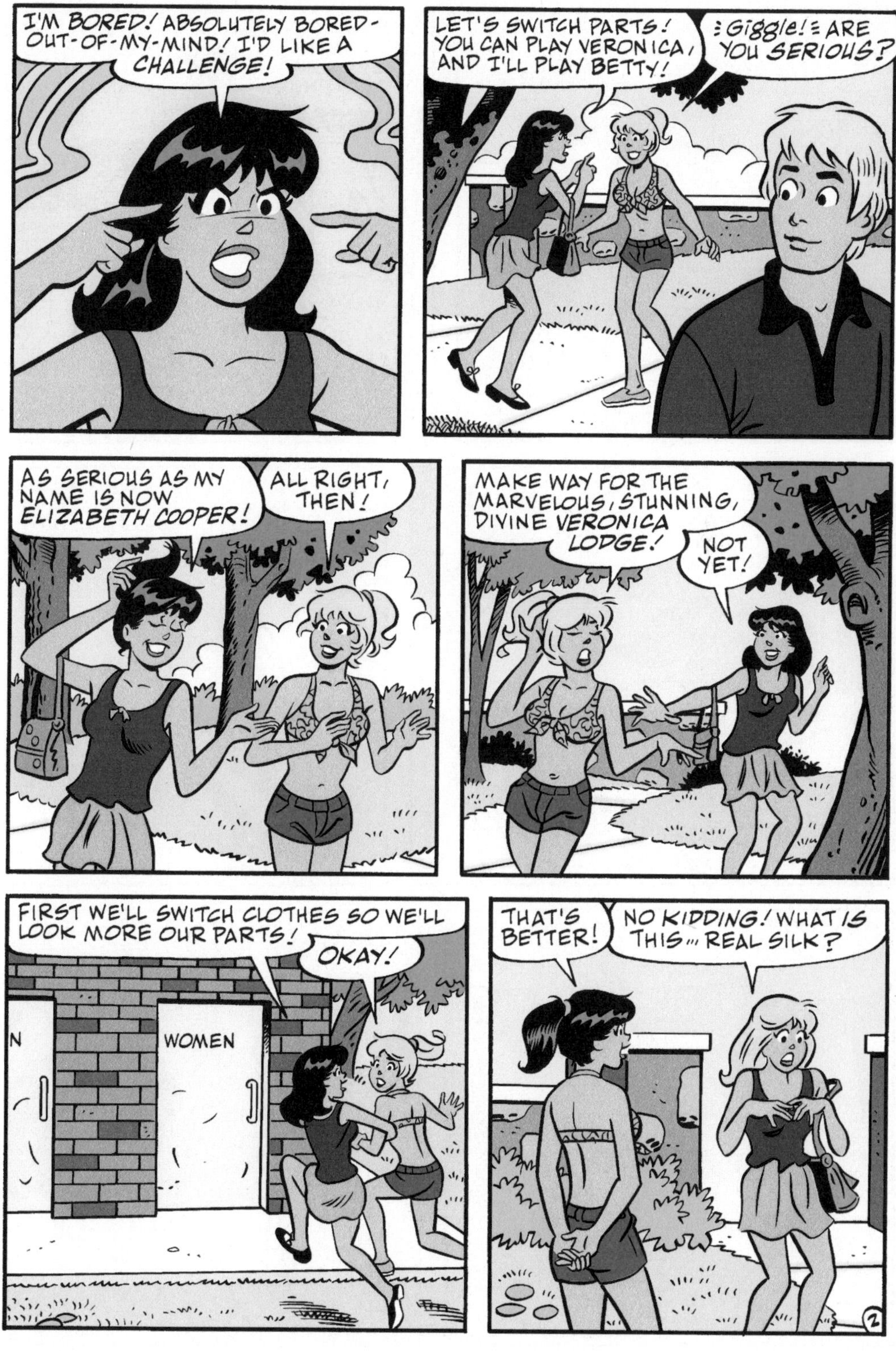

I'M BORED! ABSOLUTELY BORED-OUT-OF-MY-MIND! I'D LIKE A CHALLENGE!
LET'S SWITCH PARTS! YOU CAN PLAY VERONICA, AND I'LL PLAY BETTY!
Giggle! ARE YOU SERIOUS?
AS SERIOUS AS MY NAME IS NOW ELIZABETH COOPER!
ALL RIGHT, THEN!
MAKE WAY FOR THE MARVELOUS, STUNNING, DIVINE VERONICA LODGE!
NOT YET!
FIRST WE'LL SWITCH CLOTHES SO WE'LL LOOK MORE OUR PARTS!
OKAY!
WOMEN
THAT'S BETTER!
NO KIDDING! WHAT IS THIS... REAL SILK?
2

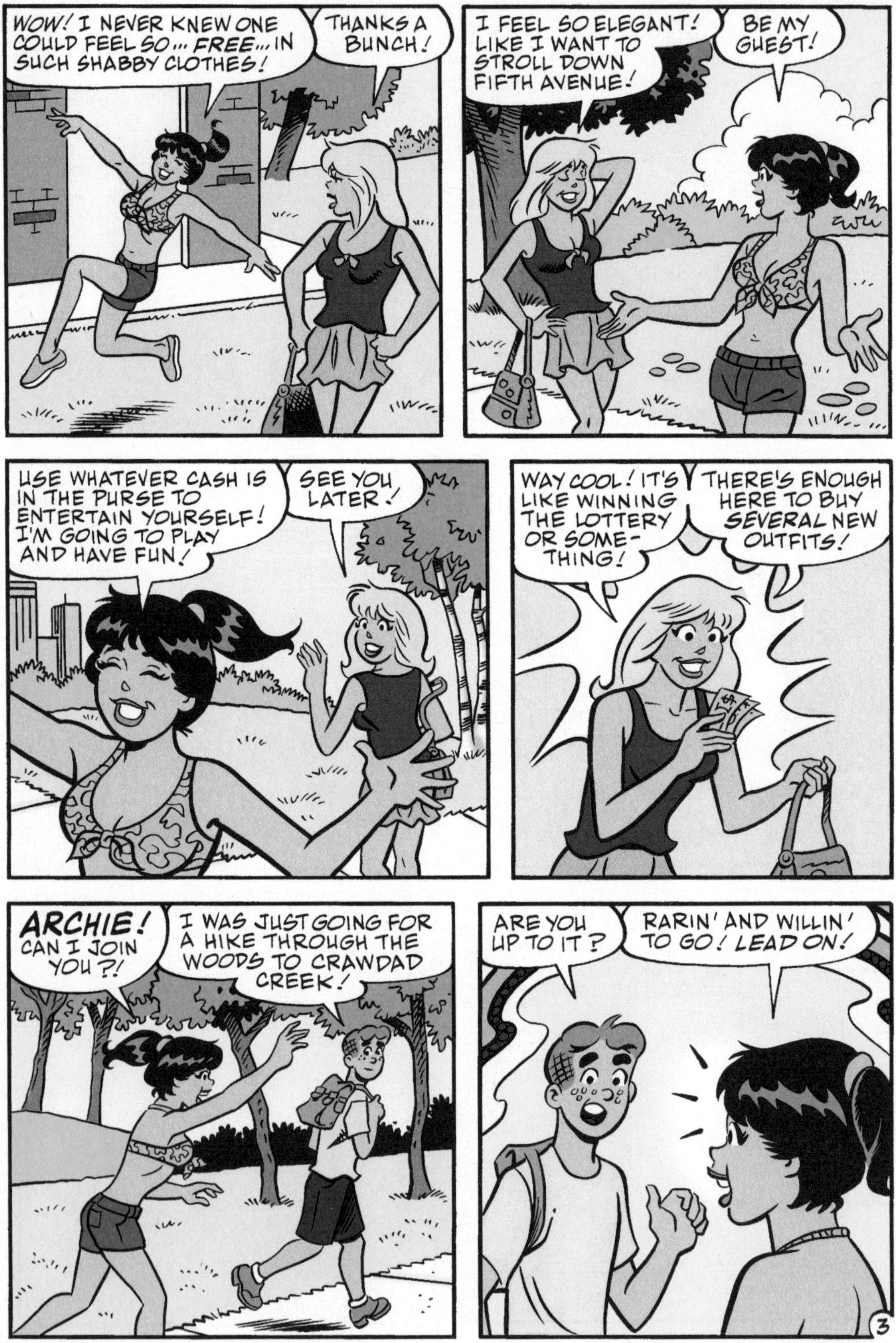
WOW! I NEVER KNEW ONE COULD FEEL SO... FREE... IN SUCH SHABBY CLOTHES!
THANKS A BUNCH!
I FEEL SO ELEGANT! LIKE I WANT TO STROLL DOWN FIFTH AVENUE!
BE MY GUEST!
USE WHATEVER CASH IS IN THE PURSE TO ENTERTAIN YOURSELF! I'M GOING TO PLAY AND HAVE FUN!
SEE YOU LATER!
WAY COOL! IT'S LIKE WINNING THE LOTTERY OR SOME-THING!
THERE'S ENOUGH HERE TO BUY SEVERAL NEW OUTFITS!
ARCHIE! CAN I JOIN YOU?!
I WAS JUST GOING FOR A HIKE THROUGH THE WOODS TO CRAWDAD CREEK!
ARE YOU UP TO IT?
RARIN' AND WILLIN' TO GO! LEAD ON!
3

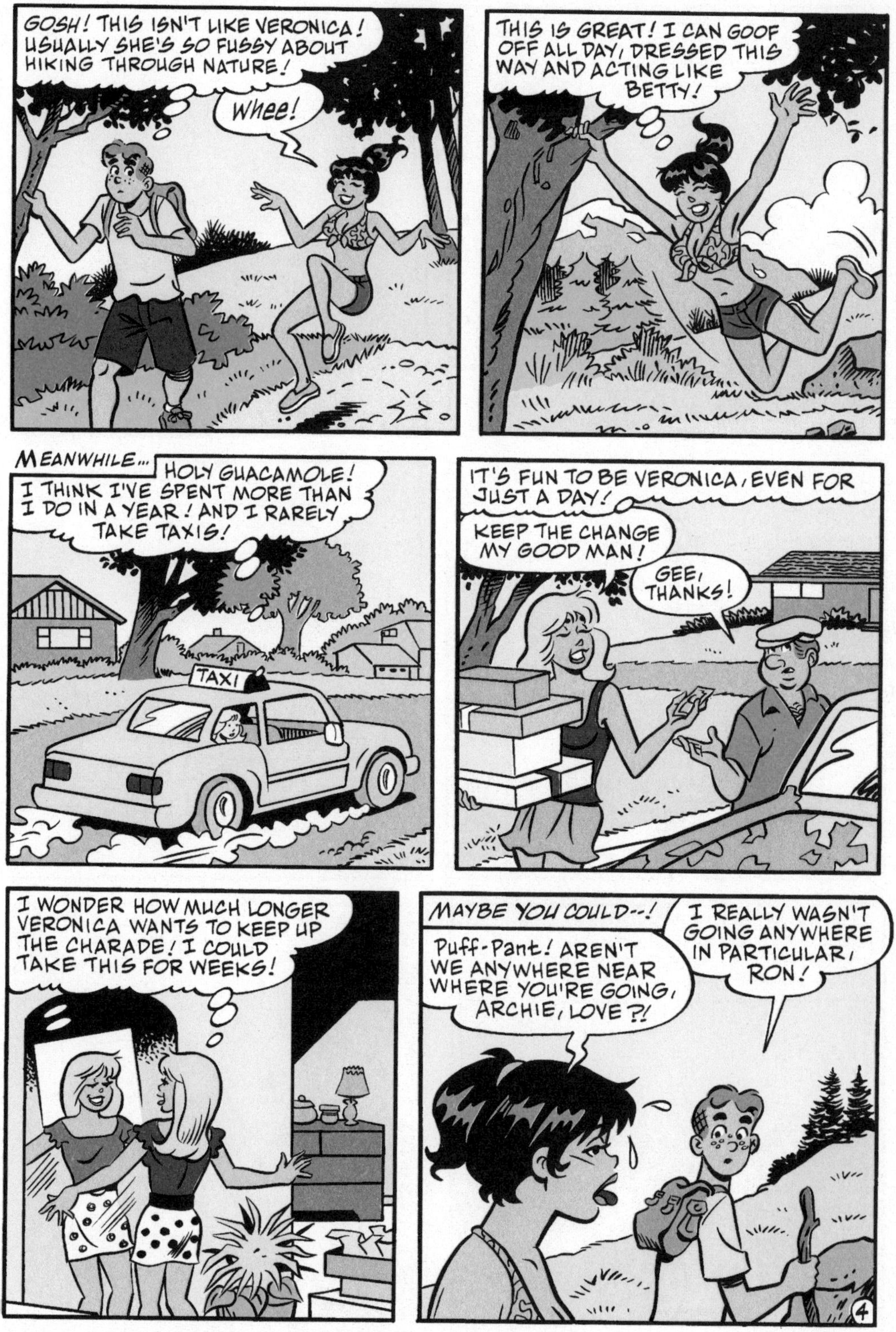

GOSH! THIS ISN'T LIKE VERONICA! USUALLY SHE'S SO FUSSY ABOUT HIKING THROUGH NATURE!
Whee!
THIS IS GREAT! I CAN GOOF OFF ALL DAY, DRESSED THIS WAY AND ACTING LIKE BETTY!
MEANWHILE...
HOLY GUACAMOLE! I THINK I'VE SPENT MORE THAN I DO IN A YEAR! AND I RARELY TAKE TAXIS!
TAXI
IT'S FUN TO BE VERONICA, EVEN FOR JUST A DAY!
KEEP THE CHANGE MY GOOD MAN!
GEE, THANKS!
I WONDER HOW MUCH LONGER VERONICA WANTS TO KEEP UP THE CHARADE! I COULD TAKE THIS FOR WEEKS!
MAYBE YOU COULD--!
I REALLY WASN'T GOING ANYWHERE IN PARTICULAR, RON!
Puff-Pant! AREN'T WE ANYWHERE NEAR WHERE YOU'RE GOING, ARCHIE, LOVE?!
4

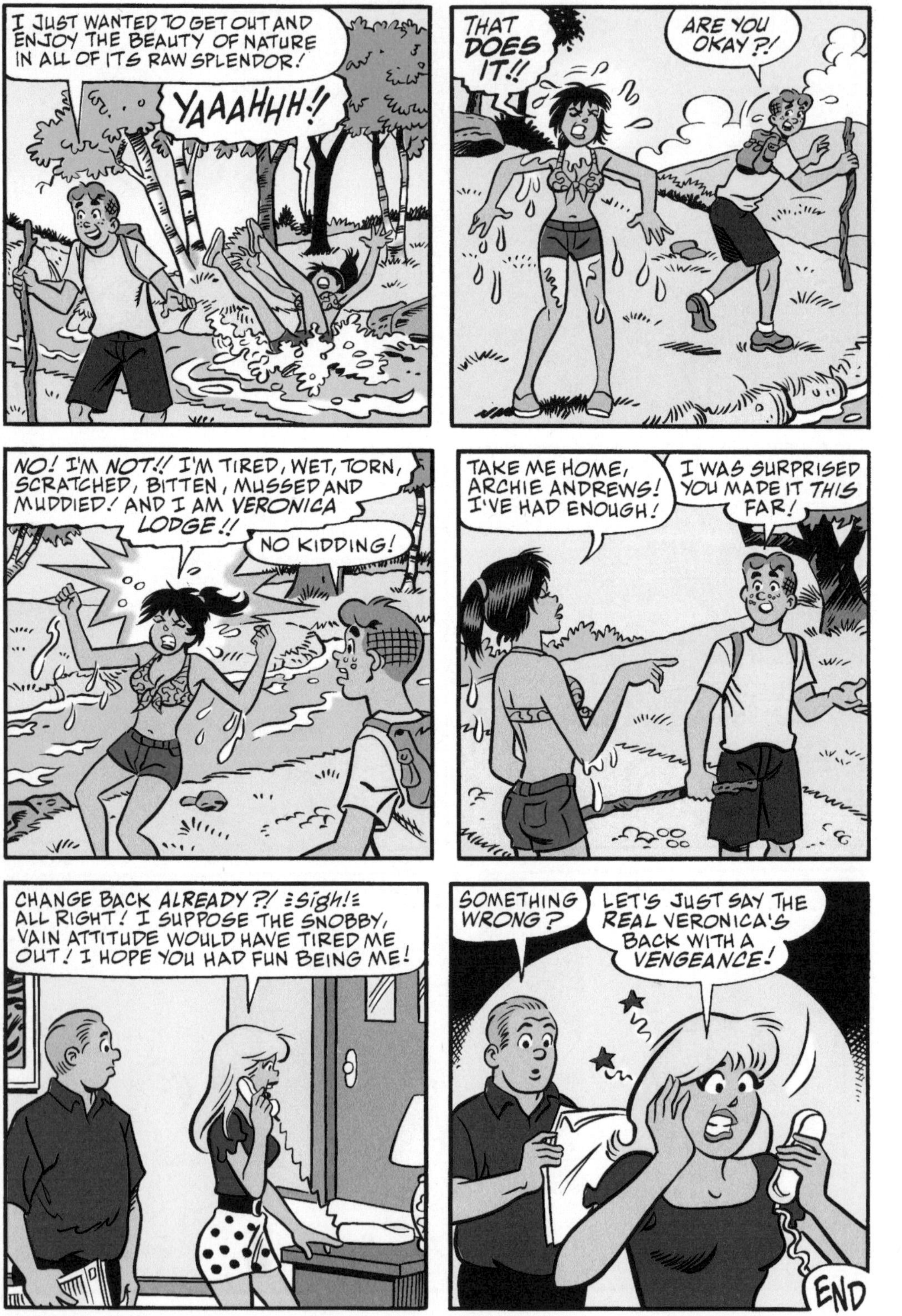
I JUST WANTED TO GET OUT AND ENJOY THE BEAUTY OF NATURE IN ALL OF ITS RAW SPLENDOR!
YAAAHHH!!
THAT DOES IT!!
ARE YOU OKAY?!
NO! I'M NOT!! I'M TIRED, WET, TORN, SCRATCHED, BITTEN, MUSSED AND MUDDIED! AND I AM VERONICA LODGE!!
NO KIDDING!
TAKE ME HOME, ARCHIE ANDREWS! I'VE HAD ENOUGH!
I WAS SURPRISED YOU MADE IT THIS FAR!
CHANGE BACK ALREADY?! sigh! ALL RIGHT! I SUPPOSE THE SNOBBY, VAIN ATTITUDE WOULD HAVE TIRED ME OUT! I HOPE YOU HAD FUN BEING ME!
SOMETHING WRONG?
LET'S JUST SAY THE REAL VERONICA'S BACK WITH A VENGEANCE!
END

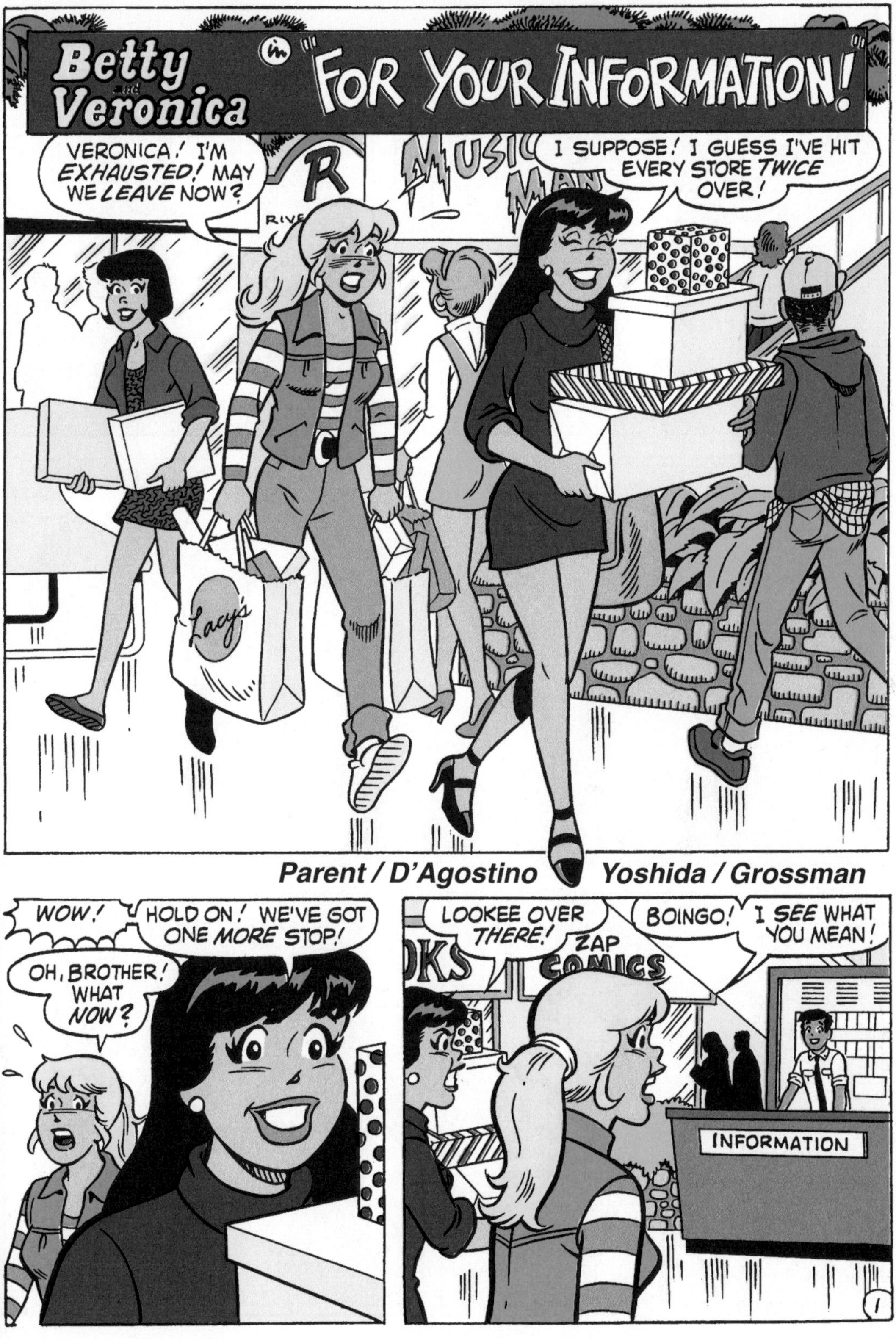
Betty and Veronica
in "FOR YOUR INFORMATION!"
VERONICA! I'M EXHAUSTED! MAY WE LEAVE NOW?
I SUPPOSE! I GUESS I'VE HIT EVERY STORE TWICE OVER!
MUSIC MAN
Lacy's
Parent / D'Agostino Yoshida / Grossman
WOW!
HOLD ON! WE'VE GOT ONE MORE STOP!
OH, BROTHER! WHAT NOW?
LOOKEE OVER THERE!
BOINGO! I SEE WHAT YOU MEAN!
ZAP COMICS
INFORMATION
1

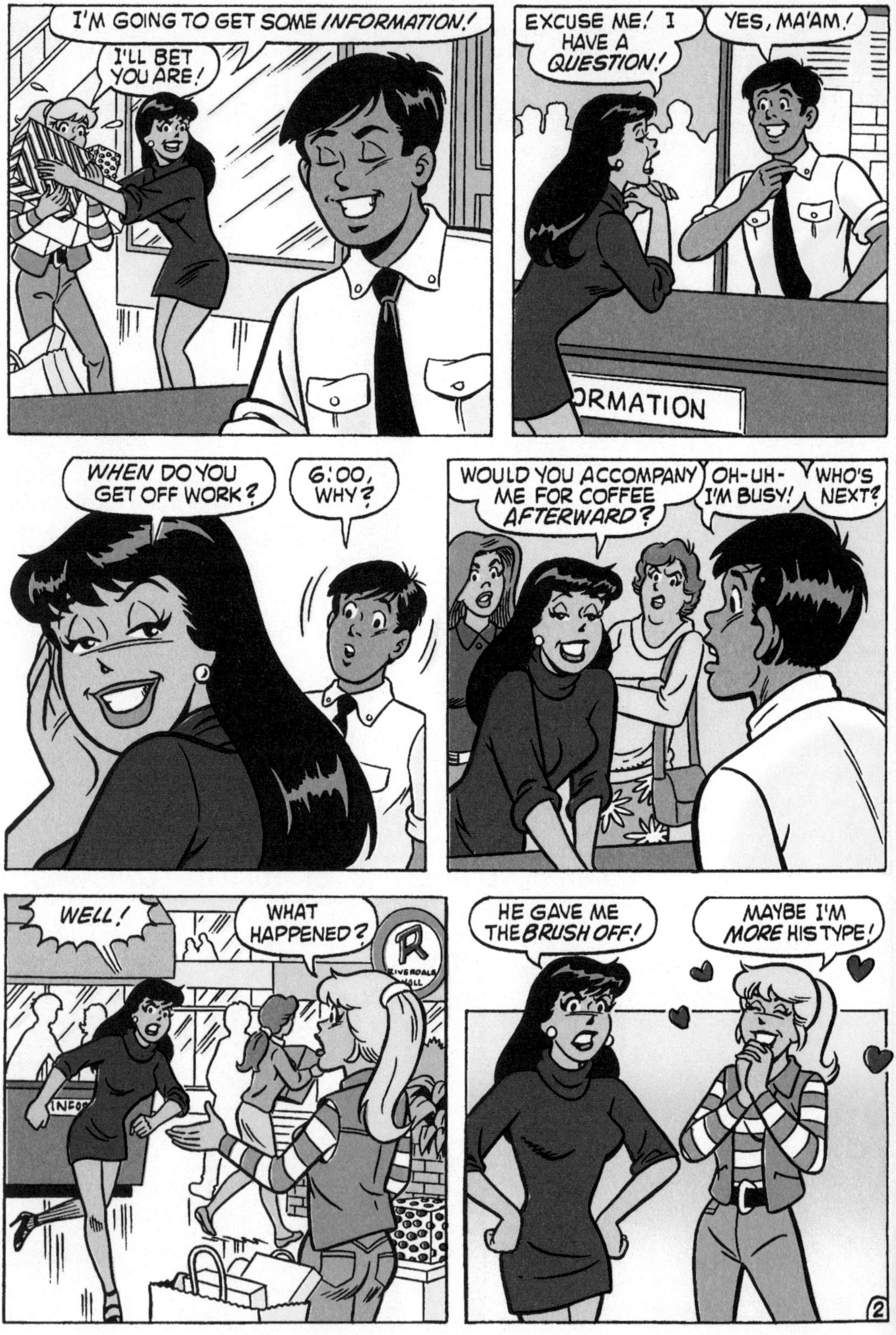
I'M GOING TO GET SOME *INFORMATION*!
I'LL BET YOU ARE!
EXCUSE ME! I HAVE A *QUESTION*!
YES, MA'AM!
ORMATION
WHEN DO YOU GET OFF WORK?
6:00, WHY?
WOULD YOU ACCOMPANY ME FOR COFFEE *AFTERWARD*?
OH-UH- I'M BUSY!
WHO'S NEXT?
WELL!
WHAT HAPPENED?
HE GAVE ME THE *BRUSH OFF*!
MAYBE I'M *MORE* HIS TYPE!
2

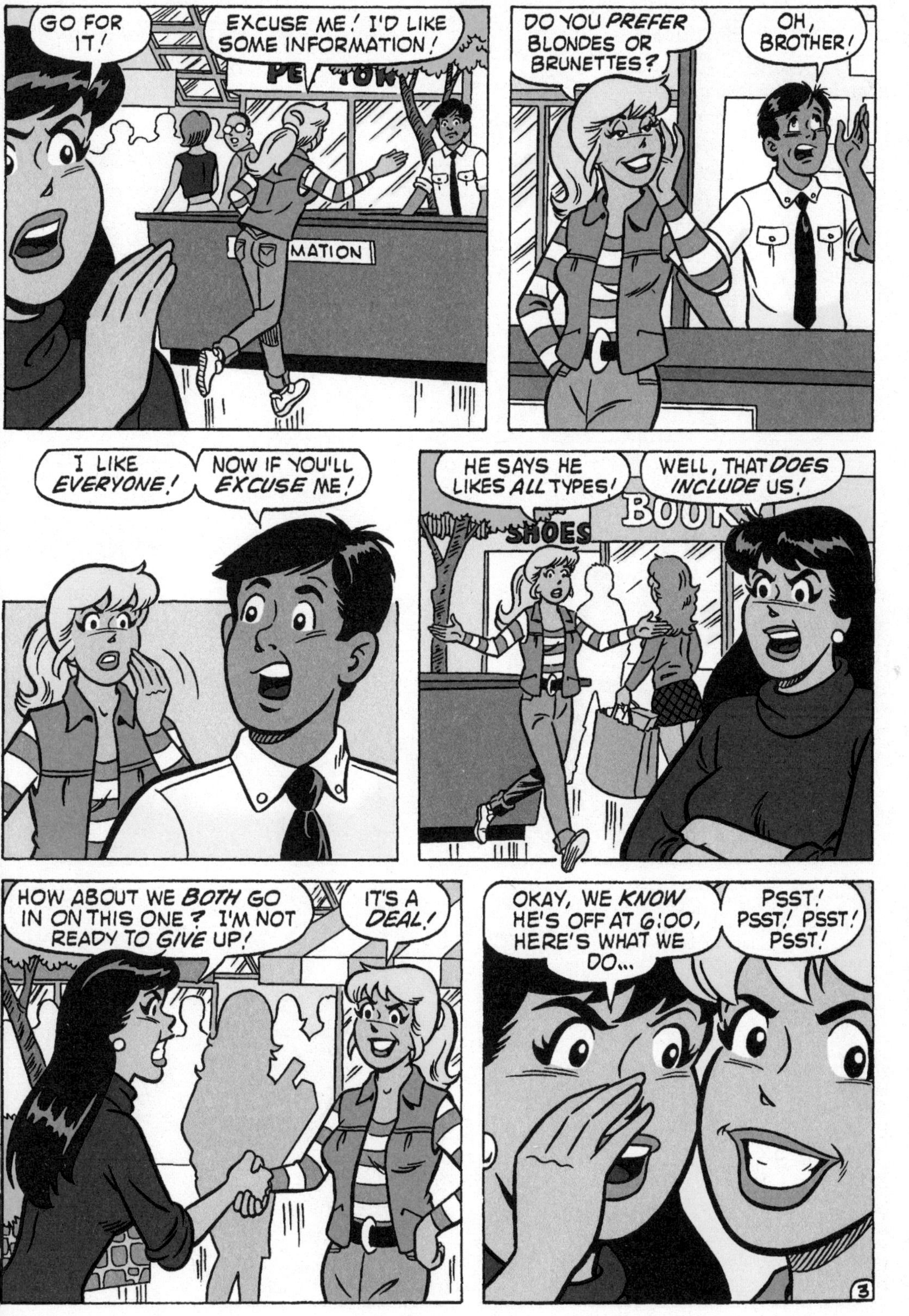
GO FOR IT!
EXCUSE ME! I'D LIKE SOME INFORMATION!
PE TOW
MATION
DO YOU PREFER BLONDES OR BRUNETTES?
OH, BROTHER!
I LIKE EVERYONE!
NOW IF YOU'LL EXCUSE ME!
HE SAYS HE LIKES ALL TYPES!
WELL, THAT DOES INCLUDE US!
SHOES
BOOK
HOW ABOUT WE BOTH GO IN ON THIS ONE? I'M NOT READY TO GIVE UP!
IT'S A DEAL!
OKAY, WE KNOW HE'S OFF AT 6:00, HERE'S WHAT WE DO...
PSST! PSST! PSST! PSST!
3

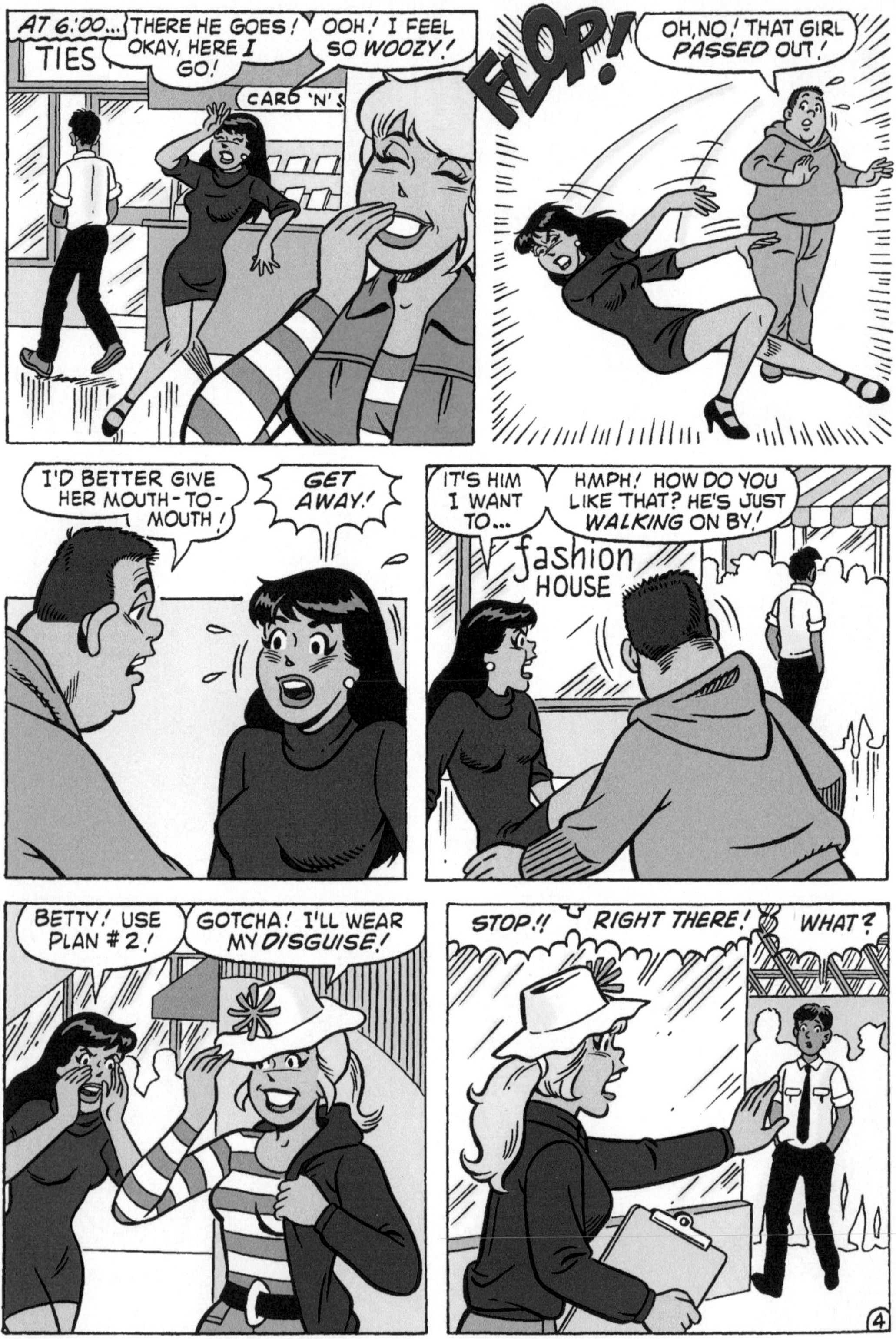
AT 6:00...
THERE HE GOES! OKAY, HERE I GO!
OOH! I FEEL SO WOOZY!
TIES
CARD 'N' S
FLOP!
OH, NO! THAT GIRL PASSED OUT!
I'D BETTER GIVE HER MOUTH-TO-MOUTH!
GET AWAY!
IT'S HIM I WANT TO...
HMPH! HOW DO YOU LIKE THAT? HE'S JUST WALKING ON BY!
fashion HOUSE
BETTY! USE PLAN # 2!
GOTCHA! I'LL WEAR MY DISGUISE!
STOP!!
RIGHT THERE!
WHAT?
4

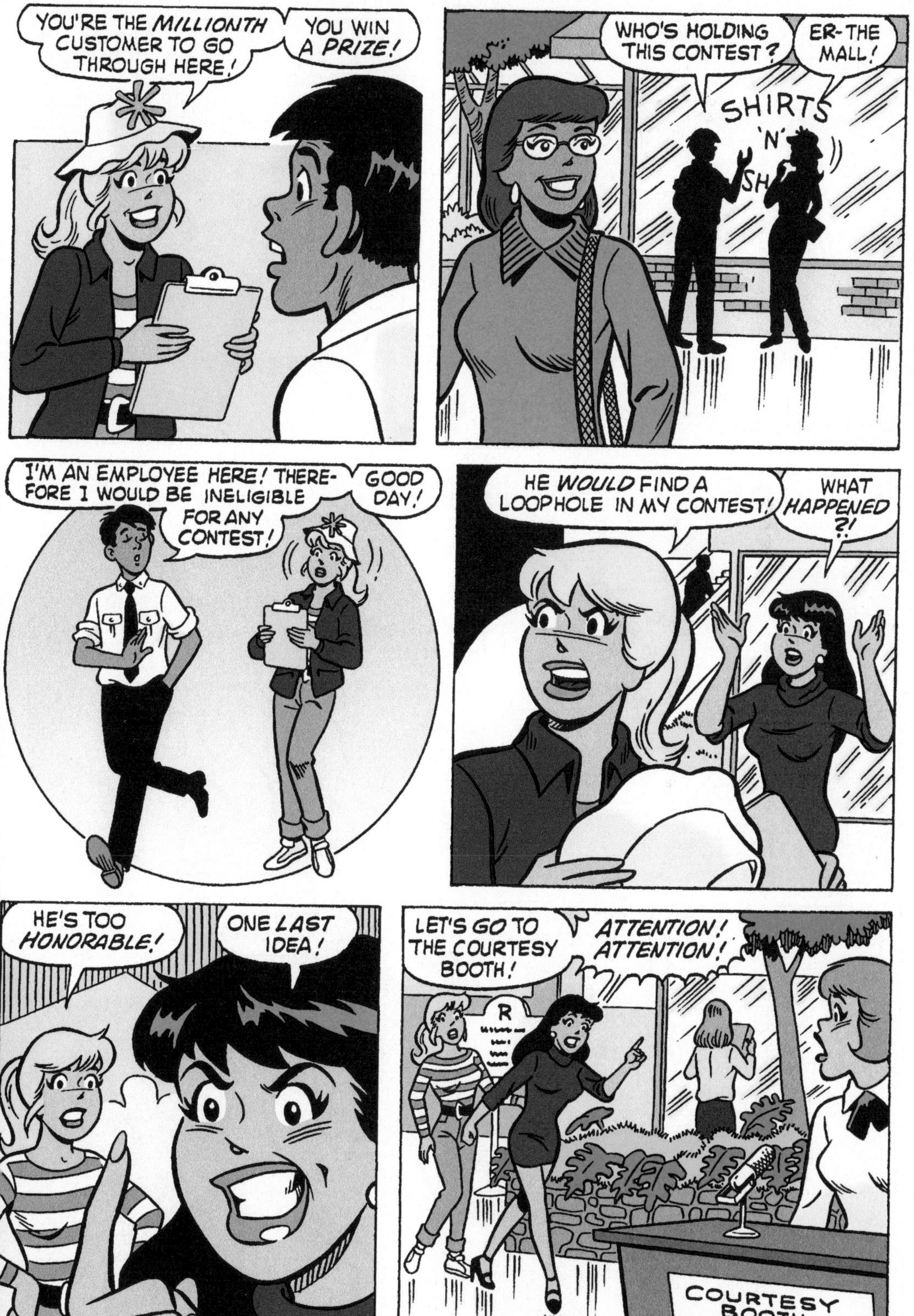
YOU'RE THE *MILLIONTH* CUSTOMER TO GO THROUGH HERE!
YOU WIN A *PRIZE*!
WHO'S HOLDING THIS CONTEST?
ER-THE MALL!
SHIRTS 'N' SH
I'M AN EMPLOYEE HERE! THEREFORE I WOULD BE INELIGIBLE FOR ANY CONTEST!
GOOD DAY!
HE *WOULD* FIND A LOOPHOLE IN MY CONTEST!
WHAT *HAPPENED* ?!
HE'S TOO *HONORABLE*!
ONE *LAST* IDEA!
LET'S *GO* TO THE COURTESY BOOTH!
ATTENTION! ATTENTION!
COURTESY BOOTH
5

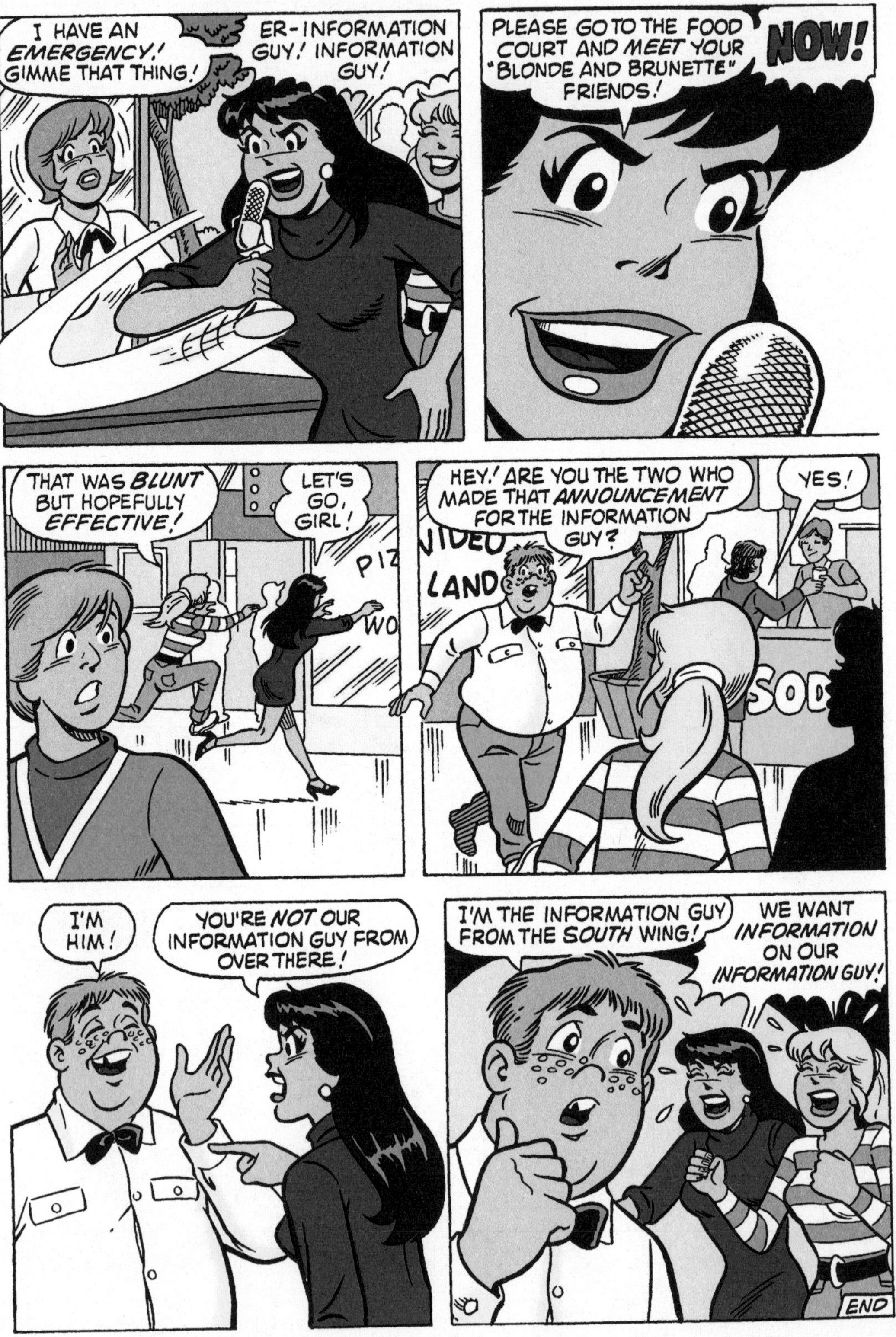
I HAVE AN EMERGENCY! GIMME THAT THING!
ER-INFORMATION GUY! INFORMATION GUY!
PLEASE GO TO THE FOOD COURT AND MEET YOUR "BLONDE AND BRUNETTE" FRIENDS!
NOW!
THAT WAS BLUNT BUT HOPEFULLY EFFECTIVE!
LET'S GO, GIRL!
HEY! ARE YOU THE TWO WHO MADE THAT ANNOUNCEMENT FOR THE INFORMATION GUY?
YES!
I'M HIM!
YOU'RE NOT OUR INFORMATION GUY FROM OVER THERE!
I'M THE INFORMATION GUY FROM THE SOUTH WING!
WE WANT INFORMATION ON OUR INFORMATION GUY!
END

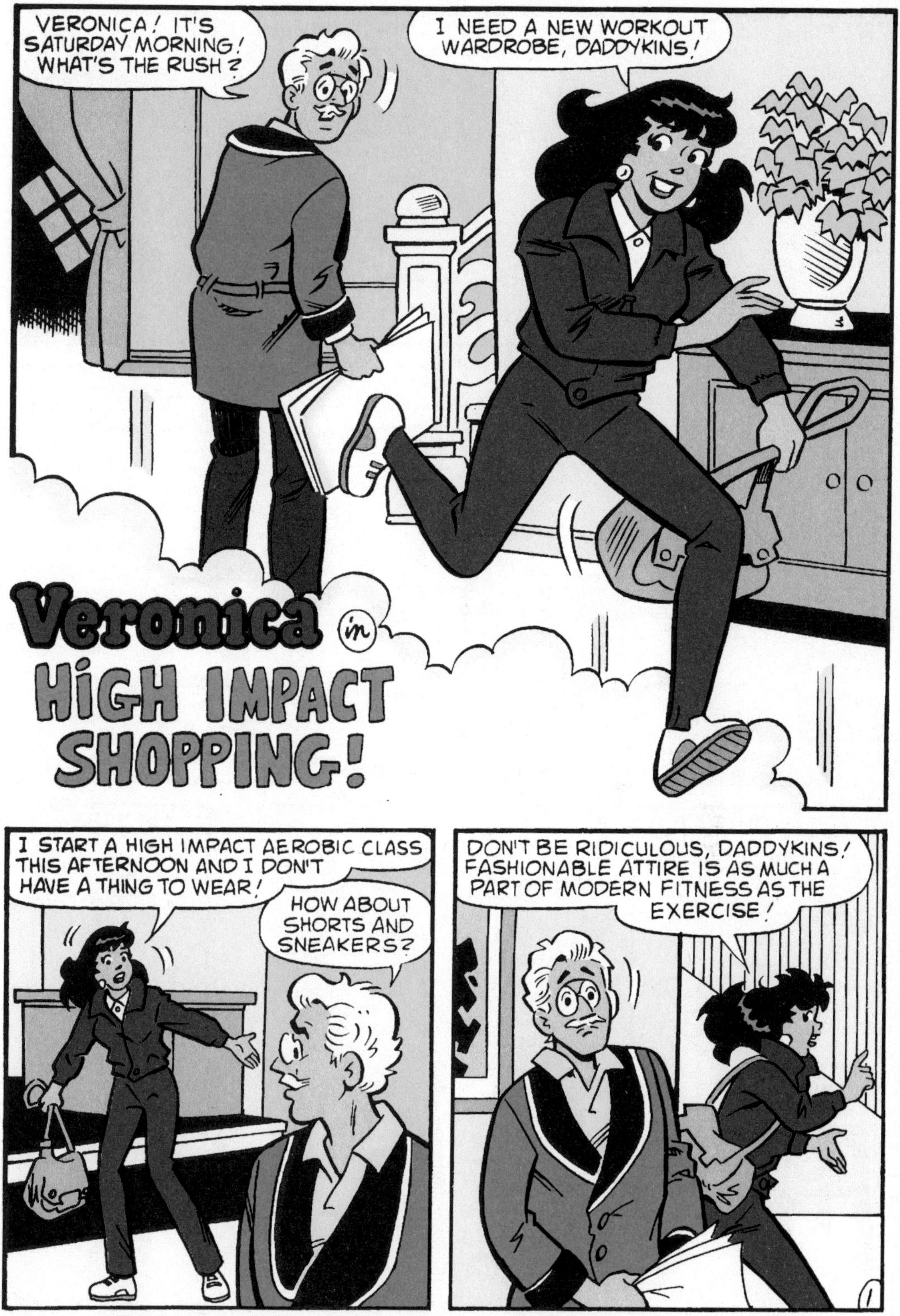
VERONICA! IT'S SATURDAY MORNING! WHAT'S THE RUSH?
I NEED A NEW WORKOUT WARDROBE, DADDYKINS!
Veronica in
HIGH IMPACT SHOPPING!
I START A HIGH IMPACT AEROBIC CLASS THIS AFTERNOON AND I DON'T HAVE A THING TO WEAR!
HOW ABOUT SHORTS AND SNEAKERS?
DON'T BE RIDICULOUS, DADDYKINS! FASHIONABLE ATTIRE IS AS MUCH A PART OF MODERN FITNESS AS THE EXERCISE!

Pellowski / Kennedy / Lapick / Yoshida / Grossman

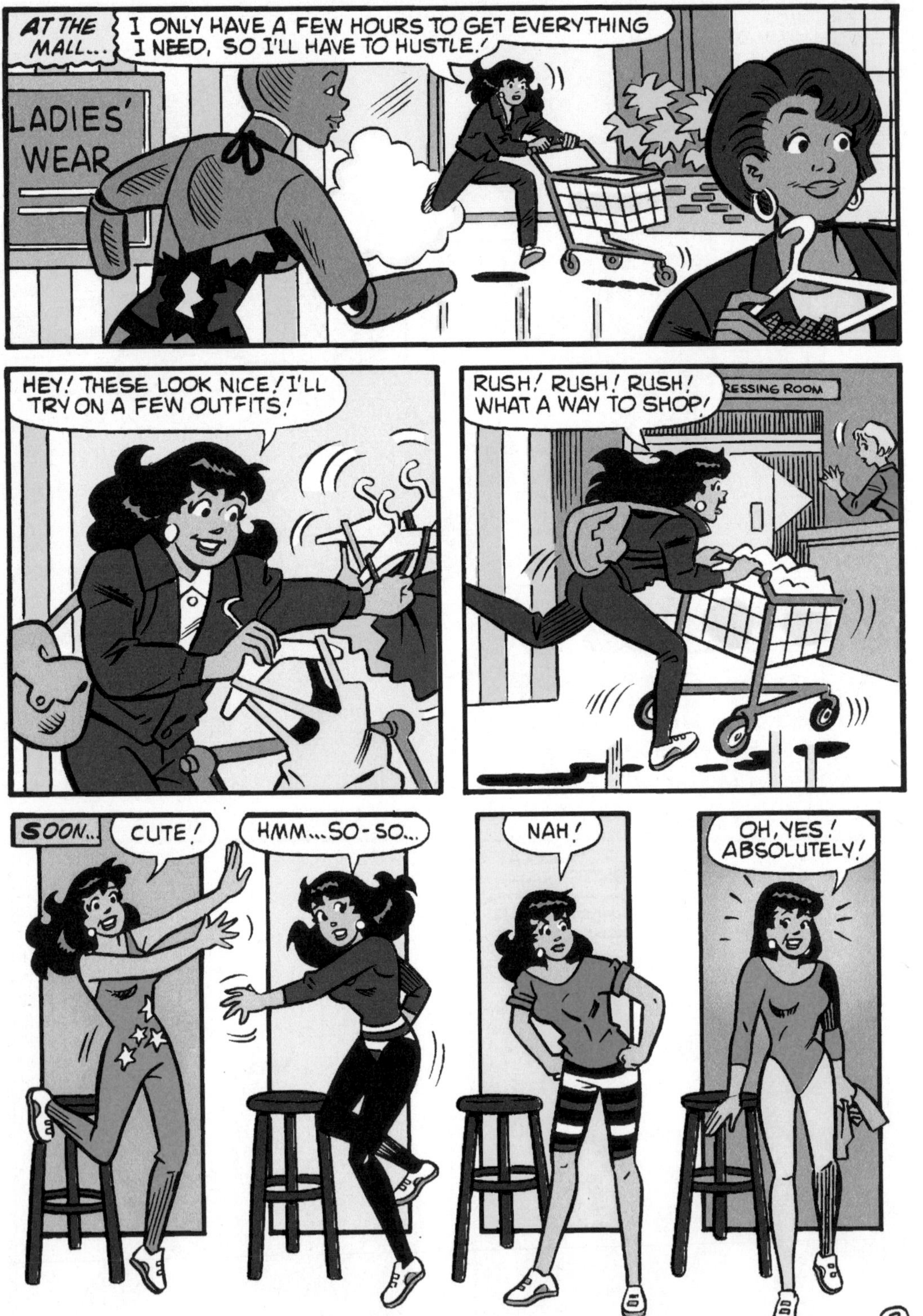
AT THE MALL...
I ONLY HAVE A FEW HOURS TO GET EVERYTHING I NEED, SO I'LL HAVE TO HUSTLE!
LADIES' WEAR
HEY! THESE LOOK NICE! I'LL TRY ON A FEW OUTFITS!
RUSH! RUSH! RUSH! WHAT A WAY TO SHOP!
RESSING ROOM
SOON...
CUTE!
HMM...SO-SO...
NAH!
OH, YES! ABSOLUTELY!
2

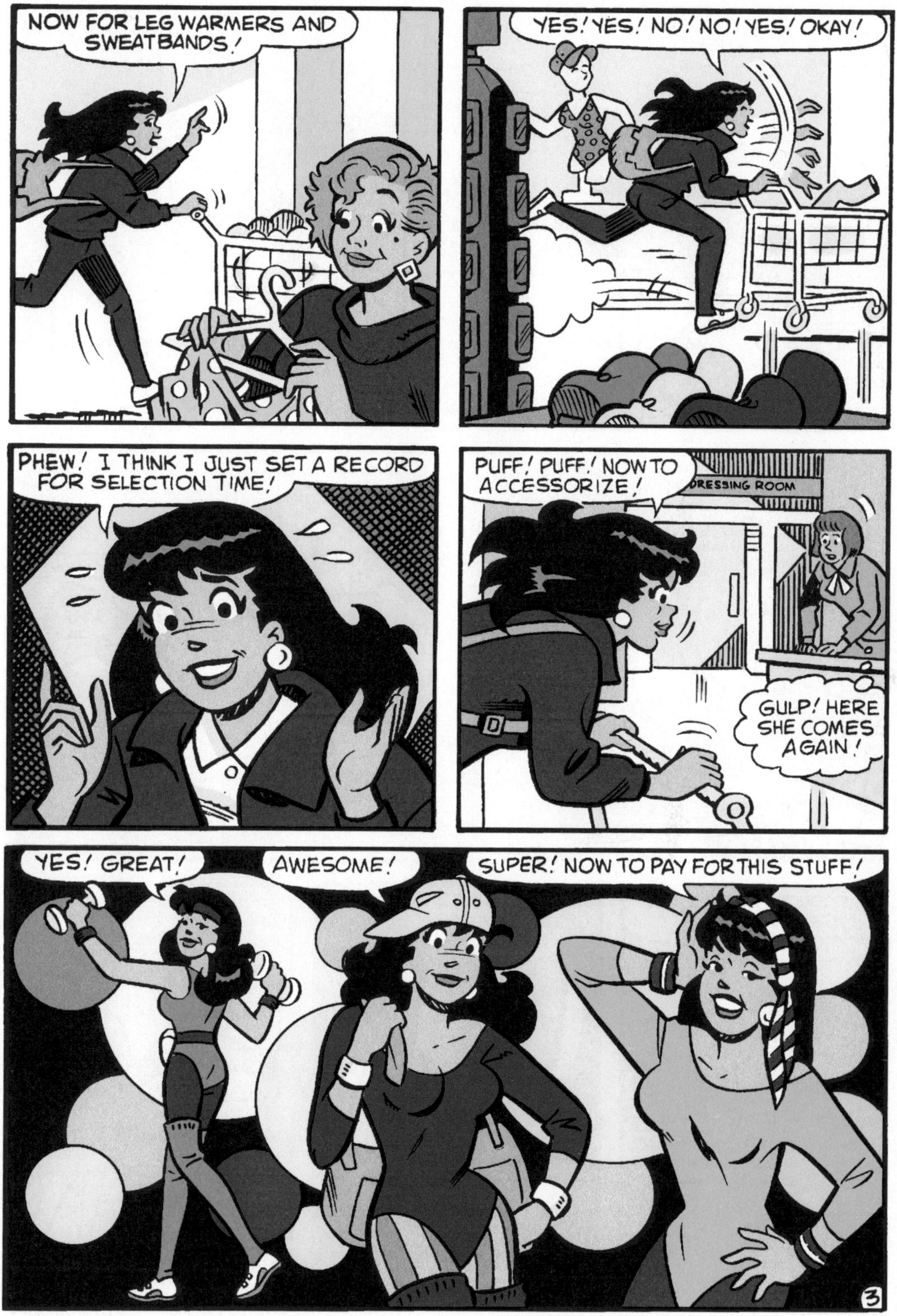
NOW FOR LEG WARMERS AND SWEATBANDS!
YES! YES! NO! NO! YES! OKAY!
PHEW! I THINK I JUST SET A RECORD FOR SELECTION TIME!
PUFF! PUFF! NOW TO ACCESSORIZE!
DRESSING ROOM
GULP! HERE SHE COMES AGAIN!
YES! GREAT!
AWESOME!
SUPER! NOW TO PAY FOR THIS STUFF!
3

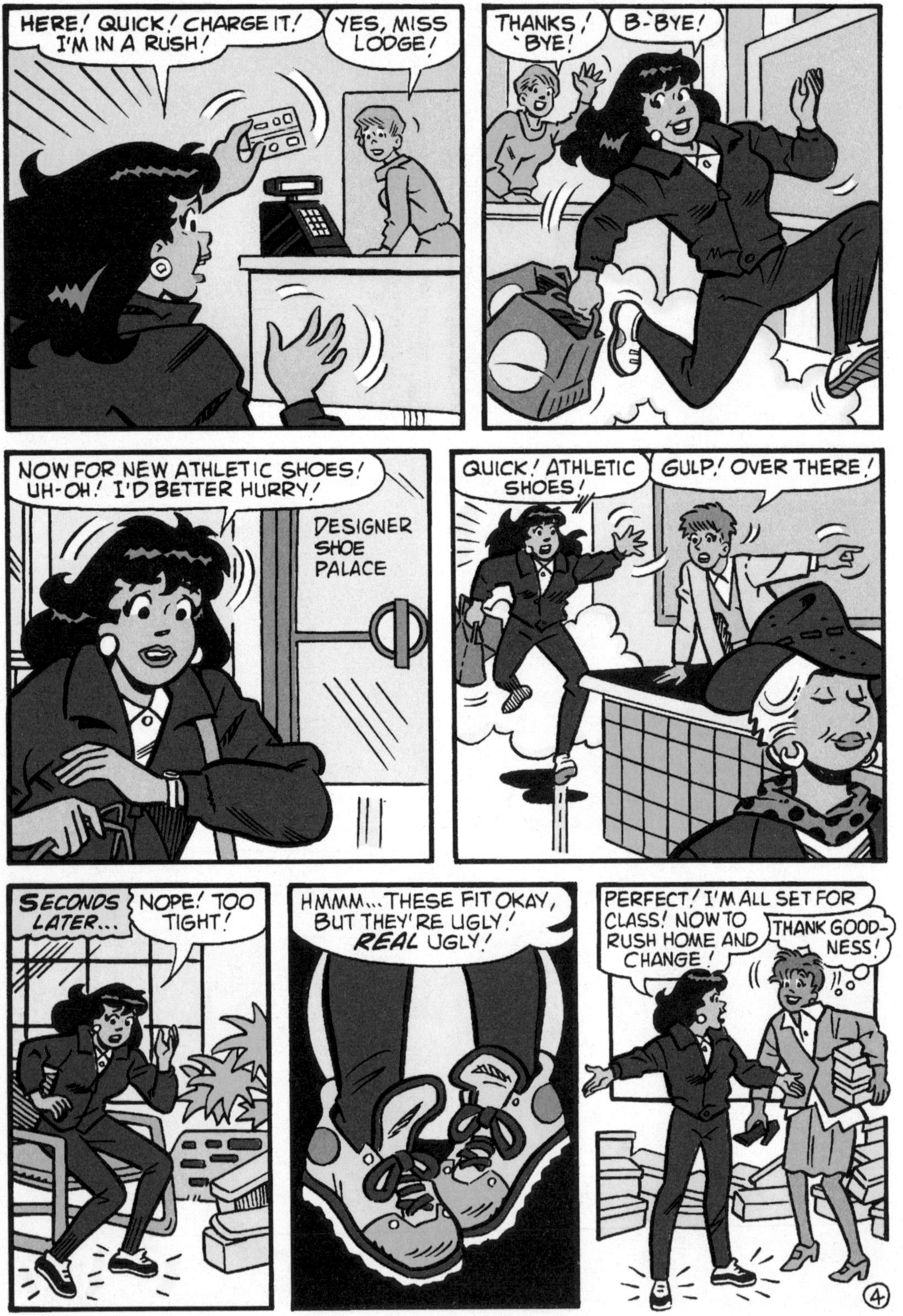
HERE! QUICK! CHARGE IT! I'M IN A RUSH!
YES, MISS LODGE!
THANKS! 'BYE!
B-'BYE!
NOW FOR NEW ATHLETIC SHOES! UH-OH! I'D BETTER HURRY!
DESIGNER SHOE PALACE
QUICK! ATHLETIC SHOES!
GULP! OVER THERE!
SECONDS LATER...
NOPE! TOO TIGHT!
HMMM... THESE FIT OKAY, BUT THEY'RE UGLY! REAL UGLY!
PERFECT! I'M ALL SET FOR CLASS! NOW TO RUSH HOME AND CHANGE!
THANK GOODNESS!
4

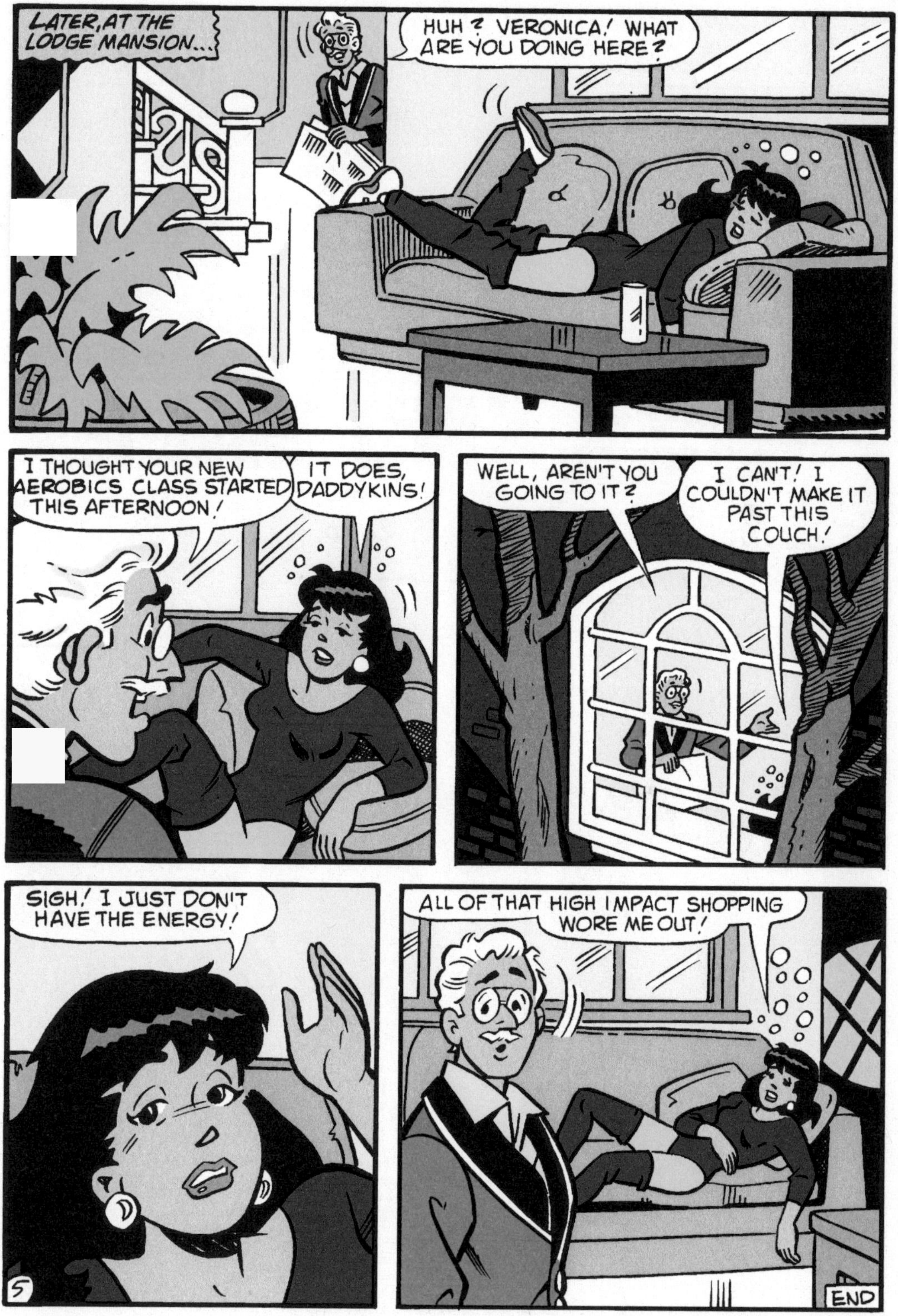

LATER, AT THE LODGE MANSION...
HUH ? VERONICA! WHAT ARE YOU DOING HERE ?
I THOUGHT YOUR NEW AEROBICS CLASS STARTED THIS AFTERNOON!
IT DOES, DADDYKINS!
WELL, AREN'T YOU GOING TO IT ?
I CAN'T! I COULDN'T MAKE IT PAST THIS COUCH!
SIGH! I JUST DON'T HAVE THE ENERGY!
ALL OF THAT HIGH IMPACT SHOPPING WORE ME OUT!
5
END

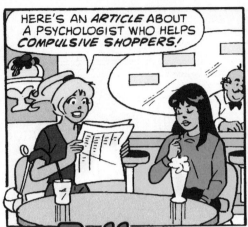

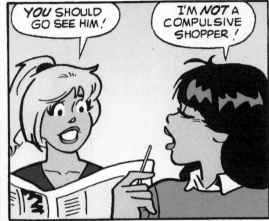

HERE'S AN ARTICLE ABOUT A PSYCHOLOGIST WHO HELPS COMPULSIVE SHOPPERS!
YOU SHOULD GO SEE HIM!
I'M NOT A COMPULSIVE SHOPPER!
Betty and Veronica in "NO SALE"
SODA
HAN
S
BAGEL
SPECIAL
OH, NO! YOU COULDN'T GO ONE DAY WITHOUT SHOPPING!
I COULD, TOO!

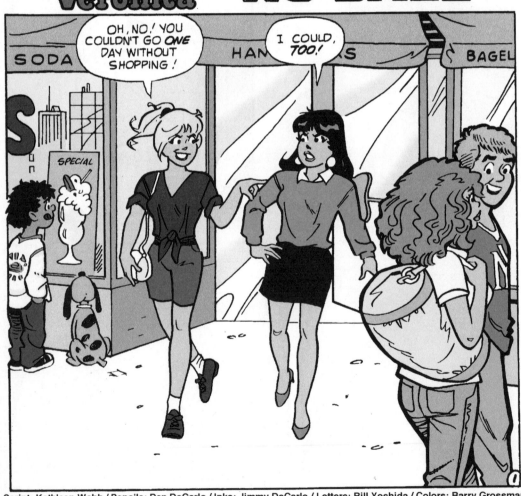

Script: Kathleen Webb / Pencils: Dan DeCarlo / Inks: Jimmy DeCarlo / Letters: Bill Yoshida / Colors: Barry Grossman

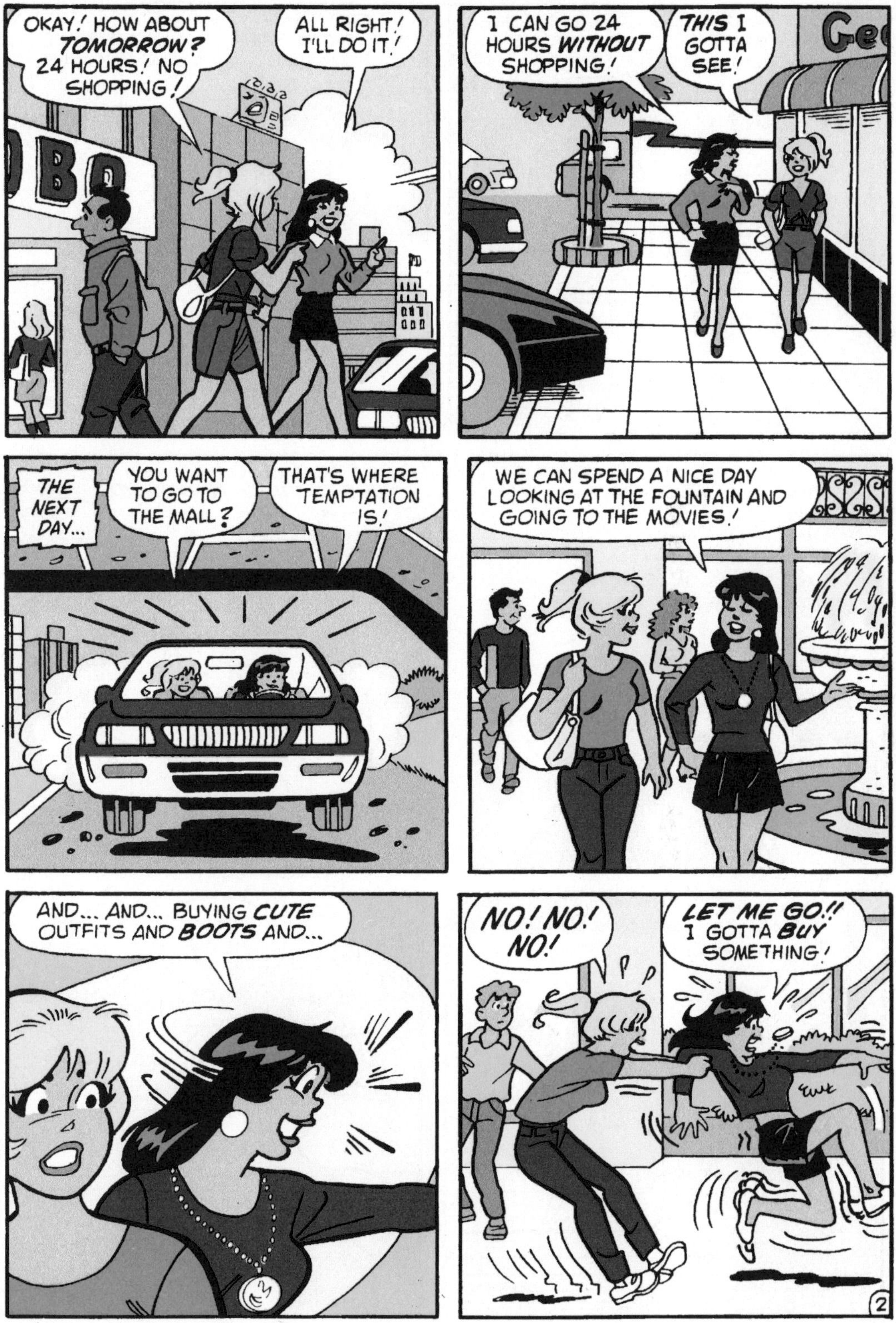

OKAY! HOW ABOUT TOMORROW? 24 HOURS! NO SHOPPING!
ALL RIGHT! I'LL DO IT!
I CAN GO 24 HOURS WITHOUT SHOPPING!
THIS I GOTTA SEE!
THE NEXT DAY...
YOU WANT TO GO TO THE MALL?
THAT'S WHERE TEMPTATION IS!
WE CAN SPEND A NICE DAY LOOKING AT THE FOUNTAIN AND GOING TO THE MOVIES!
AND... AND... BUYING CUTE OUTFITS AND BOOTS AND...
NO! NO! NO!
LET ME GO!! I GOTTA BUY SOMETHING!
2

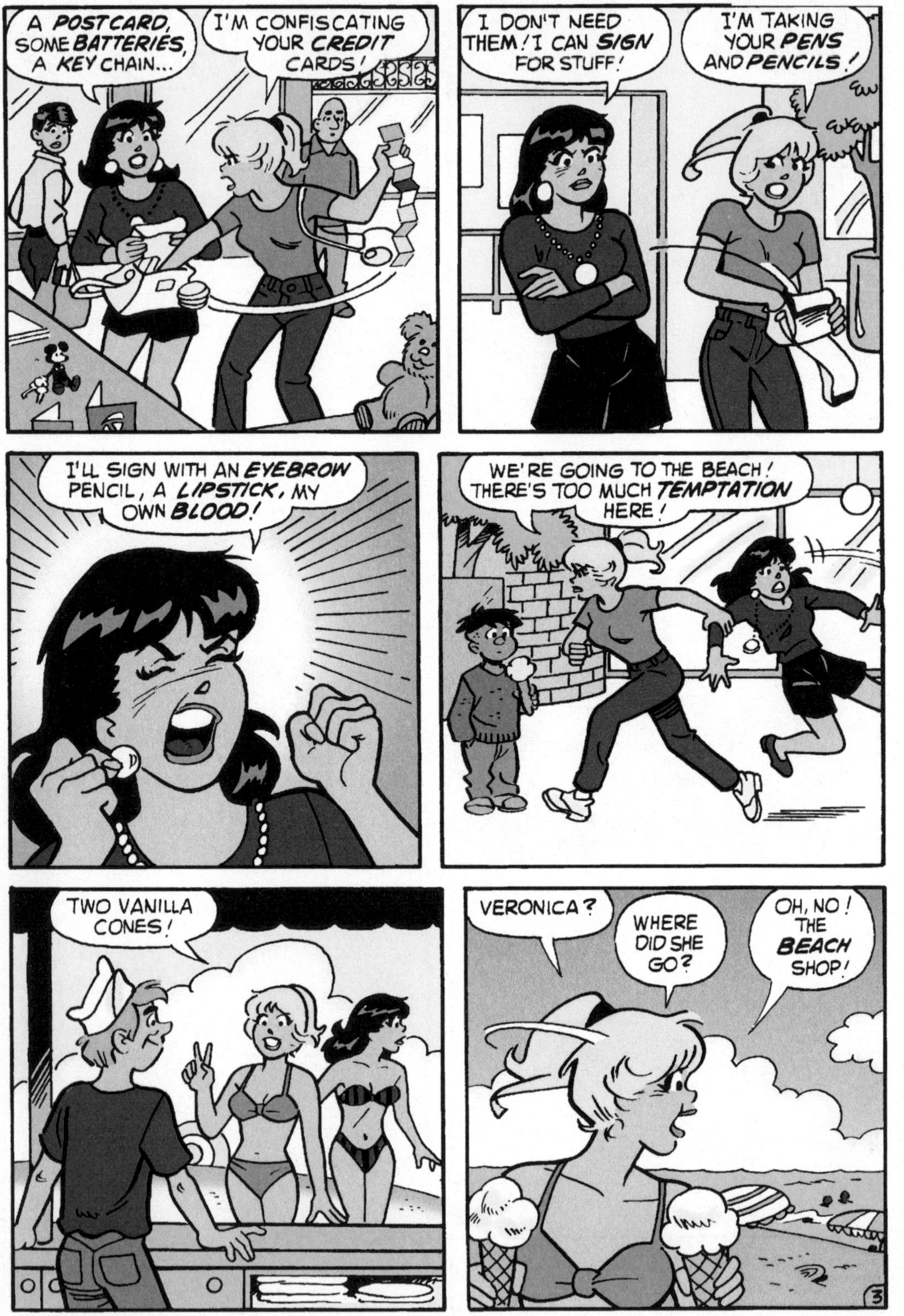

A POSTCARD, SOME BATTERIES, A KEY CHAIN...
I'M CONFISCATING YOUR CREDIT CARDS!
I DON'T NEED THEM! I CAN SIGN FOR STUFF!
I'M TAKING YOUR PENS AND PENCILS!
I'LL SIGN WITH AN EYEBROW PENCIL, A LIPSTICK, MY OWN BLOOD!
WE'RE GOING TO THE BEACH! THERE'S TOO MUCH TEMPTATION HERE!
TWO VANILLA CONES!
VERONICA?
WHERE DID SHE GO?
OH, NO! THE BEACH SHOP!
3

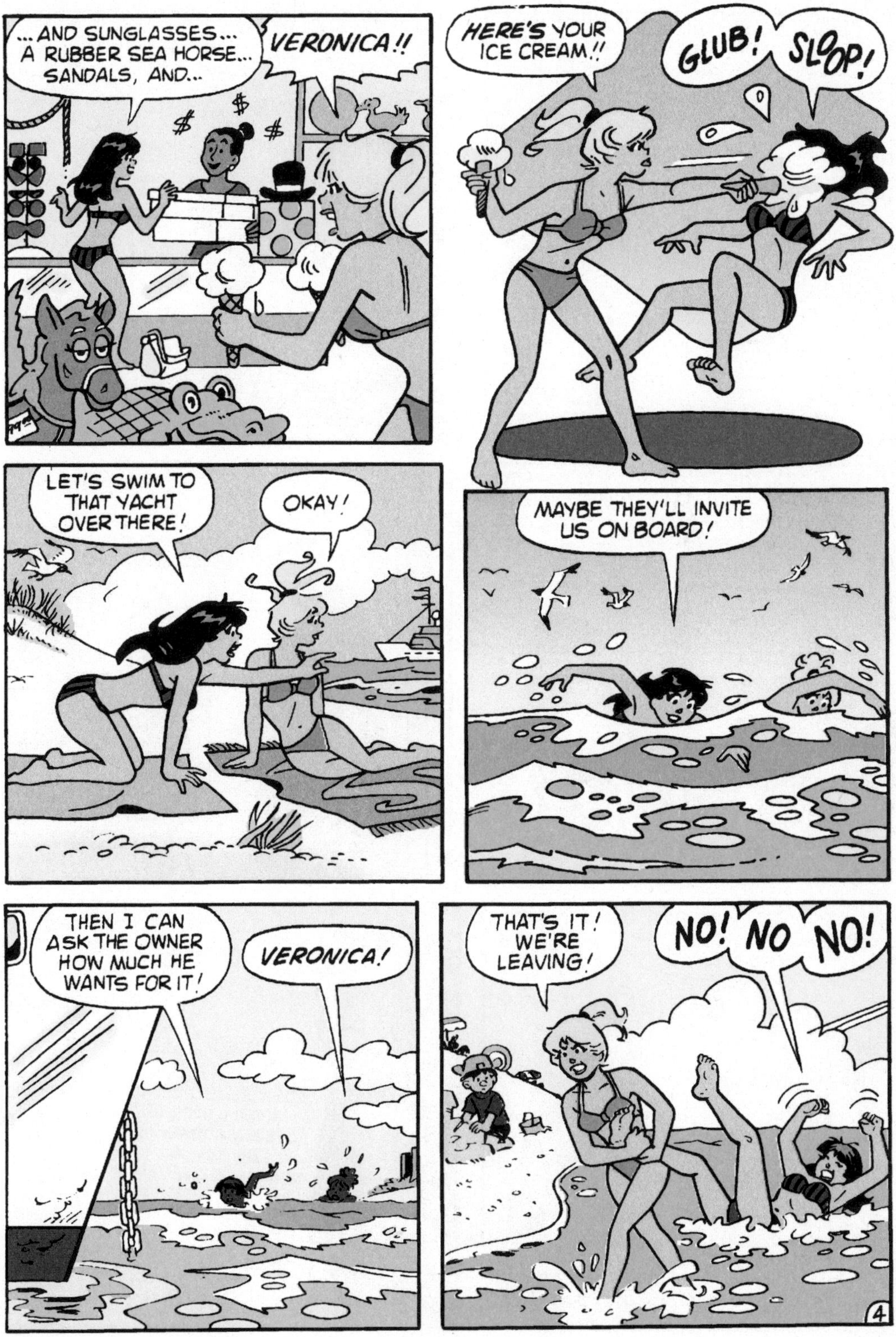
...AND SUNGLASSES... A RUBBER SEA HORSE... SANDALS, AND...
VERONICA!!
HERE'S YOUR ICE CREAM!!
GLUB!
SLOOP!
LET'S SWIM TO THAT YACHT OVER THERE!
OKAY!
MAYBE THEY'LL INVITE US ON BOARD!
THEN I CAN ASK THE OWNER HOW MUCH HE WANTS FOR IT!
VERONICA!
THAT'S IT! WE'RE LEAVING!
NO! NO NO!
4

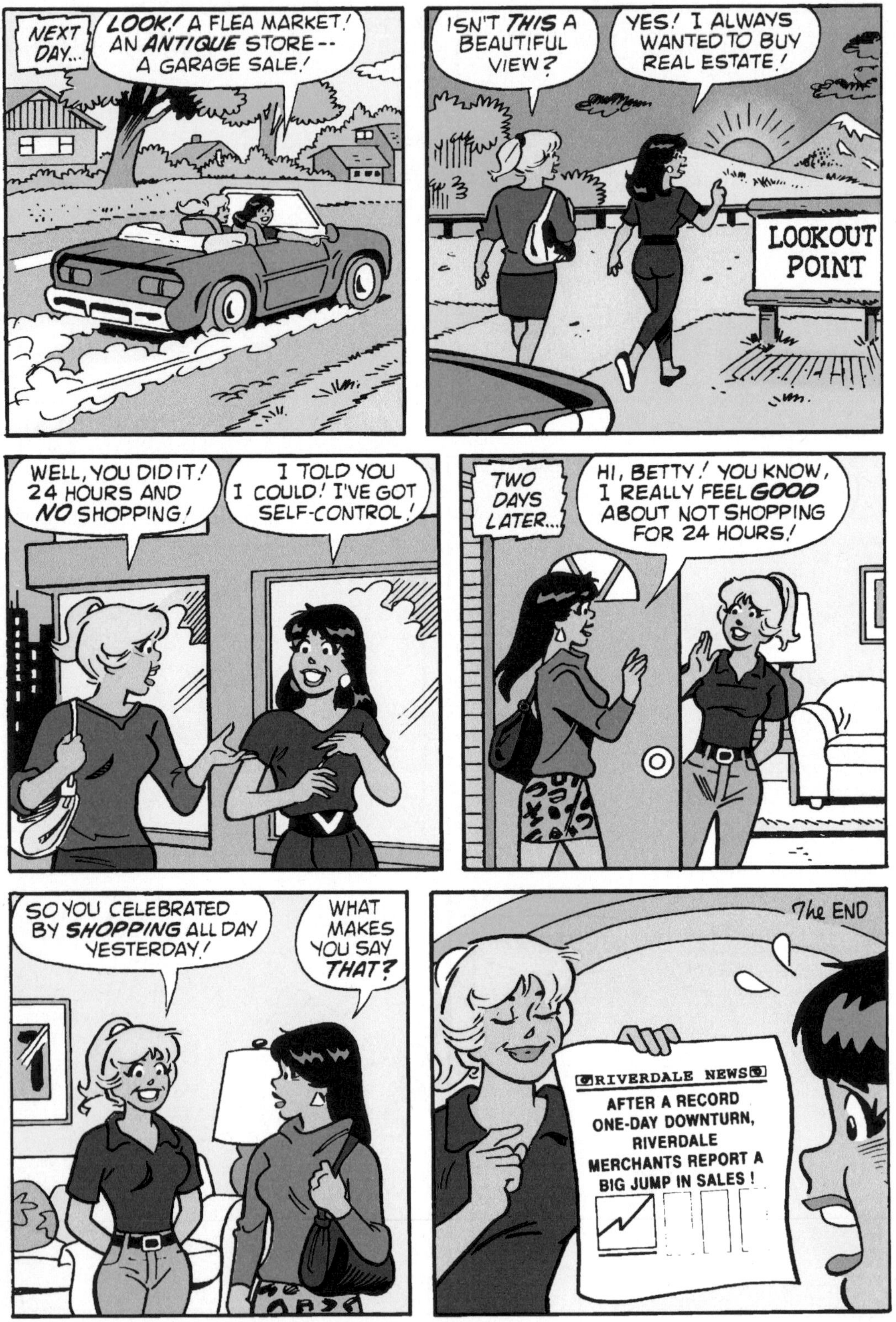
NEXT DAY...
LOOK! A FLEA MARKET! AN ANTIQUE STORE -- A GARAGE SALE!
ISN'T THIS A BEAUTIFUL VIEW?
YES! I ALWAYS WANTED TO BUY REAL ESTATE!
LOOKOUT POINT
WELL, YOU DID IT! 24 HOURS AND NO SHOPPING!
I TOLD YOU I COULD! I'VE GOT SELF-CONTROL!
TWO DAYS LATER...
HI, BETTY! YOU KNOW, I REALLY FEEL GOOD ABOUT NOT SHOPPING FOR 24 HOURS!
SO YOU CELEBRATED BY SHOPPING ALL DAY YESTERDAY!
WHAT MAKES YOU SAY THAT?
The END
RIVERDALE NEWS
AFTER A RECORD ONE-DAY DOWNTURN, RIVERDALE MERCHANTS REPORT A BIG JUMP IN SALES!

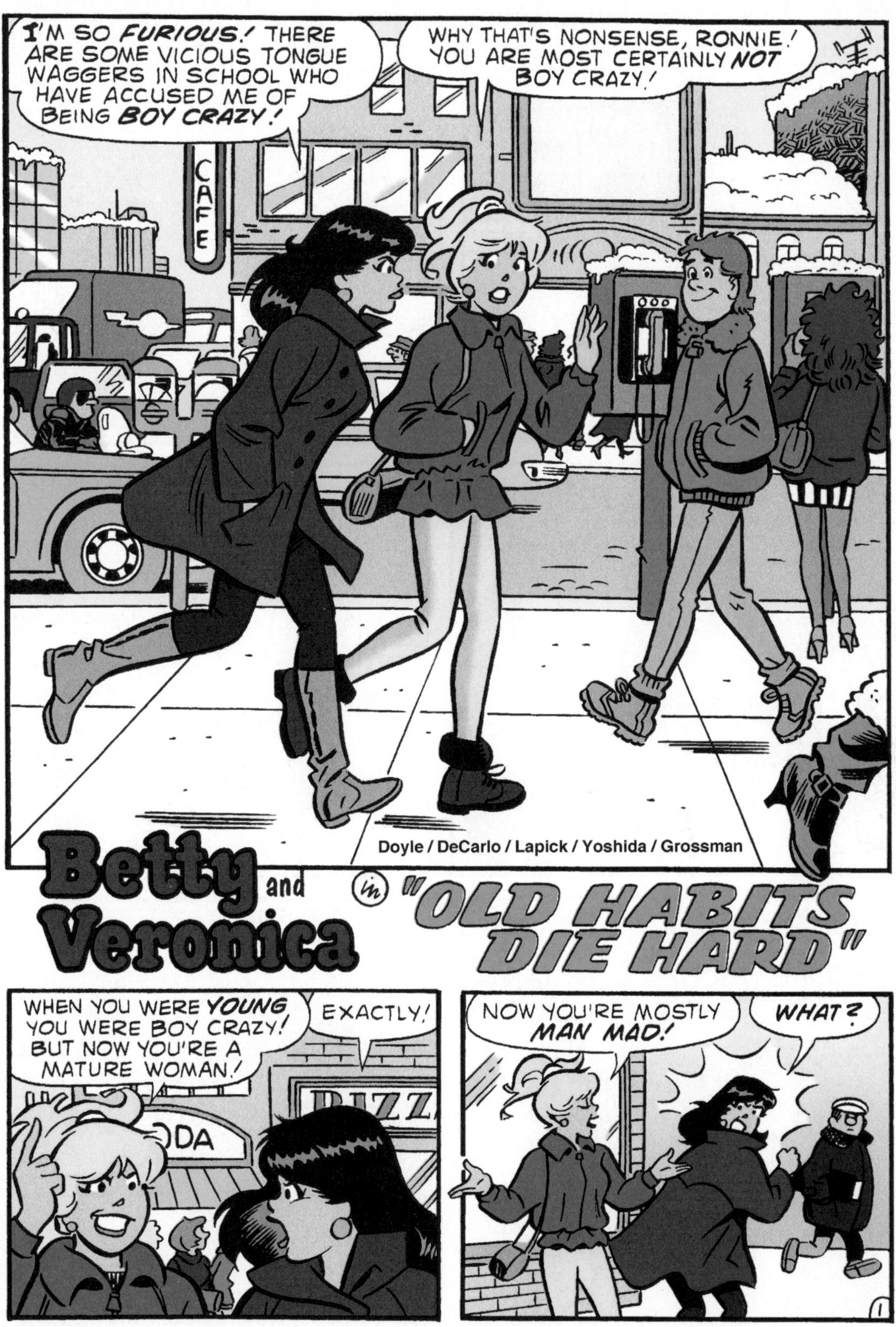
I'M SO FURIOUS! THERE ARE SOME VICIOUS TONGUE WAGGERS IN SCHOOL WHO HAVE ACCUSED ME OF BEING BOY CRAZY!
WHY THAT'S NONSENSE, RONNIE! YOU ARE MOST CERTAINLY NOT BOY CRAZY!
CAFE
Doyle / DeCarlo / Lapick / Yoshida / Grossman
Betty and Veronica
in "OLD HABITS DIE HARD"
WHEN YOU WERE YOUNG YOU WERE BOY CRAZY! BUT NOW YOU'RE A MATURE WOMAN!
EXACTLY!
ODA
PIZZ
NOW YOU'RE MOSTLY MAN MAD!
WHAT?
1

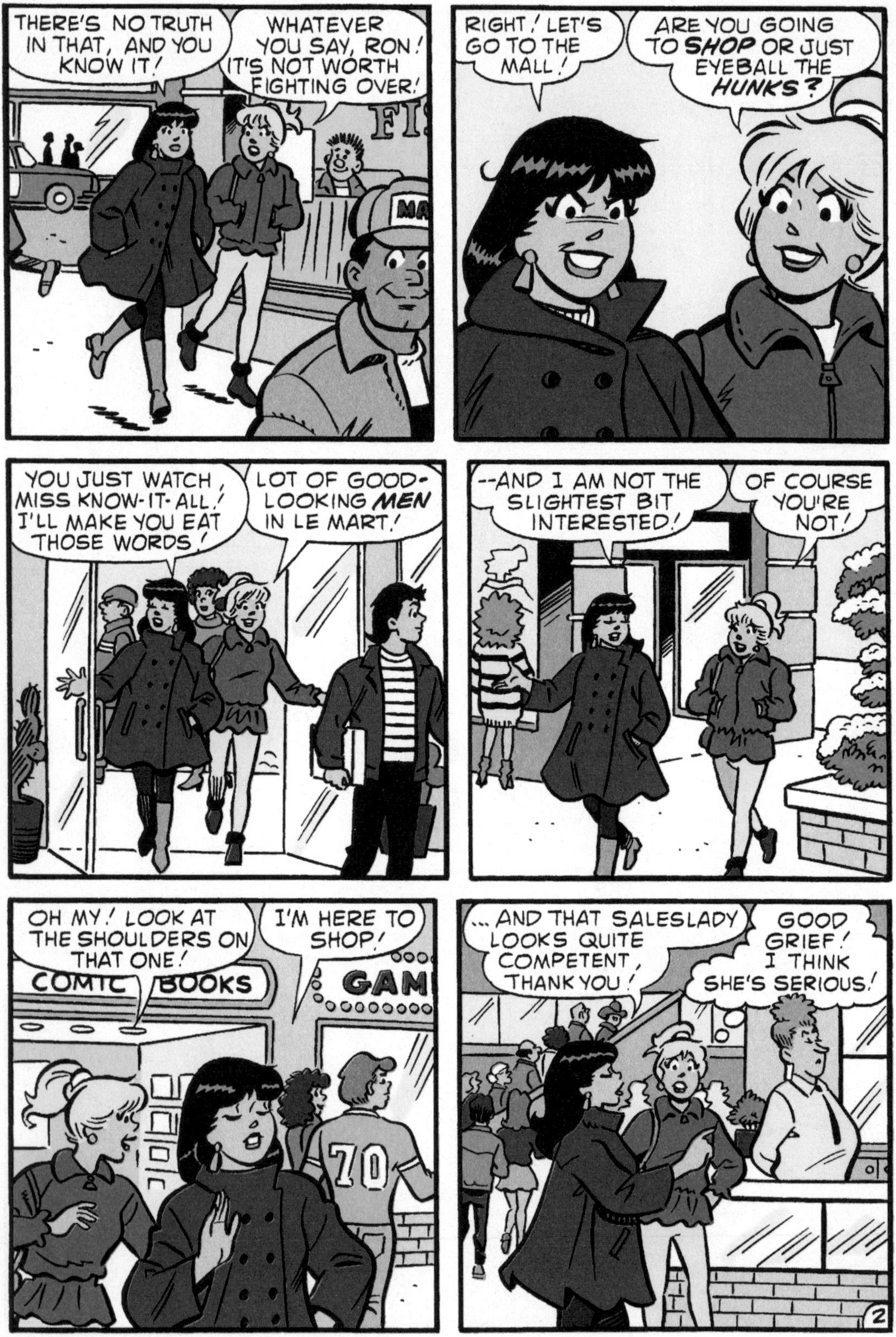
THERE'S NO TRUTH IN THAT, AND YOU KNOW IT!
WHATEVER YOU SAY, RON! IT'S NOT WORTH FIGHTING OVER!
RIGHT! LET'S GO TO THE MALL!
ARE YOU GOING TO SHOP OR JUST EYEBALL THE HUNKS?
YOU JUST WATCH, MISS KNOW-IT-ALL! I'LL MAKE YOU EAT THOSE WORDS!
LOT OF GOOD-LOOKING MEN IN LE MART!
--AND I AM NOT THE SLIGHTEST BIT INTERESTED!
OF COURSE YOU'RE NOT!
OH MY! LOOK AT THE SHOULDERS ON THAT ONE!
I'M HERE TO SHOP!
COMIC BOOKS
...AND THAT SALESLADY LOOKS QUITE COMPETENT, THANK YOU!
GOOD GRIEF! I THINK SHE'S SERIOUS!
2

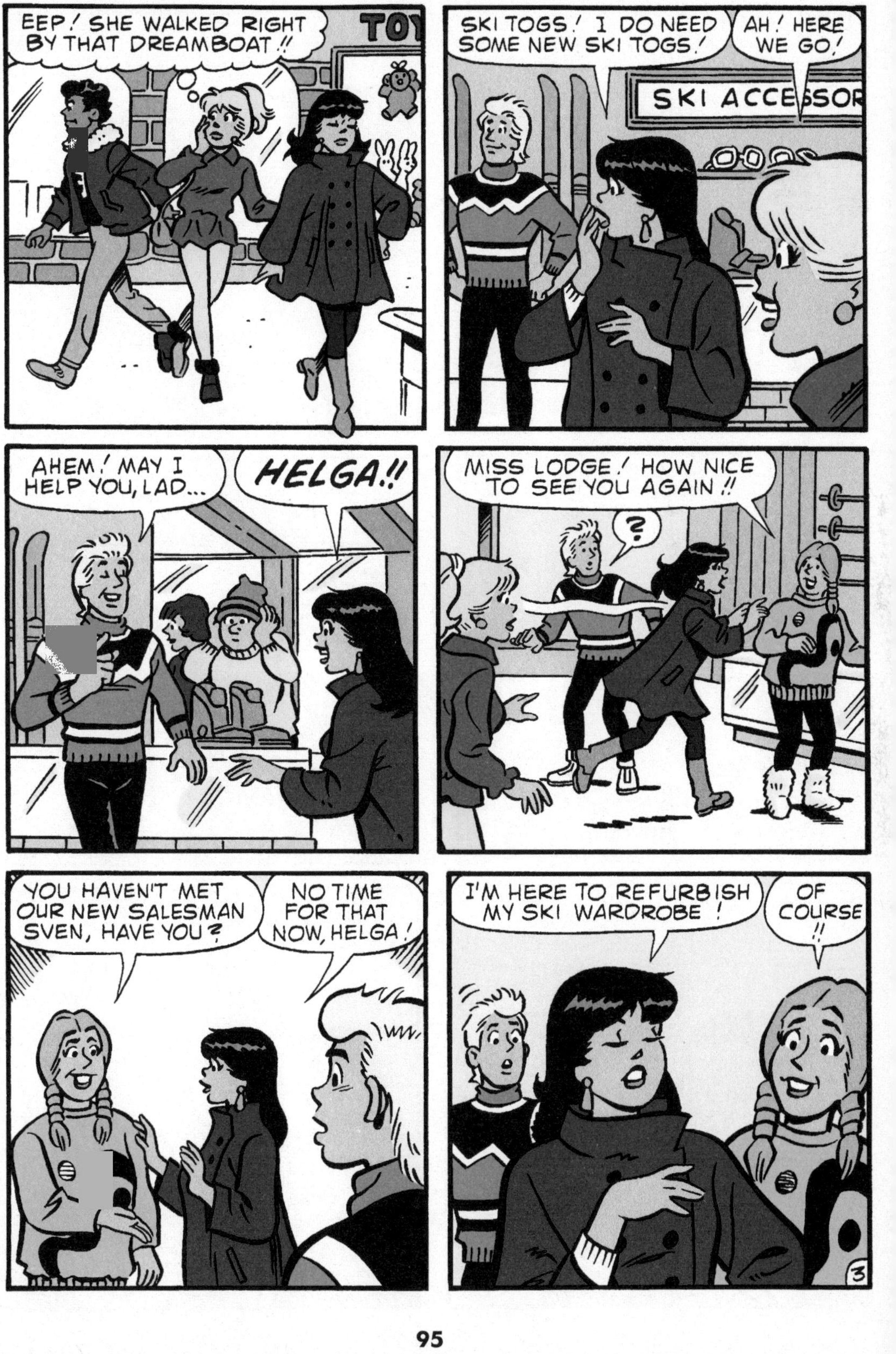
EEP! SHE WALKED RIGHT BY THAT DREAMBOAT!!
SKI TOGS! I DO NEED SOME NEW SKI TOGS!
AH! HERE WE GO!
SKI ACCESSOR
AHEM! MAY I HELP YOU, LAD...
HELGA!!
MISS LODGE! HOW NICE TO SEE YOU AGAIN!!
?
YOU HAVEN'T MET OUR NEW SALESMAN SVEN, HAVE YOU?
NO TIME FOR THAT NOW, HELGA!
I'M HERE TO REFURBISH MY SKI WARDROBE!
OF COURSE!!
3

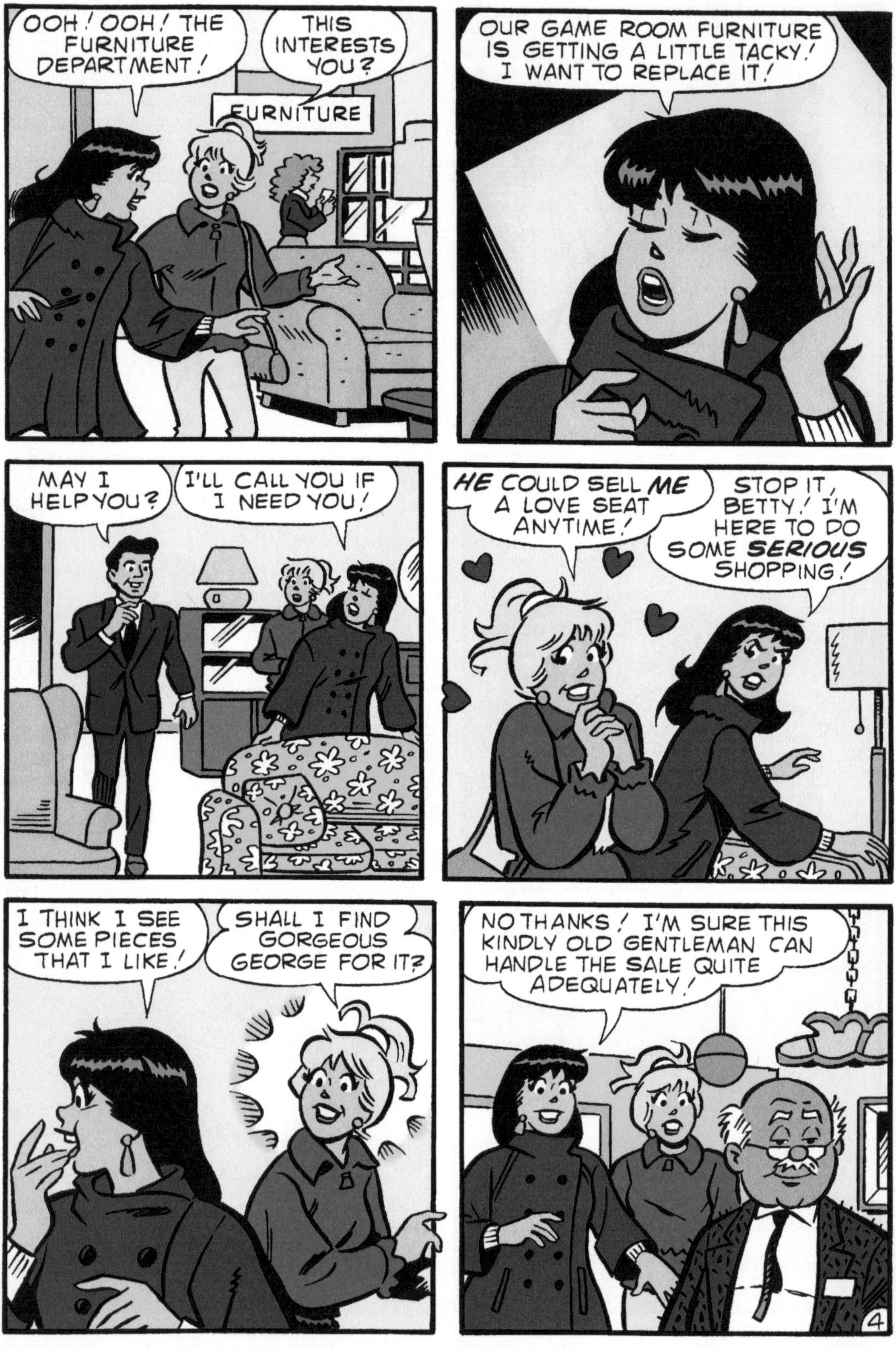
OOH! OOH! THE FURNITURE DEPARTMENT!
THIS INTERESTS YOU?
FURNITURE
OUR GAME ROOM FURNITURE IS GETTING A LITTLE TACKY! I WANT TO REPLACE IT!
MAY I HELP YOU?
I'LL CALL YOU IF I NEED YOU!
HE COULD SELL ME A LOVE SEAT ANYTIME!
STOP IT, BETTY! I'M HERE TO DO SOME SERIOUS SHOPPING!
I THINK I SEE SOME PIECES THAT I LIKE!
SHALL I FIND GORGEOUS GEORGE FOR IT?
NO THANKS! I'M SURE THIS KINDLY OLD GENTLEMAN CAN HANDLE THE SALE QUITE ADEQUATELY!
4

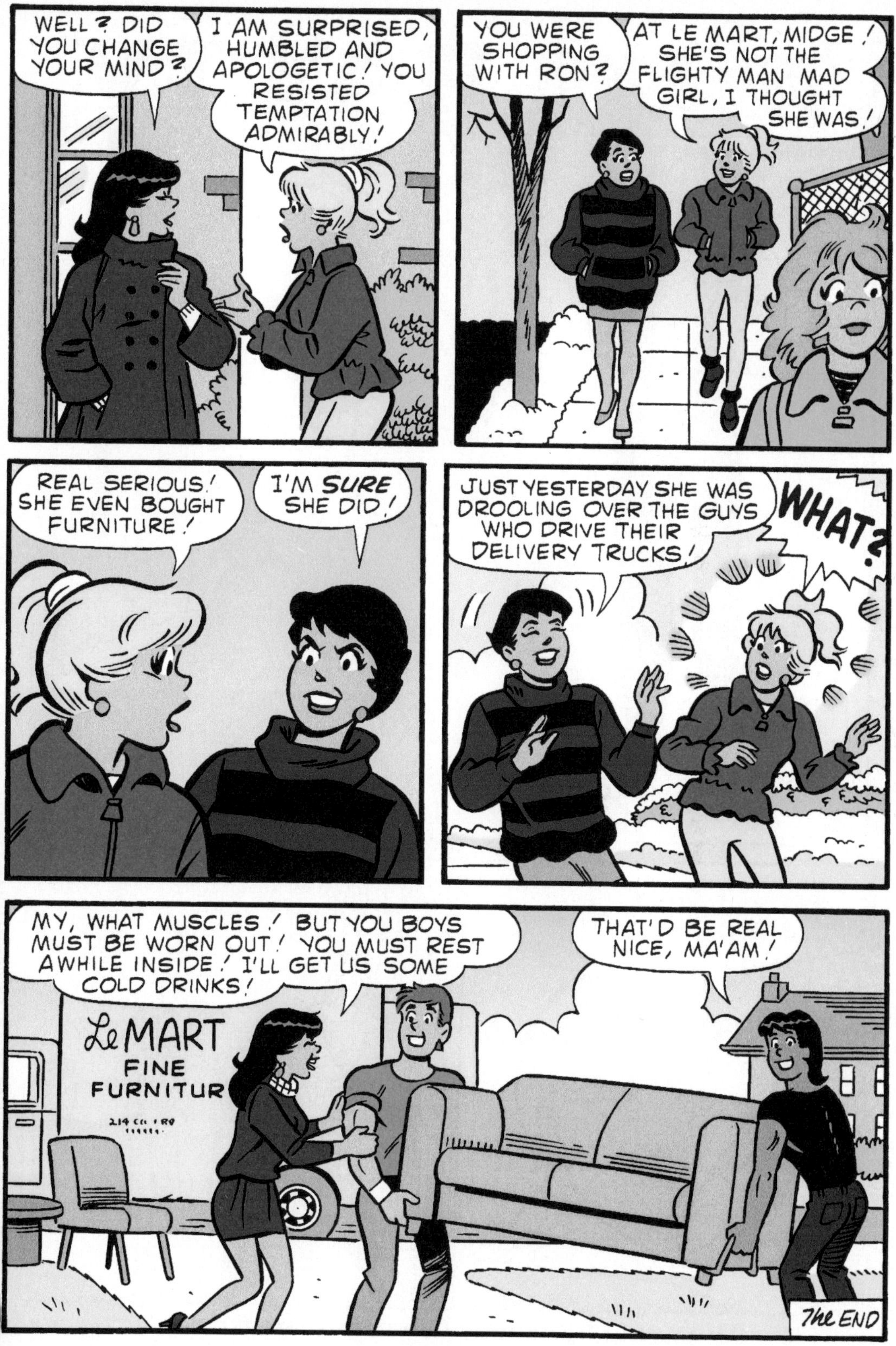
WELL? DID YOU CHANGE YOUR MIND?
I AM SURPRISED, HUMBLED AND APOLOGETIC! YOU RESISTED TEMPTATION ADMIRABLY!
YOU WERE SHOPPING WITH RON?
AT LE MART, MIDGE! SHE'S NOT THE FLIGHTY MAN MAD GIRL, I THOUGHT SHE WAS!
REAL SERIOUS! SHE EVEN BOUGHT FURNITURE!
I'M SURE SHE DID!
JUST YESTERDAY SHE WAS DROOLING OVER THE GUYS WHO DRIVE THEIR DELIVERY TRUCKS!
WHAT?
MY, WHAT MUSCLES! BUT YOU BOYS MUST BE WORN OUT! YOU MUST REST AWHILE INSIDE! I'LL GET US SOME COLD DRINKS!
THAT'D BE REAL NICE, MA'AM!
LeMART
FINE
FURNITUR
The END

Veronica in PAY T.V.

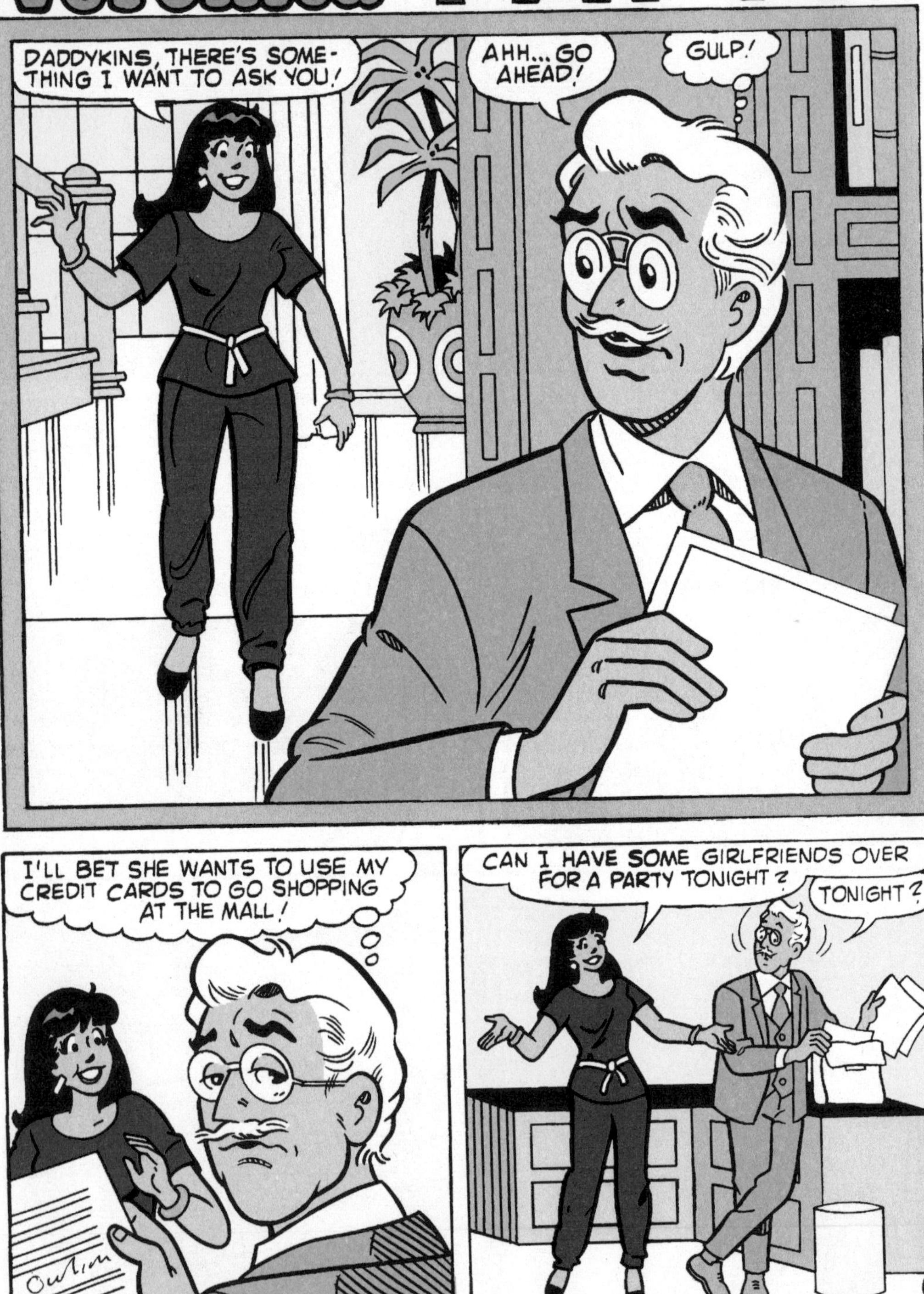
DADDYKINS, THERE'S SOMETHING I WANT TO ASK YOU!
AHH...GO AHEAD!
GULP!
I'LL BET SHE WANTS TO USE MY CREDIT CARDS TO GO SHOPPING AT THE MALL!
CAN I HAVE SOME GIRLFRIENDS OVER FOR A PARTY TONIGHT?
TONIGHT?

Pellowski / T.Kennedy / Yoshida / Grossman

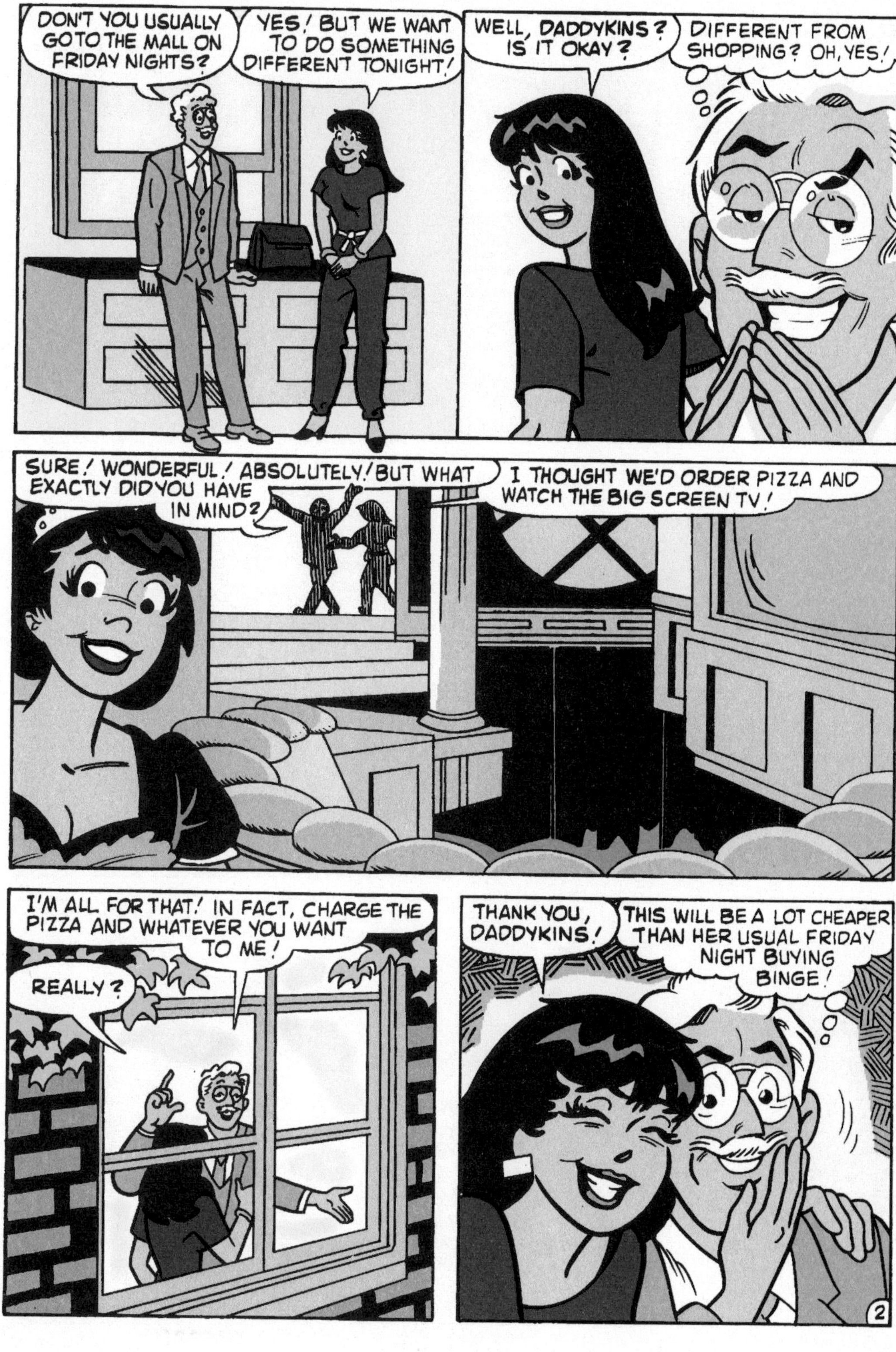
DON'T YOU USUALLY GO TO THE MALL ON FRIDAY NIGHTS?
YES! BUT WE WANT TO DO SOMETHING DIFFERENT TONIGHT!
WELL, DADDYKINS? IS IT OKAY?
DIFFERENT FROM SHOPPING? OH, YES!
SURE! WONDERFUL! ABSOLUTELY! BUT WHAT EXACTLY DID YOU HAVE IN MIND?
I THOUGHT WE'D ORDER PIZZA AND WATCH THE BIG SCREEN TV!
I'M ALL FOR THAT! IN FACT, CHARGE THE PIZZA AND WHATEVER YOU WANT TO ME!
REALLY?
THANK YOU, DADDYKINS!
THIS WILL BE A LOT CHEAPER THAN HER USUAL FRIDAY NIGHT BUYING BINGE!
2

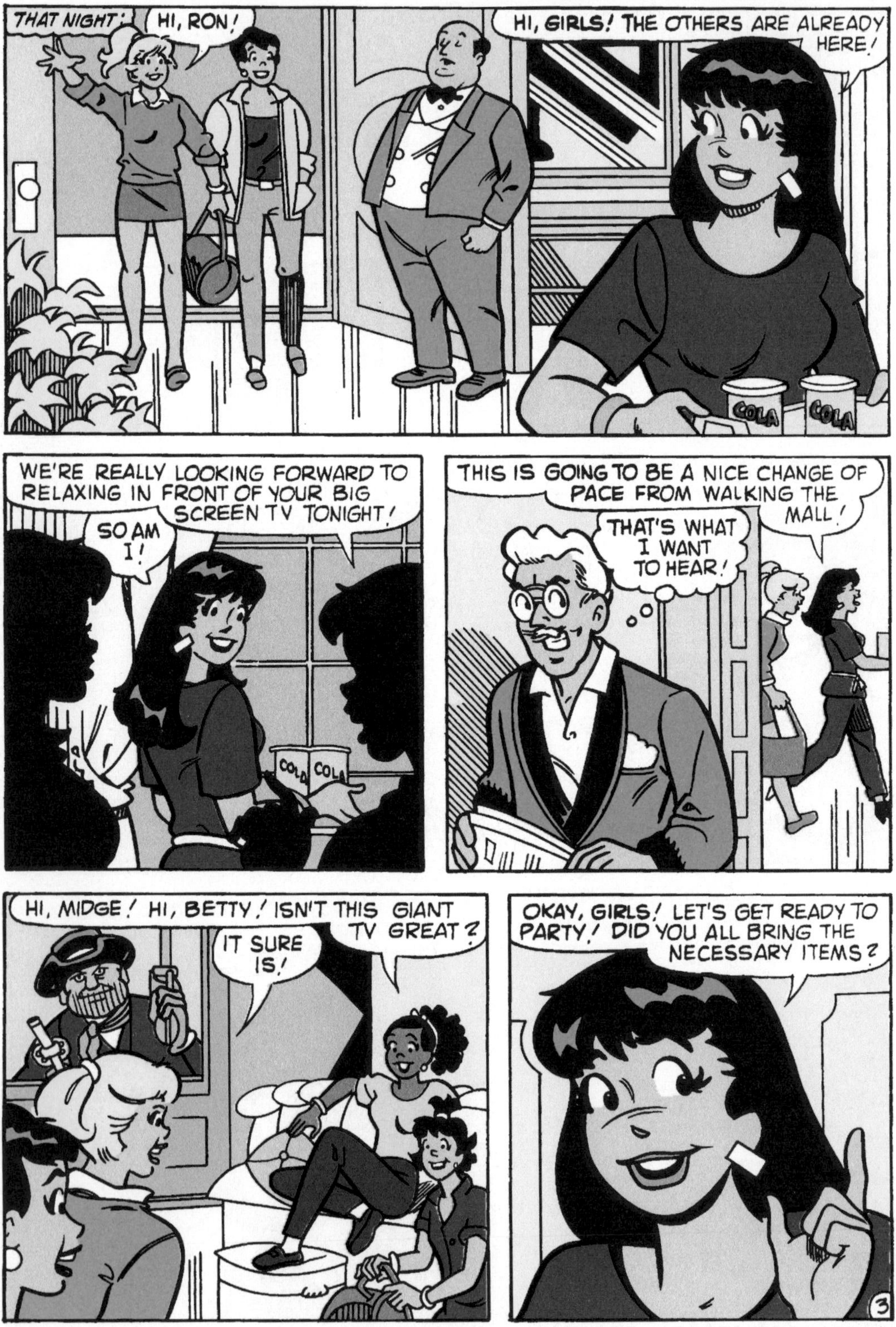
THAT NIGHT:
HI, RON!
HI, GIRLS! THE OTHERS ARE ALREADY HERE!
WE'RE REALLY LOOKING FORWARD TO RELAXING IN FRONT OF YOUR BIG SCREEN TV TONIGHT!
SO AM I!
COLA
COLA
THIS IS GOING TO BE A NICE CHANGE OF PACE FROM WALKING THE MALL!
THAT'S WHAT I WANT TO HEAR!
HI, MIDGE! HI, BETTY! ISN'T THIS GIANT TV GREAT?
IT SURE IS!
OKAY, GIRLS! LET'S GET READY TO PARTY! DID YOU ALL BRING THE NECESSARY ITEMS?
3

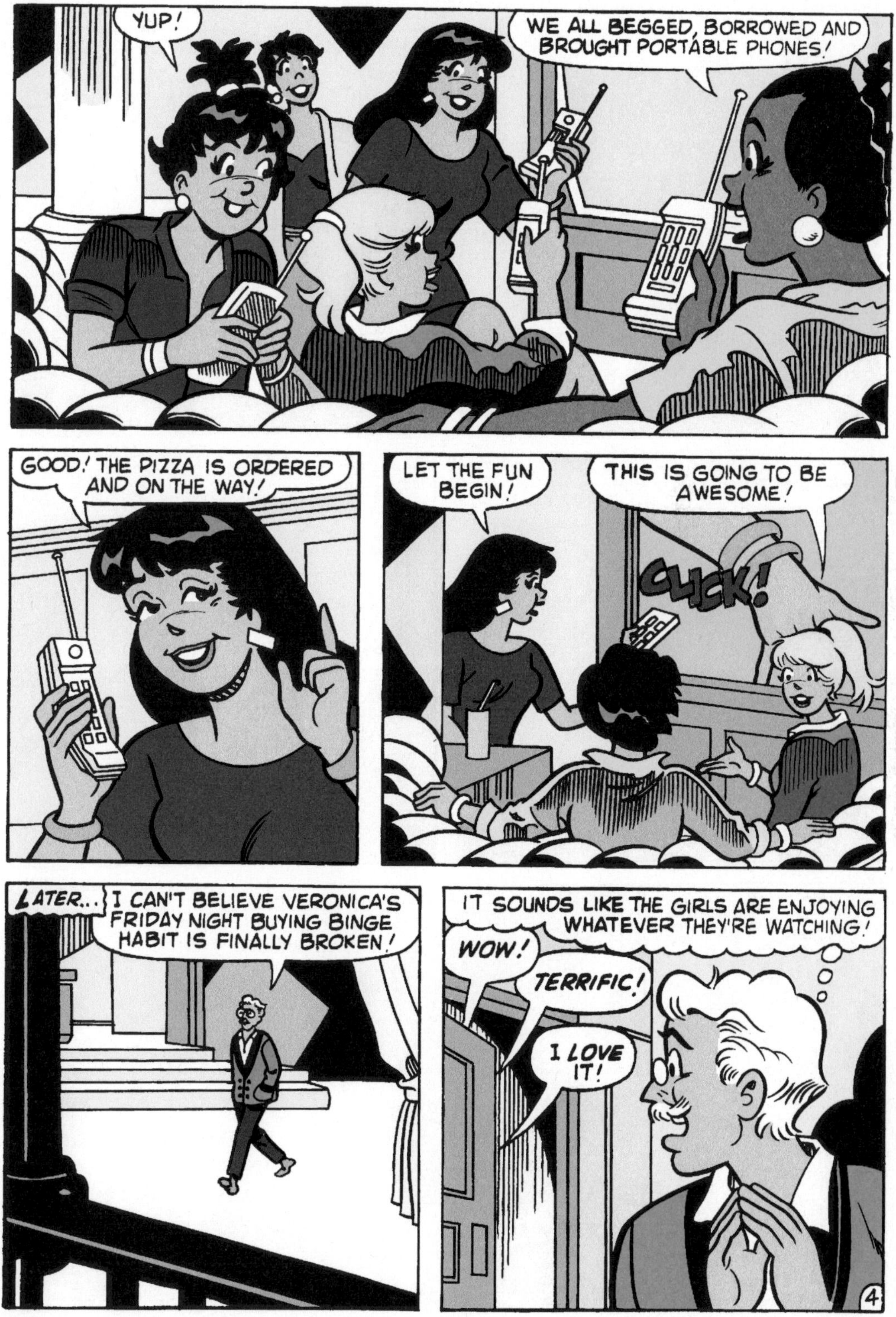
YUP!
WE ALL BEGGED, BORROWED AND BROUGHT PORTABLE PHONES!
GOOD! THE PIZZA IS ORDERED AND ON THE WAY!
LET THE FUN BEGIN!
THIS IS GOING TO BE AWESOME!
CLICK!
LATER...
I CAN'T BELIEVE VERONICA'S FRIDAY NIGHT BUYING BINGE HABIT IS FINALLY BROKEN!
IT SOUNDS LIKE THE GIRLS ARE ENJOYING WHATEVER THEY'RE WATCHING!
WOW!
TERRIFIC!
I LOVE IT!
4

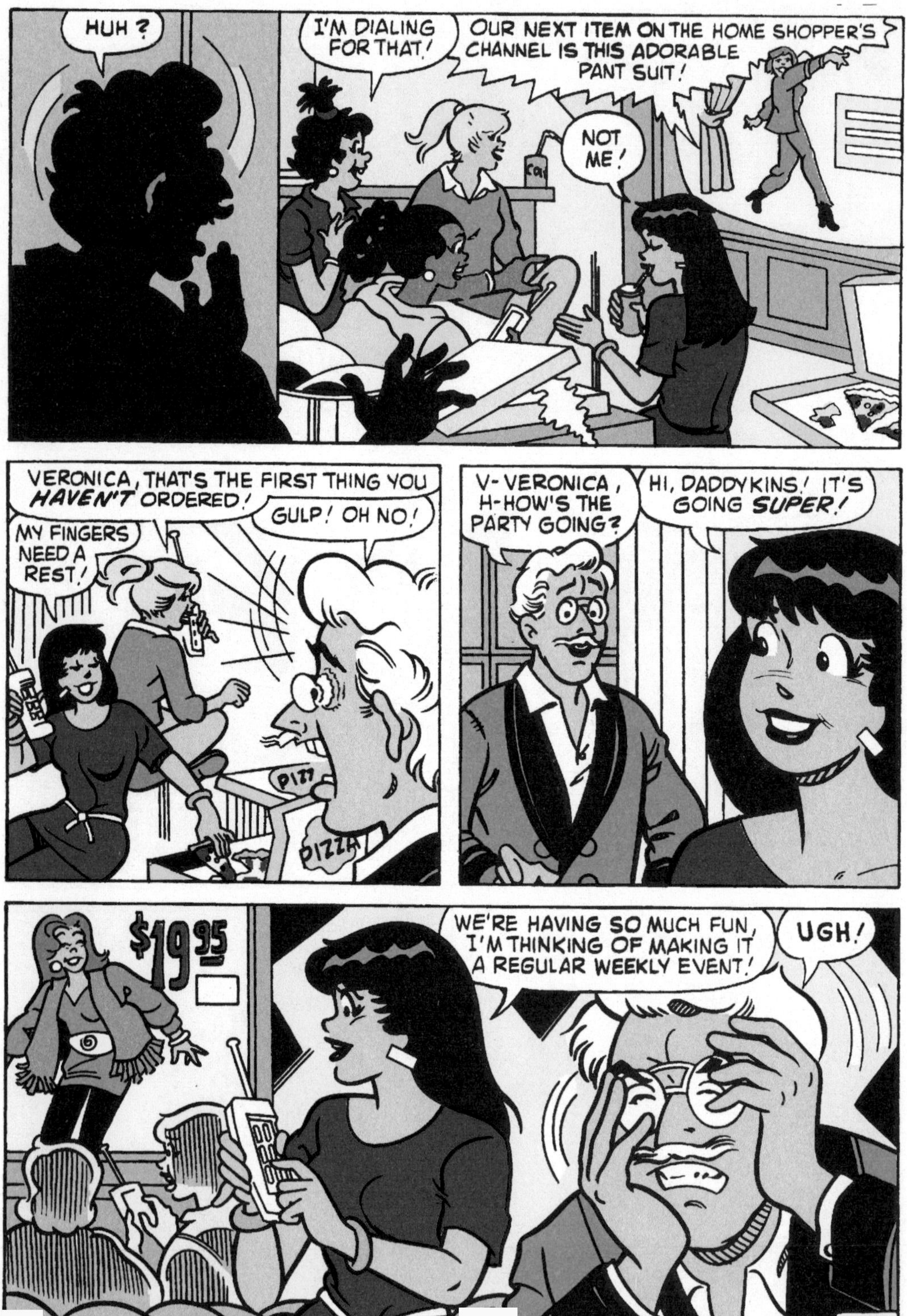
HUH ?
I'M DIALING FOR THAT!
OUR NEXT ITEM ON THE HOME SHOPPER'S CHANNEL IS THIS ADORABLE PANT SUIT!
NOT ME!
VERONICA, THAT'S THE FIRST THING YOU *HAVEN'T* ORDERED!
MY FINGERS NEED A REST!
GULP! OH NO!
PIZZA
V-VERONICA, H-HOW'S THE PARTY GOING?
HI, DADDYKINS! IT'S GOING *SUPER*!
$19.95
WE'RE HAVING SO MUCH FUN, I'M THINKING OF MAKING IT A REGULAR WEEKLY EVENT!
UGH!
END

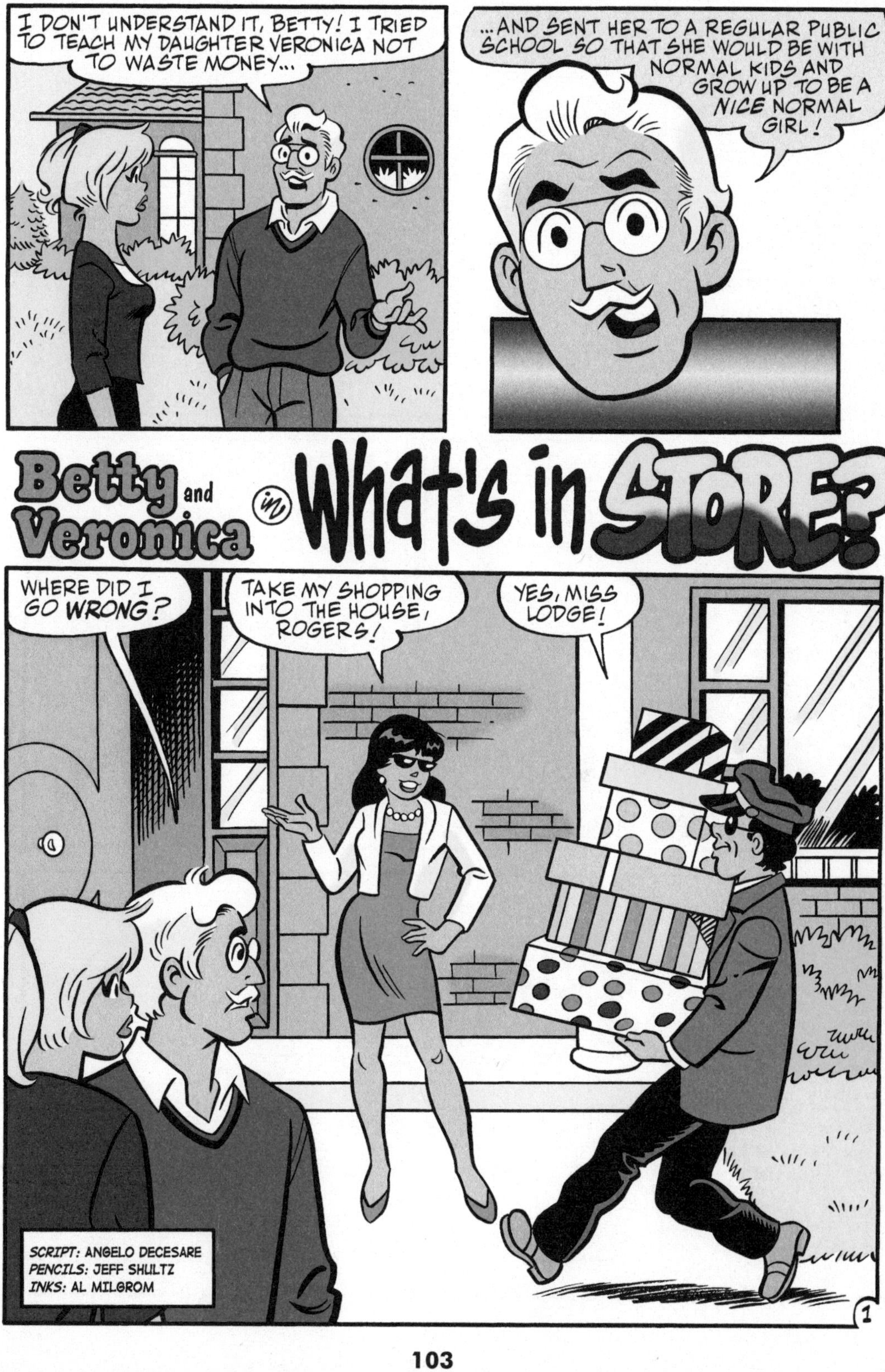
I DON'T UNDERSTAND IT, BETTY! I TRIED TO TEACH MY DAUGHTER VERONICA NOT TO WASTE MONEY...
...AND SENT HER TO A REGULAR PUBLIC SCHOOL SO THAT SHE WOULD BE WITH NORMAL KIDS AND GROW UP TO BE A NICE NORMAL GIRL!
Betty and Veronica in What's in STORE?
WHERE DID I GO WRONG?
TAKE MY SHOPPING INTO THE HOUSE, ROGERS!
YES, MISS LODGE!
SCRIPT: ANGELO DECESARE
PENCILS: JEFF SHULTZ
INKS: AL MILGROM
1

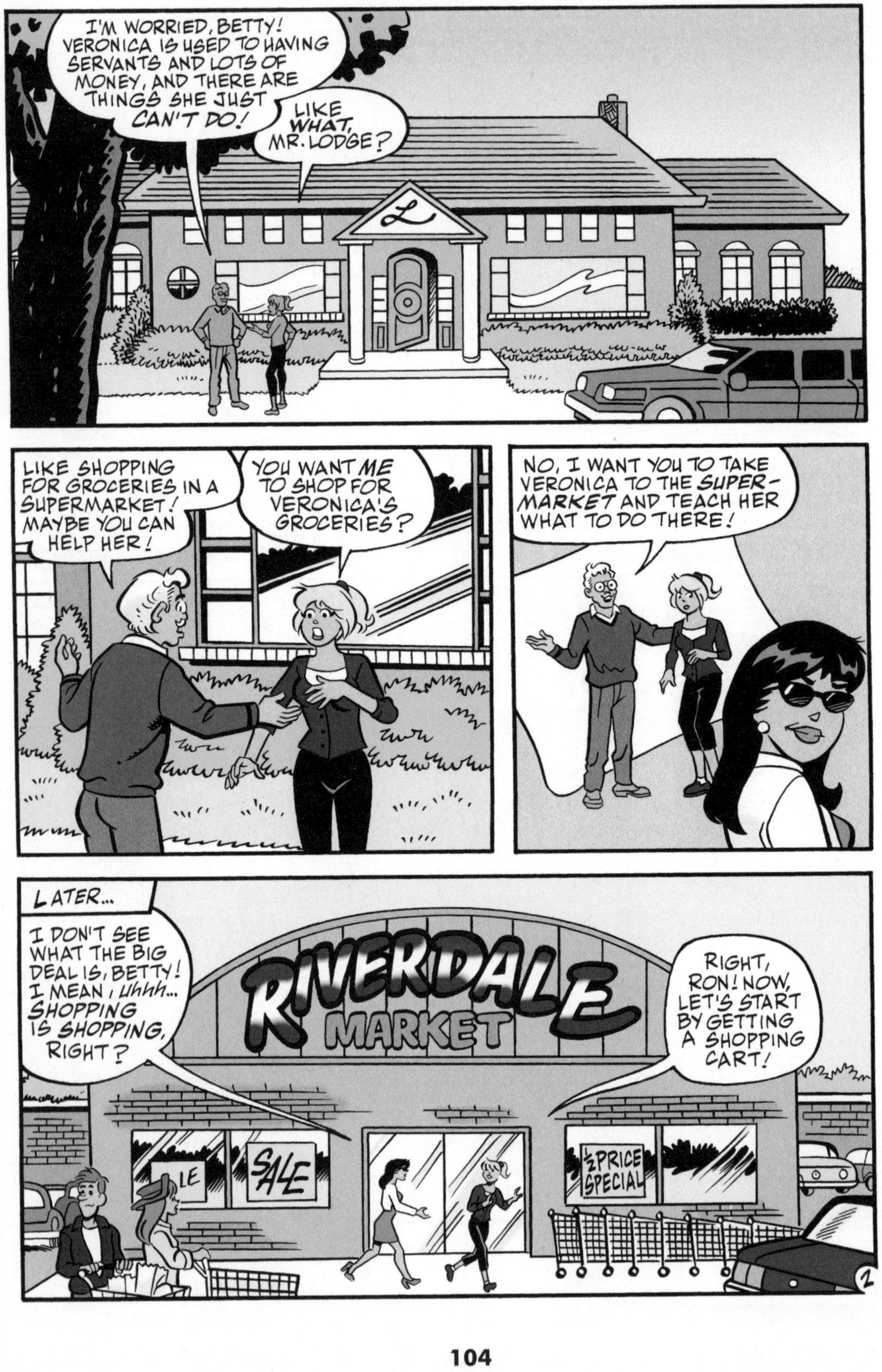
I'M WORRIED, BETTY! VERONICA IS USED TO HAVING SERVANTS AND LOTS OF MONEY, AND THERE ARE THINGS SHE JUST CAN'T DO!
LIKE WHAT, MR. LODGE?
LIKE SHOPPING FOR GROCERIES IN A SUPERMARKET! MAYBE YOU CAN HELP HER!
YOU WANT ME TO SHOP FOR VERONICA'S GROCERIES?
NO, I WANT YOU TO TAKE VERONICA TO THE SUPER-MARKET AND TEACH HER WHAT TO DO THERE!
LATER...
I DON'T SEE WHAT THE BIG DEAL IS, BETTY! I MEAN, uhhh... SHOPPING IS SHOPPING, RIGHT?
RIVERDALE MARKET
RIGHT, RON! NOW, LET'S START BY GETTING A SHOPPING CART!
SALE
½ PRICE SPECIAL
2

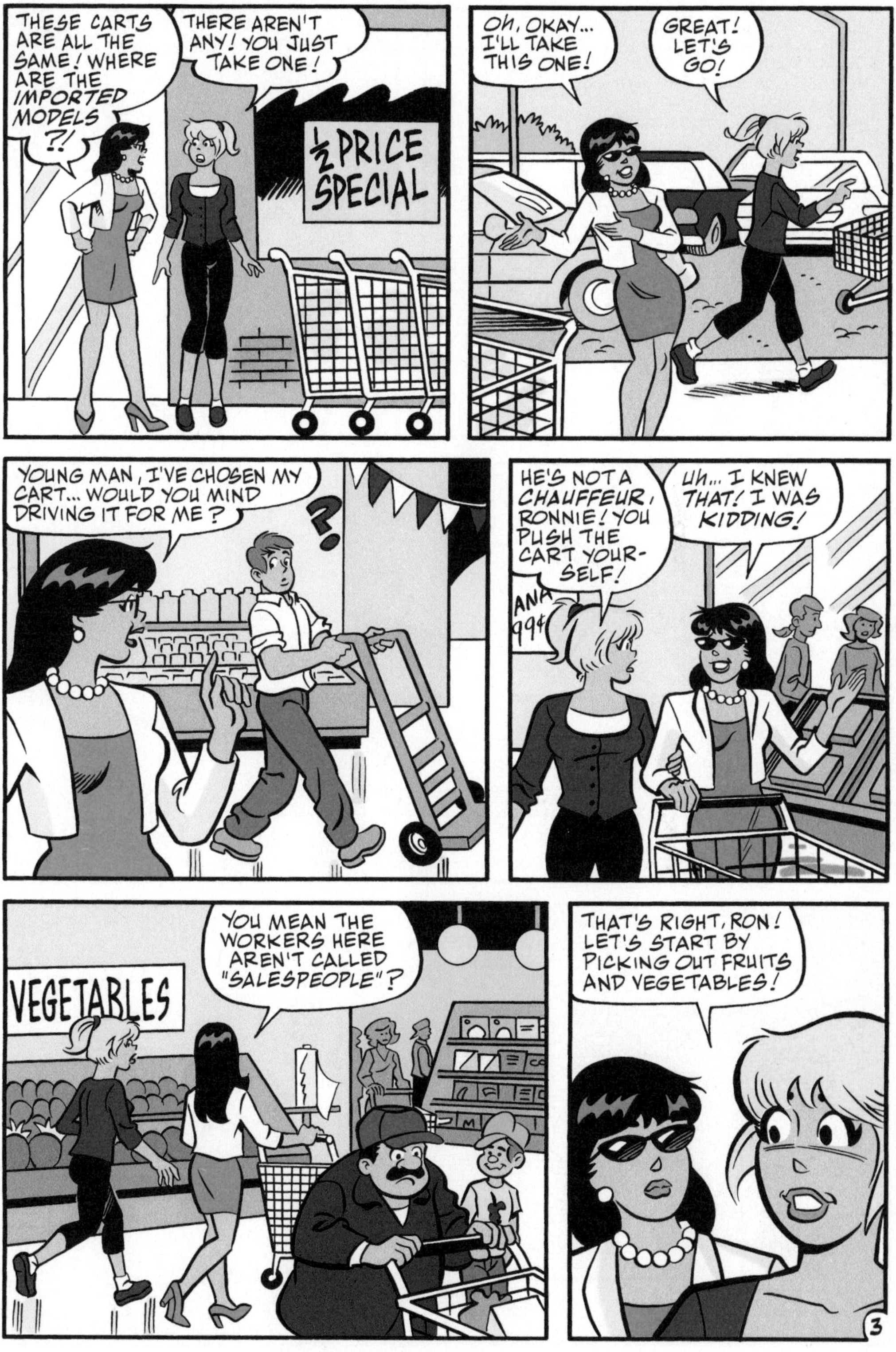
THESE CARTS ARE ALL THE SAME! WHERE ARE THE IMPORTED MODELS ?!
THERE AREN'T ANY! YOU JUST TAKE ONE!
1/2 PRICE SPECIAL
OH, OKAY... I'LL TAKE THIS ONE!
GREAT! LET'S GO!
YOUNG MAN, I'VE CHOSEN MY CART... WOULD YOU MIND DRIVING IT FOR ME?
?
HE'S NOT A CHAUFFEUR, RONNIE! YOU PUSH THE CART YOURSELF!
UH... I KNEW THAT! I WAS KIDDING!
ANA 99¢
VEGETABLES
YOU MEAN THE WORKERS HERE AREN'T CALLED "SALESPEOPLE"?
THAT'S RIGHT, RON! LET'S START BY PICKING OUT FRUITS AND VEGETABLES!
3

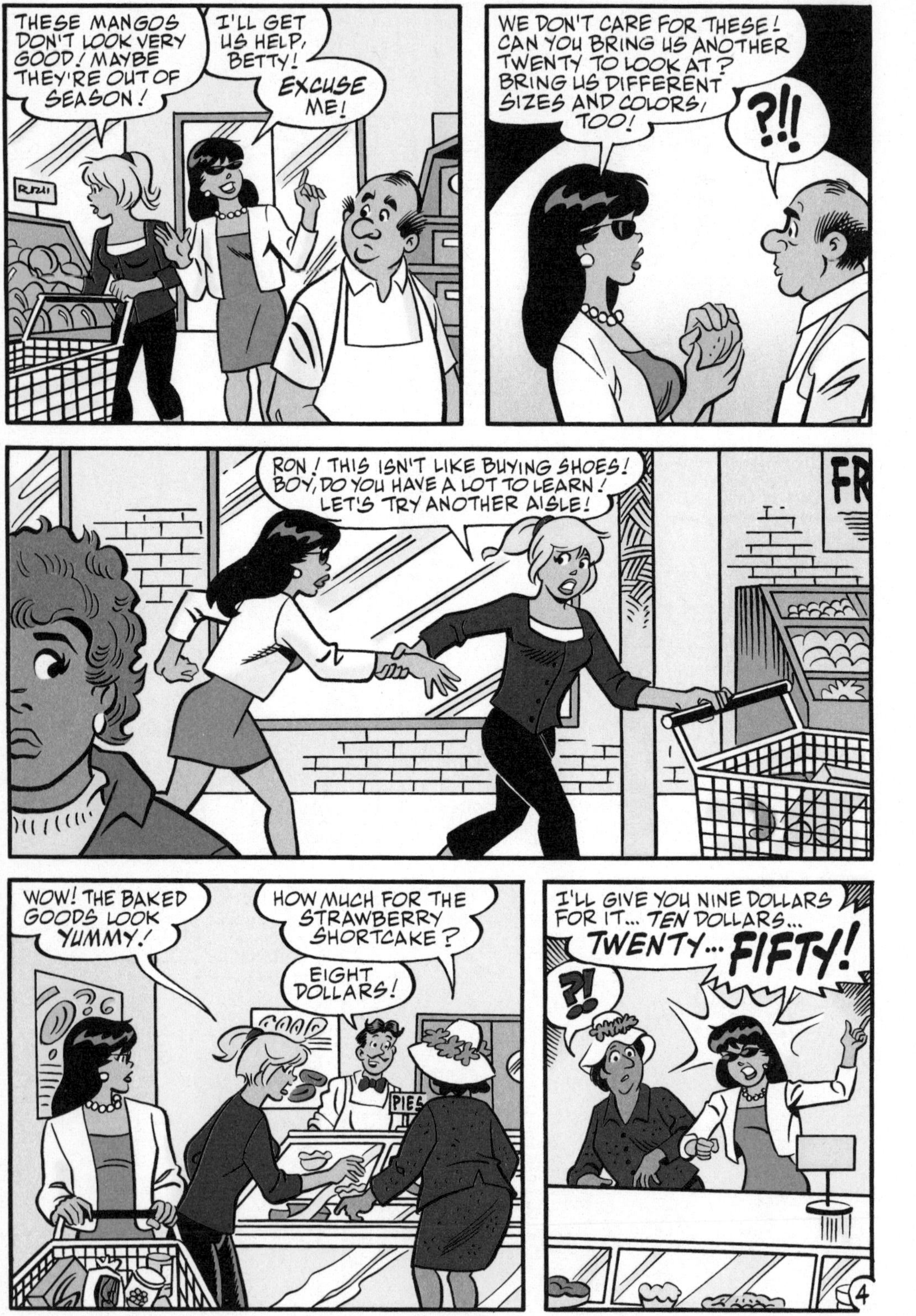
THESE MANGOS DON'T LOOK VERY GOOD! MAYBE THEY'RE OUT OF SEASON!
I'LL GET US HELP, BETTY!
EXCUSE ME!
WE DON'T CARE FOR THESE! CAN YOU BRING US ANOTHER TWENTY TO LOOK AT? BRING US DIFFERENT SIZES AND COLORS, TOO!
?!!
RON! THIS ISN'T LIKE BUYING SHOES! BOY, DO YOU HAVE A LOT TO LEARN! LET'S TRY ANOTHER AISLE!
WOW! THE BAKED GOODS LOOK YUMMY!
HOW MUCH FOR THE STRAWBERRY SHORTCAKE?
EIGHT DOLLARS!
PIES
I'LL GIVE YOU NINE DOLLARS FOR IT... TEN DOLLARS... TWENTY... FIFTY!
?!
4

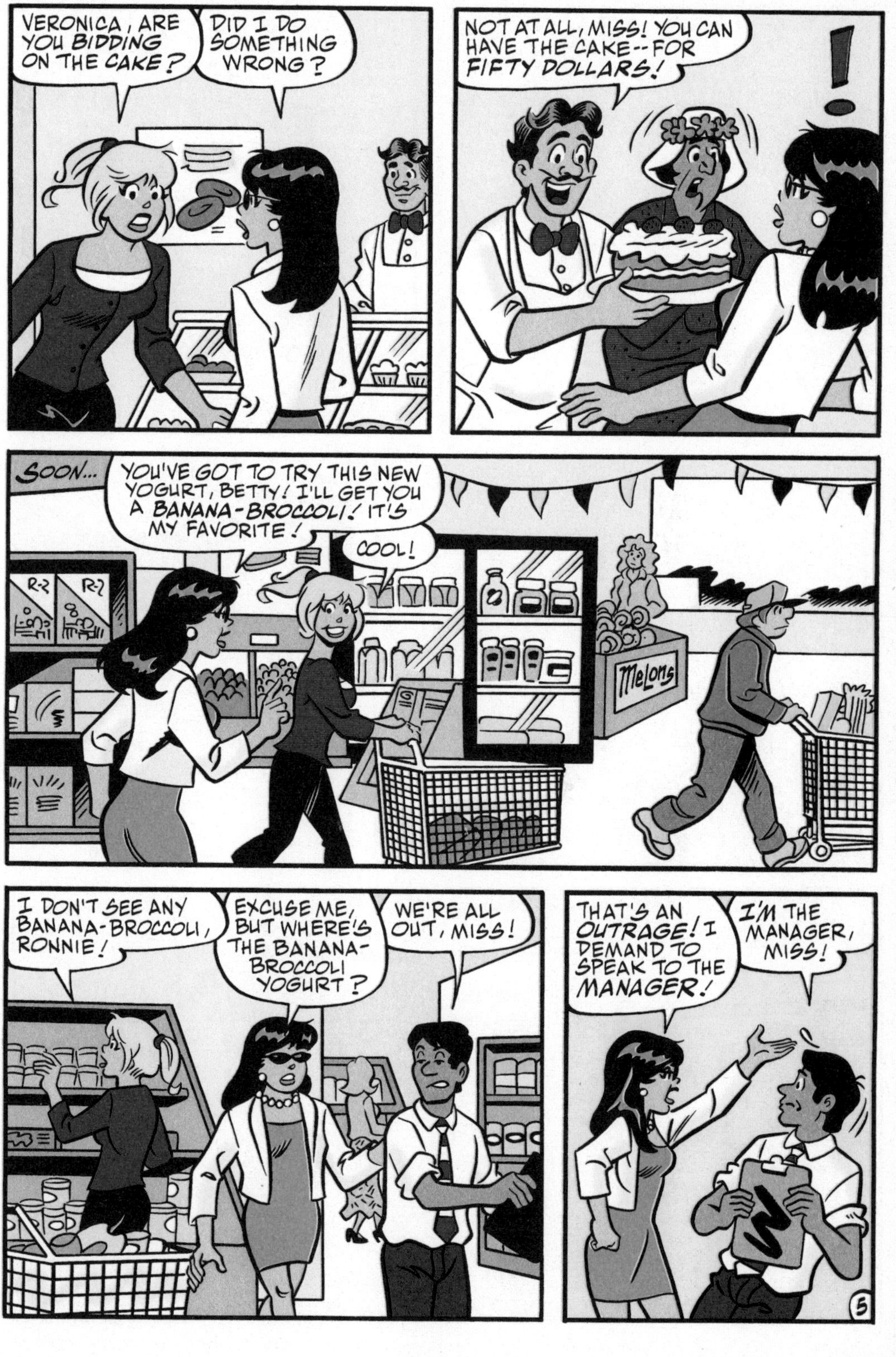
VERONICA, ARE YOU BIDDING ON THE CAKE?
DID I DO SOMETHING WRONG?
NOT AT ALL, MISS! YOU CAN HAVE THE CAKE-- FOR FIFTY DOLLARS!
!
SOON...
YOU'VE GOT TO TRY THIS NEW YOGURT, BETTY! I'LL GET YOU A BANANA-BROCCOLI! IT'S MY FAVORITE!
COOL!
MELONS
I DON'T SEE ANY BANANA-BROCCOLI, RONNIE!
EXCUSE ME, BUT WHERE'S THE BANANA-BROCCOLI YOGURT?
WE'RE ALL OUT, MISS!
THAT'S AN OUTRAGE! I DEMAND TO SPEAK TO THE MANAGER!
I'M THE MANAGER, MISS!
5

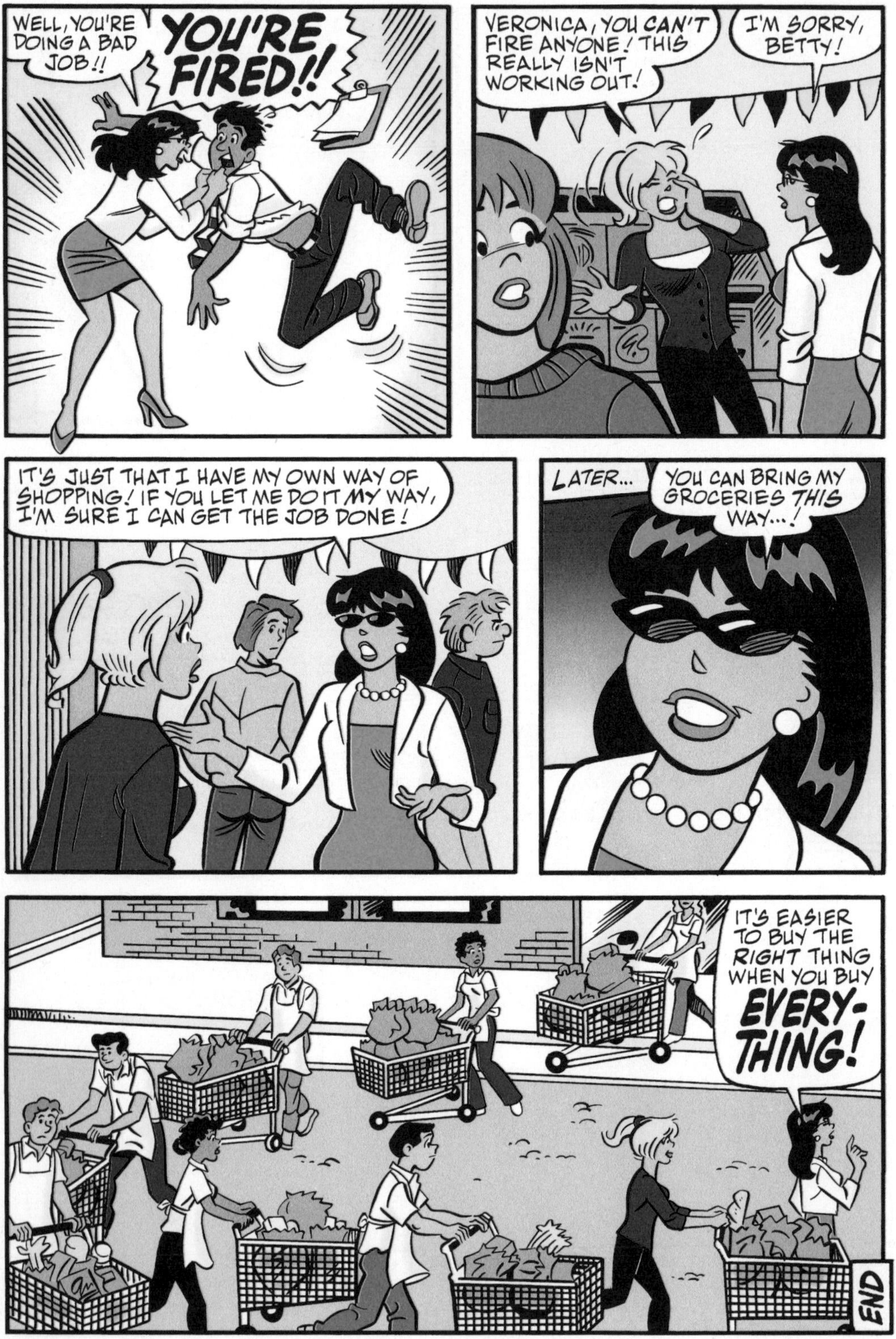
WELL, YOU'RE DOING A BAD JOB!!
YOU'RE FIRED!!
VERONICA, YOU CAN'T FIRE ANYONE! THIS REALLY ISN'T WORKING OUT!
I'M SORRY, BETTY!
IT'S JUST THAT I HAVE MY OWN WAY OF SHOPPING! IF YOU LET ME DO IT MY WAY, I'M SURE I CAN GET THE JOB DONE!
LATER...
YOU CAN BRING MY GROCERIES THIS WAY...!
IT'S EASIER TO BUY THE RIGHT THING WHEN YOU BUY EVERY-THING!
END

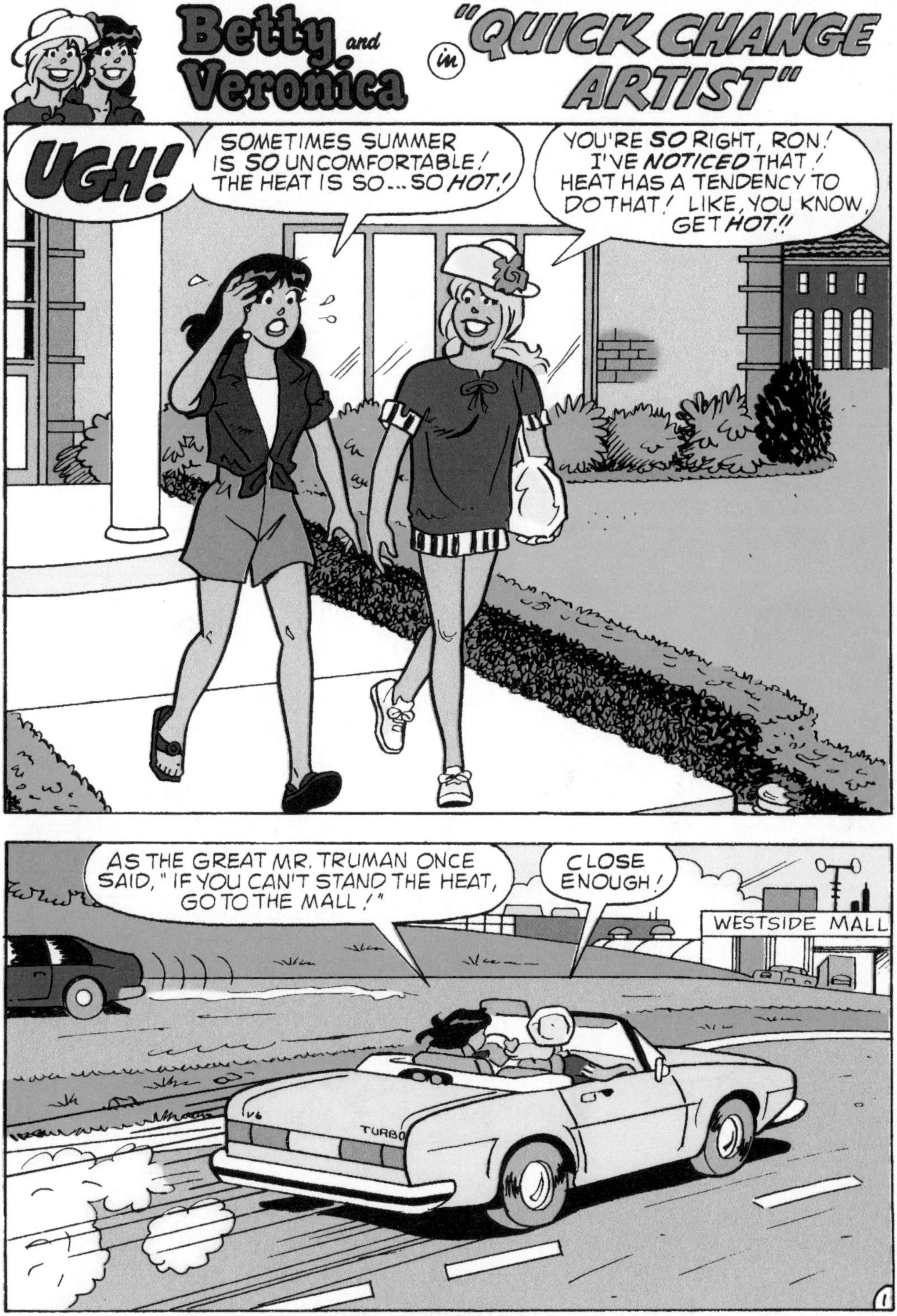
Betty and Veronica in "QUICK CHANGE ARTIST"
UGH!
SOMETIMES SUMMER IS SO UNCOMFORTABLE! THE HEAT IS SO... SO HOT!
YOU'RE SO RIGHT, RON! I'VE NOTICED THAT! HEAT HAS A TENDENCY TO DO THAT! LIKE, YOU KNOW, GET HOT!!
AS THE GREAT MR. TRUMAN ONCE SAID, "IF YOU CAN'T STAND THE HEAT, GO TO THE MALL!"
CLOSE ENOUGH!
WESTSIDE MALL
V6
TURBO
1

Webb / DeCarlo / Scarpelli / Yoshida / Grossman

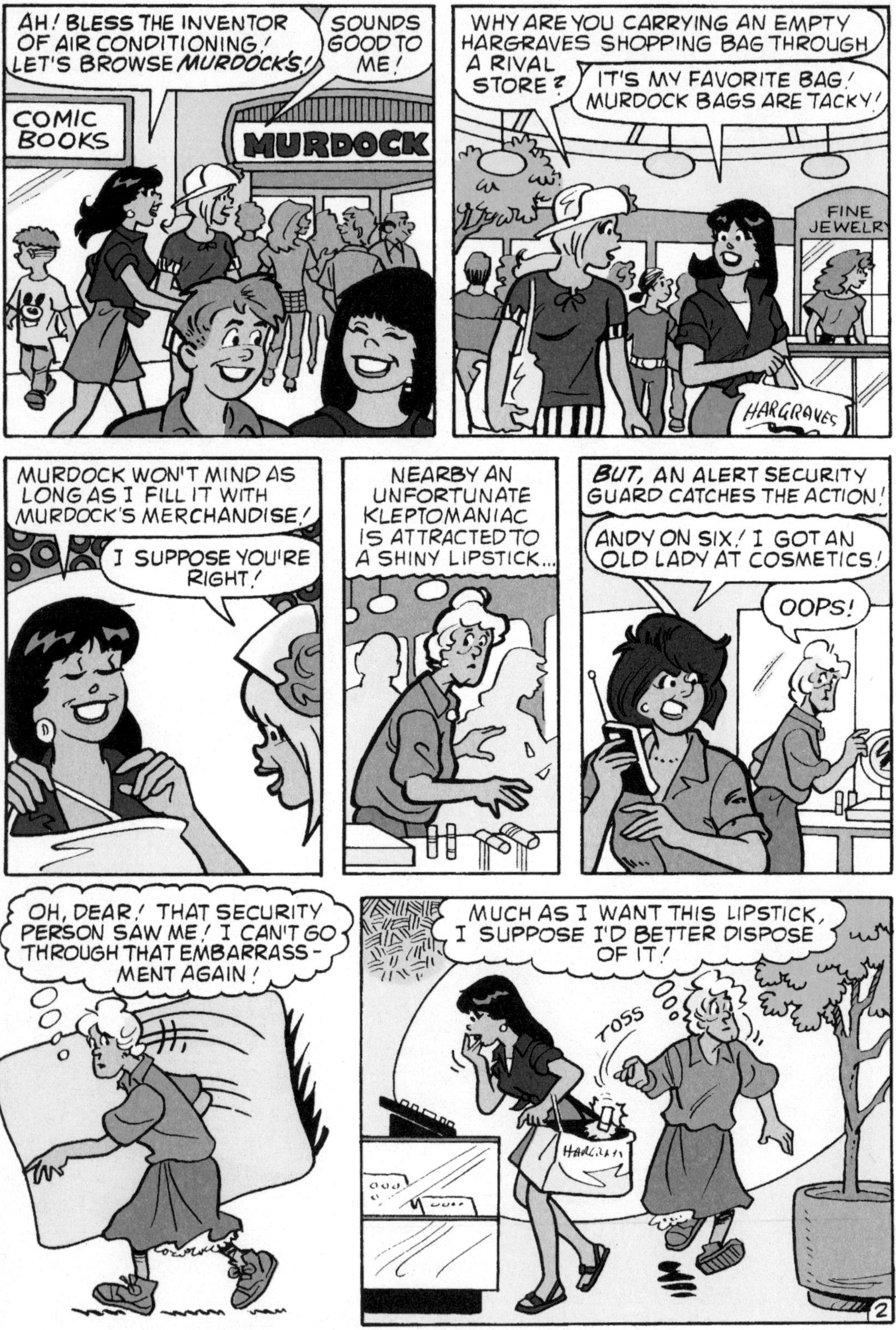
AH! BLESS THE INVENTOR OF AIR CONDITIONING! LET'S BROWSE MURDOCK'S!
SOUNDS GOOD TO ME!
COMIC BOOKS
MURDOCK
WHY ARE YOU CARRYING AN EMPTY HARGRAVES SHOPPING BAG THROUGH A RIVAL STORE?
IT'S MY FAVORITE BAG! MURDOCK BAGS ARE TACKY!
FINE JEWELRY
HARGRAVES
MURDOCK WON'T MIND AS LONG AS I FILL IT WITH MURDOCK'S MERCHANDISE!
I SUPPOSE YOU'RE RIGHT!
NEARBY AN UNFORTUNATE KLEPTOMANIAC IS ATTRACTED TO A SHINY LIPSTICK...
BUT, AN ALERT SECURITY GUARD CATCHES THE ACTION!
ANDY ON SIX! I GOT AN OLD LADY AT COSMETICS!
OOPS!
OH, DEAR! THAT SECURITY PERSON SAW ME! I CAN'T GO THROUGH THAT EMBARRASS-MENT AGAIN!
MUCH AS I WANT THIS LIPSTICK, I SUPPOSE I'D BETTER DISPOSE OF IT!
TOSS
2

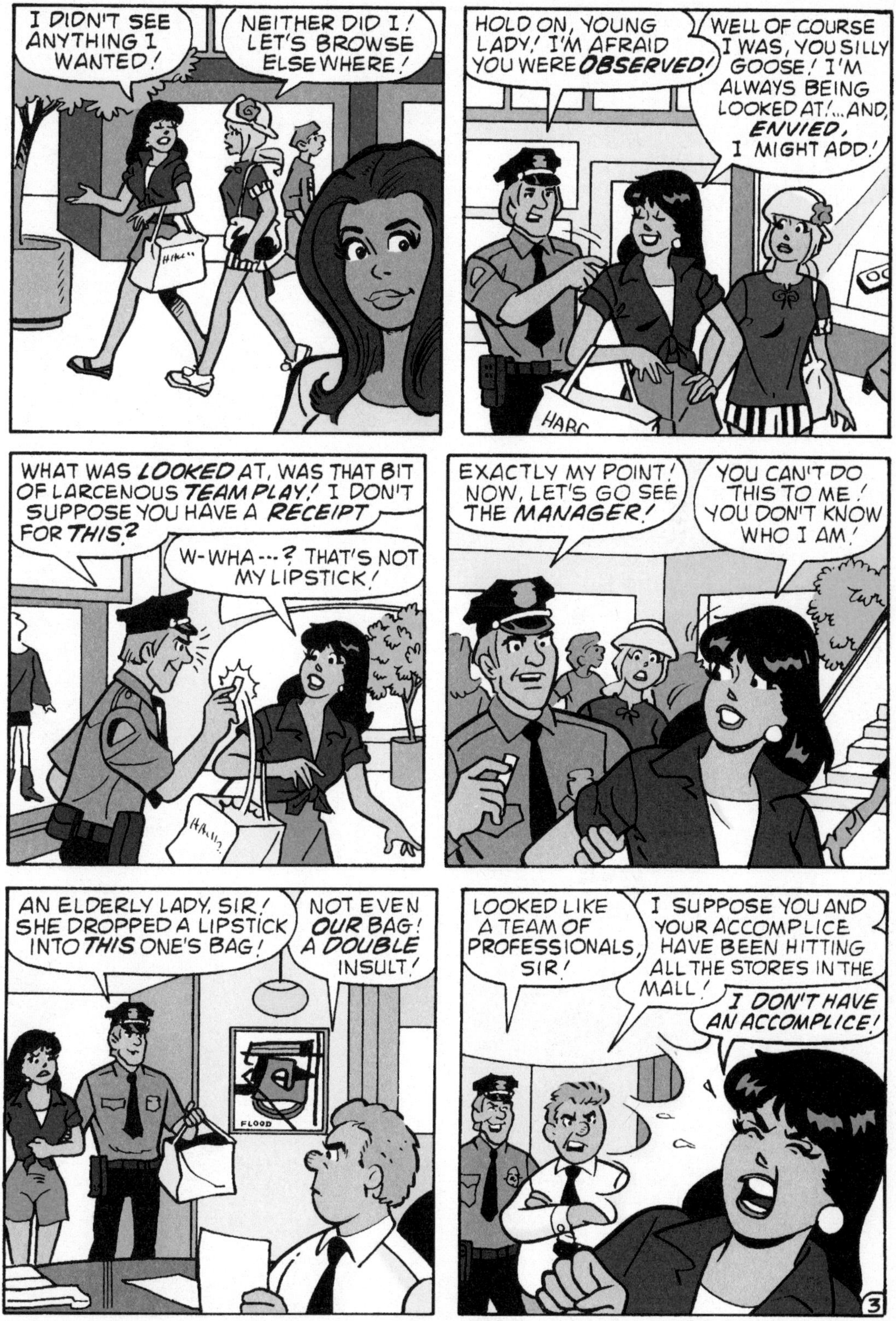
I DIDN'T SEE ANYTHING I WANTED!
NEITHER DID I! LET'S BROWSE ELSEWHERE!
HOLD ON, YOUNG LADY! I'M AFRAID YOU WERE OBSERVED!
WELL OF COURSE I WAS, YOU SILLY GOOSE! I'M ALWAYS BEING LOOKED AT!...AND, ENVIED, I MIGHT ADD!
WHAT WAS LOOKED AT, WAS THAT BIT OF LARCENOUS TEAM PLAY! I DON'T SUPPOSE YOU HAVE A RECEIPT FOR THIS?
W-WHA---? THAT'S NOT MY LIPSTICK!
EXACTLY MY POINT! NOW, LET'S GO SEE THE MANAGER!
YOU CAN'T DO THIS TO ME! YOU DON'T KNOW WHO I AM!
AN ELDERLY LADY, SIR! SHE DROPPED A LIPSTICK INTO THIS ONE'S BAG!
NOT EVEN OUR BAG! A DOUBLE INSULT!
FLOOD
LOOKED LIKE A TEAM OF PROFESSIONALS, SIR!
I SUPPOSE YOU AND YOUR ACCOMPLICE HAVE BEEN HITTING ALL THE STORES IN THE MALL!
I DON'T HAVE AN ACCOMPLICE!
3

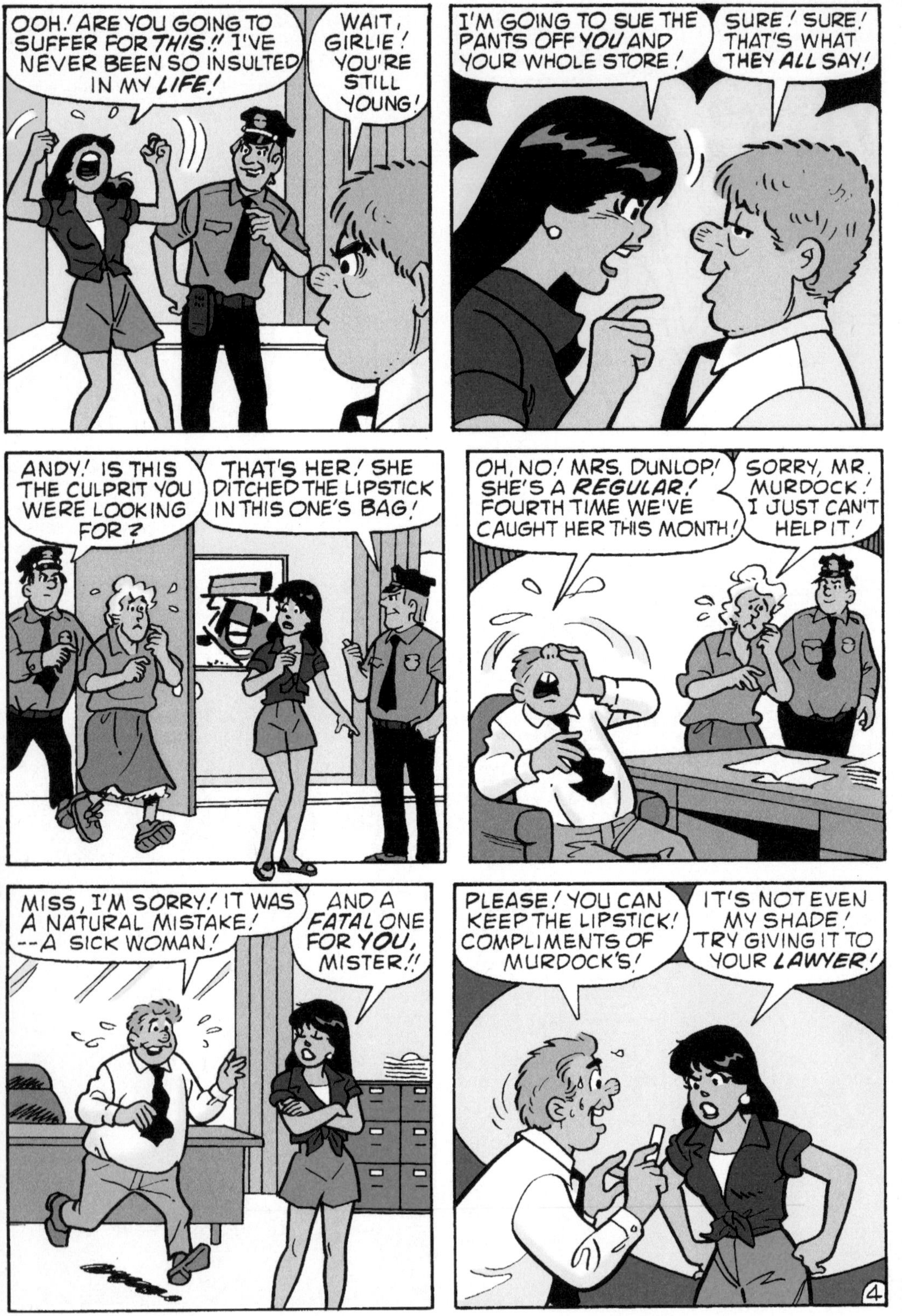
OOH! ARE YOU GOING TO SUFFER FOR THIS!! I'VE NEVER BEEN SO INSULTED IN MY LIFE!
WAIT, GIRLIE! YOU'RE STILL YOUNG!
I'M GOING TO SUE THE PANTS OFF YOU AND YOUR WHOLE STORE!
SURE! SURE! THAT'S WHAT THEY ALL SAY!
ANDY! IS THIS THE CULPRIT YOU WERE LOOKING FOR?
THAT'S HER! SHE DITCHED THE LIPSTICK IN THIS ONE'S BAG!
OH, NO! MRS. DUNLOP! SHE'S A REGULAR! FOURTH TIME WE'VE CAUGHT HER THIS MONTH!
SORRY, MR. MURDOCK! I JUST CAN'T HELP IT!
MISS, I'M SORRY! IT WAS A NATURAL MISTAKE! --A SICK WOMAN!
AND A FATAL ONE FOR YOU, MISTER!!
PLEASE! YOU CAN KEEP THE LIPSTICK! COMPLIMENTS OF MURDOCK'S!
IT'S NOT EVEN MY SHADE! TRY GIVING IT TO YOUR LAWYER!
4

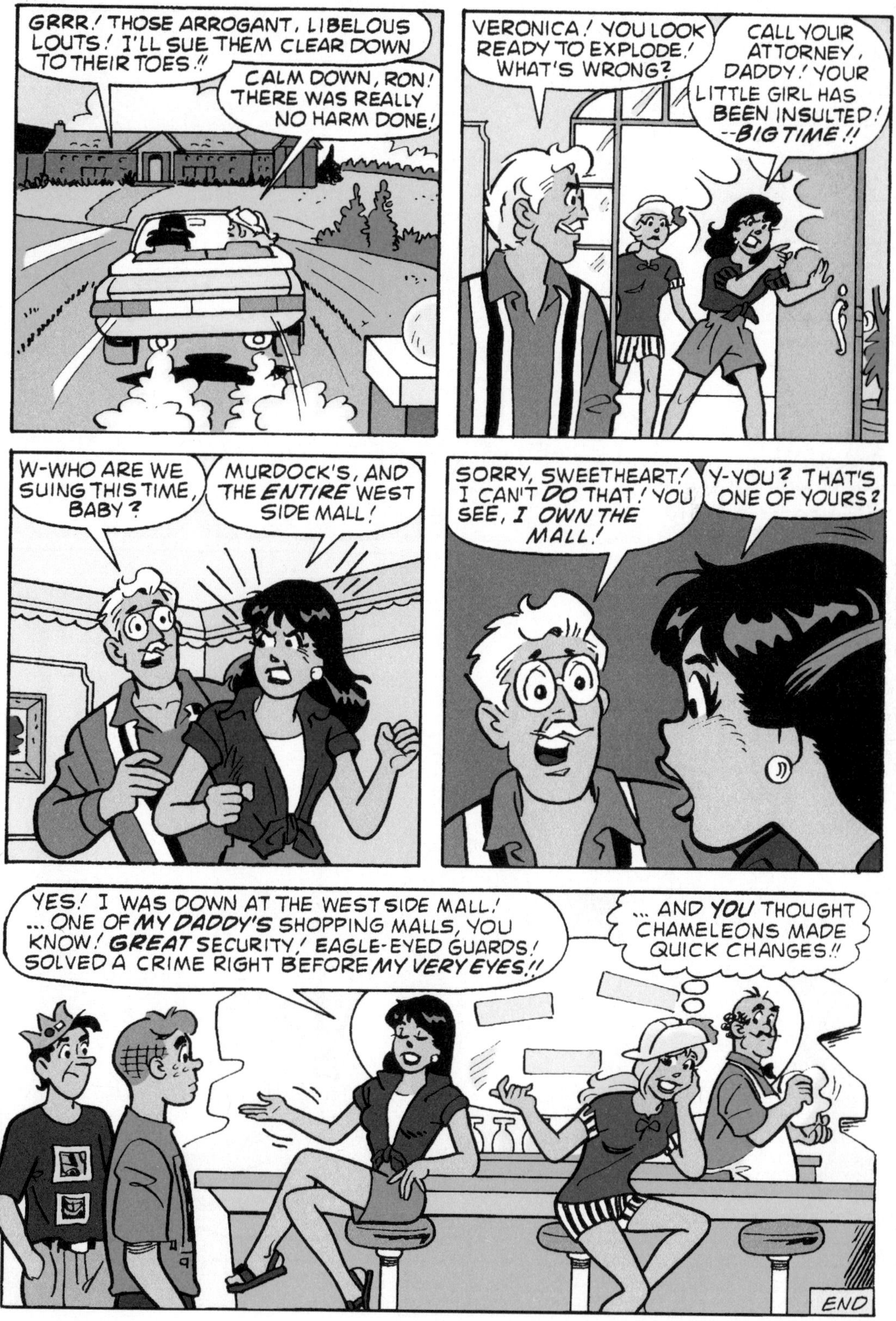
GRRR! THOSE ARROGANT, LIBELOUS LOUTS! I'LL SUE THEM CLEAR DOWN TO THEIR TOES!!
CALM DOWN, RON! THERE WAS REALLY NO HARM DONE!
VERONICA! YOU LOOK READY TO EXPLODE! WHAT'S WRONG?
CALL YOUR ATTORNEY, DADDY! YOUR LITTLE GIRL HAS BEEN INSULTED! --BIG TIME!!
W-WHO ARE WE SUING THIS TIME, BABY?
MURDOCK'S, AND THE ENTIRE WEST SIDE MALL!
SORRY, SWEETHEART! I CAN'T DO THAT! YOU SEE, I OWN THE MALL!
Y-YOU? THAT'S ONE OF YOURS?
YES! I WAS DOWN AT THE WEST SIDE MALL! ...ONE OF MY DADDY'S SHOPPING MALLS, YOU KNOW! GREAT SECURITY! EAGLE-EYED GUARDS! SOLVED A CRIME RIGHT BEFORE MY VERY EYES!!
...AND YOU THOUGHT CHAMELEONS MADE QUICK CHANGES!!
END

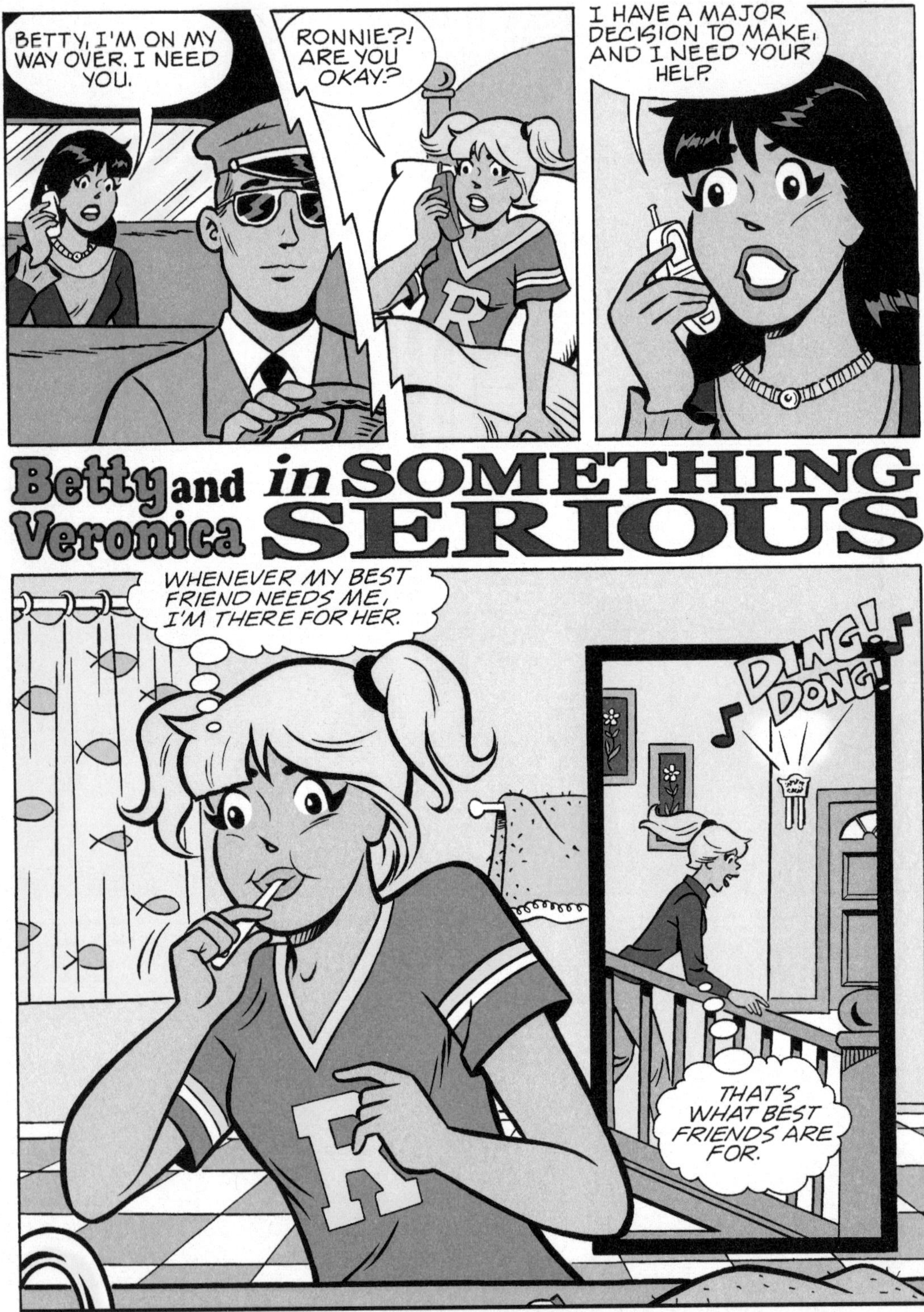
BETTY, I'M ON MY WAY OVER. I NEED YOU.
RONNIE?! ARE YOU OKAY?
I HAVE A MAJOR DECISION TO MAKE, AND I NEED YOUR HELP.
Betty and Veronica in SOMETHING SERIOUS
WHENEVER MY BEST FRIEND NEEDS ME, I'M THERE FOR HER.
DING! DONG!
THAT'S WHAT BEST FRIENDS ARE FOR.

SCRIPT: BARBARA SLATE PENCILS: DAN PARENT INKS: JON D'AGOSTINO
COLORS: BARRY GROSSMAN LETTERS: JOHN WORKMAN

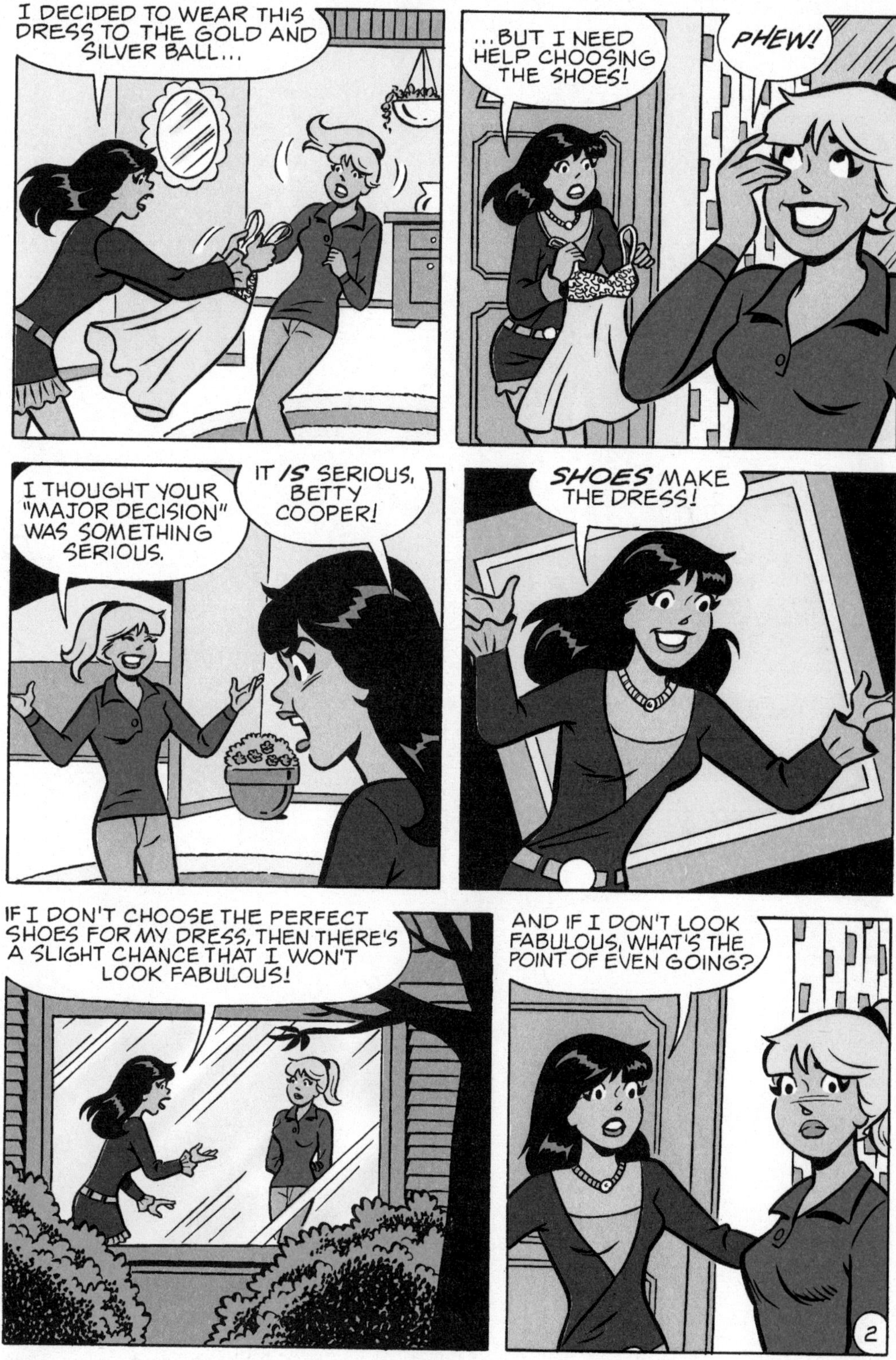
I DECIDED TO WEAR THIS DRESS TO THE GOLD AND SILVER BALL...
...BUT I NEED HELP CHOOSING THE SHOES!
PHEW!
I THOUGHT YOUR "MAJOR DECISION" WAS SOMETHING SERIOUS.
IT IS SERIOUS, BETTY COOPER!
SHOES MAKE THE DRESS!
IF I DON'T CHOOSE THE PERFECT SHOES FOR MY DRESS, THEN THERE'S A SLIGHT CHANCE THAT I WON'T LOOK FABULOUS!
AND IF I DON'T LOOK FABULOUS, WHAT'S THE POINT OF EVEN GOING?
2

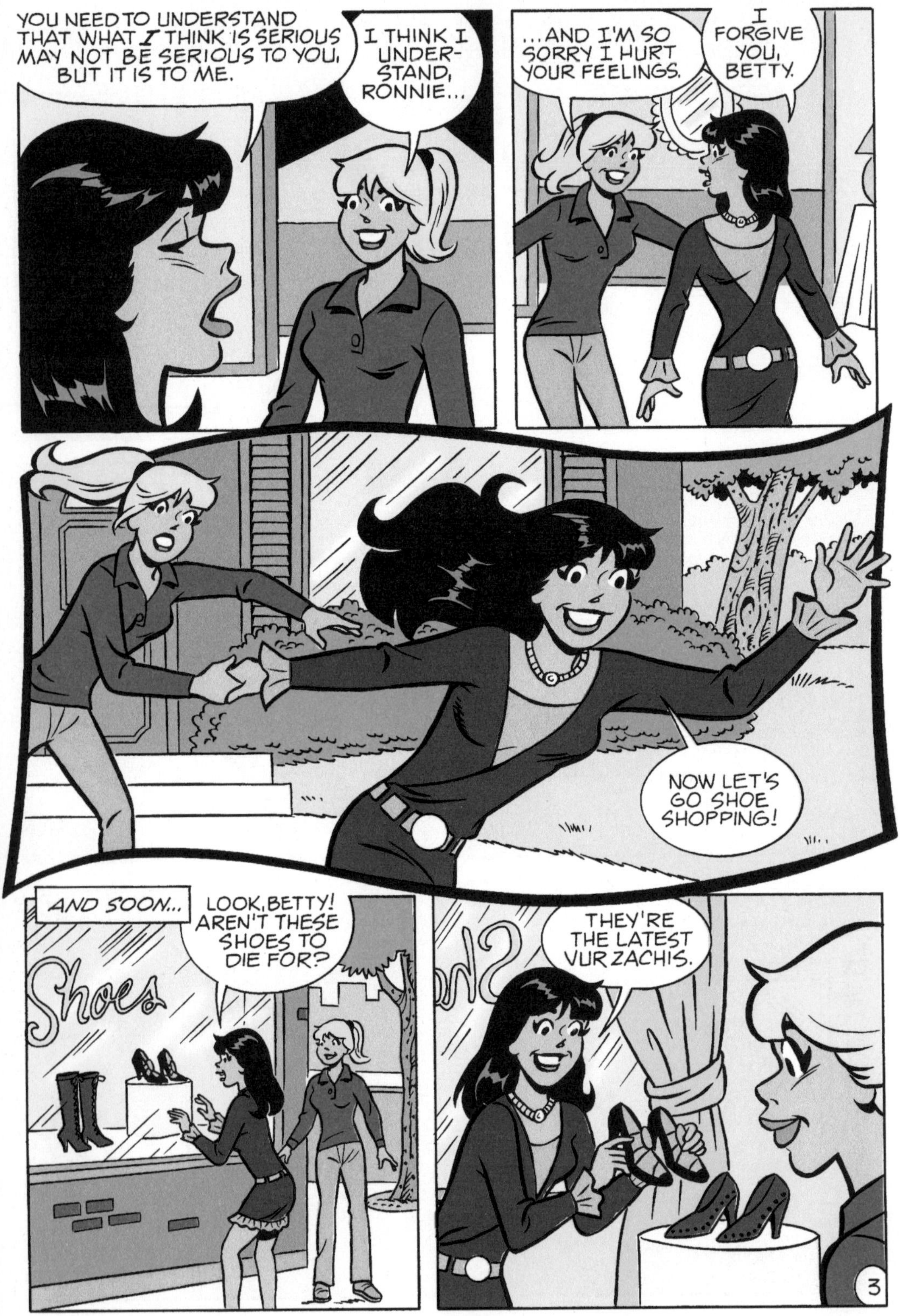
YOU NEED TO UNDERSTAND THAT WHAT I THINK IS SERIOUS MAY NOT BE SERIOUS TO YOU, BUT IT IS TO ME.
I THINK I UNDER-STAND, RONNIE...
...AND I'M SO SORRY I HURT YOUR FEELINGS.
I FORGIVE YOU, BETTY.
NOW LET'S GO SHOE SHOPPING!
AND SOON...
LOOK, BETTY! AREN'T THESE SHOES TO DIE FOR?
Shoes
THEY'RE THE LATEST VURZACHIS.
3

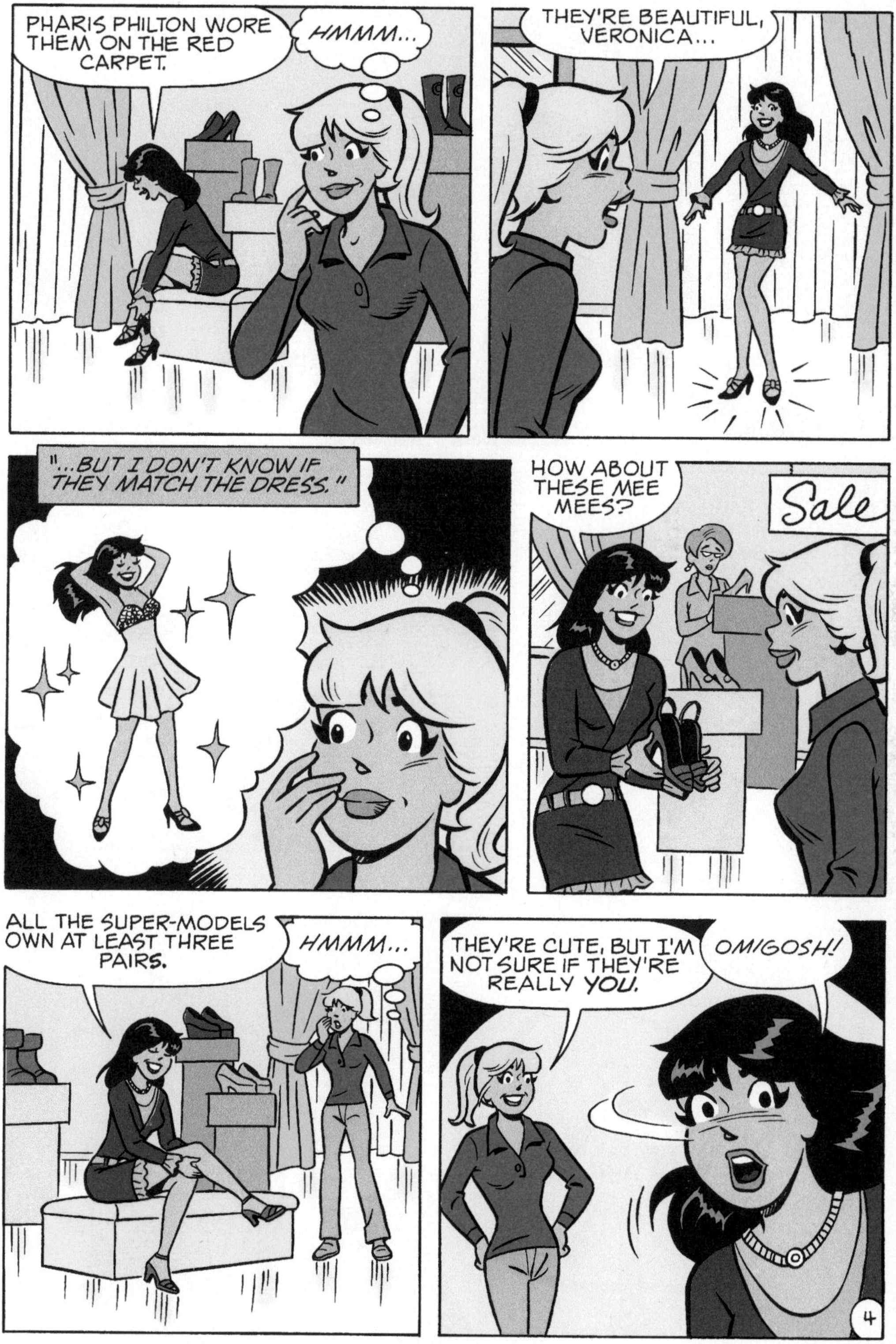
PHARIS PHILTON WORE THEM ON THE RED CARPET.
HMMM...
THEY'RE BEAUTIFUL, VERONICA...
"...BUT I DON'T KNOW IF THEY MATCH THE DRESS."
HOW ABOUT THESE MEE MEES?
Sale
ALL THE SUPER-MODELS OWN AT LEAST THREE PAIRS.
HMMM...
THEY'RE CUTE, BUT I'M NOT SURE IF THEY'RE REALLY YOU.
OMIGOSH!
4

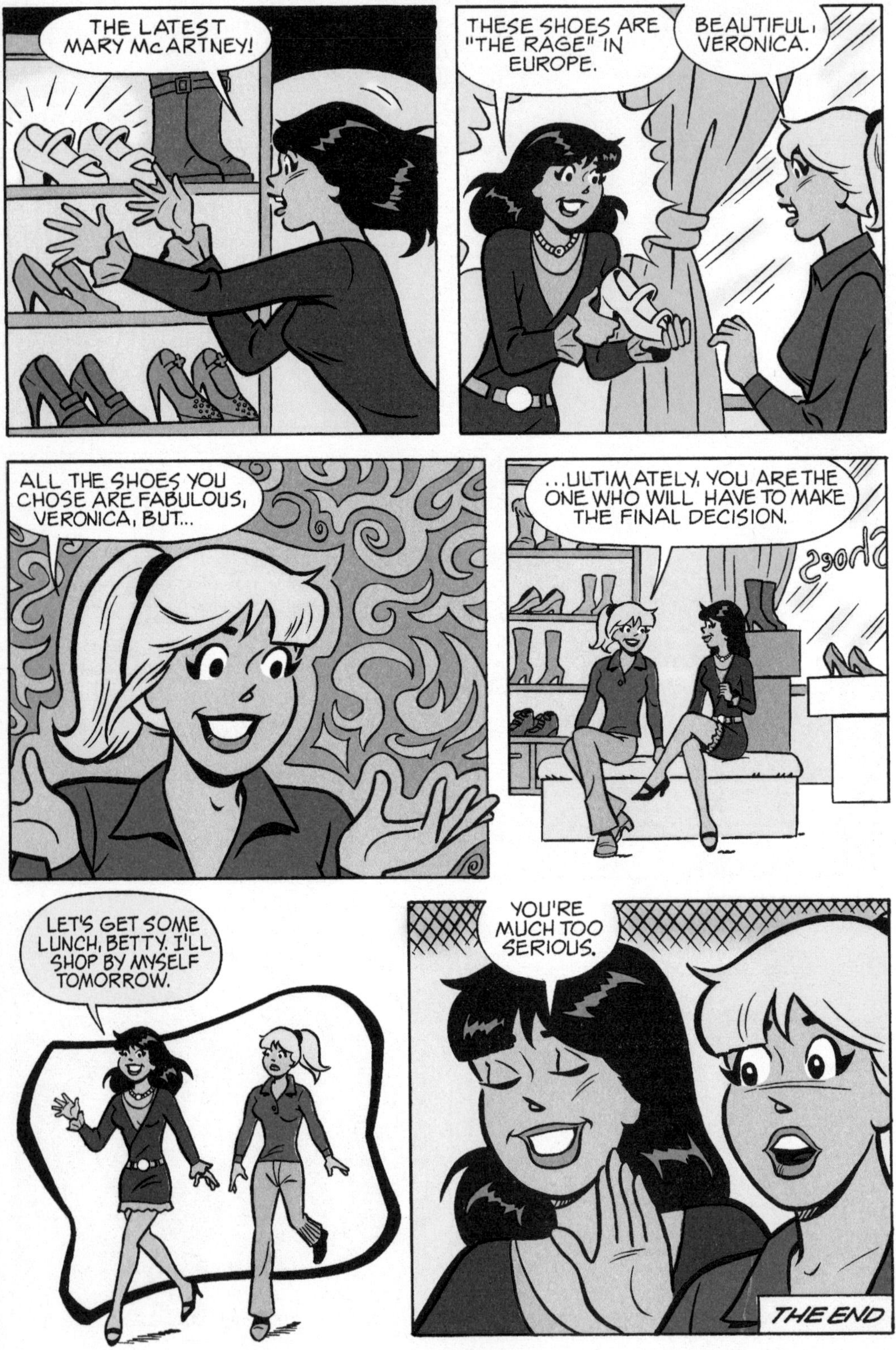
THE LATEST MARY McCARTNEY!
THESE SHOES ARE "THE RAGE" IN EUROPE.
BEAUTIFUL, VERONICA.
ALL THE SHOES YOU CHOSE ARE FABULOUS, VERONICA, BUT...
...ULTIMATELY, YOU ARE THE ONE WHO WILL HAVE TO MAKE THE FINAL DECISION.
LET'S GET SOME LUNCH, BETTY. I'LL SHOP BY MYSELF TOMORROW.
YOU'RE MUCH TOO SERIOUS.
THE END

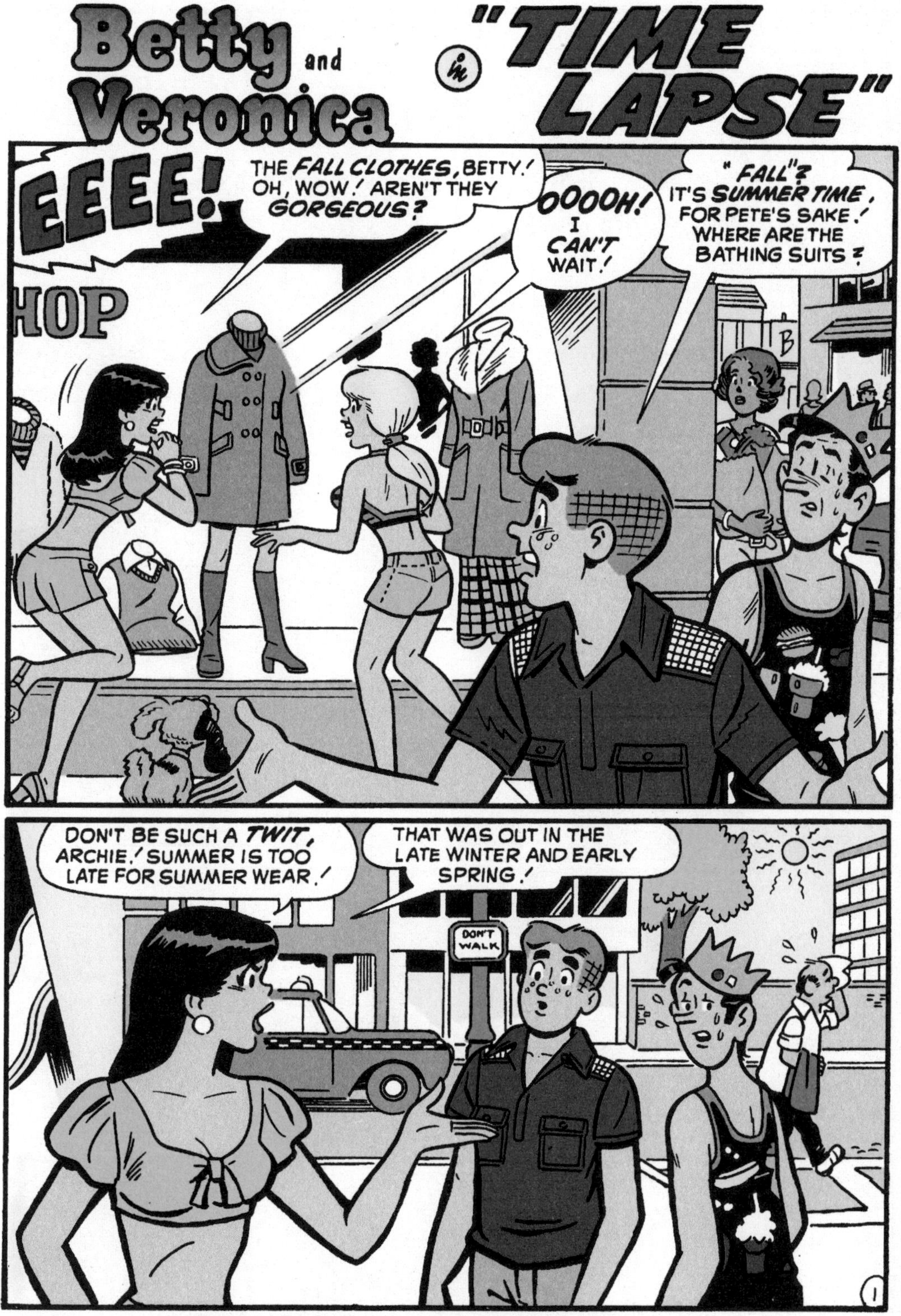
Betty and Veronica
in "TIME LAPSE"
EEEE!
THE FALL CLOTHES, BETTY! OH, WOW! AREN'T THEY GORGEOUS?
OOOOH! I CAN'T WAIT!
"FALL"? IT'S SUMMER TIME, FOR PETE'S SAKE! WHERE ARE THE BATHING SUITS?
HOP
DON'T BE SUCH A TWIT, ARCHIE! SUMMER IS TOO LATE FOR SUMMER WEAR!
THAT WAS OUT IN THE LATE WINTER AND EARLY SPRING!
DON'T WALK
1

Doyle / DeCarlo / Lapick / Yoshida / Grossman

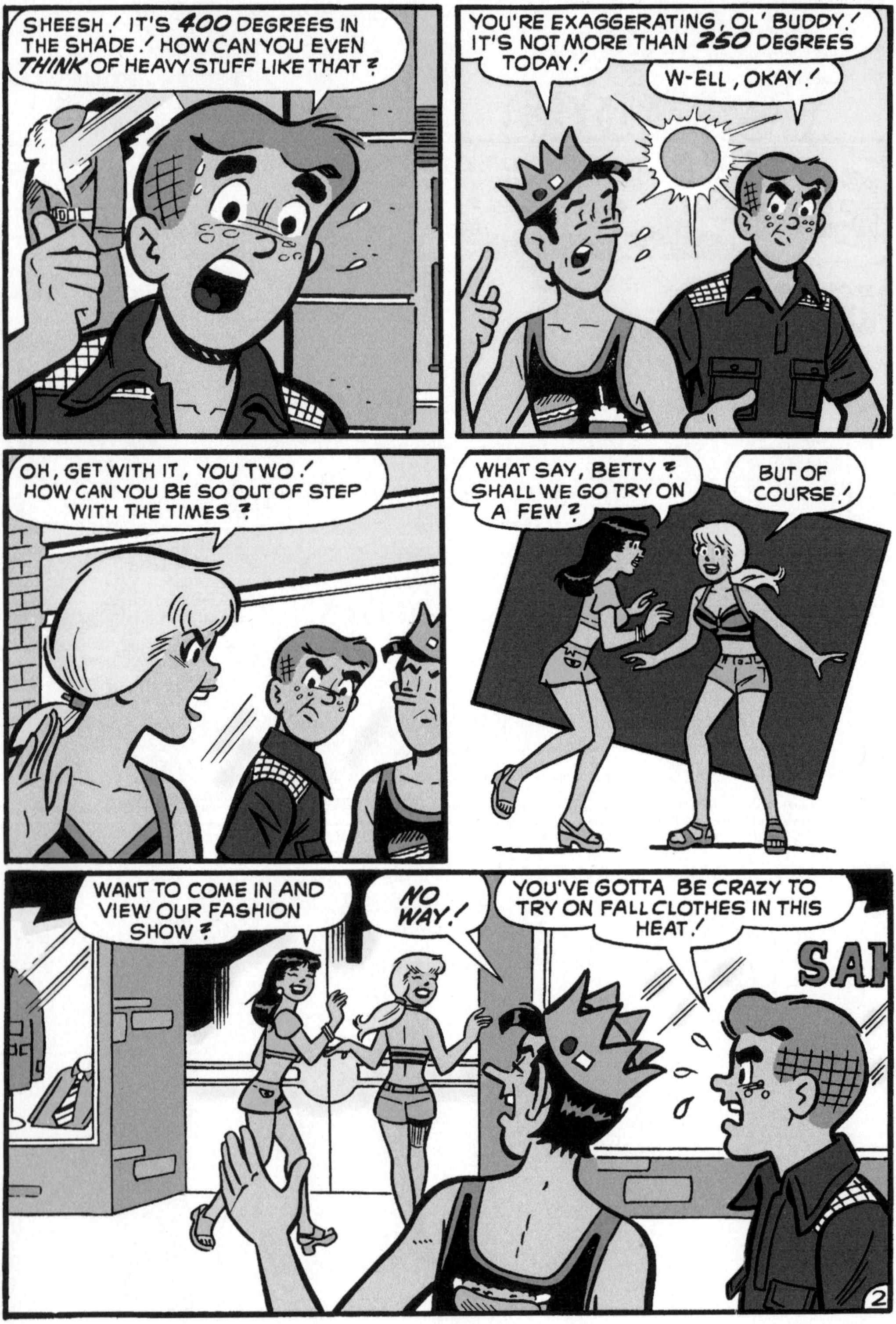
SHEESH! IT'S 400 DEGREES IN THE SHADE! HOW CAN YOU EVEN THINK OF HEAVY STUFF LIKE THAT?
YOU'RE EXAGGERATING, OL' BUDDY! IT'S NOT MORE THAN 250 DEGREES TODAY!
W-ELL, OKAY!
OH, GET WITH IT, YOU TWO! HOW CAN YOU BE SO OUT OF STEP WITH THE TIMES?
WHAT SAY, BETTY? SHALL WE GO TRY ON A FEW?
BUT OF COURSE!
WANT TO COME IN AND VIEW OUR FASHION SHOW?
NO WAY!
YOU'VE GOTTA BE CRAZY TO TRY ON FALL CLOTHES IN THIS HEAT!
SAK
2

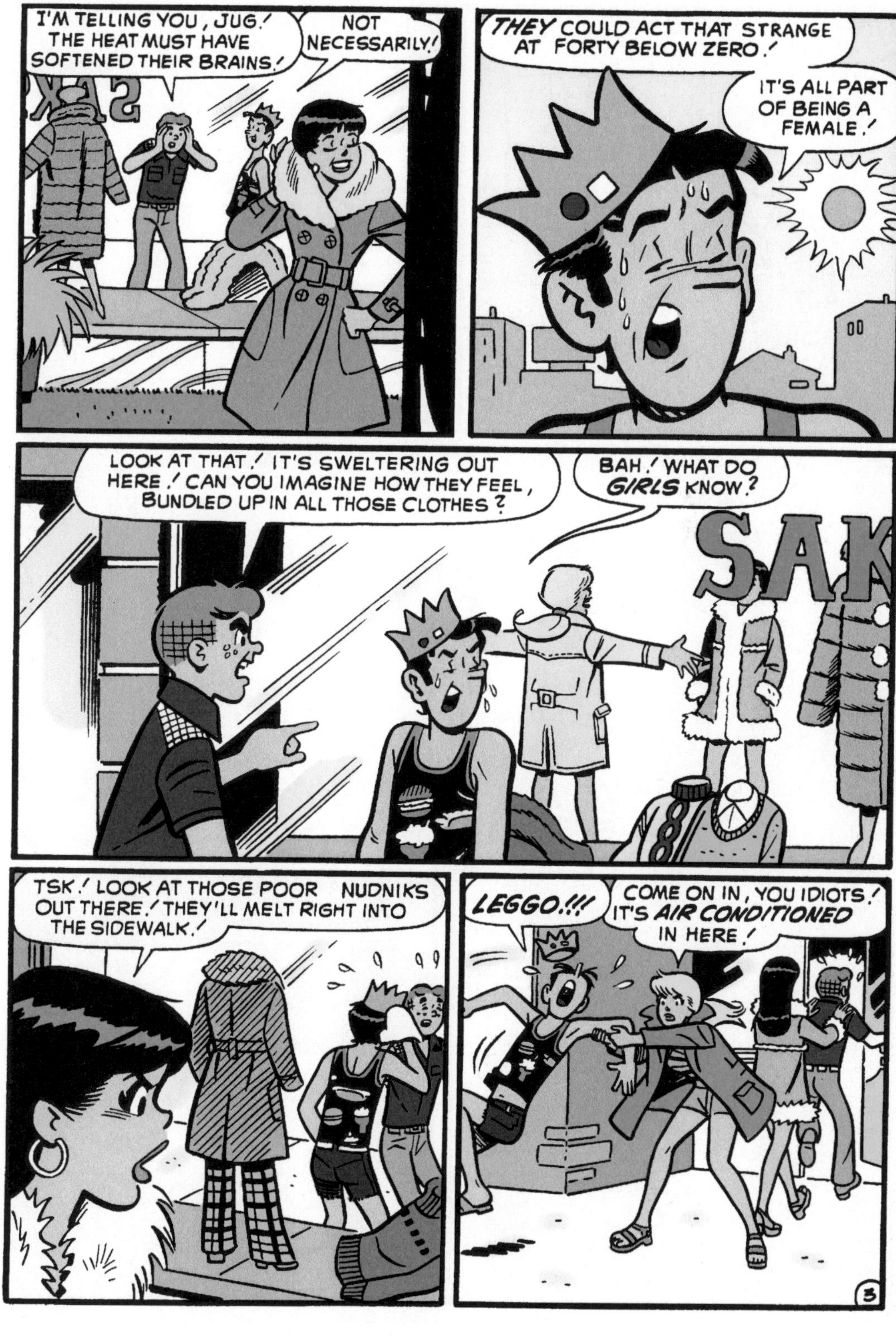

I'M TELLING YOU, JUG! THE HEAT MUST HAVE SOFTENED THEIR BRAINS!
NOT NECESSARILY!
SAK
THEY COULD ACT THAT STRANGE AT FORTY BELOW ZERO!
IT'S ALL PART OF BEING A FEMALE!
LOOK AT THAT! IT'S SWELTERING OUT HERE! CAN YOU IMAGINE HOW THEY FEEL, BUNDLED UP IN ALL THOSE CLOTHES?
BAH! WHAT DO GIRLS KNOW?
SAK
TSK! LOOK AT THOSE POOR NUDNIKS OUT THERE! THEY'LL MELT RIGHT INTO THE SIDEWALK!
LEGGO!!!
COME ON IN, YOU IDIOTS! IT'S AIR CONDITIONED IN HERE!
3

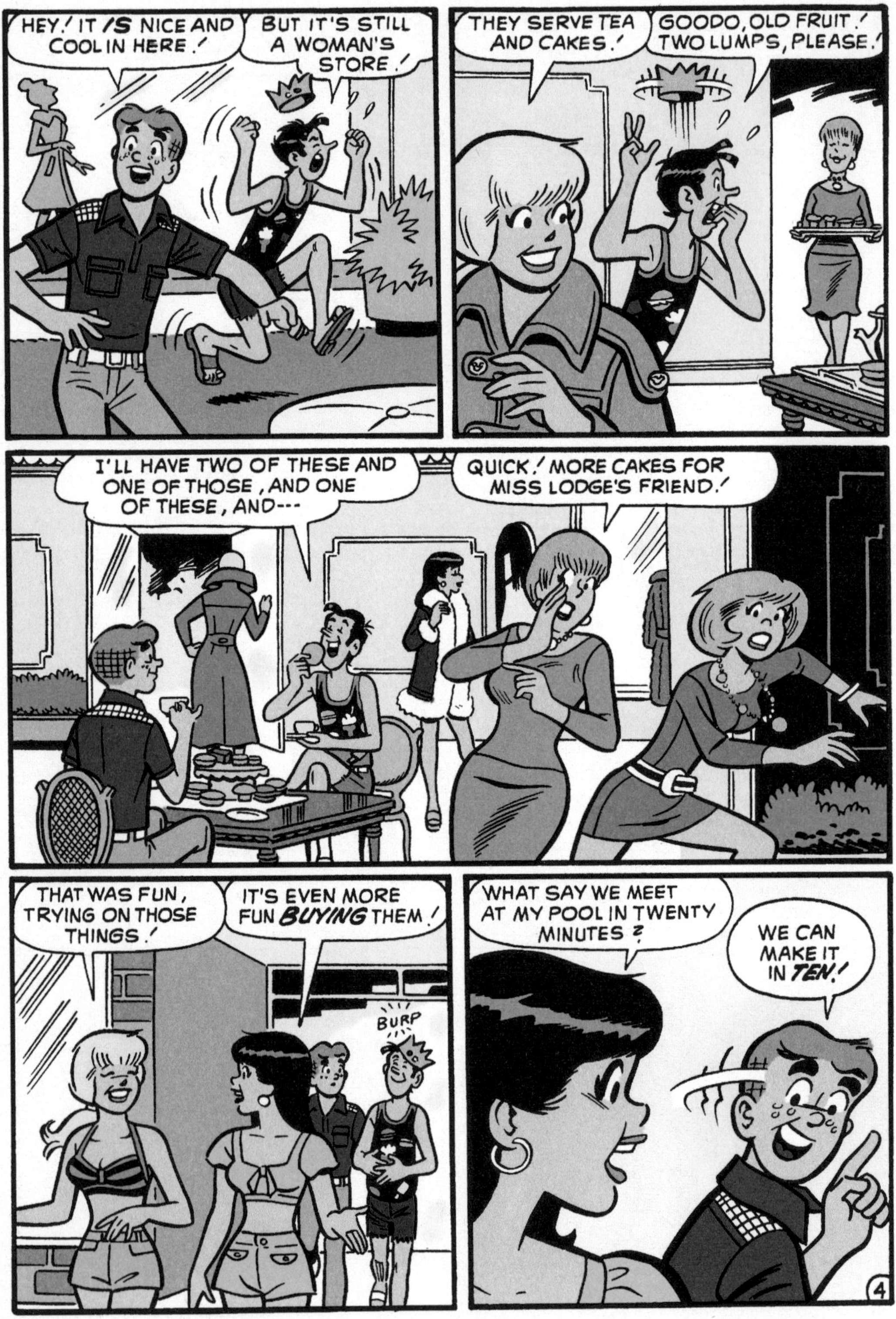
HEY! IT IS NICE AND COOL IN HERE!
BUT IT'S STILL A WOMAN'S STORE!
THEY SERVE TEA AND CAKES!
GOODO, OLD FRUIT! TWO LUMPS, PLEASE!
I'LL HAVE TWO OF THESE AND ONE OF THOSE, AND ONE OF THESE, AND---
QUICK! MORE CAKES FOR MISS LODGE'S FRIEND!
THAT WAS FUN, TRYING ON THOSE THINGS!
IT'S EVEN MORE FUN BUYING THEM!
BURP
WHAT SAY WE MEET AT MY POOL IN TWENTY MINUTES?
WE CAN MAKE IT IN TEN!
4

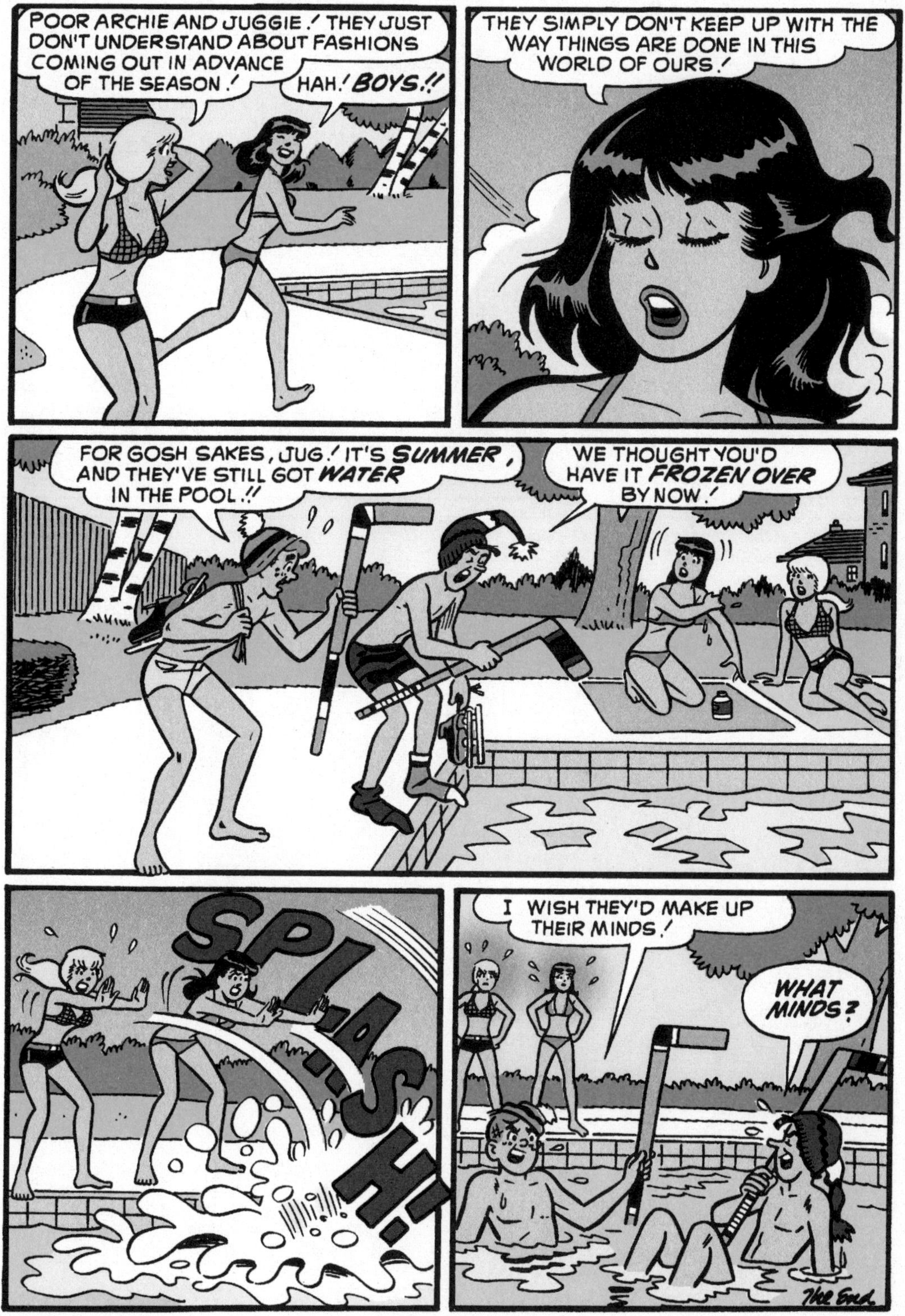
POOR ARCHIE AND JUGGIE! THEY JUST DON'T UNDERSTAND ABOUT FASHIONS COMING OUT IN ADVANCE OF THE SEASON!
HAH! BOYS!!
THEY SIMPLY DON'T KEEP UP WITH THE WAY THINGS ARE DONE IN THIS WORLD OF OURS!
FOR GOSH SAKES, JUG! IT'S SUMMER, AND THEY'VE STILL GOT WATER IN THE POOL!!
WE THOUGHT YOU'D HAVE IT FROZEN OVER BY NOW!
SPLASH!
I WISH THEY'D MAKE UP THEIR MINDS!
WHAT MINDS?
The End

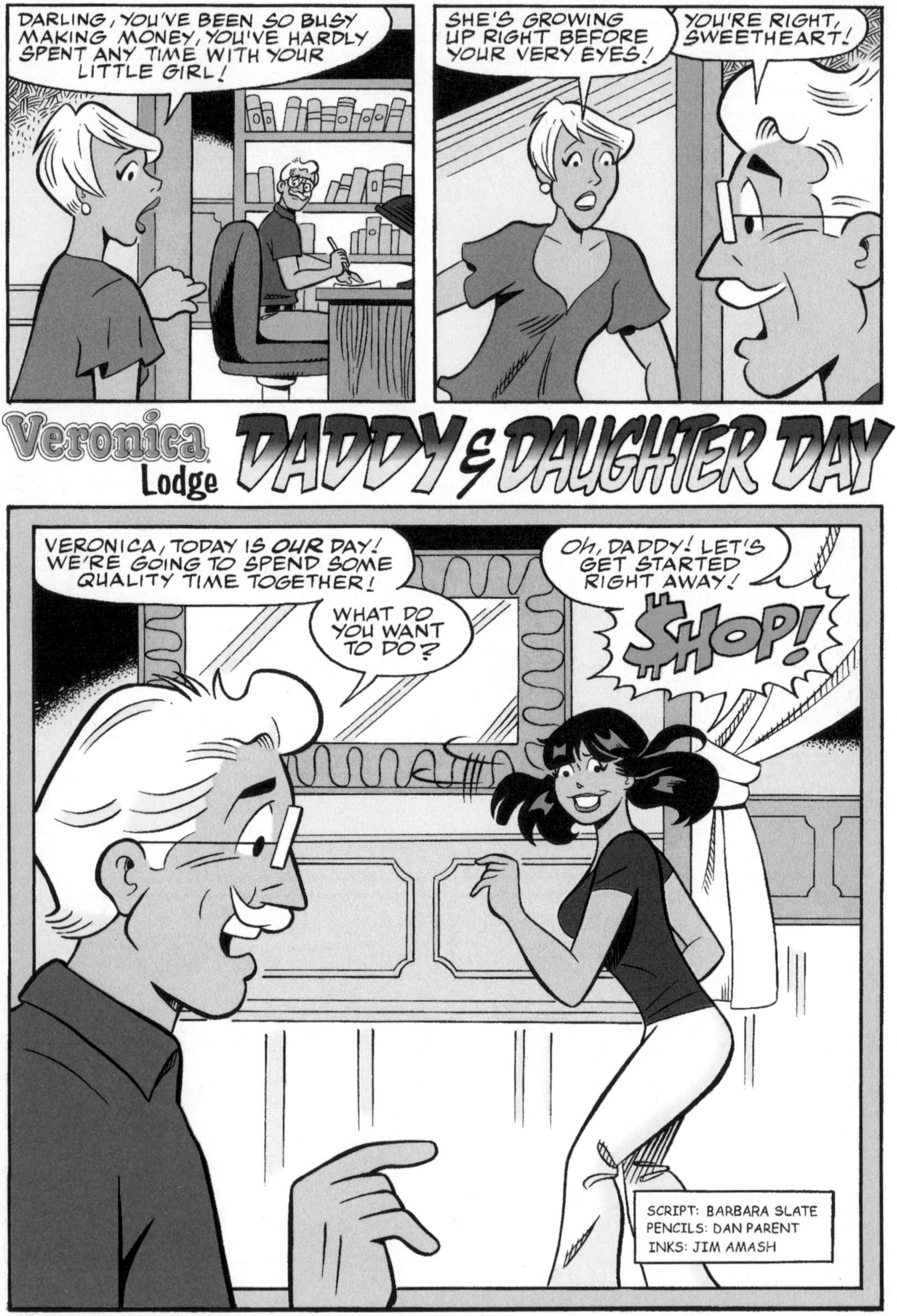
DARLING, YOU'VE BEEN SO BUSY MAKING MONEY, YOU'VE HARDLY SPENT ANY TIME WITH YOUR LITTLE GIRL!
SHE'S GROWING UP RIGHT BEFORE YOUR VERY EYES!
YOU'RE RIGHT, SWEETHEART!
Veronica Lodge
DADDY & DAUGHTER DAY
VERONICA, TODAY IS OUR DAY! WE'RE GOING TO SPEND SOME QUALITY TIME TOGETHER!
WHAT DO YOU WANT TO DO?
Oh, DADDY! LET'S GET STARTED RIGHT AWAY!
$HOP!
SCRIPT: BARBARA SLATE
PENCILS: DAN PARENT
INKS: JIM AMASH

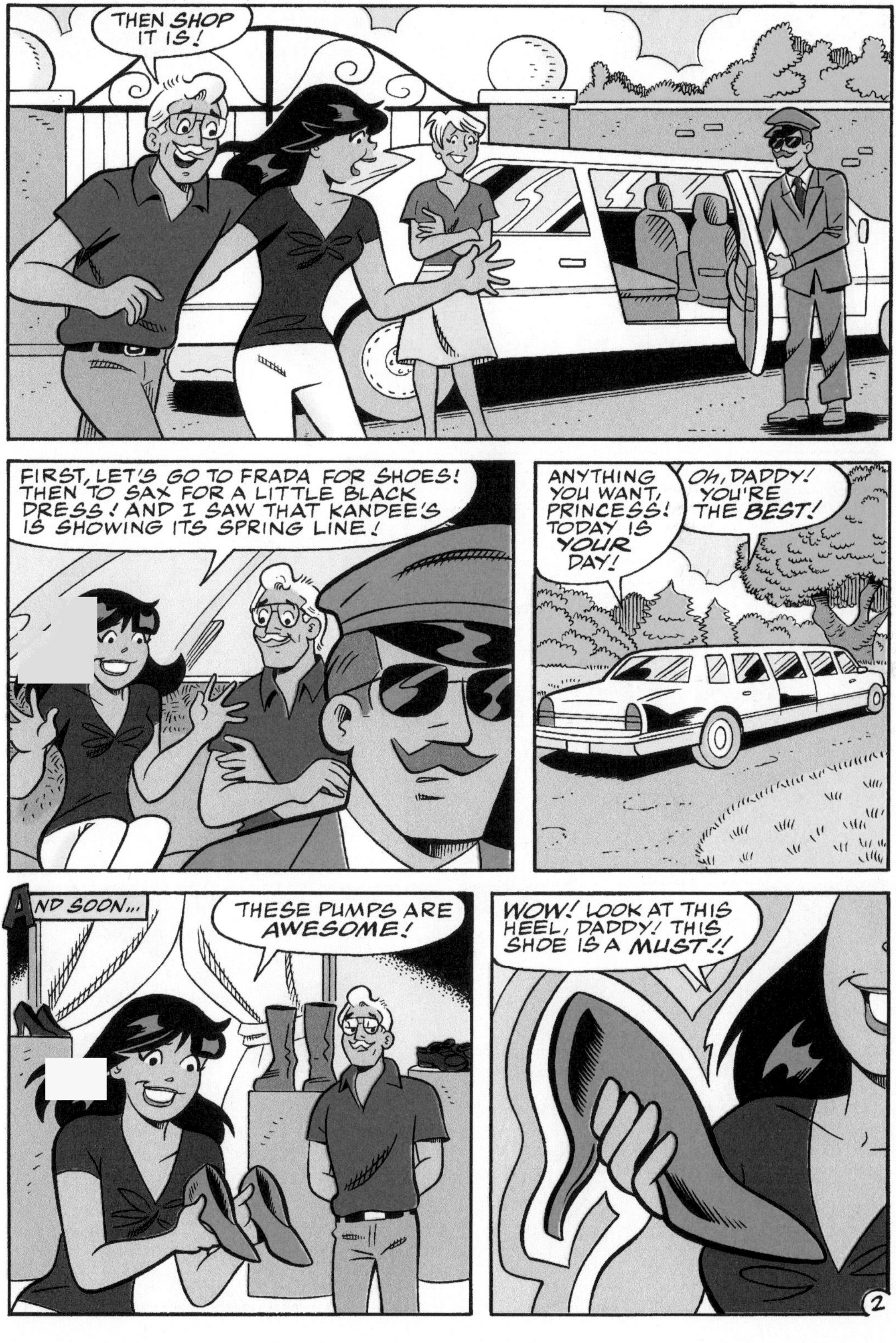
THEN SHOP IT IS!
FIRST, LET'S GO TO FRADA FOR SHOES! THEN TO SAX FOR A LITTLE BLACK DRESS! AND I SAW THAT KANDEE'S IS SHOWING ITS SPRING LINE!
ANYTHING YOU WANT, PRINCESS! TODAY IS YOUR DAY!
OH, DADDY! YOU'RE THE BEST!
AND SOON...
THESE PUMPS ARE AWESOME!
WOW! LOOK AT THIS HEEL, DADDY! THIS SHOE IS A MUST!!
2

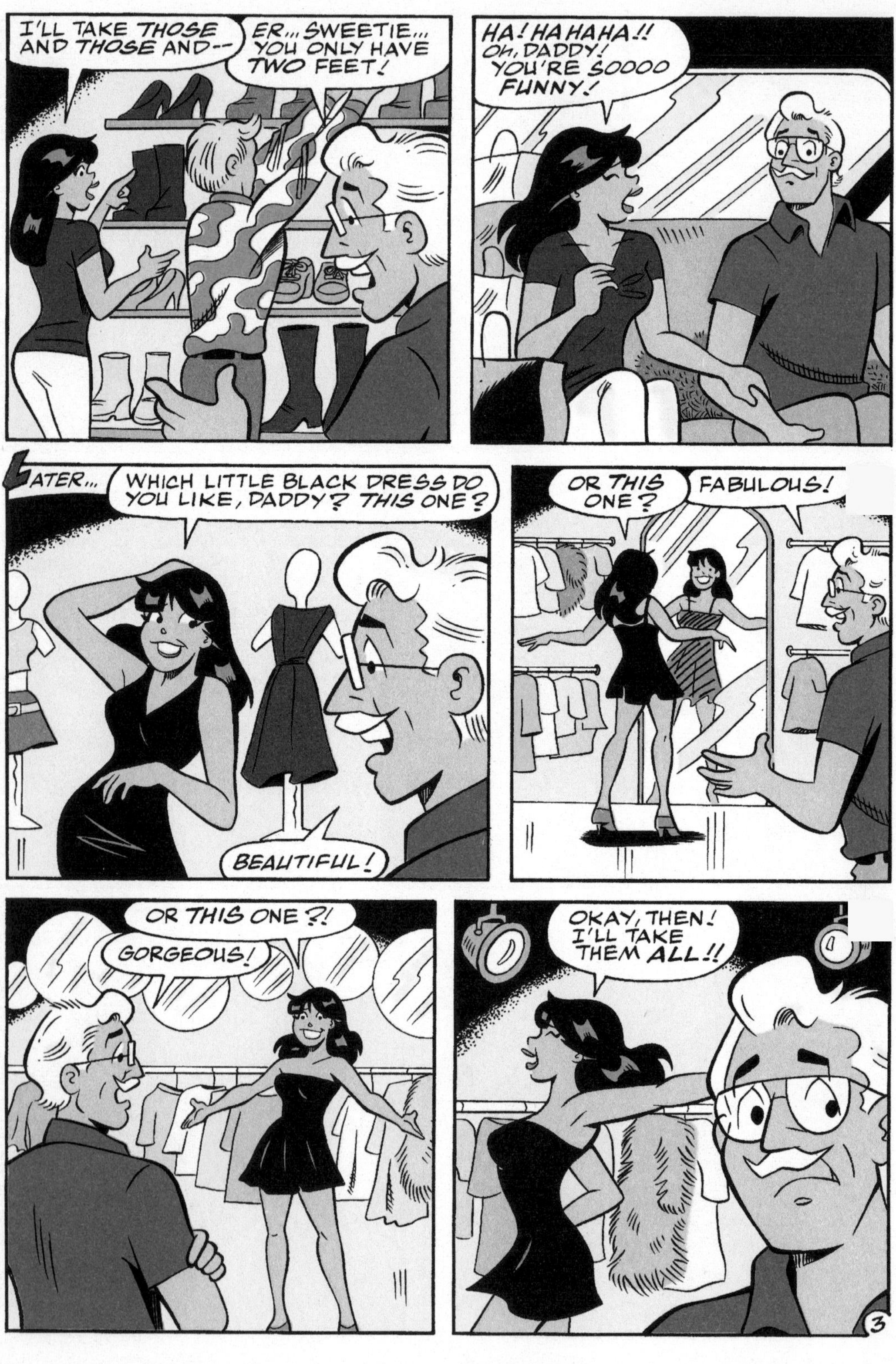
I'LL TAKE THOSE AND THOSE AND--
ER... SWEETIE... YOU ONLY HAVE TWO FEET!
HA! HAHAHA!! Oh, DADDY! YOU'RE SOOOO FUNNY!
LATER...
WHICH LITTLE BLACK DRESS DO YOU LIKE, DADDY? THIS ONE?
BEAUTIFUL!
OR THIS ONE?
FABULOUS!
OR THIS ONE?!
GORGEOUS!
OKAY, THEN! I'LL TAKE THEM ALL!!
3

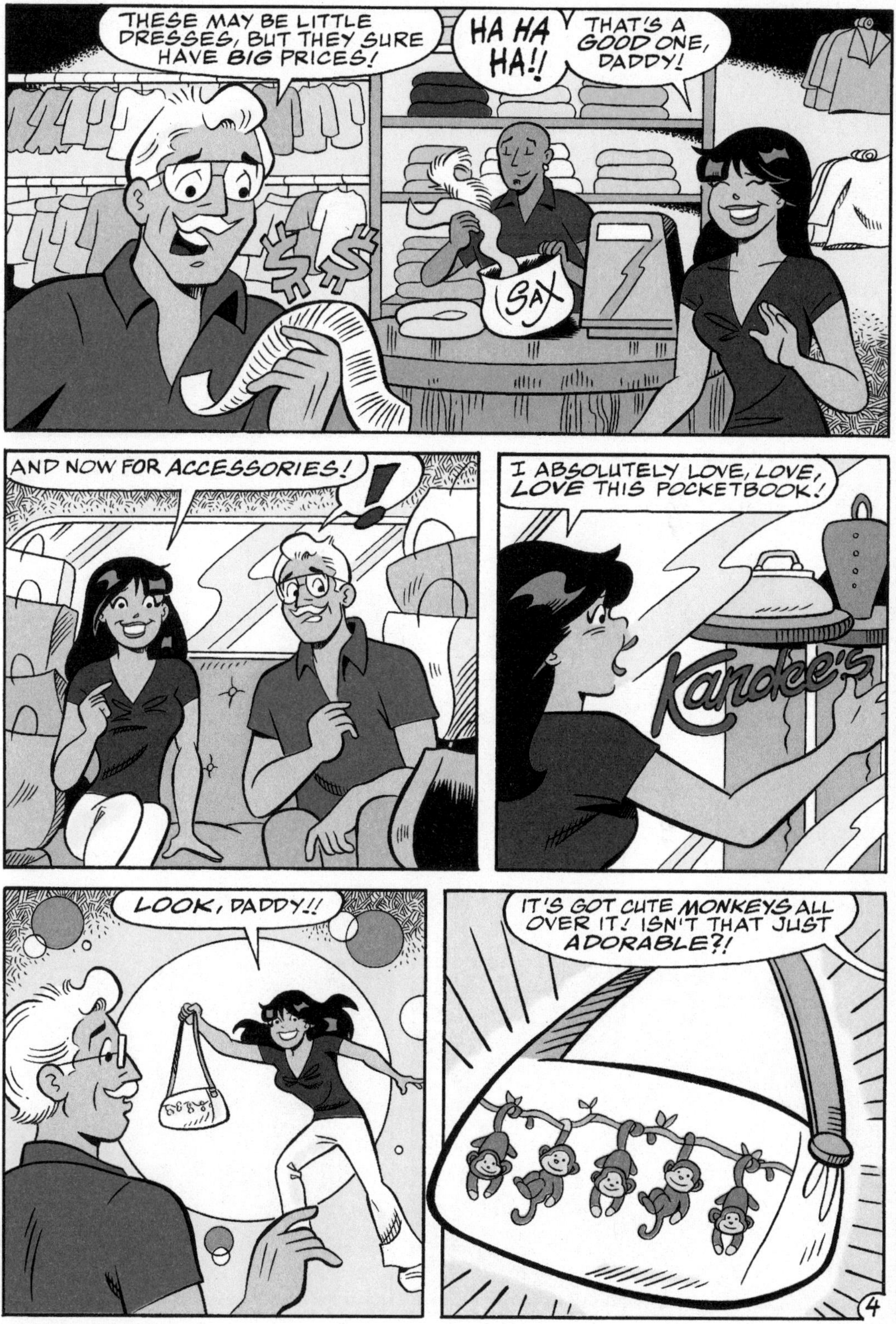
THESE MAY BE LITTLE DRESSES, BUT THEY SURE HAVE BIG PRICES!
HA HA HA!!
THAT'S A GOOD ONE, DADDY!
SAX
AND NOW FOR ACCESSORIES!
!
I ABSOLUTELY LOVE, LOVE, LOVE THIS POCKETBOOK!
Kandee's
LOOK, DADDY!!
IT'S GOT CUTE MONKEYS ALL OVER IT! ISN'T THAT JUST ADORABLE?!
4

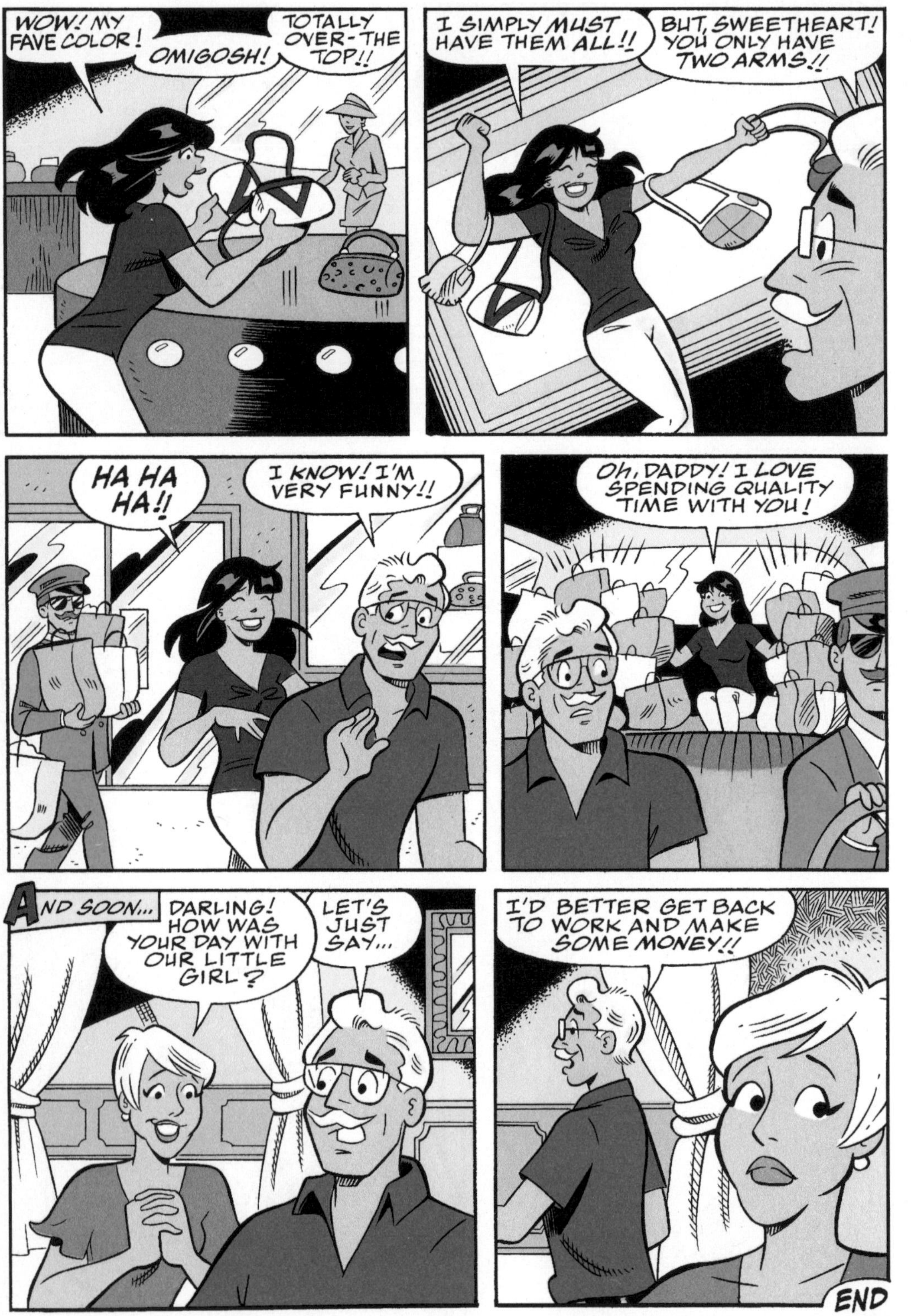
WOW! MY FAVE COLOR!
OMIGOSH!
TOTALLY OVER-THE TOP!!
I SIMPLY MUST HAVE THEM ALL!!
BUT, SWEETHEART! YOU ONLY HAVE TWO ARMS!!
HA HA HA!!
I KNOW! I'M VERY FUNNY!!
Oh, DADDY! I LOVE SPENDING QUALITY TIME WITH YOU!
AND SOON...
DARLING! HOW WAS YOUR DAY WITH OUR LITTLE GIRL?
LET'S JUST SAY...
I'D BETTER GET BACK TO WORK AND MAKE SOME MONEY!!
END

ARCHIE GRAPHIC NOVEL CHECKLIST

Available at your local comic book store, fine bookstores near you, and online @ ArchieComics.com!

OVER 50 GRAPHIC NOVELS AVAILABLE AND COUNTING • BILLIONS OF ARCHIE COMICS SOLD

FAVORITES

With over 70 years of stories, it's hard to pick a favorite, but we think we may have narrowed it down.

- ☐ Archie: Cyber Adventures (978-1-879794-83-2)
- ☐ Archie: Freshman Year Book 1 (978-1-879794-40-5)
- ☐ Archie: Freshman Year Book 2 (978-1-879794-71-9)
- ☐ Adventures of Little Archie Book 1 (978-1-879794-17-7)
- ☐ Adventures of Little Archie Book 2 (978-1-879794-28-3)
- ☐ Katy Keene: Model Behavior (978-1-879794-33-7)
- ☐ Cartoon Life of Chuck Clayton (978-1-879794-48-1)
- ☐ Betty's Diary (978-1-879794-46-7)
- ☐ Archie: The Man from R.I.V.E.R.D.A.L.E. (978-1-879794-68-9)
- ☐ Veronica's Passport (978-1-879794-43-6)
- ☐ Jinx: Little Jinx Grows Up (978-1-879794-91-7)
- ☐ Jinx: Little Miss Steps (978-1-936975-41-9)
- ☐ Archie: Obama & Palin in Riverdale (978-1-879794-87-0)
- ☐ Archie's Giant Kids' Joke Book (978-1-936975-28-0)
- ☐ Archie's Even Funnier Kids' Joke Book (978-1-936975-67-9)
- ☐ Archie's Fun 'N' Games Activity Book (978-1-936975-51-8)
- ☐ Diary of A Girl Next Door: Betty (978-1-936975-37-2)

SABRINA: THE TEENAGE WITCH

Capture the magic with these spell-binding titles, featuring everyone's favorite teenage witch!

- ☐ The Magic of Sabrina the Teenage Witch (978-1-879794-75-7)
- ☐ Sabrina: Based on the Animated Series (978-1-879794-80-1)
- ☐ Sabrina the Teenage Witch: The Magic Within vol.1 (978-1-936975-39-6)
- ☐ Sabrina the Teenage Witch: The Magic Within vol.2 (978-1-936975-54-9)
- ☐ Sabrina the Teenage Witch: The Magic Within vol.3 (978-1-936975-60-0)
- ☐ Sabrina the Teenage Witch: The Magic Within vol.4 (978-1-936975-76-1)

MUST HAVES

Whether you're already a fan or just getting started, these titles are essential to any graphic novel collection.

- ☐ Archie: Clash of the New Kids (978-1-936975-09-9)
- ☐ Archie: Love Showdown (978-1-936975-21-1)
- ☐ Archie: World Tour (978-1-879794-73-3)
- ☐ Archie & Friends: Night at the Comic Shop (978-1-879794-69-6)
- ☐ Archie: Christmas Classics (978-1-879794-78-8)
- ☐ Archie Americana: Best of the 90s Book 1 (978-1-879794-35-1)
- ☐ Archie Americana: Best of the 90s Book 2 (978-1-879794-66-5)
- ☐ Archie Americana: Best of the 80s Book 1 (978-1-879794-06-1)
- ☐ Archie Americana: Best of the 80s Book 2 (978-1-879794-58-0)

ART BOOKS

High-quality collections of classic and current Archie Comics images.

- ☐ The Art of Betty & Veronica (978-1-936975-03-7) HC
- ☐ The Art of Archie: The Covers (978-1-936975-79-2) HC

Archie COMICS

ARCHIECOMICS.COM

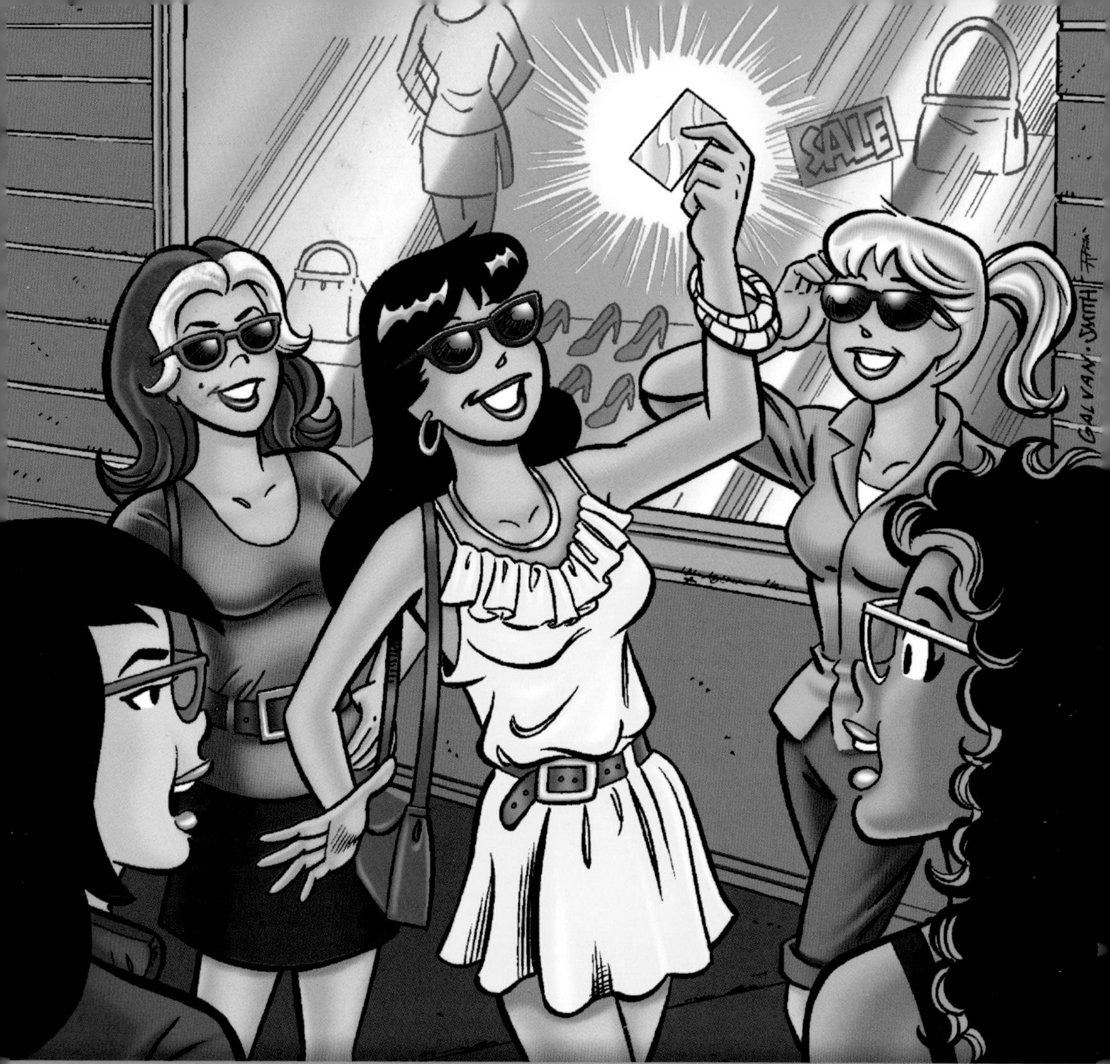
SALE
GALVAN·SMITH

What could Betty & Veronica possibly love more than Archie? That's easy–shopping!

Get ready to hit the mall with Betty & Veronica! Begin your very own shopping spree with this graphic novel collec some of the funniest stories featuring Riverdale's res super-shoppers! Shop till you drop in this hilarious collection!

$9.99 US / $10.99 CAN
ISBN 978-1-61988-904-0
50999 >
EAN
9 781619 889040
ARCHIECOMICS.COM

OVER 2 BILLION ARCHIE COMICS SOLD WORLD WIDE